Santa Lucia

MICHELLE DAMIANI

RIALTO
PRESS

SANTA LUCIA

Rialto Press
P.O. Box 1472
Charlottesville, VA 22902

michelledamiani.com

For Keith, my silver and green

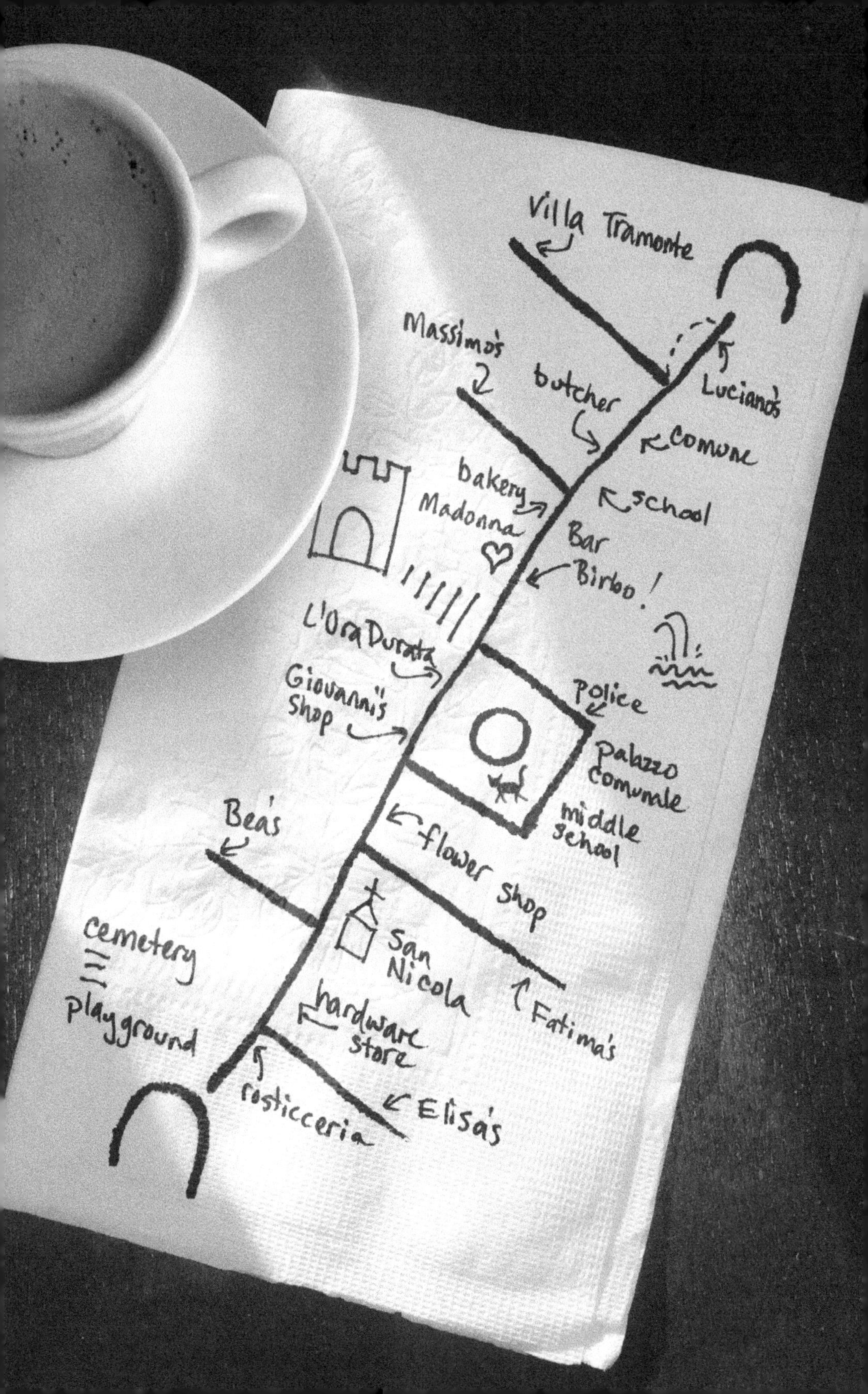
Villa Tramonte
Massimo's
butcher
Luciano's
Comune
bakery
Madonna
school
Bar
Birbo!
L'Ora Durata
Giovanni's
Shop
Police
Palazzo
Comunale
middle
school
Bea's
flower shop
cemetery
San
Nicola
Fatima's
playground
hardware
store
rosticceria
Elisa's

A NOTE ON THE ITALIAN

Italian words in the text are followed by the English translation or can be understood by context. For interested readers, there is a glossary in the back of this book.

~

CAST OF CHARACTERS

MAIN CHARACTERS

Chiara	*The owner of Bar Birbo, she therefore hears all the rumors and secrets.*
Edo	*Chiara's nephew who works at Bar Birbo*
Luciano	*A retired schoolteacher.*
Massimo	*The women in his life are Anna, Margherita, Giulia, and Isotta.*
Anna	*Massimo's mother.*
Elisa	*An 11-year-old girl who struggles in school. She is Fatima's best friend.*
Fatima	*A 12-year-old immigrant girl from Morocco. She is Elisa's best friend.*
Magda	*Moved to Santa Lucia from Germany years ago with her husband who has since disappeared in Thailand.*
Isotta	*A transplant to Santa Lucia from Florence.*
Fabrizio	*A mysterious stranger.*
Patrizia	*Chiara's best friend who helps her husband, Giuseppe, in his butcher shop.*

VILLAGERS

Ava — *Santa Lucia's guerrilla gardener, perennially unlucky in love.*

Bea — *Santa Lucia's source of fresh eggs and fresh gossip.*

Giuseppe — *Patrizia's husband and the maker of Santa Lucia's famous chicken sausages.*

Sauro — *Santa Lucia's baker.*

Giovanni — *The joke-telling owner of the little shop on the piazza.*

Concetta — *Elisa's mother, married to Carlo with two sons, Guido and Matteo*

Arturo — *Older villager who is sure his French wife is cheating on him.*

Rosetta — *The school principal.*

Paola — *The owner of the fruit and vegetable market.*

Marcello — *The town cop.*

Dante — *The mayor.*

Stella — *The mayor's wife and Chiara's childhood friend.*

Vale — *The town handyman.*

THE LAST OF SEPTEMBER

On the crest of a hill, surrounded by glimmering olive groves, lies Santa Lucia. It is a typical Italian hill town, if smaller than those on the tourist trail. Even if you have never traveled to Italy, you no doubt have seen enough movies with lush soundtracks and sweeping camera work to have an instant picture in your mind—imagine stone arches framing panoramas, exuberant locals fiercely debating the chance of rain, and the scent of rosemary floating high above ancient streets. As you stroll through flower-lined alleys, it is easy to assume that Santa Lucia is as serene as it appears. But life here is like life anywhere, and the town's idyllic facade masks love, betrayal, scandal, innuendo, mystery, romance, and heartbreak.

Rest easy, none of that will mar a passing visit to Santa Lucia. Those travelers who merely stop by will notice the light before anything else. Of course, there aren't all that many visitors to a village this removed from Rome or Florence, so rarely will you hear voices raised in wonder at the shimmering air. Only one tourist has gone home and attempted to describe the light: "like sky warping upon meeting land." He rubbed his temples and abandoned the attempt, as well as his fledgling dream of writing poetry.

The villagers themselves stopped remarking on the heavy, churning light generations ago. Nowadays, their voices intertwine with its fluctuations without their awareness. In the morning, the cadence of their greetings rises with the honeying of the golden air. They pass each other on their way to their jobs as gardener, teacher, baker, and shopkeeper, their voices lifting, "*Buongiorno!*" The lilt on that second o. They knot together in the street, gesturing at the billboard in the town *comune* announcing another possible strike, before separating with a staccato, "*Ciao! Ciao! Cia-o!*" Honestly, they sound like Bea's clutch of chickens celebrating the approach of a food pail. Meanwhile, the glow pools in alley corners and gleams from the alabaster stones tugged from the Apennine mountains.

The light swells and shifts throughout the day, until it is a rich blue in the late afternoon, almost navy. As if the ink of night were dipped onto a paintbrush and touched to the watery air of Santa Lucia. Conversations mute, as the cobalt sheen sinks into the town. Even when the old women gather on their plastic chairs under stone arches while sorting greens, their voices blur, in time to the gathering blue of night.

Yes, the opalescent light certainly makes dusk a stirring time to visit Santa Lucia, but it must be said that Santa Lucia is at her best, her most tourist-ready, in the mornings. Especially if you stand right here on Via Romana. From this spot you can watch as the painter and the butcher meet in the street and angle into Bar Birbo. As they continue their debate on the proper care of olive trees during this unseasonable drought, they fishtail their hips to create space at the bar. Chatter continues to the beat of shaking sugar packets, with a final plunk as Chiara serves each *espresso* with a smile and an "*Eccolo*," here it is. Her crescendoing welcome twines with the luminescent morning. With a nod, they acknowledge the arrival of white cups of dark and nutty coffee before resuming their discussion. In mere moments, the new arrivals transform into scenery, as the next pair or trio of villagers meet in the street and nod into Bar Birbo.

It is like this every morning. Every morning save Mondays, when the bar is closed. Bar Birbo has always been closed on Mondays, ever since Chiara's great-grandfather converted the downstairs of their ancient *palazzo* to serve coffee. What had been a desperate attempt to resolve his family's financial crisis became the jewel of Santa Lucia (after the falls, of course). Bar Birbo, the villagers crow at any opportunity, had the distinction of being the first bar in the *zona*. Yet, even though the bar's *giorno di chiusura* hasn't changed in almost 100 years, the people of Santa Lucia still stop and gape, confused, as they propel a friend by the arm toward the waxed wooden front of Bar Birbo, only to find the door shut tight. Their eyes drift upward to the open window of the residence above the bar, where Chiara is undoubtedly making her heavenly pistachio yogurt cake for herself and whatever niece or nephew has come for a visit. Grumbling, the disappointed *espresso*-seeker shuffles to the *tabaccheria*, where the coffee lacks the sweet roundness of Bar Birbo's, and the owner, Cesare, scowls at the once-weekly swelling in his coffee clientele. Mondays lack a certain wholeness for the citizens of Santa Lucia, but one can pick up a *giornale* to read, and the *marca da bollo* stamp for whatever piece of bureaucracy has been put off for too long.

And so every day but one, villagers stroll out of Bar Birbo with their minds sharpened by Chiara's coffee, and their days knit with their neighbors'. Perhaps they no longer notice the light. But on particularly iridescent days, they may pause on the low step leading from Bar Birbo to the cobblestone street. In that brief moment, they take in the sunset-hued stucco buildings' murmur of color alongside the predominately creamy stone walls, the splash of red geranium-filled flowerpots, and how the children with backpacks as unwieldy as turtle shells race to school, their laughter weaving through the sound of the church bells.

Such are mornings in Santa Lucia. Just as they have been for generations.

"*Buongiorno*, Massimo, *un caffè?*"

"*Sì, certo*, Chiara, of course." The clustered villagers looked over their shoulders at the man silhouetted against the glowing doorway. With a rustling burble, they parted to allow Massimo to approach the bar, the women twitching their skirts to fall more becomingly. The man ignored the bustle his presence created. He stepped into the opening at the bar, and pulled back his blue-striped shirtsleeve to consult his watch. His grandfather's watch, really, but he knew the scratches in the gold and the imperfections in the leather as well as he knew his own hand. He straightened his tie and then gazed over the heads of the other patrons, seeing none of them. He didn't hear the hushed voices of Sauro, the baker, and Rosetta, the school principal, as they lowered their heads to whisper confidentially.

"*Guarda*, Rosetta," Sauro murmured, gesturing with his chin. "It's Massimo."

Rosetta fought the urge to smooth down her hair as she cast a quick glance at Massimo, standing like a signal fire over the crowd, his strong jaw echoing his strong brows. "Mmm . . ." she responded, noncommittally.

Sauro watched his friend with a bemused expression. He murmured, "I wonder, will he ever smile again?"

This got Rosetta's attention. "Massimo's a serious person. You know that."

"*Sì*, but the seriousness, it's different now. Like he'll never know joy."

"Such drama. He was never a cheerful man, even before."

Sauro paused to consider the foam left clinging to the side of his *cappuccino* cup, before venturing with a loftily raised eyebrow, "If I remember correctly, that didn't stop you from tagging after him like Carosello follows a pork bone."

Rosetta shifted uncomfortably. "So now you're comparing me to a one-eyed dog?"

Sauro shrugged. "You know what I mean."

Rosetta decided to glide over the implied comparison to the flea-bitten creature that jogged about town looking for scraps. "Anyway, that was years ago! And besides, it's not like it was just me. All the girls had crushes on him. But he wouldn't give any of us the time of day."

Sauro nodded and said, "Only Giulia."

Rosetta struggled not to roll her eyes and add a cutting comment as Sauro mused, "I never understood that attraction. Massimo is so tall, so . . . well, you know."

Unfortunately, Rosetta heard none of this fascinating narration. Her eyes were half-lidded, and her vision trained on Massimo.

Unaware, Sauro stirred his coffee. "And Giulia. She was very sweet, but . . ." Sauro leaned past Rosetta's shoulder to assess Massimo. His thick, dark hair that waved away from his bronze forehead and then swooped roguishly to the left, past eyelashes as thick as paintbrushes. His broad chest narrowing to a neat waist. It seemed unfair that Massimo had lost none of his good looks. Even after the tragedy.

As Sauro's elbow brushed her own, Rosetta caught her cue. She said, dreamily, "*Comunque*, she was a sweet girl. And in love with him since we were children. Besides, you know what they say about Italian men and their mothers. Is it any wonder he chose Giulia?"

Sauro said, "And they never found out what happened to her. So strange."

Eyes still fixed on Massimo, sipping his coffee with authority, Rosetta said, "Yes, well. Strange things happen. God's will."

The conversation shifted back and forth easily. After all, they'd had it at least once a week for the past year. But neither Rosetta nor Sauro seemed to notice the pattern. Only Chiara registered a familiarity with the turns of the dialogue, and that only by smiling to herself, the gap between her two front teeth winking, as she dried a glass with extra care.

Massimo spooned the last of the coffee-soaked sugar into his mouth and stepped to the register to drop his euro on a scuffed copper plate. His smile flashed briefly at Chiara, but it didn't reach his eyes, which remained fixed to some distant point. He turned on his heel and with military briskness he started out the door looking neither right nor left, but determinedly walking up the hill to one of the two lots where the villagers parked their cars.

He didn't notice the man pressed against the shadows, waiting for him.

Elisa hurried to school, late. This was unfortunately the standard state of affairs for little Elisa. Always behind, which would cause her no end of heartache. But more on that later.

As Elisa struggled to hang onto the papers wriggling out of her notebook (why, oh, why, hadn't she organized them yesterday like she'd planned?), she tripped through the *piazza*, dappled with buttery light, and jogged around a couple that looked to be American judging from their fanny packs. The tourists paused in the middle of the street to take a picture up the wide stone steps to the castle. That abandoned castle never failed to reverberate in Elisa's imagination, even though she must have passed it thousands of times in her eleven years. On quiet afternoons, when no one would notice her absence, she often peered in the glassless windows, filling her mind with the ghosts of twirling gowns and long tables groaning under the weight of hundreds of platters of pastas and grilled meats and roasted birds, still plumed.

Elisa hastened her steps to force her mind to the task ahead, narrowly avoiding the man striding out of Bar Birbo. Elisa cut her eyes to the flower boxes set against the windows of the *gelateria* to avoid the look of annoyance that no doubt twisted the man's face. The morning had already been difficult enough. But she couldn't avoid his heavy hand on her shoulder. She looked up at Massimo and tried not to cower.

"*Piano*," he told her, his voice almost soft. Elisa nodded and focused on reining in her legs' frantic energy. She peeked up at the familiar face of the Madonna leaning out of her blue niche, but Elisa wouldn't stop to touch her, no matter how much luck she believed it would bring. After a few dramatically slowed steps, the thought of the school door closing consumed her once again and her steps quickened as she hurried down Via Romana.

The scent of almonds wafted above her as she passed L'Antico Forno, the town's bakery. She would *not* allow herself the pleasure of stopping to inhale. Or to check if the window display of baked goods had changed from the late summer design of a sun made of bread and flowers constructed from *biscotti*, to the boar-shaped cookies the *forno* always created in honor of Santa Lucia's autumnal festival of *cinghiale*.

She wove around parents chatting beside parked scooters and through the blessedly still-open door of the school. The school secretary, who had unhinged the door to prepare it for closing, began reprimanding the latecomer, until she realized it was Elisa. It was often Elisa, but how could she be angry at a child that thin, with eyes that haunted.

Instead she offered an encouraging smile and called after Elisa's receding back, "*Tranquilla!*" Be calm.

Elisa gave no sign of having heard her, and instead stumbled up the steps, scurried across the catwalk situated above the dank hole offering glimpses of the Roman blocks below, through the linoleum-lined hallway smelling faintly of disinfectant with a curious cat food muskiness. She paused outside the door of her classroom. Her head darted over her shoulder, and she furtively tucked a strand of her no-particular-color hair behind her ear as she surveyed the jackets stretched down the wall like offerings. No one could see her—did she dare?

At the sound of squeaking chalk, Elisa quickly shrugged off her coat, deposited it on a hook, and ducked into the classroom. She dropped into her seat as Maestra Cocinelli turned away from the board to face the class.

Massimo leaned down to buff an imagined smudge off his relentlessly shiny left shoe. He stood and considered the polished leather before tucking his handkerchief back into his pocket and pulling back his sleeve once again to check the time.

He smelled Luciano before he saw him—the air became ripe with the dinginess of potatoes forgotten at the back of a dark cupboard. Massimo quickened his footsteps. If Luciano was as drunk as usual, Massimo could outstrip him without too much fuss. But the lurch of footsteps gained on him. Before he could formulate an escape plan, Luciano stood before him, shouting and waving his hands.

"You devil! You did this! Of all the games in all the fields you had to befoul me! *Mine!*"

Massimo rolled his eyes and glanced about to see if there were any bystanders. Only Carosello turned from an alley onto the road, steadfastly trotting toward the school. Massimo noticed that the tuft of fur that covered the dog's missing eye was coated with coffee grounds.

Luciano continued, crying, "You are not a man! Just a pile of empty, a twisted sack . . . no standing, no morals, you . . . you are mouse feces! Yes, that with the cat and the pile and all the defecation under the couch . . ." The rest of his words collapsed into garbled slosh.

Satisfied that he was alone, Massimo grabbed Luciano's lapel and pulled him close to his gritted teeth. "No more, old man. You will get out of my sight. You are nothing. You are worthless. You are nobody. Get out of here before I call the police and tell them everything."

Luciano shivered, whispering, "Everything? What . . . what? But, it was you!"

Massimo sneered, "Who will listen to you? Now get away from me! *Vai!*" Massimo pushed Luciano backward. The older man's arms pinwheeled as he fought to keep his balance. Stumbling over the uneven cobblestones, Luciano collapsed, a fall of rags.

Luciano clutched his ears and moaned, "No! It's unhinging the bell. It's *you.*"

"Massimo!"

Massimo's head twisted. He straightened and uncreased his forehead with an easy smile. "Patrizia! How good to see you. Perhaps you can help? Luciano seems to have fallen and I must get to Rome."

Patrizia took in the huddle of Luciano. "Why is he crying?" Her gaze narrowed. "Massimo? What happened?"

"Who can say?" Massimo pulled back his sleeve to consult his watch. "He attacked me, running at me with his hands waving, screaming something about mouse droppings under his couch, or some such. Insane, yes? Then he just tripped and fell. A loose cobblestone, perhaps. Anyway, he's fine." Massimo stepped around Luciano who was leaning on Patrizia's arm to rise. As he walked away he called over his shoulder, "I certainly am grateful that you came along when you did. I didn't want to leave him there, but," he chuckled, "I couldn't really see him home either. Please send my regards to Giuseppe. My mother will be by later today for sausages."

Patrizia shook her head as she helped wipe the dirt off Luciano's pants and coat. "Luciano? What happened?"

Luciano's cloudy gaze cleared as he looked into Patrizia's familiar eyes, the crow's feet deeper than he remembered. "Patrizia?"

"Yes, it's me. Luciano, what happened? With Massimo?"

Luciano mouth twitched as he thought for a moment. "I . . . the cobblestone and the water."

Patrizia frowned. "The water?"

Luciano sagged.

Patrizia pulled him up. "Luciano, when did you last eat?"

Luciano just shook his head.

Speaking softly, Patrizia said, "Maestro, you need to eat. Here, come to the shop. Let's find you something."

Luciano shook his head again, more forcefully. This seemed to clear some of the cobwebs. "I couldn't."

Patrizia scoffed, "Of course you can! The *porchetta* just arrived, let me make you a sandwich."

Luciano ducked his head, a gesture that hearkened back to his old charm. "Patrizia. Such an angel."

As he walked down Via Romana, Edoardo nudged his hair forward from the crown of his head, gathering up the front like he'd seen in *Uomo Moderno*. Approaching Bar Birbo, he practiced smiling, trying to loosen the tightness in his cheeks. He wished for some gum. Or even a mint.

Several calls of "Edo!" met him as he opened the door.

"*Ciao, ciao, ciao,*" he waved and called to the collection of coffee drinkers, dropping a kiss on the cheek of his aunt, Chiara, and murmuring an affectionate, "*Buongiorno, cara.*" Chiara smiled up at her nephew and patted his artfully stubbled cheek. She saw so much of his baby sweetness in him, still, at 19. It was sometimes shocking to notice his wiry frame and arresting features and recognize him as a man almost fully grown.

Edoardo opened a drawer with a swift motion and withdrew a freshly laundered apron. He snapped it open with one easy tip of his left hand, while his right plucked the string out of the air. He clicked his feet together as he rested the apron over his trim hips, crossed the strings in the back, and then swiftly knotted them together at the level of his navel. The florist's daughter, Ava, who had lingered in Bar Birbo in the hopes of catching a glimpse of Edoardo, sighed inwardly at his fluid movements. No longer able to pretend to be savoring the last few bubbles in her *cappuccino,* she reluctantly abandoned her place at the bar.

As Chiara was frothing milk for the two newly arrived police officers, Edoardo turned sideways to slip past her to the register.

"*Il solito?* Your usual?" he asked Ava with a smile.

Ava fought the image of herself leaning over the copper plate and running her fingers over that full lower lip. Instead she stammered, "*Sì, grazie*, Edo."

Edoardo's hands flew over the cash register, but it didn't open. He sighed and tried again, calling out, "Chiara! When are you going to get a cash register built this century?"

Chiara looked up at her nephew's words laced with uncharacteristic bitterness. She bit the corner of her cheek, as she took in Edo's clenching jaw. He scowled and avoided her gaze, punching at the yellowing button again and again. The register finally flung open with a homely binging sound. The patrons released their attention back to their conversations. Ava scrambled through her purse, looking for exact change, as Edoardo drummed his fingers on the bar and whistled tunelessly to the tinny music spooling out of Chiara's faded radio. Fumbling, Ava found the coins that rolled infuriatingly around her purse and handed them to Edoardo, who caught them with a tight grin. Ava jolted a bit when her fingers brushed Edoardo's palm. But he didn't blink as his hands closed around the coins and dropped them in the till.

Magda tugged the door behind her. She started to turn away, but then stopped and pushed one more time against the solid wood. Satisfied, she wrapped her cardigan around her narrow frame to ward off the morning breeze, cool as a lizard's belly. She considered watering the pots of flowers that lined the rental property beside her apartment but, squinting at the sky, decided it would likely rain and save her the trouble. Besides, she wanted to get to Bar Birbo and show Chiara the article. Eagerness propelled her steps down Via Romana.

Despite that anticipation, she couldn't help but stall when she saw tourists on the steps that led to the dilapidated castle. A quick survey established that these weren't the renters staying in her larger apartment. She seemed to remember that those were Australian. She wondered where these were lodging. A scowl crossed her already furrowed face as she thought about her other rental property standing empty, this one with a *terrazza* overlooking the deep valley to the rolling hills and stark mountains beyond. Why didn't these tourists book with her?

She ran her hands over her face to iron out the creases and approached the couple as they took turns pointing into their guidebook.

"I am afraid you will find little information about that castle in any book!" she called gaily.

Startled, the tourists looked up.

"How did you know we spoke English?" the man asked.

Magda briefly flirted with the idea of pointing out their running shoes, the bags strapped to their waists like udders, their shorts, or his wife's flyaway hair, but instead doled out a measured laugh and said, "Lucky guess. I am always looking for a chance to practice my English. You see, I have a rental property in Santa Lucia and I know how valuable it is to have an English-speaking host."

The woman nodded companionably, but the man shifted his weight and frowned.

Magda's smile stretched further as she asked, "Are you staying in Santa Lucia?"

Ah, that's where this was going. Even just knowing Magda in a cursory way, one probably should have known.

The woman, however, did not know Magda even in a cursory way. Or, at least she didn't remember that she did. "No, unfortunately. We wanted to stay here, but the room we were interested in didn't have a dryer." The man nudged his wife's foot with his own.

Magda made the connection just as the wife blushed faintly. Magda barked in a way that the man assumed must be a laugh. "Yes! You are that American couple! I remember! I told you that if you wanted to dry your clothes as easily as picking up a burger, you should stay in America! Oh, that was very funny!" Magda laughed, her mouth open wide.

The tourists exchanged alarmed expressions.

Magda sighed, quite pleased with herself. "You are so lucky. I almost did not write again, but then I decided to be charitable, and I referred you to the hotel in Girona, where I send guests when my apartments are full. As they so often are." Magda nodded at her generosity. "Yes, I send many people to that hotel, and they always thank me. So does the hotel. 'Oh, Magda!' they say, 'Before you sent us all these tourists, no one knew us! But now we are on the TripAdvisor with many positive ratings! All because of you!'"

Magda pulled her shoulders back and beamed at the tourists who smiled woodenly.

"Now, this castle you are looking at. It was built in the 1500s to protect the citizens of Santa Lucia from the constant battle between the Pope and the Baglioni in Perugia. The people of Santa Lucia have never wanted to be part of conflict, that's why they built their town so far off the Via Flaminia. Hoping they could rest—how do you say? Uncorrupted?—away from the battling armies. In larger wars, like the salt war, not even Santa Lucia's distant location protected the town from being pulled to support one side or another. So the castle was built by the Duke. As a castle, it is fairly small, but the walls circled the town, which makes it special. With the natural spring bringing water from the mountain caves, the people of Santa Lucia could live under siege for some time. Have you seen where the water was routed to create our famous falls?"

The couple shook their heads and the man's arm wound around his wife's waist. Magda failed to notice the man's grip, the firm pull away from the scene. She droned on, "Yes, it's not visible from the drive, the only real place to see it is from Bar Birbo's *terrazza*. I am on my way there now. Come with me! You can buy me a coffee for all my wasted time helping you!" Magda laughed. This time the couple did not smile. Instead they both started talking about wanting to get something to eat at that charming bakery, so perhaps another time.

Magda stepped between them and linked her elbows with theirs, pulling them toward the bar. "No! Oh, I am saving you from a disaster. The *forno*, how do I say? It is too old, too antique. They bake their bread in the traditional Umbrian way, without salt, and tourists find it not possible to eat. And their pastries are too dry. Besides, Sauro the baker is not a good man. He plays the horn for the Santa Lucia band and refused to play at the party I hosted for my 70th birthday! Anyway, to understand Santa Lucia you must see the falls. People come from all over the world and say that the falls, though less sculptured than Trevi fountain in Rome, are more special, more beautiful."

She led them firmly down the steps.

As the couple shared a moment of panicked eye rolling behind Magda's back, their expressions changed. Where once they registered comedy-infused horror ("Just wait until we tell our friends back home about this!"), their eyes widened in confusion, before cringing with incredulity tinged with disgust. For Magda was passing gas with every few steps. Step, step, toot. Step, step, toot.

The tourists leaned forward and away, trying desperately to gain distance from any possible odor. Magda appeared not to notice as she directed the couple through the doorway of Bar Birbo.

"*Ciao, Chiara, ho trovato clienti per te!*" she greeted Chiara, congratulating herself on bringing customers into the busy establishment.

Chiara nodded and smiled at the tourists, gesturing that they were welcome to sit on the stone *terrazza* with a view of the falls. The faces of the villagers followed the tourists, pulled along by Magda.

"Poor tourists," muttered the construction worker to the *sindaco*, the mayor.

The mayor, Dante, sighed and sipped his coffee.

The heavy iron bells of San Nicola carved the blurry sky in ten even strokes. The last stragglers from the morning rush stretched out their goodbyes before heading to work. Even the tourists left, Chiara distracting Magda by asking her opinion on the school system's decision to keep to a six-day-a-week schedule, allowing Edo to gracefully escort the American couple out the door. He waved off their attempts to pay. He was just sorry that the final press of customers prevented him from intervening earlier. Nodding and waving them out of the bar, Edo offered up a prayer that they wouldn't tell their friends back in America that Santa Lucia was full of *blooming idiots*. He remembered very little of his middle school English classes, but *blooming idiots* had somehow stuck. Probably because he and his friends had delighted in adopting mock British accents and announcing that the others were *blooming idiots.*

Magda finally bent her steps out the door, but only after haranguing the old man affixing a poster to the wall advertising the *cinghiale* hunt that presaged the town's November festival. The man grumbled to himself, and continued hanging the poster. He called out a merry, "*Ciao! Come state?*" to Edo and Chiara above the continued chastising at his wasteful use of tape. Magda scowled before cinching her sweater around her narrow waist. Then she bustled out the door, head cocked to glare at the sky. The aged hunter followed with a harrumph.

The bar stood quiet.

Chiara ran a snowy linen under warm water and began scrubbing at the bits of dried milk on the La Pavoni *espresso* machine. She deliberated before asking, "*Tutto a posto*, Edo?"

"What do you mean? Of course. Everything is fine."

Chiara chewed her right cheek and said nothing.

Edo put his hands up. "Okay! Okay! Enough with the third degree. I'll tell you."

Smiling, Chiara turned around and rested her damp rag on the sink as she gazed searchingly at her nephew's face.

He grinned, but then his smile faltered. He ran his hand over his forehead with a sigh.

"Tell me, Edo."

"I don't know how to. I mean, where to begin? It's just . . . not good at home. They don't get me. I don't get them. I know you have to side with them because Papà's your brother. So I'm not sure why we're even having this conversation." He finished, lamely.

Chiara reached out to place her palm on Edo's arm. "It's okay. I love my brother, but we all know he can be a bit bullish. Tell me what happened."

Edo put his other hand on Chiara's before slipping away to pour a glass of mineral water. Chiara watched him, hoping nobody would enter the bar.

Draining the glass, Edo deposited it in the sink before turning back to Chiara.

"They hate me."

"Oh, Edo. No. They don't hate you."

"No. Yes. I know you're right, but it really seems like they hate me. I've been such a disappointment. I never played soccer. I never got great grades, I didn't even finish high school. Plus, they can't stand my friends. The ones I've dared to bring home." Edo sighed and ran his hand along his well-defined cheekbones. "Isn't this the plot of every bad American movie? Is this the part where I say I'm so misunderstood?" He offered up a wry smile, which Chiara didn't bother returning.

She glanced at the door before saying, softly, "Edo, love. They want you to be happy, and they're worried about you not finding your way. I know they probably act angry, but—"

"He told me to move out."

"No."

"Yes."

Chiara felt the ground slip beneath her. She clutched the bar for support.

Edo went on, "I got home late last night. Not so late that I'd have a hard time getting here on time, obviously, but too late for them, I guess. They were up waiting for me and told me I was wasting my life and to get out."

"Wasting your life?"

"Because all I do is party and work here at the bar."

Chiara closed her eyes against this fresh assault. She always wondered if her brother and his elegant Milanese wife looked down on her for working the family business.

"Oh, I'm sorry, Chiara, I didn't think."

"No, it's okay. Your father has always been strange with me about the bar, and I could never decide if that's because he thought it was worthless or because he was jealous that it was left to me."

Edo considered. "I don't know. Both, maybe?"

"Maybe. It doesn't matter now."

"I mean, remember all those Christmases that he and Mamma stormed out of here complaining that you got all the special treatment? We all tried to tell them that of course the family doted on you, after . . ." Edo's voice collapsed as Chiara's eyes shot toward him. "*Oddio*, Chiara, I'm sorry, I didn't mean—my foot is living in my mouth."

Chiara shook her head and patted Edo's hand. "It's okay, Edo. I know what you mean. It doesn't matter. Too many years ago. Anyway, your father probably isn't a fan of you working here. With me."

"I am though."

"I know, *caro*, I know."

A pause. Each of them exhaled in relief at skirting an edge neither of them wanted to cross.

Chiara began again, "So what are you going to do?"

"Do?"

"Yes. Go, I mean. Was your father serious? Do you have to move out?"

Edo considered. "I don't know. I'd like to anyway, to be honest. At home, I can't breathe."

The bell over the door rang, startling them to attention.

"*Buongiorno*, Bea," Chiara said. "*Un cappuccino?*"

"Just *un caffè* today, Chiara." The older woman said, plopping down onto a stool to re-roll her thick knee-high compression stockings. "I have to get to the farm and get chicken feed. Almost out. Do you need eggs this week?"

Chiara moved to make the coffee, but Edo swatted her out of the way, leaving Chiara to turn to the older woman who was rooting through the bowl of sugar packets. Bea scowled, "Don't you have any diet sugar?"

Chiara reached for the bowl at the other end of the counter, and her fingers skipped through the white and brown packets searching for—"Yes, here you go. We haven't had a chance to refill since the morning rush."

Bea thanked Chiara before taking the blue packet and tapping it on the counter. She looked up at Chiara expectantly.

Chiara wondered what Bea was waiting for and then realized. "Oh! The eggs. No, I still have most of the dozen you brought me a week or two ago."

"No pistachio yogurt cake for you lately? No *frittatas?*"

Chiara smiled and leaned to the left, allowing Edo to place the cup in front of Bea. "No, no visitors for awhile and when it's just me, I don't have the energy enough to do more than boil pasta."

Bea snorted. "Yes, I know. When Paolo goes fishing with his cousins, my dinner is toast with Nutella. Don't tell my grandchildren." Bea knocked back her *espresso* in three hearty swigs. She sighed as she wrenched herself off of the stool. "*Uffa* . . . ugh, I hate being old and fat. Remember Chiara, when I was young?"

Chiara smiled and accepted the euro as Bea turned and swung open the door to draw in the smell of low lying clouds that had begun framing the street.

Chiara scraped a bit of *cornetto* off her shirt sleeve before venturing, "You know, Edo. You could live here."

Edo looked up at Chiara, eyebrows knotted together. "Here? Really?"

"Sure, if you want to. I have more than enough space upstairs. It's not new construction, you know. There are some oddities that come with age, and you'd have to be okay that."

"I'm okay with that."

"Really?"

"Yes, really. If you're sure you want me here. Apparently I'm not that easy to live with."

Chiara leaned towards Edo, pressed her check against his and said, "I'm not worried."

It was the second hour of math, and Elisa decided to abandon paying attention. The numbers refused to behave. No matter how much she squinted her eyes or pushed her temples or bit her tongue, understanding danced teasingly out of reach. Her brothers had drilled her on basic math functions until she could do simple calculations. Beyond these, she was in the dark. The teacher wrote an equation with a decimal point on the board, and though Elisa, like all the children, copied down the information dutifully with her blue pen, she allowed her mind to roam, imagining a castle inhabited by birds wearing fanny packs, pecking at decorative towers of birdseed.

The flutter of umbrella pines whispered, pulling her gaze through the window. Chin on her hand, she could practically feel the breeze caress her skin as she imagined dancing with clouds. The fog, sweet and cool, swirled around her, enveloping her, until she felt coddled and safe, insulated from the world. The music was the music of stars, high and clear. The air smelled of ice caps and the underside of stones and the trails of stars, blazing across the sky.

An alley cat leapt onto the window ledge, startling Elisa out of her reverie.

"*Oh!*" She jumped in her seat, knocking over her papers. A quick survey of the room revealed that her *quaderno* lacked the large sections copied in red pen that her fellow students had filled in their notes.

Her heart sank into the silence that followed her yelp.

"Elisa!" shouted the teacher.

"*Sì, Professore?*" answered Elisa, hoping the term of respect would buy her some mercy.

"Come here. Bring your notebook."

It did not appear to buy her any mercy whatsoever.

Hoping to delay the inevitable, Elisa slowly leaned to pick up her *quaderno*. The teacher barked, "Now!" and Elisa flinched.

She scooped up the notebook, furtively trying to push the papers back into the leaves. Papers she once again wished she had remembered to organize and glue in last night. Elisa placed the notebook into the teacher's outstretched hand, and a ruler came down hard, across her wrist. The teacher quickly flipped through the papers, and with an aggrieved sigh and a roll of his eyes, he pointed at the notes on today's lesson.

"Look at this! Half of your numbers are still facing the wrong way! You are far too old for this babyish habit, Elisa. I've been trying to get you to learn this since first grade! Are you an imbecile?"

Elisa seethed. Yes, she used to write her numbers backward. But she had worked at it, and now only the 3's were backward, and that only when she was in a hurry. Or not paying attention.

"You will stand in the corner, so everyone can see what happens to students who hold up the class with their unwillingness to learn. Move, Elisa. *Avanti!*"

Elisa's cheeks flushed as she stumbled. She wanted to ask if her *maestro* would be calling her mother. She needed to prepare, to get her mother out of the house again. Her teacher shoved the notebook back at her.

"You think I want this garbage? Take your 'notebook.'"

Elisa reached for her *quaderno*, but failed to make contact with it before the teacher released it to the floor in a flurry of papers. Elisa could hardly see as her eyes swam with tears. Suddenly she noticed another set of hands brushing the papers into a neat pile. Elisa looked up and saw the new girl, the one from Morocco—Alina? Salina?—on her knees carefully collecting the loose sheets. The girl looked into Elisa's eyes and gave a sympathetic smile. Papers gathered, she handed the notebook back to Elisa. Who took it.

Hundreds of rolling hills away, in what Romans would tell you is the unassailable birthplace of the civilized world, fourteen men and one woman rose in unison from the long, gleaming table to stretch and organize lunch plans. Massimo flicked his wrist forward and back to expose his watch's face and calculated. If he called now, would he wake Margherita from her afternoon repose? Imagining her petulant expression when wrested from sleep, he decided not to risk it. He'd see her when he got home. Turning toward the door, he almost stumbled into the lone woman, slowly arranging papers in her folio.

"Did everyone leave?" he asked. Isotta, he suddenly remembered her name.

She looked up, surprised at being addressed. "Yes. I think they all went to Leo's. If you want to catch up with them."

Massimo considered. Another hour discussing bank business sounded deadly dull. He studied Isotta, realizing his gaze had slid over the one person in the room not wearing shoulder pads. Now, he narrowed his eyes, as she took her time placing pens in the correct slot of her briefcase and zipping her folio. His breath caught. Her features lack conventional beauty, perhaps, but had a certain quality. A shadow briefly clouded his vision before he impulsively said, "Leo's will be crowded. I'd like to unwind a bit before diving back into it. I'll find someplace quieter, if you'd care to join me?"

Isotta's forehead wrinkled in confusion. She fought the urge to peer over her shoulder at the person Massimo must be addressing. It seemed impossible that he meant that slow smile for her. On a good day she might be the recipient of a man's jocular bump on the shoulder, but no more than that, and certainly by no one like Massimo. She bit her lip and wondered if he was joking. As he waited patiently for a response, she decided that he must simply be friendly. Her heart beat too fervently for caution. "Sure," she said, shrugging on her coat.

"Great," Massimo said, straightening her coat collar before nestling his hand at the small of her back to steer her past the chairs left in disarray around the table. "Bankers," he joked. "So careful in every way except the state of a room when they leave it."

Massimo's sense of humor was not as polished as his appearance. Then again, we don't exactly expect Dolce & Gabbana models to send a room into spasms of laughter. Massimo's good neighbors never mentioned it; perhaps that's the wisest course of action.

Isotta laughed nervously, trying not to focus on the way her skin seemed to melt under Massimo's touch. She hoped that he wouldn't feel the sudden heat through her polyester knit dress and her light wool coat.

They walked toward the elevator, and Massimo's hand slipped off her back. Did Isotta imagine that he brushed against her hip a little longer than necessary before letting his arm swing in time to his walk? He gestured her into the elevator and pressed the button for the ground floor before asking, "Any place you like in the neighborhood?"

"No, actually this is my first time in Rome."

Massimo paused as he exited the elevator, "It is? How can that be?"

Isotta smiled. "Strange, I know. But I grew up in Florence, and Florentines never think there is an adequate reason to leave the region. And my promotion is recent, so I'm only now invited to these meetings."

"But you must have gone for a school *gita*. A trip to see the *Colosseo*? I can't believe you've never been here."

"There was a school trip, that's true. I think, two? But I didn't go."

"Why not?"

Isotta knew it was a nosy question, but it was impossible to be affronted when she looked up into Massimo's face and saw his eyes crinkled in concern. She focused on not stumbling down the steps to the sidewalk to give herself time to answer. "Well, my parents lost the permission form."

"They lost the form? More than once?"

"That probably makes them sound like bad people. They aren't. I'm the youngest of five, and my sisters kept my mother busy, and anyway she never really recovered from the last miscarriage." Isotta stopped herself. "I'm sorry, that's probably far more than you wanted to know." Her face flushed. Talking about miscarriages in front of this man with movie star good looks. Her foolishness knew no bounds.

Massimo reached for her hand to stop her from walking. When Isotta rallied her courage to look up at him, he gazed at her and used one finger to move a stray tendril of blond hair from her cheek to behind her ear. "I asked," he said, simply. Isotta nodded and smoothed her dress over her hips. She tried to force out a nonchalant laugh, as she'd seen girls do on the street, but it came out as more of a gasp. Coughing to cover the strange set of noises emanating distressingly from her throat, Isotta started walking. Far too aware that Massimo still held her hand.

"Well, my novice traveler," Massimo said with a grin, "It is my duty to make sure this first trip to Rome is a good one."

"Are you here a lot?"

"Just for meetings. I discovered this excellent *trattoria* on the next block a few years ago. It's not elegant, but it is a comfortable place to eat, and the chef makes a worthwhile plate of *gnocchi* on Thursdays."

"That sounds perfect."

They walked in silence, still hand in hand, until Massimo gestured to the restaurant and broke contact to open the door for her. As she passed him, she imagined she felt his gaze on her back. As a realist, Isotta knew that plain might be the best word to describe her, but she'd worked at her figure and dressed to highlight her assets. Her cropped coat, for instance, flared at the waist. She flushed at the possibility that Massimo might like what he saw. That self-conscious glow suffused her features, and as she sat down she had no idea how ethereal she looked—blond hair floating around her shoulders, large blue eyes that were usually hooded now open and bright, drawing attention toward her burnished complexion and away from the nose that she knew was a bit too large and the chin that she knew was a bit too small. As Massimo sat down across from her, he thought that she looked like a Renaissance angel.

Isotta beamed at him and their gaze held. The waiter noted the quiet intensity of the moment and moved away with their menus, resolving to drop them on their table when the spell broke. All thought fled from Isotta's skittering brain. She was lost, drowning in the blissful sea created by this potent, intangible contact. Finally, Massimo reached for Isotta's hand, and she slipped her fingers between his. When he pressed his other hand over hers, she felt an explosion of warmth low in her belly.

Finally Massimo arched one eyebrow and suggestively whispered, "Do *gnocchi* sound good?"

Isotta laughed, not nervously this time, but full-throated. Yes, *gnocchi* sounded very good indeed.

Magda grumbled as she hefted her bags from the *macelleria* counter. Yes, Giuseppe the butcher had saved her the capon as he'd promised, but he had failed to implement even *one* of the suggestions she'd made to increase tourist traffic. Seething, she'd once again pointed out that making a sign that advertised his famous *porchetta*, sandwiches stuffed with rolled and roasted pork, thick with herbs, would draw in new visitors. Who would undoubtedly also purchase the vacuum-packed salami and glass containers of special, locally made grape jam or *tartufata* sauce of olives, mushrooms, and truffles. Yes, especially the *tartufata*. Tourists went bananas for anything with truffles in it, even the old and woody stuff, or the infinitesimal pinch of truffles added to rancid olive oil and touted as "truffle oil." Add a sign for the dumbos who couldn't connect *tartufata* to truffle, and he could be raking in euros.

Giuseppe laughed off her advice, as usual, and tried to change the subject. As usual. Magda had noticed a chill descend over the patrons waiting for him to grind beef or slice *prosciutto*.

How infuriating, she thought, as she looked up into the sky now gaining clarity, the fog evaporating.

Why work so hard to bring in tourist dollars if the whole town fought her at every turn?

They were all stuck in the old ways. As an outsider, she could see the potential for this storybook village. But she would never keep her rental apartments as full as they should be, and therefore she would never make the money she deserved, if TripAdvisor only showed a handful of establishments and attractions.

That castle. If only she could persuade the town council to restore it. The Duke's family owned it on paper, but in reality it belonged to the townspeople who sneaked into its ghost-lined walls for a spot of adventure or as a destination for furtive lovemaking away from prying eyes. Yes, she'd seen evidence of that when she sneaked in herself and poked around. She had also noticed the pile of dirty brocade in a corner of the room with the cavernous fireplace still littered with ashes. She'd run her hands along the long dining table and wondered why it had never been stolen. She'd roamed from room to room, examining the brackets for candles and the tumbled pile of what looked like charred remains of a canopy bed. No amount of reading had revealed to her the secrets tucked deep within the walls of the dilapidated castle. Yes, she had learned the publicly sanctioned stories about the Duke and his wars. But she wanted to know when it all went wrong, when the family legacy twisted back on itself. She had heard a smattering of gossip about how and why the castle was abandoned, but the stories didn't make sense. She was sure there'd be more information about the last in the ducal line if he'd really left Santa Lucia in order to pursue his career as an Olympic fencer.

The castle could be a real draw into this backwater town. More than once she had seen tourists picnicking on the grounds. They must assume it to be public property. Indeed, Lorenzo, the town gardener, did keep the grass short and the bushes pruned on his own time. And she'd seen Ava, the florist's daughter, planting yellow flowers around its crumbling walls. She wondered if Ava was responsible for keeping the wisteria tidy. It must be somebody, or else the vine would have taken over the whole building by now. As it was, a well-formed cascade of grape-smelling flowers covered the west wall, as well as the arbor that lined the walkway between the main building and the kitchens.

It really was a treasure, that castle. If only she could capitalize on its antique charm.

Magda sighed and continued down the shaded alley to her apartment.

Chiara returned from wiping down the tables on the *terrazza*.

"The wind's picking up. Autumn is around the corner."

Edoardo looked up from rearranging the pastries in the case to make the display appear fuller. "Already? Didn't the students just return to school?"

"*Sì*, but nonetheless, there is a cool edge to the breeze. Summer is over."

"Well, it's about time, the heat destroys my hair." Edoardo waggled his eyebrows at Chiara, who grinned.

"Edo, there is so much product in your hair, I'm pretty sure a land mine wouldn't budge it."

Edoardo snorted a quiet laugh. Chiara patted him affectionately on the shoulder. "*Caro*, why don't you take a break. Go for a *passeggiata*."

"I'm okay. I don't need a break."

Chiara studied the boy. Was the fight this morning so painful? Why didn't he want to go? "Sure you do. What young man wants to be cooped up all day with his spinster aunt. Now go!"

"You're not exactly a spinster."

"Oh, two different words for the same pasta. Now *vai!*" Chiara spun her drying towel into a whip and snapped it at her nephew. When Edo still hesitated, Chiara lowered her voice and added, seriousness tinging the apparent lightness of her words, "I need to call your father. I'm more likely to bungle it if I have an audience."

Edoardo chewed his lower lip. He nodded and took off his apron slowly. "Okay if I take a few euros for a *gelato?*"

"At the wages I pay you? I'm lucky you aren't robbing me blind."

"*Grazie*, Chiara." Edoardo opened the register and took out a few coins. Dropping the money into his pocket, he moved to press his stubbled cheek against Chiara's, then strode purposely toward the door. For a brief instant, he stood silhouetted against the light. Tall and lean, hands on his hips, his head turned in profile, he gazed down the street. Chiara watched her nephew stand in thought. As a baby, he had lacked the snub nose and baby roundness of her other nieces and nephews. In fact, she'd wondered if he would ever grow into his deep set eyes, long nose, and full lips. He certainly had. Backlit, his features appeared almost carved. He was a beautiful boy.

A surge in sunshine left Chiara momentarily blinded. She pressed her hands against her eyelids. When she looked up, the doorway stood empty.

She sighed and took the phone out from under the counter. Rolling her head from shoulder to shoulder, she took in a shuddering breath, and dialed. "Filippo? It's me."

"Chiara? What's going on? Did something happen to Edo?"

"No, no. Edo is out for a walk." She paused. "He told me about the fight."

"What exactly did he tell you?"

"Not much. Just that."

"Oh."

"And that you asked him to leave."

Silence.

"Filippo?"

"I'm here. I don't know what to do. I know I shouldn't have threatened him, but his mother is beside herself, and it got out of control."

Chiara nodded, forgetting Filippo couldn't see her. He went on, "Besides, what business is this of yours?"

"We're family."

"So? That doesn't give you the right to pry like *nonna* used to. That bar isn't a license to insert your opinion."

"I didn't give you an opinion."

"Oh. What do you want then?"

Chiara took a breath, her eyes flitting to the door. Ava hesitated outside, and then seemed to change her mind, probably when she realized Edo wasn't in. Not for the first time, Chiara wished Edo would notice how sweet Ava was on him. She watched Ava walk away, head tipped back to catch the sunshine. "I want Edo to live with me."

"Live with you? What do you know about being a mother?"

A pause. "Uncalled for, Filippo."

Another pause. "You're right, I'm sorry."

"I'm not pretending to be his mother. There's no part of me that wants to be his mother. But I am his aunt, and your sister. You all need some space from each other, and I have all this room."

"I don't know, Chiara. You're all heart, but I don't see you taking a firm hand, making sure he keeps to curfew and stays away from those derelicts.”

Chiara stifled a snort, and said, “Mmhmm. Filippo, how is your ‘firm hand’ working?”

“Not well,” Filippo admitted.

“Look, I’m not saying I have the answer. Like you so kindly remind me, it’s not like I’ve done this before.” Chiara fought to keep the resentment out of her voice. It was hard to ignore the quills that only family could hurl. “Maybe it’s time for a different strategy. Maybe we should let Edo find his own way through the groves.”

“Maybe. But what would I tell his mother?”

Chiara rolled her eyes. “Honestly, Filippo, that’s up to you. Tell her that Edo is staying here for a bit to save on gas, and we can see how it goes.”

“Okay. I can do that.”

Chiara straightened as she watched one of the *scopa*-playing old men standing outside the bar, counting his coins. “I have to go, brother. I’ll have Edo call you about details.”

“All right. And Chiara? Tell him I love him.

“I will.”

“And . . . thank you.”

“My pleasure.”

Lunch in Rome passed in a blur of talking. Mostly Massimo talking and Isotta watching his face transform with his mood. She listened to the cadence of his voice ebb and flow like the movement of shifting sunlight across a forest floor. The *gnocchi* were probably delicious but not half as delicious as watching this man’s eyes move from snapping in anger at a remembered affront at the last meeting to lilting with humor as he made a self-deprecating comment about his often-misguided need to be right.

Not until he reached for the olive oil to dress his salad did she notice the ring. She wondered how she could've missed it given the number of times he had taken her hand in his and stroked her fingers. The air seemed to go out of the room, and Isotta sagged in her seat. She knew it was too good to be true. No man like this, perhaps any man ever, would want her as more than a lunchtime dalliance. She had been an idiot to imagine a chemistry between them.

Massimo noticed Isotta's face lose its animated watchfulness. "Is anything the matter?" He asked, frowning. He certainly hoped Isotta wasn't moody. He couldn't abide moodiness.

Isotta didn't answer, but Massimo noticed her eyes pulling away from his wedding ring to gaze up at him with an expression of mute betrayal. Well, at least she didn't yell and make a scene. That was an excellent sign. In fact, he couldn't have designed a better test of her temperament.

"I see you've noticed my wedding band."

Isotta's eyes widened.

"I was married. I'm not anymore."

The sentence hung in the air between them. Isotta tried to decide if this could be a ploy of some kind. She'd never been the victim of a ploy, of course, but she'd read about them. And her sisters would often gossip about the tricks men used to lure women into bed.

The silence stretched into uncomfortable shapes, prompting Isotta to finally whisper, "What happened?"

A darkness troubled Massimo's features. He rubbed his jaw before continuing. "She died."

"She died?" Isotta breathed, pulled between the hope that this was true and Massimo hadn't been toying with her, and the fear that he'd really lost his wife at such a young age. "Can I ask . . ."

Massimo studied her for a moment, and continued to run his thumb along his jawbone. "Yes, okay. It's right that I tell you. We were on the Adriatic, at Numana, swimming, and all of a sudden she wasn't there. I ran all over the coastline calling her. People came, the police boats. A helicopter found her, 500 meters from the shoreline." His voice broke and he stared at the tablecloth, brushing the crumbs distractedly across the red tablecloth.

"Oh, Massimo. I am so, *so* sorry."

Massimo nodded, absently making a pile with the crumbs.

Isotta ventured, "But ... Numana, it's so mild, isn't it? Shallow? How ..."

Massimo's voice hardened. "It just happened."

Reaching for his hand, Isotta whispered, sadness heavy in her voice, "When?"

"About a year ago. I know I should take off the ring, but ..."

"Of course you haven't taken off the ring. You must miss her terribly."

"I do. Particularly since I assumed I'd never want to be with another woman. But Isotta, with you—"

Isotta's heart dropped.

Massimo continued, "With you, for the first time in a long time, I feel happy. I know we met only this morning. I know I seem like a complete jerk even talking like this." Massimo smiled easily before fluttering his eyes down to the table. "It may be ridiculous. But it's the truth."

He spread his fingers wide on the tablecloth and then gazed levelly at Isotta. "Sitting here, with you, I am happy. And I feel like if I could touch you, your hand, your, cheek, I would feel happier still."

Isotta could hardly believe his words. And yet she could not deny the melting she felt in her chest. Didn't that mean that there was something real between them? Despite this tragedy he carried, and despite the fact that they had only known each other for a few hours and despite the fact that he was far out of her league? This must be something worth pursuing.

She leaned across the table and turned her face toward him, offering him her cheek. It was a bold move, far more daring than she would ever have dreamed of being. Far more daring than anybody who knew her would believe possible. No wonder that in the space of a breath, her heart tightened in her chest until it ached.

Massimo stretched his hand across the table, and stroked a line between Isotta's light eyes and her delicate mouth. His other hand joined the first and together they cupped her face. Impulsively Isotta took one of his hands in her own and turned her face to kiss his palm, slowly, while watching his expression, scared that she had now crossed a line.

Instead, she heard Massimo's breath turn ragged. He whispered, "Let's get out of here."

Isotta stood, so suddenly she surprised not only the waiter passing behind her, but also herself. "Okay."

Massimo tossed his napkin onto the table and rose, looking down into Isotta's beseeching eyes. He leaned down and gently pressed his lips close to her ear before whispering, "You won't regret this."

Isotta held the table to keep from falling. Massimo pulled away from her and smiled his wide and perfect smile. He took his wallet out of his pocket and dropped a handful of bills on the table.

The sight of the money snapped Isotta out of the spell. "Wait! What about the afternoon meetings?" Massimo wound his arm around her waist and pulled her close before helping her into her coat. "We'll call in, say that you got food poisoning and I'm taking you home."

"Am I going home?"

"Oh, I can't tolerate a two hour train ride. There's a hotel by the train station, we'll go there."

Isotta tried to think, but there seemed to be too much blood in her brain. "Okay."

"Okay," Massimo agreed. "Now, I'll call the bank. While I am doing that, why don't you pop into that shop and buy us some bottles of water?" Massimo almost held his breath, hoping. If she didn't do it without complaint, he wasn't sure this would work.

But she nodded as if hypnotized and made her way through the electric doors of the grocery store. Massimo flipped open his phone and quickly dialed. "Mamma? I'm not coming home tonight."

"What do you mean you're not coming home?" His mother's voice pitched high. "What's going on?"

Massimo paused, not wanting to break the charm of the moment by speaking of it aloud. "I think I found her."

He grinned as his mother gasped and said, "Is it like the time in February in Milano?"

He laughed easily. "No, it's more like the time in July in Perugia. Only better. I was careful."

"Okay," his mother answered slowly. "But, what am I supposed to tell Margherita?"

"Tell her, tell her something. It doesn't matter what. I'll be home in the morning."

At this point, you must be wondering, "Who is Margherita? And what does he mean 'July in Perugia'?" You are right to wonder.

At 1:15 the end-of-day school bell clanged, echoing through the corridor. Elisa clutched her papers to her chest, hefted her backpack onto her shoulder, and bolted out of the classroom.

"Elisa!" a girl's voice called.

Her steps slowed. At the doorway of the school, she took a breath and turned around.

The Moroccan girl caught up to her and took her hand. Her face watchful, she said, "What Maestro did today? It was ugly."

Elisa bit her lip and tried to control the tears that threatened to spill over her lashes. She nodded.

"He was always like this?"

Elisa paused, not sure how to answer the question she'd never considered.

The other students eddied around them, a few stopping at this source of stalled movement. Elisa caught the gaze of Mario, one of her classmates. He'd heard the Moroccan girl's question, and answered, "No, he wasn't. I mean, he was never really fun. But in fourth grade—before you moved here, maybe?—he started shouting more. And remember, Elisa? When he spanked you?"

It's true. He did that. It is appalling, isn't it, how adults can dehumanize children?

The Moroccan girl's gaze shifted from Mario to Elisa, studying her response. Elisa just nodded again, her chin trembling.

Mario patted Elisa's shoulder before continuing to the *piedibus* that would take him to his home in the hills above Santa Lucia where his mother waited with a hot lunch. Elisa watched Mario and his friend Angelo grab hands and run, no doubt racing to the *alimentari* for candy. Elisa ducked her head trying to force back the easy tears. As her classmates whirled past her, she felt more pats on the shoulder and squeezes of her hand.

Finally, the crowd thinned. Elisa looked up to see the Moroccan girl, her face glowing like good caramel. Elisa mumbled, "I'm sorry, I don't remember your name."

The girl answered "Fatima," with a smile that revealed a row of perfect teeth. Elisa wondered if people in Morocco had more teeth than people in Italy.

"I'm Elisa."

"I know."

Elisa ventured a smile. "I should know your name. I'm so empty headed."

"Oh, I don't think your head is empty. I think you found some better spots to be."

Elisa laughed.

Fatima tugged Elisa's hand. "Come on! The fog has gone *arrivederci!*

The sun is happy, let's get *gelato!* There are so many kinds! I want to try every *gelato* flavor in the world. But today I'm getting *gianduja*. It will be hard to try every flavor because I always get *gianduja*. It's my favorite. What's yours?"

Elisa laughed again at Fatima's whirling, and increasingly accented, speech. "I like *gianduja* too. But I can't."

"Your mother needs you home?"

Elisa closed her eyes at the thought of her mother getting a phone call in her absence. "No."

"Then come with me. We'll get one big one and share it."

"You have money?" Elisa asked, doubtfully.

Fatima patted the right pocket of her long skirt. "Yes, from helping Mamma with the cleaning."

At Elisa's lack of response, Fatima squeezed her hand and pulled her. Making sure she spoke clearly she added, "Come on! If we are going to argue, let's have it be about which *gelato* is best with *gianduja*. I say banana." Fatima grinned, her cheeks flushed like young persimmons.

Elisa hesitated for barely a moment, before squeezing Fatima's hand in return. "Banana! *Che schifo!*"

Whatever awaited her at home would probably be easier to bear with a sweetened stomach.

Edoardo rounded the doorway back into Bar Birbo. "*Ciao*, Chiara!"

Chiara kept her gaze on the tin shaker she was filling with cacao powder while answering, "*Ciao*, Edo! Did you get *gelato?*"

For a moment he was tempted to confide in his aunt, to tell her how he'd seen the boys from his school days. The ones that would make fun of everything from the color of his shoes to his awkwardness during wrestling. He'd lost his appetite. He supposed he could have gotten a *gelato* on his way back to the bar, but he'd gotten distracted by the sight of two girls sitting on the *comune* steps beside the *gelateria*. One was the girl who he always spotted running to and from school. He almost didn't recognize her, Elisa he thought her name was. She'd pushed her hair off her face, behind her ears, as she leaned forward to listen to the other girl. He'd even seen a brief flash of a smile. It occurred to him that he'd never before seen that girl smile. Which was a shame, her smile was lovely, softening the hard angles of her face and bringing a golden cast to her pallid features. The other, foreign, girl was new to Santa Lucia, but he'd seen her sauntering back and forth to school, eyes often gazing upward to catch sight of the underside of the roof overhangs and the trim around the windows. Her curiosity at her surroundings always prompted him to peer into the same shadows to see what she saw.

He'd been so charmed, he'd paused to watch the girls. Ava, who had been passing with a box of lavender seedlings, had stopped beside him. The two of them had stood there, silent, just watching. As he'd said goodbye to Ava, he'd noticed she looked wistful. He wondered if her youth had been any easier than his. It should be noted that Ava's youth was ripe with its share of tragedy. But that's a story for another day.

Deciding not to burden his aunt, who was already laden with the confidences of Santa Lucia's coffee drinkers, he smacked his stomach and declared, "Nah. I decided that a few moments of sweet bliss aren't worth losing my girlish figure." Here he put one hand behind his head and the other on his waist like a pinup model next to a Ferrari.

Chiara laughed easily. "No chance of that, Edo, what with all the weights you lift and those long bike rides."

"Well, one never knows," Edoardo waggled his eyebrows and grinned. "Just one *gelato* could be the thing that sends my trim body running for the hills."

Chiara looked down at the substantial flesh straining a bit against her shirt and sighed. "Maybe that's what happened to me. One too many *gelati.*"

Edoardo cried in mock horror and then ran to throw his arms around his aunt. "You are beautiful. Always have been, always will be. No amount of *gelato* will change that."

Chiara squeezed her nephew, then pulled away to pat his cheek affectionately. "You are a sweet boy, Edo. Now get to work."

Edoardo dropped the three euros back in the register before removing a fresh apron and tying it briskly around his hips. He asked, nonchalantly, "Did you get a hold of my father?"

"Yes. It's all set. You should go home early today though and talk to them. Plus, you'll need to pack."

"Really? He wasn't angry?"

"He wasn't pleased, but he doesn't like the tension any more than you do. He made sure to order me to tell you that he loves you."

Edo grinned. "I can't believe it. When can I move in?"

"Tonight? Tomorrow? It won't take me long to clear out the spare room. It's just full of boxes of water right now."

"I can move those, let me do it."

Chiara nodded.

Edo sighed and shook his head, surprised at how expansive he felt without the weight he hadn't realized he had been lugging. "Any action while I was gone?"

"Let's see. Vincenzo came in and complained that Roberta in the apartment above him is watering her plants just when he looks out the window. He's sure it's deliberate."

"Ha! Does he think Roberta waits all day for him to put his head out of the window? Though come to think of it, I wouldn't put it past her. That woman has the patience and tenacity of a *ragno*."

Chiara poked Edoardo on the shoulder, "Don't let Roberta hear you compare her to a spider! But, yes, agreed. Then again, she's a tea drinker, and they are a shifty lot." Chiara mugged. "What else? Oh! Laura came in ostensibly for a *marocchino*, but really because she's just so full of excitement that Marcello—you know her son? He's not that much older than you, and a police officer—he passed his exams and is beginning work in Santa Lucia. She wanted to talk more about how they are overworking him already, but Dante, the mayor, not the bricklayer, dropped in for a glass of wine."

"It's early for him, isn't it? He usually drinks wine in the evening."

"Yes, but he needed some relaxation. He just got word from VUS that they are going to be repairing the water lines that run under the *piazza* through November, maybe even December."

"Okay. And? That's good right? People have been grumbling about the lack of water pressure for years."

"Yes, but Edo—the festival. Where will the men roast the *cinghiale*? Or set up the tables?"

"*Madonna mia!* I'd forgotten! *Cavolo*, Chiara, won't that be bad for the bar, too?"

"Certainly, unless the council figures out a place to hold the *sagra*. That income gets us through the winter."

Edo bit his lip and thought as he emptied the little round dishwasher. "I suppose our *terrazza* is too small."

"Far too small. But maybe we can do the roast out there, and set the tables throughout the streets."

"That might work." Edoardo's vision was caught by a man in mismatched pants and coat bustling down the street, checkered hat pulled low over his brow. "Oh, no. Gird yourself, Chiara. Here comes Arturo, no doubt upset again because he found yet more evidence that his Parisian wife is cheating on him."

Chiara looked up. "Oh, poor Arturo. What heartache." She readied her warm smile and flipped the switch to pull a shot of *espresso*.

As Arturo entered the bar, unbuttoning his jacket, he was pushed out of the way by Luciano, lurching up to the counter. He waved his arm wildly, his voice harsh and guttural. "Let alone, pedestrian wingbats! There's nothing—*nothing!*—and I don't propagate the garden with loam or salt. No! I don't! Whatever the chattering monkeys say. They portend evil, as everyone knows."

The words made no sense, but Edo knew what Luciano wanted. Nodding, Edo placed a cup under the La Pavoni to catch the thick drops of *espresso*, while reaching for the bottle of *grappa*.

Arturo minced his steps to the end of the bar and shot a look of revulsion at Luciano. "Honestly, Chiara," he whispered, "He just gets worse and worse. He was blind drunk this *morning*, trying to attack Massimo. Don't shake your head, I saw it myself! Luckily, Patrizia stepped in, probably offered him food like always. Really, how much longer are we supposed to pretend this is normal?"

Chiara bit the corner of her lip and watched as Edo placed the cup on the saucer, handle pointed to his left before he poured a generous slug of the distilled liquor into the cup. Replacing the *grappa*, he set the cup in front of Luciano, ignoring the rumpled odor of unwashed tweed.

"Here you go, Maestro Luciano," he said gently.

Luciano blinked at the honorific and for an instant his eyes seemed to see Edo as if through a veil. The moment passed and he grunted before setting his cane to hang on the bar while he blew delicately into his coffee.

Isotta and Massimo walked out of the hotel into Rome's clean, early morning air. Isotta inhaled deeply. She felt different, somehow. More awake, more solid. It was because of this man. Impossible that less than 24 hours ago she had been walking to the bank meeting, nervous about her new position, nervous about meeting new people, nervous about getting lost and being late. Now her insides felt so fluid, so warm, she couldn't imagine ever feeling nervous again. Not with Massimo beside her.

She turned toward him, craving his arm around her again. Smiling, she stretched on her tiptoes for a kiss.

Massimo squinted at his watch and patted her shoulder, "*Un caffè* before we head to the train station?"

Isotta's smile dissolved. "Um, okay. Sure. *Un caffè.*"

"*Allora*, there's a bar on the corner. I want to check the paper, see how Inter Milan did in last night's game." He grumbled and began walking, leaving her standing outside the hotel.

Ouch. That had to sting. The last thing you want after a night of passion is to realize that your lover sums it up by regretting not watching a soccer game.

Isotta's legs started to give out. Was Massimo already regretting their night together? She ran her fingertips over her lips, still tender from pressing against Massimo's, her cheek still abraded from his morning stubble rubbing against her as he breathed in her ear. She had planned to close her eyes on the train and remember every moment of their love-making. Her bruised lips and raw cheek were talismans she had planned to treasure. In the shower this morning, she'd even imagined bringing Massimo home to her family and seeing their looks of surprise that she could attract a such a man. Those thoughts had been interrupted by Massimo opening the steamed shower door and joining her. The next hour had been a foggy blur of sensation, of passion rising and passion spent and passion rising again.

And now.

She was still standing outside the hotel, watching Massimo's broad shoulders recede down the street.

Was he expecting her to catch up? Did he notice she wasn't beside him? Or was he hoping she would stay behind and let the connection between them, the memories of last night, fade away like the heat from stone walls at the end of the day?

Massimo turned, "Isotta? Are you coming? You have a train to catch and I need to get back to Santa Lucia before traffic gets heavy. If we want coffee we'd better hustle."

Isotta's legs moved as if pulled by marionette strings. Jerkily, and without her input.

When she was standing beside him again, he smiled down at her and touched her chin with his forefinger. Was it her imagination, or was that smile colder, almost forbidding? "I apologize for my distraction, darling. My head is already in the car, away from you, missing you. I know I should enjoy our last few moments together before we head home, but I can't help feeling how lonely I'll be in less than an hour."

Relief flooded Isotta. That was it. It wasn't that he was ready to toss her aside. Her eyes filled with tears, and she ducked her head so Massimo wouldn't see and think her a fool. But he lifted her chin and used his thumbs to stroke the tears from her cheeks before kissing each of her eyes in turn. "Isotta? What is it, *tesoro mio*, my treasure?"

A cry escaped Isotta's throat and she clapped her hand over her mouth and shook her head, finally whispering, "Nothing, nothing, Massimo. It's just that I will miss you." Her voice gained strength. "When can we see each other again?"

His broad smile took her breath away. "How about next weekend? When I come to Florence and ask for your hand in marriage?"

Morning dawned fresh in Santa Lucia. The edges of leaves on trees across the valley were in clear relief, and the landscape absorbed the shadows, leaving the air rinsed and pure. Chiara yawned as she flicked on the lights of Bar Birbo, switching on the radio on her way to warm up the La Pavoni. The shop filled with a distant music.

Brushing chestnut-colored bangs off her forehead, she walked to the door to greet Roberto, arriving in his three-wheeled truck with a box of pastries, *focaccia*, and *tramezzini*, little crustless sandwiches so popular at lunch time. Chiara checked to make sure the tuna and artichoke *tramezzini* were included, since she had just changed her order from tuna and olive, once Edo confessed a fondness for artichokes. Yes, all good, she nodded, signed the proffered form, and bid Roberto goodbye. He leapt back into his Ape to deliver a box to Luigi, the owner of l'Ora Durata, Santa Lucia's lone trattoria. Chiara's ears briefly filled with the rattling engine noise, before quiet again descended over the gleaming surfaces of the bar. The song playing was one of her favorites from her youth, and she swayed and hummed as she filled her display case with the freshly arrived baked goods. Every once in a while, a piece of the song bubbled out and she sang, sending her resonant alto across the still air.

It was her favorite time of day. The empty bar spoke of possibility. The light washed away the difficult feelings that often slithered in at night. She was alone with her morning thoughts, and those thoughts were simple, manageable. Edo was moving in today, and she was already looking forward to sharing dinner with him. There was a clean, new-day smell in the air.

Chiara looked up when the door opened, and Stella, the mayor's wife, entered.

"*Un cappuccino*, Stella?"

"*Sì, grazie.*"

"Why the long face?"

Stella bit her lip and waved her hand, as if batting away irritating insects.

Chiara chewed her cheek and continued preparing the coffee, waiting for Stella to gather herself.

"*Eccolo.*"

Stella nodded, then burst out, "It's Dante."

Chiara nodded, "*Sì?*"

"Well, I just don't think he's into me anymore."

"What do you mean?" Chiara tried not to laugh at the phrasing. Stella must've been watching American romantic comedies again.

"I don't know. He ignores me. I make him dinner, he takes it to eat in front of the TV. Says after a day of hobnobbing with big and important people and being the big and important mayor," Stella puffed our her chest and mimed swaggering with her shoulders before collapsing over the cup and stirring disconsolately, "he just wants to be entertained in peace. I cut my hair, he doesn't notice. If I point it out, he'll nod, but it's almost like he resents my making him look at me."

At Chiara's skeptical expression, Stella added, "Seriously, Chiara! It's like it's painful to look at me." Stella drew her face up like a prune to demonstrate. Chiara reached for Stella's hand and held it.

Stella blinked back tears. "And I can hardly blame him. Look at me! Who has seven children anymore? Nobody! And this is why! Look what it does to a woman's body! I don't know why I had to be the only woman who obeyed the church's teachings on birth control. Damn church." Stella looked aghast at her own words. "Oh, I didn't mean that Chiara, you know I love the church."

"I know, *cara*, I know."

"And I love my children."

"Of course."

"But I don't love what seven births have done to my body." Stella held out her hands and stepped back from the bar, looking down at herself with revulsion. She shivered and whispered, "Well, it can't be helped. What sags can't be made tight. It's no wonder Dante won't sleep with me. I'm hideous."

"Stella! That's enough! You are absolutely not hideous. No, you aren't a nubile young girl anymore, but who among us is?" Chiara held out her own arms, forcing Stella to regard her rounded figure.

"Oh, Chiara, you'll always be beautiful. You have those grey eyes everyone is bewitched by."

Chiara snorted with laughter. "Now you are just being ridiculous. I'm fairly certain I haven't bewitched anybody in at least, oh, 20 or 30 years."

"Well, you could, you know. If you were interested."

"Maybe," Chiara mused. "It feels like I'm related to everyone in Santa Lucia, whether I actually am or not, and when do I ever leave?"

The women stood silent on either side of the bar, Stella sipping her *cappuccino*, Chiara with her elbow on the bar to rest her chin in thought.

She broke free of her ruminations. "Anyway, this isn't about me. What I meant to say is that you are still an attractive woman. Striking. I can't imagine Dante finds you repulsive."

"Well, you could have fooled me. When I was young, I thought men were so desperate for constant sex that I'd have to beat my husband back with a wooden spoon at my time of the month. Now? I'd give anything to have him touch me. I don't know, Chiara. Maybe he looks at dirty magazines or that pornography on the computer, and who am I to compete with that?"

"You think he does that?"

"Maybe. How would I know? I'm not allowed in his office. All I know is he barely acknowledges me now that the children are out of the house and there is nothing to talk about."

"I'm sorry, Stella."

"Me too." Stella spooned up the last of the sugar in her cup and licked it from her spoon like a lollipop. "But thanks for listening."

Chiara reached again to hold Stella's hand for a moment.

"No problem. And the coffee is on me."

"What? Marriage?" a strangled cry escaped Isotta's lips. "You can't be serious."

Massimo's expression darkened. "Oh, I'm very serious. I thought you were, too. Otherwise what was all this for?" He gestured vaguely in the direction of the elegant hotel behind them. Suddenly Isotta was conscious of the people hurrying past them with briefcases and luggage. She felt an ironic spotlight around her conversation with Massimo. Like they each had the wrong part in a play. What was happening? Was this how relationships progressed? She'd never heard of anything like this, but her sphere of experience was admittedly limited.

She did not know how to answer the man who suddenly felt like a stranger, despite the fact that she had kissed every mole on his body and knew the exact direction that his chest hair whorled. Images from last night smacked into the confusion of the moment to leave her mute. It is understandable, the images from last night are indeed quite distracting.

"Look, Isotta, I'm not the kind of man to mess around. Once I make a decision, I never vary. I've decided that I want to be with you. If that's not what you want, then last night clearly didn't mean to you what it meant to me."

"It did! Oh, Massimo, it did! I just . . . I'm just surprised."

"How can you be surprised? Do you imagine I do what we did together last night without thinking of marriage?"

"I don't know! I don't know! I don't know how these things work! It's not like I've been . . . it's not like I've been with others," Isotta stammered.

Massimo's face lightened. "Really? I was your first? Oh, how sweet." He moved closer to her until his body was so close she could feel his heat. He continued stepping forward, forcing Isotta backward until she felt the hardness of the rose-colored stucco wall behind her. Massimo pressed against her, his arm above her head, smoothing her hair. He murmured, "This does explain some things."

"Explain some things? Bad things? You mean I wasn't . . . good?"

"Oh, you were wonderful, but the beginning did feel a little, well, how can I say this delicately? A bit bound."

Isotta felt her cheeks redden.

He murmured, "*Tesoro*, it's nothing to be ashamed of. It only makes me want you more. Again. Now." Isotta darted a glance at his face, to see if he was mocking her. But his eyes were inviting, like they were last night. He stroked her cheek and let his hand drift down her body as he pressed more snugly against her, until she could feel him, firm and insistent. She hated herself for wanting him again. Massimo rested his warm lips against her ear and whispered, "I wish you didn't have a train to catch."

He pulled away. Taking her hand he led her down the street and said, "So let's talk about the wedding."

Magda tried to burrow back under the covers, ignoring the sunlight piling on her windowsill. But sleep eluded her, no matter how much she chased it through the blind alleys of her mind. She sighed and heaved herself up, stretching her arms above her and yawning loudly. As her feet searched for her slippers, she pushed one under the bed. Sighing in resignation, Magda got down on the floor to find her slipper, now shrouded in shadows. Her hand swept the space, and her outstretched fingers brushed against a cardboard box.

She snapped her hand away as if burned. She pressed that hand against her mouth and sat up on her knees, her body a dark smudge ensconced in a voluminous white nightgown. Gingerly she reached again under the bed and found her slipper. Not bothering to perch back on her tousled blankets, she swung her feet around and placed each in its own warm and woolly slipper.

A wave of sound began crescendoing from the base of her skull, threatening to overwhelm her. She forced down the mental static and tried to slow her heart rate.

Don't think of the box.

Don't think of the box.

Blast.

All she could do was think of that damned box.

She stood and strode purposely into the bathroom. She hadn't shared a home with anyone since her husband had wandered off like an idiot during their trip to Thailand ten years ago, never to be heard from again. And yet she still locked the bathroom door with a satisfying click. Magda turned on the faucet to full capacity and hummed loudly as she ran a line of toothpaste over the bristles of her toothbrush. Vigorously she scoured her teeth, delighting in the foam and the ensuing need to concentrate on not letting a dribble of toothpaste ruin her nightgown.

She swished water as if it was full of pixies she had to stun by tossing them roughly in her mouth. Then she spat. Stepping to the shower, she turned on the water as hot as possible. If she were lucky, by the time she exited the shower the memory of the box brushing against her fingertips would have receded. She would be ready to face another day.

Fatima paused in the *piazza* to take in the view of the distant hills. She inhaled. The air smelled of flowers pulling into themselves, concentrating before they began to wither. She watched the burnished light leap and play across the hills. Fatima noticed all of this without joy or interest.

A grumble from her stomach reminded her that she needed to get a *cornetto* at the *forno* before school. Her mother hadn't made their customary breakfast of fried eggs with cumin this morning. When Fatima had raised her hand to knock on her parents' bedroom door, she'd heard hushed voices and crying. Instead of knocking, Fatima had stroked the door and offered up a prayer for her family. Then she'd taken coins out of the scuffed bowl and closed the front door softly behind her.

Outside the bakery, Fatima noticed Maestro Luciano. He was shuffling a little with his cane, staring intently at the summertime baked-dough display. Silently, Fatima sidled past him through the strings of brown and blue beads hung to keep out the flies. She waited behind the butcher, who was choosing loaves for his shop's *panini*. Fatima's eyes roamed between the shelves full of crusty loaves and the faded pictures of Italy's coastline torn from calendars. When Sauro was finished ringing up the butcher's bread order, Fatima stepped to the register and asked for *due cornetti con crema*. She realized that she had not only pointed at the *cornetti*, she had also lofted her thumb and forefinger high into the baker's vision. A hold-over from when she was new to town and worried about not being under-stood.

Sauro nodded as he put the cream-filled pastries in a brown wax bag. Fatima noticed that he slipped an almond *biscotti* alongside the *cornetti* before placing the bag on the counter. The baker lofted a finger over his lips with a genial smile. Fatima grinned in thanks. She pushed the euros across the glass display case, exact change, just like the baker preferred. He dropped the coins in the register and wished her *buona giornata*.

Fatima tilted her body sidewise as she left the bakery, as usual calcu-lating how many fewer bead strands she displaced than when she entered. She was relieved to notice Maestro still outside gazing up—seemingly without seeing—at the Madonna, safe in her heavenly niche in the stone wall. Fatima approached him and put a hand on his arm. He startled. The haze in his eyes lifted a bit, and before it could crash back, Fatima reached into her bag and drew out a *cornetto*, handing it to Luciano.

He started to hesitate, but then hunger took over. "*Grazie,*" he whis-pered before gingerly taking the pastry from Fatima's hands. She nodded and gently guided him to the benches in the *piazza*. Once they were seated, she pulled out her own *cornetto* from the bag as well as the napkins she'd remembered to bring from the bakery. These *cornetti* were always over-flowing with cream.

Fatima concentrated on eating her own pastry to give Maestro an opportunity to devour his. She worried about how long it had been since he'd eaten. She hid her concern by swinging her legs and chatting. She wanted to tell him what happened to her cousins in Perugia, the ones who owned the kebab shop, the way she would have confided in him before. No, she needed to keep it light. She prattled on about a new pop song she'd heard on the radio. Time was, Luciano would have raise an eyebrow, knowing how her parents disapproved of Western influences. She and Luciano would have engaged in a long-ranging conversation about variations in culture, perhaps touching on her fear of both immersing herself in her new home and leaving the old behind. But this time he said nothing. She spoke about how the song reminded her of a book she'd read years ago, so she'd started reading the Italian version. She confessed she still struggled with the *passato remoto* tense. It used to be a joke between them, but now Luciano's eyes simply grew unfocused and soft. Fatima patted his hand, which made him blink and sit up. "Okay, time for school. *Ciao,* Maestro!" She lifted her heavy backpack over her thin shoulders and ducked nimbly out of the *piazza*, startling Carosello who had been deep into his project of driving an empty plastic tub lined with dried cat food along the stones of the *piazza* with his nose.

Luciano watched Fatima's receding back.. His insides quickly twisted again into their customary clenched shape. He doubled over, desperate to numb the pain.

He rose, shambling toward the *alimentari*. Wine, he needed wine. As grateful as he'd just been for the nourishment in his stomach, now he railed. All that cream would impede the buzz from silencing his brain, from untangling his heartstrings.

Plunging his hands into his pockets, he felt nothing. Nothing except a withered olive still attached to its stem and leaves. Luciano turned the leaves over, from the light green side to the dark green side.

You should know that an olive leaf is a remarkable thing. Amazing, in fact, how the two shades of green translate to the silver halos that float around the trees. There was a time when Luciano would have marveled at those slightly dried out leaves, even though he'd had the identical admiration of the green-to-silver scores of times in his life. Now, he merely thrust the debris deep into his pocket without noting its color at all.

Wine, he needed wine.

There were ways to get liquor, even with no money. He had done it before—slip in with a group of customers, and when Giovanni was ringing up purchases he'd pluck a bottle of wine and step out.

The odds of getting caught were slim. What would Giovanni do if he caught him anyway?

He needed to slow his racing heart first.

A challenge, when the promise of sweet oblivion was jostling his temples.

Edoardo watched the little girl dash into school. He had seen her slip a pastry to Maestro, and his heart warmed. He wondered at the connection between them, and then remembered that for years Luciano had made it his mission to teach foreigners Italian. There had been an influx of Moroccan families settling around Santa Lucia in the last five or ten years and Luciano had always cushioned their adjustment, usually by volunteering to teach them Italian. Edo remembered Luciano telling him that fathers and sons were his usual takers, but sometimes he was allowed to work with the mothers. Rarely the daughters.

Reaching back in his memory, Edo remembered now having a conversation with Luciano before everything went dim for his old teacher. They had stood in the streaming sunlight, Luciano had laughingly told him about a family he was tutoring. The father, he'd said, was a bit less stringent in his religious doctrine than other Moroccan men. He'd sigh in exasperation, but accepted his daughter and wife learning alongside the males at the kitchen table.

It was that girl that Luciano spoke about animatedly, his eyes glimmering with fondness. The girl who was quicker than anyone in the family. Luciano said, affection warming his voice, that the parents and brothers didn't seem to mind being outshone by the girl. In fact, they took pride in her quick mastery of difficult concepts.

More than her facility for learning, Luciano relished her questions. Moving from Morocco had made her insatiably curious about how many more ways there were of living in the world. When she'd heard that Luciano had once visited Vietnam as part of a tour group, she'd wanted to understand how the Vietnamese prayed, what communism was, what people ate for breakfast, was pork forbidden? As Luciano relayed the story to Edo, he'd guffawed, mimicking how wide the girl's eyes had grown.

This must be that same girl.

Rubbing at the bar to remove streaks in the buffed stone, Edo thought about when Luciano was his own teacher. It was painful for Edo remember his childhood. The children had been merciless, treating him like the wounded member of the pack. He was teased and rejected, and didn't know how to understand it beyond his stupid beak-like nose and forehead like a dumb shelf over his eyes. He knew he looked weird, but was he monstrous?

It was Luciano who noticed Edo shuffling on the edge of the playground and asked him to stay after school. Luciano sat Edo down on the child-size seat beside his sturdy teacher's chair. Opening a drawer, he pulled out a glass jar of candy and set it carefully on the desk. "You mustn't tell the others, Edo, but I have a fondness for *caramelle*. I always indulge in a piece or two after school. Would you care for one?"

"Or two." Edo smiled at him through his lashes, still dewy with tears.

Luciano roared his approval.

"Or two, my child."

Off came the lid and Luciano offered the jar to Edo who rooted around until he found a strawberry chew and a lemon hard candy. As Edoardo removed the wrapper from his strawberry candy, Luciano foraged through the crinkling sweets and asked, "So tell me, Edo. What happened today?"

"I don't know, Maestro. The same thing that happens every day, I guess. The kids chose me last for soccer during *ginnastica*. Then made crude jokes that I can't say out loud."

"Why not?" Luciano asked, considering the cherry drop he pulled out of the jar.

"Because then I'd have to tell the priest I said bad words."

Luciano fought a grin. "Fair enough. What does Maestro Andrea do when the children mock you?"

"Nothing. Laughs. And then knocks me on the shoulder and says a little ribbing is just what I need to make me a man."

Luciano chewed his candy thoughtfully. "I wonder, why do the children say these things to you?"

"I don't know!" Little Edo's voice quivered. "I'm not mean or anything. I know I play more with the girls, but that's because they are nice to me. Mamma says I need to eat more *tagliatelle* so I'm not so skinny and weak. Then they won't pick on me. And anyway, I don't even like soccer. I don't see why we have to play."

"Yes, well, not all foods can be *caramelle*."

Edo's brow bent as he asked, "What does that mean?"

"Just that sometimes in our day we get *caramelle* and sometimes we get liver. It is the way of the world. This is easy to understand when we are eating *caramelle*, harder when we are eating liver."

"But Maestro, I like liver."

"Then you are a truly exceptional child." Luciano said, his eyes dancing. "So, what to do about this teasing. I believe I'll have a talk with your Maestro Andrea. He may need to remember how children once teased him for wearing his big brother's far-too-large hand-me-downs."

Edo smiled tenuously. Luciano went on, "But let's let that stay between you and me. Safeguarding the wounds of others is the purview and practice of real men. Will you honor that?"

Edo nodded and to this day he'd never divulged a word.

He never knew what Luciano had done behind the scenes, but the teasing stopped. He wasn't popular, at least until high school when he grew into his nose and his feet. Even then, he never seemed to shake off the perception of being awkward, gangly, weak. Older villagers still saw him that way.

He wondered now what Luciano had said to his *ginnastica* teacher. It almost didn't matter, actually. The magic of that afternoon was in Luciano's kindness. Edo had carried that with him for years.

Edoardo angrily wiped at the tears that leapt unbidden into his eyes. His *maestro* deserved better.

Massimo gently opened the front door.

His mother clicked off the television and looked up expectantly, "Well?"

"Where's Margherita?"

"Asleep. I expected you home an hour ago."

"I stopped at the Autogrill for lunch. It was a long night," Massimo smirked.

Anna held up a hand to forestall him. "I don't need details. But tell me the rest." She gestured for him to sit beside her.

"Mamma, I just got home." The schoolboy whine was at odds with his knowing grin.

"*Ma dai*, Massimo. This is important. And once Margherita wakes up, you know we can hardly have this conversation."

Massimo dropped his briefcase on the chair and stepped over his mother's outstretched legs to drop onto the couch. "What do you want to know?"

"What do you mean what do I want to know? Everything!"

"Let's see." He stretched out, considering. "She's beautiful." Anna's sharp intake of breath prompted Massimo to reach toward her and tuck a loose strand of hair behind her ear. "You know what I mean."

Anna gripped her hands in her lap and nodded. "Really beautiful?"

"Well, not exactly," Massimo conceded. His equivocation was justified, if a touch unkind to his betrothed. After all, Isotta was easily overlooked, but you'll remember there were those moments of radiance. Massimo considered, "Her hair is blond for one thing."

"Blond? How odd. Is that her natural color?"

Massimo gave an easy laugh and leaned back a bit. "How should I know? But she doesn't seem the type to dye it. She's an innocent. Pure, or she was until last night." Massimo gave a dramatic wink.

Anna shoved his leg in annoyance. "Really, Massimo."

Massimo snickered. "Anyway, I think that's what makes her so beautiful. She's hungry to be loved."

"That's what you said in February. And July."

"No, those *looked* right. Isotta *is* right. That's the difference. Anyway, July wasn't my fault. Her parents interfered."

"But February."

"Yes, I was wrong about Veronica. But this time I was careful."

Anna furrowed her brow. "Isotta? That's a strange name."

Massimo smiled. "She's from Florence."

"Ah." Anna paused. "And you're sure."

"Very sure."

"Because Margherita . . ."

"I know, Mamma, I know.

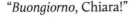

"*Buongiorno*, Chiara!"

"*Buongiorno*, Patrizia! *Come stai?*"

"Pretty well. Edo watching the bar?"

"Yes, but our walk shouldn't be too long today, he looks exhausted from moving in last night. I'd like to get back before the morning rush. Let him unpack and get settled."

"Sure, that's no problem. I need to do the shopping before this rain comes."

Chiara tipped her head back, squinting against the sun. "Rain?"

"I know, there's not that many clouds. But the sunrise was pink, so."

"Oh, Patrizia, you believe that?"

"Well, *funziona!*" Patrizia retorted defensively. "It works at least as well as the news."

"Which is to say, not at all." Chiara linked her arm through her friend's. "I'm just teasing, *cara*. I'm sure you are right. Now, which path today?"

"Let's do the one with the statue of St. Francis. It'll take us past both of our *uliveti,* and I want to check my olive trees for that blasted bacteria making its way up from Puglia. I can't bear to think what will happen if our trees get hit. I'm already worried that the drought this summer is going to decrease oil production."

Chiara nodded, "Sure. Remember, though, the trees have stood for centuries. They'll be okay."

Patrizia answered, "I want to be optimistic, too, but my cousin's grove in Salento was hit and it was a disaster."

As they began walking, Patrizia went on, "Anyway, that way is flatter and my legs are tired from walking to Girona yesterday."

"All that way? Why in the name of the Madonna would you do that?"

"Well, Giuseppe needed the car to pick up supplies for the *macelleria*."

"He's not carting pig carcasses in your Fiat again is he?"

Patrizia laughed, her snorting cackle bringing the twitch of a smile to Chiara's lips. "No, no. He hasn't done that in ten years—since I threatened him with sleeping in that damned display case he's so proud of." Patrizia took a breath to slow her laughing, "No, he had to get eggs since Bea's chickens won't be laying so much with the cooler weather, and also a few crates of wine and boxes of pasta. You know, the small stuff."

"Okay, so Giuseppe had the car. But where did you have to go that couldn't wait?"

"*Ai*, Chiara. I didn't want to burden you with this."

Chiara stopped along the path, and placed her hand on her friend's arm. They stood, through this touch connected to a friendship that had carried them their whole lives, since they were schoolgirls in pinafores. The olive trees surrounding them like a rolling quilt shimmered dully now in a light that was growing progressively stonier. Heavy clouds threatened to spill over the surrounding mountains.

"Patrizia? What is it?"

Patrizia blinked furiously and looked away, "I swore to myself I wouldn't talk about this with you."

"Tell me."

"It's Filamena."

Chiara's hand on Patrizia's arm tightened. "Is she okay? Please tell me she's okay."

"Yes, she's okay. I mean, she's physically well enough, I suppose. She's worried about little Marco. Frankly, I am too."

"What's happening?"

Patrizia sighed. "You know he was never really a normal baby. We kept waiting for him to catch up, but he's only falling more behind. His teachers at the *asilo*, his preschool, keep calling Filamena and . . . oh, Chiara, they are saying there is something wrong with him. That he's special, and not in a good way. He makes strange noises and rocks while waving his hands in front of his face and runs on his tiptoes." Patrizia took in a shaky breath.

"We knew all that, I guess. We hoped he'd grow out of it. But now, the teachers say he doesn't get along well with the other children. He hits them when they have something he wants, and then he doesn't seem to understand why he's in trouble. He howls. It's too much for Filamena, and to hear that pain in the voice of my own daughter. Oh, Chiara, I'm so sorry! That was thoughtless of me."

"Patrizia, stop. I love Filamena like she's blood, I've been part of her life since she was born. I'm her godmother, for heaven's sake! To own the truth, I've been worried about Marco, too. I feel like there's a piece that struggles to be a regular baby, but that part is buried under so much else."

"Exactly. You understand," Patrizia assented, before they began walking again. "So yesterday, Filamena called me hysterical. Marco wouldn't go to school, he couldn't say why. You know he doesn't have all that many words anyway. Paolo is on another trip, so she has no help. I had to go." The rustle of the wind through the olive branches stalled the women for a moment before Patrizia said, "Here let's speed up, the sky is looking *brutto*." She started moving along the path, Chiara beside her so she could continue to touch her friend's arm from time to time.

"Marco had calmed down by the time my train arrived. Once he knew he wouldn't have to go to school, he settled right down. And there was this moment, Chiara, I don't know how to explain it. But there was this moment where I just felt like he clicked. I had pricked my finger on the embroidery I was doing, and he brought me a washcloth, and then he kept coming over and checking my finger. Even one time, resting my finger against his cheek. And I thought, he's in there! There's a loving little boy lost in there." Her words turned jagged, and she pulled a tissue out from her sleeve to wipe her eyes as she walked.

"Oh, Patrizia. Of course there is. How is Filamena?"

"She was glad I came, of course. Made a big deal of my bringing her *mortadella* from Giuseppe's shop. I know she misses seeing us every day, but it did make sense for them to move to Rieti. So much closer to Rome for Paolo's work. But I worry about her, there with no family."

"I wish she could come here when Paolo is traveling, have some help."

"I know. Me too. But with Marco and school."

"Did he go back today?"

"He did, actually. Like nothing ever happened. It's a good school. They are just worried about him. I am too, but Filamena—I'm more worried about her. Who takes care of the mother, except her own mother?"

Chiara laughed and then watched her footing over the spot where the stones were loose. "That's true. I miss my mother every day."

"So do I, Chiara. So do I."

They paused in front of the statue of St. Francis.

Chiara sent up a prayer that the saint of small creatures would ease Marco's way.

A large drop of rain plopped onto Chiara's nose, and her eyes flew open. She and Patrizia stared at each other, as the large drops began falling faster. The dusty path quickly polka-dotted with splatters of rain. Chiara and Patrizia held hands and tipped their heads back to feel the drops of water explode against their cheeks. And in their sudden joy, the years fell away from them, lightening their faces as they laughed like girls and raced back to Santa Lucia.

From her seat, Elisa watched the sky clot with clouds, tremble with a steely grayness, and then begin pelting rain down like a recrimination. She loved rain. Everyone slowed down in the rain, and she was less likely to attract attention. She felt enveloped in a protective shroud, distant from trouble.

The class, however, groaned in unison as the fat raindrops flung themselves faster at the windows. Elisa heard someone mutter, "There goes recess. Again!"

"Silence!" commanded *Maestra*, smiling. She knew how restless the children were, how hard it was to focus on geography when the sudden downpour threatened their short burst of free time. She pretended to finish the lesson early to give the students a bit of extra time to grouse before they shoved their desks together.

At the release, Elisa avoided Fatima's eye contact and slipped out to the bathroom. Once outside the classroom, she quickly crept her hands into jacket pockets, closing her fingers around each found coin. She hesitated at Fatima's puffy purple jacket, but the promise of those coins she'd seen when Fatima bought *gelato* pushed her to dip her fingers into the lip of the pocket. An image of her mother standing over her shouting about her poor school performance hastened her hand, and she closed her fist around the cool and welcoming metal. Withdrawing her hand at the sound of voices approaching the hallway, Elisa dashed to the bathroom. She whipped around to lock the door. Holding her breath as much to avoid the vapors from the open hole in the floor as to slow her heartbeat, she opened her hand. She'd stolen a total of six coins, though only five looked to be euros. One didn't look familiar, and bending to look more closely at it, Elisa noticed the back had a star made out of double lines. Could this be Fatima's? A Moroccan coin, maybe? She couldn't use that, and even if she could, she was still far short of what she needed. If she didn't get twenty euros together soon—she shuddered at the thought of what might happen.

Shoving the coins deep into her jeans pocket, she unlatched the door to admit two giggling girls.

Elisa chewed her lip as she walked back to the classroom. How much did she have at home? Almost five euros she was sure. Today's catch would bring her to six. Not enough. Not nearly enough.

If only she could do better in school. She had been so sure this year she'd focus for real. But if anything, this year was proving to be harder than last. It seemed like the more she tried, the more her thoughts slid away like wet ribbons down a stream.

She fought back aggravation. And what was she supposed to do with a Moroccan coin? It was useless, and Fatima was sure to notice it was missing. Her new friend missed nothing. Elisa had to figure out a way to get it back into Fatima's pocket, but the hallway was now filled with students pulling snacks from their backpacks.

There was nothing in her backpack, save papers that induced panic. She walked into the classroom, trying to swallow her irritation, when she saw Fatima waving at her and pointing at an empty seat beside her. She liked Fatima, she really did. She supposed that if she asked Fatima for money, Fatima might willingly hand it over. For some reason, this annoyed Elisa.

She waved back at Fatima and the grin that spread across her friend's face soothed some of Elisa's jangled nerves. She snaked through the classroom, through the hodgepodge arrangement of desks and around the boys surreptitiously playing soccer with a water bottle. As she picked her way around girls perched around the ancient boombox, arguing over radio stations, one of the boys, Mario, trapped the water bottle with his feet. He peeked over to see if Fatima was watching. She was. He thwacked the makeshift ball with decided strength. Mario cast a shy smile at Fatima. Who suddenly found the floor impossibly interesting. Can anyone quite forget the exquisite pain of young love?

Elisa plopped into her seat. "Boys," she sighed. "My brothers are just the same."

Fatima stammered. "Mine too." She cleared her throat. "In Morocco it was handball, but now they kick anything not stuck down."

The girls giggled.

Fatima unfolded the wax paper wrapped around her focaccia. She gestured at Elisa's shirt. "I like that."

Elisa looked down, surprised. "What? This shirt?"

"Yes, it's a pretty color." Fatima took a bite of her bread spangled with rosemary and chewed thoughtfully.

Elisa looked down again, sure they must be talking about different things. "Oh. I don't remember where I got it."

Fatima swallowed and hesitated before saying, "I wish I could wear short sleeves."

Elisa furrowed her brows. "Why can't you?"

Fatima tucked her hair behind her ears and said, "Girls don't wear short sleeves in Morocco."

Elisa said, "Oh! So you don't have any."

Fatima answered, "Right."

Elisa drummed her fingers on the desk for a minute, trying to ignore the rumbling in her belly. "You could make your own, you know. Just cut the sleeves off."

Fatima hesitated. "Maybe."

Elisa smiled. "It's easy! Bring a shirt tomorrow, and we can cut it together!"

Fatima repeated, "Maybe."

Elisa bounced a little at the prospect of a project. "That would be fun. Actually I have a bunch of shirts my brothers don't wear anymore. We can cut one of those. So you don't have to spoil one of your shirts."

Fatima nodded slowly. "We could try."

Elisa said, "I'll look for a good one when I get home. Also, after school, can you do that thing where we make a list of all my homework so I don't forget any?"

Fatima smiled, "*Certo!*"

Elisa smiled, "Thanks. That really helped."

"No more zeroes."

"No more zeroes!"

Fatima tore her focaccia offered half to Elisa. "Want some?"

"Oh, thanks," said Elisa. "I forgot to pack mine."

Fatima didn't look like she believed her. But she smiled and said nothing.

Chiara stepped down the final step, opened the door to the bar, and rubbed the tops of her arms. Yes, it was definitely autumn. She slipped on the sweater she kept downstairs.

She switched on the radio and hummed as she put away the dishes from the small round dishwasher. She stopped, listening as the pipes squeaked to life. Was that Edo? He'd gotten home so late she figured he would lag getting up.

At the rumble of the Ape, she unlocked the door and accepted her box of pastries and *tramezzini*, scrawling her signature across the form. She unpacked the delivery then stacked the last of the cups and saucers next to the La Pavoni. Switching it on to make herself a coffee, she wrapped her sweater more fully across her chest.

As the bell over the door chimed, she started to say hello to her neighbor until she realized it wasn't a neighbor. It was a stranger. A stranger with a full head of salt and pepper hair brushed back from his forehead to fall in soft waves to below his ears. Longer than men in Santa Lucia wore their hair. She wasn't totally convinced he was Italian until his voice lilted in a fluid, "*Buongiorno signora, un caffè lungo, per favore.*" He had an accent, difficult to place. It had the blurriness of the east of Italy, with some of the bitten-off quality of the south and the muted cadence of the north. Chiara realized she had yet to respond to his request, so she nodded and stepped to the La Pavoni to pull the shot that she'd intended as her own.

The stranger tucked his newspaper under his arm as he flipped through the sugar packets, pulling out the tan raw sugar. He silently watched Chiara as she turned the handle of the *espresso* cup and set the saucer in front of him. She smiled at him curiously, but he said nothing as he carried his coffee to the table.

This was unusual. Italians never sat down in the bar. Unless they were tourists, in which case they always sat on the *terrazza*. The price of sitting was only worth it for a view. The man smoothed his fingers across his eyebrows before sitting back, dropping his newspaper on the table. Chiara got the sense that he was waiting.

But waiting for what?

Normally she would strike up conversation, but she was uncharacteristically tongue-tied in the face of this stranger. Yes, he was attractive, with his deep-set eyes and square jaw. But that wasn't it. Something about him made her want to check in the mirror to assure herself that she didn't carry the vestiges of her restless night.

The bell over the door chimed again and Stella rushed in, trailing the scent of woodsmoke curled into fog. Before Chiara could alert her friend to the presence of the newcomer, Stella was overflowing with words.

"Chiara, you are not going to believe this. Last night, not only did Dante not say a single word to me—what? What is it?"

Chiara was raising her eyebrows and gesturing with her chin toward the table, where the stranger was watching, jaw cocked to the side. Stella turned quickly to stare at him. He tipped his head in greeting before assuming a sleepy expression and snapping his paper open. Stella turned back to Chiara, a questioning expression on her face. Chiara shrugged.

"Well," Stella stammered. "Anyway, um. Oh! There's Vale, I needed to talk to him about something. I'll see you later, Chiara."

As she hurried out, Stella shot a final accusatory glance at the stranger. He blithely turned the page of the newspaper while taking an infinitesimal sip of his coffee.

Chiara watched Stella catch up with Vale, the town handyman. She started to prepare her own coffee when her attention was caught by the warm smile creasing Vale's thin, sun-lined face. Stella was gesturing up the street, her hands fluttering even more than usual, and Vale followed her movements, nodding once in awhile. Finally he put his hand on Stella's shoulder and her hands fell to her side. He leaned down and spoke, softly it seemed. Stella nodded seriously. Vale's hand fell from her shoulder and they spoke for a few moments before turning toward the *piazza*, walking in step, arms almost brushing.

Chiara peered after them, chewing her cheek. Vale seemed the same age as Stella, but he must be closer to Chiara's age. He had always been quiet, a bit detached. Perhaps it was this that made him seem older. Chiara turned to pull her coffee and noticed that the stranger's eyes darted quickly down to his paper.

Elisa and Fatima held hands as they walked out of school. "Do you want to come over?" Elisa impulsively asked.

"Right now?"

"Or another time."

"Oh, Elisa, I'd love to, but my parents would not let me."

"They don't like me?"

Fatima smiled at her friend's ludicrousness. "I can't go to houses that they don't know."

"Oh."

Fatima stopped walking and rubbed her bottom lip with her teeth. "I have an idea."

"For what?"

"So we can see each other after school."

"Oh! Really? What is it?"

"Well, do you know Maestro Luciano?"

"The drunk?"

"Elisa! *Che maleducata*, that's so mean!"

Elisa threw up her hands to shield her face. She yelped, "Well, it's true! It's not mean if it's true!"

Fatima glared at Elisa, who looked away, scowling. Elisa wondered, was it mean? If Fatima said so, it must be. A moment's reflection convinced her that she wouldn't want one of her brothers called a name, even if it were true. "I'm sorry, Fatima, I don't know him. It's what my parents say. And doesn't he smell like old wine?"

"Well, maybe," Fatima conceded. "But he wasn't always like that. You don't remember?"

Elisa screwed her face up in concentration. "Yes, that's right. It's been so long I thought he'd always been this way, but he used to be different."

Fatima nodded. "Maestro Luciano taught my family Italian when we moved here. But then all these bad things happened, and since then he's been like sink water going in a circle. I don't know how to say that in Italian." Fatima made a slow circular motion with her finger and then made the circle faster and tighter.

Elisa nodded that she knew what Fatima meant.

Fatima shrugged, "I want everyone to be nice to him."

Elisa thought about this, imagining that shuffling old man patiently teaching Fatima Italian, which, now that she thought of it, was really good compared to Elisa's English that she'd been learning in school for years. She felt sad for him. And for Fatima. She wondered what the bad thing was that happened to him but supposed it didn't matter.

Goodness, children can be aggravatingly non-curious. An adult would have rabidly pushed for details and then nodded over this juicy bit of back-story.

Elisa said, "I'm really sorry."

The girls stood against the damp wall of the school. The rain had lightened, and eased away over the course of the day, and now the blue-tinged afternoon light warmed their upturned faces.

"Fatima?" Elisa ventured, "Why are we talking about Maestro Luciano?"

"Oh! Right, I forgot."

Elisa grinned, "That's okay. I know all about that."

Fatima gently shoved Elisa's shoulder. "*Basta!*" She laughed. "Anyway,

I like to visit him after school. He has a house with a garden. Sometimes I pull up the bad plants. He loves it when I bring sweets." Her rough little laugh rang out. "Maybe you can come with me. If it's okay with your parents. We could cut the shirt you brought me!"

Elisa scrunched her eyes at the sun that was hiding again behind a navy rimmed cloud. "Maybe. Sometimes my mom notices and sometimes she doesn't. I guess I could tell her I was getting tutored. She'd definitely believe that."

"Yes! Great idea. Actually, I bet he *can* tutor you. He's a great teacher and that way it won't be lying."

"I don't mind lying to my parents."

"You don't?"

"No. Why? Do you?"

Fatima stared at her feet. "Well, yes. My family is always honest. Always. My parents say that without honesty we can never believe each other or trust each other. Or love each other. "

"Oh. So you tell them everything?"

"No."

"No? But—"

"I don't lie to them. But there are some things I don't tell them." Fatima flushed, wondering if her friend could read the secrets written across her face—the hours logged beside the hushed radio memorizing pop song lyrics, the catch in her chest when she caught Mario looking at her, the longing to one day belong to a band of young adults who gathered around the tables of l'Ora Durata to eat whatever they wanted while sipping currant-red wine, the dreams of one day breakfasting on pastries as the sun rose over the Seine and at sunset gazing out over a Japanese temple, like the one she saw in a book at Luciano's.

"There are some things I don't tell my parents either." Elisa hoped Fatima wouldn't ask what. That coin burned in her pocket still, a reminder of the bundle of euros in her underwear drawer. Not enough, still not enough. Stefano would start hounding her soon if she didn't give him the money. If only she could pass her classes, maybe it would be okay. If Luciano could really help . . .

She ventured, "Fatima, do you really think Maestro Luciano could help me? I mean, whenever I see him, he looks so . . . well, foggier than me."

"He has good days and bad days," Fatima said, firmly. "He is so nice, and he has the best stories. He knows everything. Plus, he talks to me like I'm a grown up."

"Do you think he'll actually be okay with you bringing me? I don't want to be mean, but he doesn't look very friendly."

"I know what you mean." Her face wrinkled in thought. "But it'll be okay. I think he'd really like you. I bet he'll be glad to help! This could really be good for him."

"You think so?"

"I do. Anyway, just in case, I'll bring sweets."

Hundreds of rolling hills away, Florentines scoff at the Roman belief that Rome is the unassailable birthplace of the civilized world. What is a crumbling, glorified fighting pit in comparison with Dante and the creation of the world's most beautiful language?

Unfortunately, Isotta could take no solace in the fact that her footsteps might well be treading in the same arc as Michelangelo's and the breath she drew could well be laced with the same dust as Brunelleschi's. She was simply a young woman waiting for the phone to ring. When it did, she startled violently, which seems at odds with how fervently she'd been wishing for this call. But then, Isotta was not used to getting what she wanted.

She ran into the bathroom before answering with a breathless, *"Pronto."*

"Buona sera, cara."

Isotta's hand gripped the phone, and she involuntarily double checked to make sure the bathroom door was firmly locked.

She whispered, "*Buona sera.*"

On the train, she had convinced herself that her encounter with the tall, brooding stranger was a delusion, born out of her desire for a love interest of her own. She hadn't breathed a word about Massimo to anybody, just told them that yes, she was feeling better, the food poisoning had passed. No more than that. Partly because she knew that her parents would backhand her if they found out she'd spent the night with a man in a hotel. Also, she couldn't risk shattering the image of her interlude by demeaning it with something as casual as conversation.

Massimo's inviting voice tugged her back into that dream state. There wasn't a hint of the cool remove he demonstrated in the board room, or the following morning. Isotta stopped herself. Better not to think of that. He was just tired from their night, she was sure. Anyway, the dominance he exhibited was not only justified, it was passing. Far outstripped by the pleasure of his fingertips stroking her face and neck, his warm kiss on her lips when he said goodbye. That canceled out the pluck of worry at his aloofness as they sipped their *espresso*, him flipping the pink pages of the sports news while she looked around casually and tried not to care.

Now his deep voice filled the space of her ribcage. She imagined his firm and gentle fingers. From above a deep well she heard him say, "I told her about you. She can't wait to meet you."

Isotta startled. "I'm sorry. Who can't wait to meet me?"

She could hear him bristling in the silence. "Massimo? I'm sorry, the phone, um. The connection isn't great."

"I said my mother can't wait to meet you."

"Oh!" Isotta tapped her teeth while she considered what to say. Really, what *can* one say when suddenly confronted with the reality that their lover has a mother?

Massimo sighed and added, "So when are you coming?"

"You're not coming here? I thought you wanted to meet my family?"

"Yes, I do." A pause. "But it is important that my mother meet you as soon as possible. Next Saturday, there is a train from Firenze to Perugia at 8:45, where you can change for the train to Girona, arriving at the station at 13:05. I can meet you then. You can spend the night, and I'll put you on the first Sunday train."

Isotta's thoughts swept into a cycling eddy of confusion. Only one thing was clear—her desire to see Massimo again. "I would love to."

Massimo intoned, "Excellent," as Isotta rushed on, "But I'm not sure how I would explain this to my parents."

Isotta was sure Massimo's exhale was the tonal version of an eye roll. "What do you mean?" He asked.

"I don't think they would take well to the idea of their youngest daughter traveling across Italy to spend the night with a man they've never met." Isotta gagged out an awkward laugh.

"I see your point. But it is imperative that you come soon. I cannot wait any longer."

"Is there a hurry?" Isotta wondered why they couldn't conduct their courtship like other couples, talk by phone and send texts, visits planned and anticipated.

"I am not like other men." He seemed to have read her mind. "We cannot be like other couples. The sooner this is clear between us the better. I don't waste time. I know what I want. I want you. I want you in my bed. I want to hold you in the darkness, to run my lips down your collarbone, and run my hands down your body."

Isotta fought back a moan. Massimo added, "Don't you want that, too?"

Isotta was ashamed of how quickly she felt flames of desire licking from the base of her spine. "Yes."

"Then come."

In Isotta's hesitation, Massimo added, "I have an idea, tell your parents you have a training at the Perugia branch. You are new, this is plausible."

She closed her eyes, imagining being in Massimo's arms again. He hadn't mentioned getting married. Had he forgotten? Changed his mind? Realized it was foolish? Realized *she* was foolish? Was she just a fling after all? She needed to see him, she needed to know.

"*Sì.* Okay. I'll try," Isotta paused. "But I'm not good at lying. They may not let me come."

"You're an adult, Isotta. Nobody can tell you what to do."

"I know. But you know how parents can be. With the church, and the family—"

"Yes, that's true." Massimo considered. "But you'll be fine." His voice grew softer, more playful. "Now, tell me what you're wearing."

Elisa rubbed her eyes until yellow splotches exploded against her darkened lids. Then she blinked rapidly to regain her vision. Nope, it didn't work. She couldn't focus. She rubbed her scratchy sweater against her thin arms vigorously. But the burn subsided quickly, leaving behind nothing but exhaustion.

She caught Fatima watching her from across the classroom as she pinched herself all over her arms and wrists. Her friend frowned in concern. Elisa just shook her head, and redoubled her effort to crowd all the thoughts out of her mind. Her teacher's voice strengthened, as if she had aimed an antenna at him. But she caught no more than a sentence or two about decimals before the voice faded back out.

And the ugly sounds took over.

Her father, barking at her mother, his voice deep and rasping.

Her mother's voice high in apology and pleading.

The sound of a belt withdrawing from belt loops like a snake loosed from its skin.

Then banging on her parents' bedroom door as her brother demanded their father stop, STOP!

The sound of leather, slicing through the air and landing with a sickening wet sound.

Her brothers, sobbing, sliding their backs down the door to huddle on the floor.

Her thrashing bedclothes as she tossed furiously on the bed, trying to muffle the rhythmic cries of pain interspersed with rough moans from her parents' bedroom. Her name muttered in anger, and then shouted, once.

"Elisa!"

Her attention snapped into place.

"*Sì*, Maestro."

"I asked you to demonstrate this problem on the board. Didn't you hear me the first time I asked you?"

Elisa hung her head, "No, *Professore, mi dispiace*."

"Huh. And how about the second, third, and fourth times I asked you?"

"*Mi dispiace*, Maestro. I'll try to do better."

"You'll try! You'll try!" the teacher jeered in a mocking voice. "Elisa, if I had a euro for every time you've tried and failed." He mugged to the rest of the class while rubbing his thumb against his fingertips to indicate riches, encouraging the laughter of his students. Most stared at him, eyes round, but some managed to laugh weakly, hoping the sound would protect them.

Elisa just hung her head and closed her eyes, willing the tears not to fall. If she started crying, she wouldn't be able to stop. She couldn't dissolve in front of the class. She just couldn't.

"Maestro!" Mario's voice rang out from across the classroom. "Maestro, quick! Something's wrong with Fatima!"

All heads whipped to stare at the new girl, who was shaking and flapping. Her dark eyes rolled back into her head as her body went suddenly rigid, arched out of the seat and flung onto the floor with a bang.

The teacher paled and raced to her side, placing his hands against her face. Elisa stood on her chair to see over Maestro's head to her friend lying limp on the floor.

"Fatima!" Maestro yelled, trying to shake her. "Fatima!"

A girl at the front of the class screamed and Maestro yelled, "Shut up!"

Elisa's fingers moved to her mouth involuntarily. She noticed her hands were shaking so much she was jerking.

Fatima moved a little, as if waking up. She opened her eyes, "I . . . I think I'm sick."

Maestro laughed in relief. "Yes, yes you are! But you're awake. Thank the Madonna." His eyes found the crucifix above the door. He whispered a prayer of gratitude.

Fatima rose to sitting and croaked out, "I think I need to go to the office."

Elisa jumped down from the chair and took Fatima's arm, guiding her to standing.

"Yes, yes," Maestro repeated, distractedly. "Yes, take her to the office."

Fatima nodded solemnly and shot a wink at Elisa.

Looking up from brushing her skirt, Fatima considered her teacher. "Thank you, Maestro. You're very . . . kind."

The light shifted and swayed as it filtered through the olive trees, tossing filigreed shadows over the lines of Luciano's face. His eyes twitched open a crack and he moaned, throwing an arm over his dusty glasses to block out the invasive sunlight.

How did he get here? What time was it? What day?

Rolling onto his back, Luciano forced his eyes to peer into the endless sky. Bright, it was so bright. Midmorning perhaps?

Luciano pushed himself toward sitting and rested his head against his crooked knees. It wasn't the first time he wound up in the *uliveto*, though he never remembered exactly how he got here. Something seemed to pull him like a trout on a line. His brain sludged forward.

His mind was clearing.

The pain was back.

Giulia.

It was Giulia who beckoned him here, among the trees that she'd cared for since she was old enough to grasp the shears. Her fingers would run over the knobs of the trees, gliding over the velvety softness of the silver leaves. How she cried when they hard-pruned the trees so that their gnarled forms were unrecognizable. And how she sagged in relief when he told her that olive trees were warriors. They thrived on stress. The jolt of deep pruning would bolster the tree to produce marvelous oil. She'd wiped her tears and nodded, her face shining. After that, he'd often find her in the kitchen with a teaspoon, savoring a little touch of the oil. She claimed she could taste the wind in the sleek peppery gold.

Yes, the groves were full of his daughter. Full of his family's laughter as the three of them cared for the trees, surrounded by neighbors calling out invitations to stop for a meal of beans cooked in crockery settled in ashes.

But now the groves were empty, empty. There was nothing for him here. Someone kept the weeds down. Probably Ava. She'd been particularly solicitous of him since his daughter died. And in the corner by the oldest tree, someone collected the amethyst heads of *boragine*, likely less out of kindness and more to top their sausage sandwiches with the silky, slightly bitter greens.

Luciano stood, desperate to quell the memories, to block out the image of his wife handing down bunches of olives to his daughter. Both with their hair held back in kerchiefs, the same ones that his wife's grandmother had used. He saw their faces, hair working out from the fabric in loose tendrils, turn toward him—jeering. Mocking him for his traitorous adherence to life. They were there, beyond the veil, out of reach. And now they were sneering, cursing him for living while they were cold and buried on the other side of Santa Lucia.

Carosello passed Luciano, brushing against his knees. Startled, Luciano flung out an arm for balance, and the dog cowered, loosing an eggshell from the scruff of his fur. The one-eyed dog gazed up at Luciano reproachfully before jogging away without a backward glance.

Luciano shook his head to free it from the shadows, and stumbled toward the town walls. Once at his doorway he fumbled for his keys before remembering he'd lost them long ago. He jiggled the bar of the doorknob until it released, and he flung himself inside. The house was musty and smelled of dead flowers. It would always smell of dead flowers—the cosmic pile-up of funerals impossible to erase.

He reached toward the light switch to banish the webs of darkness clogging the rancid air. Though there was an obliging click of the switch, there was no answering light.

Magda squeezed a heavy, thick-skinned lemon before scowling and selecting another. Four lemons later, she found one with the right amount of give and nestled it in her red basket. She rummaged in the white cardboard box for another lemon and began the process again. This time she was luckier. She only had to glower at two lemons before finding one that met her standards. She placed the lemon beside the first, and then moved on to onions with fat white bulbs and shoots so green and springy they seemed aquatic. As she scanned the shelves for the least expensive kind of prunes, she realized that there were several customers engaged with the vendor at the register. She couldn't make out their words—was her hearing going?—but could tell they were leaning toward each other to speak with more ease than anyone ever spoke with her.

It was frustrating, frankly.

She worked hard to be a useful member of her community, attending town meetings to offer the wisdom of her more global experience. She was always ready to share her extensive business acumen with local vendors. She wanted nothing more than to put Santa Lucia on the tourist map. And yet she was never included in anything. Not really. Her advice was laughed off. Attempts at intimacy with townspeople were met with awkward discomfort.

Such small-minded xenophobes. They just couldn't stand that she was an outsider, succeeding in their community when so many of them lacked the creature comforts she provided to her guests. Yes, they were jealous xenophobes. And, she thought, placing the bag of prunes in her basket, they probably still held it against her that she was from a wealthy country. Small-minded, jealous xenophobes. She should have settled in Rome. That was a city with an open mind. But no, her stupid husband insisted on a stupid small town. Said it would be easier to integrate with the locals. Ha! How many locals did they befriend?

If she was going to be honest, Gustav befriended a few. But that was obviously because he threw his money around like an obnoxious American. Everyone likes the guy who never haggles and always buys the priciest bottle of wine. She had been able to control her husband in many ways, but never when it came to finances. He had insisted that his family money was to be managed by him alone, which meant settling in this dusty village, and overspending. Overspending, that is, until he wandered off in Thailand. Who knew what he was doing for money now.

Magda turned toward the potatoes and tried to find three with dry, curling peels. She wondered if Gustav was dead. Time was, that thought sent a shiver of horror through her heart. Now, it did nothing but raise her curiosity. If he wasn't dead, what was he doing? Was he still in Thailand? Had he spent years funneling money into an account that she didn't know about so he could disappear and live off savings without her being the wiser? After all, when she'd gone to investigate the contents of his trust, it had been empty. Well, if he wanted to live among people who ate dog (they all denied it, but she knew better—poor people would stop at nothing for a bit of protein and didn't have the sense to be disgusted by it) and bathed in stagnant bays of algae-filled water then more power to him.

Magda's fists clutched around the basket handles as she remembered walking into her in-laws kitchen after Gustav's "funeral". Her mother-in-law, in a carrying whisper, was telling her friends that Gustav's bank account was empty thanks to the purchase of the property in Italy, a purchase made to accommodate Magda's need to get out of Germany. And it was that empty bank account, coupled with his sour wife, that drove him to escape. Kill himself or wander off, Magda was never sure of her mother-in-law's meaning. She could hardly ask for clarification after she walked into the kitchen to fetch a bottle of what Germans pass off as wine, scattering their gossip.

She tossed the last potato in her basket with enough force that all eyes turned to her. Throwing her shoulders back, she strode toward the counter and lofted her basket beside the register. Paola began ringing up her produce, and Magda bit back a remark about the poor quality of the lemons. Instead she attempted to crack a joke about how stupid Giuseppe was to not put a sign in his window advertising *panini*. Magda looked around with a broad smile, but everyone's faces registered mute annoyance. One by one, their eyes began looking in other directions.

Handing her money to Paola, Magda defiantly snatched up her bag of produce and stalked to the door.

But her disdainful exit was marred by her own released gas. Magda paused. As she pushed through the door, she told herself that it wasn't laughter she heard, just a rising up of more stupid, irrelevant chatter.

Arturo paused before paying for his coffee, ready to evaluate the next patrons for their likelihood of having some gossip, or a willing ear to listen to his newest proof that his wife was lying with another man. But there was just Magda hurtling by with her bag of produce as two *vigili* drifted into the bar. Arturo nodded at the officers with a resentful smile, and continued out the door. He paused momentarily when he noticed that Fabio, who worked at the hardware store, accompanied the police officers. Fabio was usually good for a few tales. But Fabio was looking stern today. Arturo sighed and left the bar.

Chiara wiped her hands on the soft white cloth as she greeted the men. The officers were looking particularly dapper in their creased pants with the red stripe down the side matching the trim on their jackets, their shined shoes, and their jaunty caps. Chiara grinned. She knew people in other towns that resented their police officers, but she had always felt affection for the *vigili* of Santa Lucia. The old, crusty ones that waved their sticks when an Ape drove by at too fast a clip as well as the young ones with their springy beards that seemed surprised to be on cheeks still rounded with the remnants of babyhood. These were the two young ones. Chiara leaned forward with a grin.

"What can I get you gentlemen?"

The smile faded from her face as she noted the mens' somber expressions.

Fabio stepped to the bar and said in a carrying whisper, "Marcello's coffee is on me, Chiara. I'll leave a five with you for whatever he wants." He pushed the money toward Chiara before turning to pat Marcello's shoulder and stepping out of the bar, down the street to the hardware shop.

Marcello sighed. "*Solo un caffè*, Chiara, *grazie*."

Chiara hesitated, before she turned to prepare the *espresso*.

When she turned back with their jots of coffee, she saw that the shorter one, Alessandro, was holding Marcello's hand like they were boys in grade school again. Marcello was wiping his eyes on the thin waxy napkins from the bar's dispenser.

Chiara reached for her purse which always held a packet of tissues. She wordlessly offered the packet to Marcello.

"*Grazie*, Chiara," murmured Marcello, while Alessandro smiled weakly at her.

"*Non fa niente*, it's nothing."

"I'm sorry, Chiara, I shouldn't be crying, especially on the job, but Mamma . . . Mamma is in the hospital, and I'm so worried." Marcello's voice sank into a whisper and he pulled another tissue from the pack and wiped his eyes angrily. "I'm sorry."

"Nobody apologizes for crying in my bar. Now, what happened to Laura? I saw her yesterday, and she seemed fine."

"*Sì*, when I went home for dinner last night, too. But my father called me at 2:00 in the morning to say that she had heart pain and he was taking her to the hospital. I met him there, and the doctors admitted her. They think it was a heart attack. A mild one, but you know Mamma has never been strong."

Chiara closed her hand over Marcello's fist, which was gripping the tissue.

"How is she now?"

"I don't know." He sniffed, "I had to leave to go to work."

"You could've taken the day off."

"I know, that's what Alessandro was just telling me. But the doctors are doing tests, and I can't be in there. If I was sitting in the waiting room, I'd be a mess. Which I guess isn't any different from how I am now, eh?"

Marcello looked up at Chiara with blurry eyes. He offered her a half smile, and Chiara remembered how thin he'd been as a child. How Laura was always trying to get him to finish his *cornetto* or *panino*, how she fussed over the crumbs and made sure he drank the last drop of his *latte caldo*, warm milk, which she sprinkled liberally with cocoa powder, believing the chocolate to be salubrious. She'd fussed over her daughter too, but once Marcello was born, he'd been the child she wrung her hands over. And then she took a mother's pride in his tallness once he reached adolescence and filled out. He'd never been as smart as his sister, but his family didn't care. He was smart enough to pass the exams to become a *poliziotto*, and how pleased they had been when he'd been able to find work in Santa Lucia.

Chiara remembered how Laura had been saddened when Marcello decided to move out, citing his late hours and not wanting to inconvenience the family. But even while Laura sniffled at the thought of her baby leaving home, she also swelled with pride. This was her little Marcello striding through the town, his baton swinging at his side.

Alessandro patted Marcello's back again, and then sipped his coffee. Chiara asked, "Does your sister know?"

"No. Damn! I should call her. But she hasn't spoken to Mamma in almost a year. Since she moved to Brussels, I think. And what can she do from there?"

"Probably nothing. But she needs to know."

"After the words she and Mamma exchanged before she moved, I'm not sure."

"*Ma dai*, Marcello, come on. You know how hard it was for her, always being in your shadow. She'd been the center of your mom's world for six years before you were born. Maybe she didn't handle it well, but to work as hard as she did, getting a doctorate in linguistics at such a young age, and yet never making her mother feel a tenth the pride she felt for you . . ."

Marcello's face clouded and he pulled his hand away from Chiara. "You shouldn't say bad things about my Mamma. Especially when she's sick."

Chiara leaned forward to catch his eye, "I'm not, Marcé, I promise. I love Laura, and I'll go visit her tonight. I'm just saying, maybe try to understand that your sister's anger at your mom is probably hurt. Because she loves her mother. She just wants to feel loved, too."

Marcello nodded and wiped his eyes. "Okay. Okay, yes, you're right. I'll call her."

"Good. Now, I'll bring a bottle of water and some pastries to Laura later today, but let me go upstairs to get the book I was telling her about last time. You can bring it to her this afternoon, and let her know I'm coming."

"Okay, Chiara. Thank you."

"It's nothing, Marcé. Your mom will be okay. She loves you too much to go anywhere."

～

Massimo

You up?

Isotta

Yes.

You told your parents you're coming?

Yes. All set.

You see? Just as I said.

I don't think they believe me though. I wasn't convincing.

You're coming aren't you?

Yes. They weren't really paying attention.

Soon you'll be in my arms and attention will be paid.

Still there?

Yes sorry dropped the phone.

After school, Fatima and Elisa parted ways at the *piazza* with a wave.

As she watched Elisa stroll down the sunlit street, Fatima felt a pang of gratitude. The last year had been lonely. People were nice in Santa Lucia, friendly even. Friendlier than she expected, and far more so than her own classmates in Morocco had been to the Palestinian kid who had moved to her neighborhood. Fatima wondered, not for the first time, what on earth could have prompted a Palestinian family to move to Morocco? Were they an Embassy family? But those kids tended to go to the International School. Were they displaced by the fighting with Israel? Or did their family just crave adventure? Fatima never found out because she wasn't allowed to speak to boys. He was ignored, as far as she could tell. She remembered seeing him alone much of the time. Just sitting and staring at his shoes, which were so different from her classmates' shoes. Maybe he knew that. Maybe it bothered him.

During their entire move to Europe she had thought about that boy, panicked that her experience would mirror his. What a surprise when her fellow students spoke to her, asked her questions, pulled her hand to join their playground games. When she mumbled that she couldn't speak Italian, they laughed and tugged her hand all the more insistently. With Luciano's lessons, and working to open her mind during school to allow the language to sink in, her Italian progressed far more quickly than she expected.

She had thought this would lead to greater intimacy with the Santa Lucia girls. But in fact, they seemed to tire of her once she was no longer novel. Fatima admitted to herself that her initial uneasiness at their fast gestures and loud words probably didn't help. Nor did the fact that she was never allowed to visit anyone's house. In fact, it was just since she started fifth grade that she was allowed to walk the five minutes to and from school on her own.

It was no wonder she and Elisa had found each other. Yes, Elisa was Italian and of average appearance and she had lived in the town for probably her whole life, but she was . . . what was the word? Spacey. Dreamy. And that set her apart. While Fatima felt pushed out of the margins, Elisa floated around them. People seemed friendly with her, as they did with Fatima, but they both had been wandering out of school alone while the rest of the students clustered outside the door to make afternoon plans.

Fatima paused in the *piazza* and breathed in the thinning sunshine. Her days felt entirely different now. She had somebody to sing pop songs with at recess, rolled up paper serving as impromptu microphones. Someone to flip through magazines with and scrutinize the outfits celebrities wore. Someone to make her her first short sleeve shirt. Playing hopscotch on the playground with her arms bare was the most free Fatima had ever felt. Suddenly, the view of her world that had been prized open by the move across the ocean was nudged a little wider. There was so much more to see and experience. She hadn't realized how much she'd craved having a friend to share that with.

Movement outside the *alimentari* on the *piazza* caught her notice. Giovanni, the grocer, was leading Luciano out of the store firmly, his arm tight around Luciano's shoulders. Fatima frowned and moved toward them.

"Maestro, are you okay?"

Luciano shook his fist at Giovanni, shouting gibberish, "How dare you! Your stench, like a walnut rotted from the core. Acid. Infecting me! You are that poison, you! Your words, vile! Cheating, lying . . . For years I suffered, watching your jars, you evil, shatter—you took her! You took her away from me, and now I've got nothing, *nothing*, and now you have the . . . the . . ." Luciano paused to hunt through his addled brain for words as Giovanni continued to murmur and aim the old man into the center of the *piazza*, "the consummate venom! Yes, to pack me out of this meat! Where is the . . . the . . . *approbation* for the aged? Where is the *benevolence* for the fallen?"

Giovanni turned to Patrizia, who had swiftly appeared behind Fatima, "There are wine bottles everywhere."

Patrizia nodded, "I'll take him home. Do you need help cleaning up?"

Giovanni shook his head. "No, Papà's already got the mop out. You can really take him home? I don't want to leave him here and have him turn around and come back in."

Patrizia said, "We were just closing the *macelleria* for *pranzo*, but I can get Luciano home first."

Giovanni sighed, "I tried not to let him near the wine, but . . ."

Luciano stumbled again and yelled at the men gathered on the benches. The pigeons bolted away into the wash-worn sky. Carosello peered up from his tour of the *piazza* to watch them arc overhead.

Fatima tore at her hangnail. She ventured, "I can take him home."

Patrizia regarded the child, frowning. "Are you sure, Fatima? He's not in great shape."

Fatima reached for Luciano's elbow to help him balance. "I can do it."

Patrizia and Giovanni exchanged looks over her head. Patrizia said, "Tell you what, we'll walk him together."

Chiara yawned as she entered Bar Birbo. Edoardo glanced up at her and smiled. "Nice *pausa?*"

"Oh, yes."

"Did you sleep?"

"Surprisingly, yes. I must have needed it. Thanks for handling the lunch rush."

"No problem, now the bar is ready for you to receive the post-*pausa* rush." Edoardo grinned, and started sweeping up the stray sugar packets on the ground. Something bright glinted among the dust and debris.

Edoardo stopped and plucked the gold shape into his palm and held it out to Chiara. "Look at this. Does it look familiar?"

Chiara took what looked to be some sort of a jewelry charm and studied it. "Hmm, I don't think so. Does it mean anything? I've never seen this shape before."

"It looks like a letter, but also not."

"A 'Y' maybe? With an extra prong in the middle? I haven't seen it either. The gold is heavy though. Looks valuable. Look, the circle at the top is open. Must have fallen off a chain or something."

Chiara smoothed down her hair. "Who was in while I was upstairs? It would have to be one of those customers who lost it, right? Or I would have seen it when I cleaned up before lunch."

Edo leaned against the broom while he thought. "Right. Hmm, let's see. Luciano, but he just barged in and then lumbered out. Looks like he's in the same state he was yesterday when he busted up Giovanni's shop. Who else? Giuseppe, Patrizia, Luciano, Magda, Ava, a few tourists—I don't think they are staying in town—Dante, a couple of *vigili*, I don't remember which ones. Oh! And the principal, I can never remember her name."

"Rosetta. Of course you don't remember her name, she's only lived here for five years." Chiara smiled.

"Well, it was after my time," Edoardo responded airily, assuming a posture of profound exhaustion at the pace of the world.

Chiara grinned.

Edo looked down at the trinket still in his palm. "Should I put it in the left-behind box?"

Chiara shook her head. "It'll get lost. Put it in the register, someone will come looking for it."

Edo nodded and moved around the counter to open the register with a sprightly *bing!*

Chiara looked up as a man entered the bar. It was the stranger from, what was it? Yesterday? The day before? Frankly, in a town like Santa Lucia when everything and nothing always seem to be happening in concert, it can be hard to keep track.

"*Buona sera,*" she said, taking the gold trinket from Edoardo and dropping it into the register.

"*Buona sera, signora, signore.* I see you found something curious?"

"Nothing, just a trinket somebody dropped."

The man's forehead creased in interest.

Chiara asked, "What can I get for you?" as she firmly closed the register.

"*Un caffè lungo, per favore.*"

Chiara nodded and began clicking the grinds into the filter basket to prepare the shot of *espresso* pulled extra slowly to make a fuller cup. The newcomer sat down at the table to wait, nudging the newspaper toward himself.

Edoardo shot Chiara a confused stare mouthing, "*Chi é?* Who is he?" Chiara shrugged. Edoardo wiped down the bar, studying the stranger, taking in his light green button down shirt. The jeans were crisp, almost as if they had been ironed, but the leather shoes were scuffed, and one was missing a tassel. The man glanced up and caught Edoardo studying him. Edoardo assiduously rubbed a stubborn spot on the bar.

Chiara smiled. She placed the cup on the saucer and impulsively decided to walk the coffee to the table, rather than leaving it for him on the counter.

"*Eccolo,*" she offered.

The man looked at her, a little surprised, but a slow grin softened his expression. He looked directly into her eyes and softly said, "*Grazie.*" At the simple word, Chiara felt her heart lurch to the right.

"*Prego,*" she answered, wanting to add something, but not knowing what. She ordered herself to look away, even as she found herself fascinated by the green and gold flecks cavorting in his hazel eyes. There was an expression in them that she couldn't read. And Chiara was used to reading everyone's expressions. She was surprised to feel herself beginning to blush.

Edoardo's voice asking her where she'd put the ginseng syrup fractured the delicate moment. She blinked and walked to the bar, pointing wordlessly at the bottle hidden behind the new delivery of wine. When she surreptitiously darted her eyes at the man again, he was sipping his coffee and reading the newspaper. Chiara sighed, not sure if she wanted the moment to have been a figment of her imagination, or if she wanted it to be real.

She washed dishes and hummed sporadically, debating if she could expect enough people to keep Edo at the bar, or if she should release him.

The door opened, and Dante strode in. "*Un caffè*, Chiara! And quickly please, *sono in fretta*, I'm in a hurry."

Chiara nodded and said, "*Subito*, right away."

She tapped the grinds flat into the filter basket and slipped it into the La Pavoni. Edoardo asked if Dante wanted anything to eat, but Dante just shook his head, annoyed at the question. Edoardo turned and grinned at Chiara, rolling his eyes a touch.

Chiara placed the coffee in front of Dante and couldn't resist asking, "How is Stella?"

"Stella? She's fine. Why wouldn't she be?" Dante narrowed his eyes as he stirred his sugar into his *espresso.*

"Just wondering. I haven't seen her lately."

Dante waved the question away. "She's busy. Last night she had a meeting."

"A meeting?"

"Yes, the women's *bocce* league."

Chiara was pretty sure there wasn't a women's bocce league.

She straightened the napkins on the bar, deep in thought. When she glanced up, she found the newcomer observing Dante.

Feeling Chiara's eyes on him, the man looked at her and smiled, a slow and slightly crooked smile. Again, Chiara felt her heart lurch. This was ridiculous. She wasn't some schoolgirl. She was a grown woman with a bar to manage, a nephew to worry over, and a town to look after. What were these quivery feelings when there was so much to occupy her? Still. She couldn't help but be aware of nerve endings she thought had died long ago.

Darting a glance at him, she noticed the stranger watching her, the smile still playing around his sensitive lips. This time she held his gaze.

Luciano winced and opened his eyes. His vision was blurry, pained, and he reached for his glasses. His hand stumbled over the coffee table and then he felt his glasses slide into his hand. He looked up into Fatima's worried, brown eyes.

"What time is it?" he croaked, then coughed, clearing what felt like a week's worth of debris out of his throat.

"I'm not sure. Almost dinner time."

"What are you doing here? Shouldn't you be home?"

"It's okay. After Patrizia and I brought you home from the *alimentari*, I went home and told Mamma you were sick, and she sent me back to you with this bottle of broth. It's still warm, do you want some?"

Luciano wasn't really hungry. It felt like he'd never be hungry again, but he nodded.

Fatima rose, "Let me get a glass of water for you."

Luciano's thoughts pinwheeled, and then he remembered that he couldn't let Fatima turn on the water, she'd notice, she'd see. But before he could formulate the right words, Fatima was back with a glass. "I brought some water with gas, that always helps me when I don't feel well."

The fizzing and popping of the water made Luciano wince anew, but he endeavored to smile and nod before taking an experimental sip. Fatima handed him a cup of warm broth with unusual spices that reminded him of Christmas. He took tentative taste, surprised at how easily the broth slid into his stomach, gilding his insides. "This is delicious, Fatima. Please thank your mother for me."

Her thin face lit up as she sat on the coffee table.

"Maestro?"

"Hmm?"

"I wish you weren't . . . sick . . . so often."

"*Allora*, Fatima." He patted her hand and then returned to sipping his broth.

"I know you are sad." Fatima said quickly, as if not wanting to lose her nerve. "I know you're sad and you miss them, but I don't think they'd want you . . . like this."

Luciano looked up at Fatima's abrupt speech. He sighed and looked down at the dust clotting the lines of his hands. "Sometimes I wonder. I don't know, Fatima. I simply don't know how to wake up into a world that doesn't have them in it." His speech turned ragged and he choked back a sob.

Fatima moved next to him and patted his shoulder.

"I think you do know, Maestro. It's like you told me about learning Italian. You said I had to trust myself to understand one day and not get tangled into how hard it was. Remember? You said that I had to let the words and the music of the language surround me, and not fight it, but trust that one day the pieces would fall into place. And they did. Remember?"

Luciano fought back tears.

Fatima went on, "Maestro, you need to put one foot in front of the other. And you don't expect perfection, you just expect to move a little. Just a little. *Piano, piano.*"

Luciano ran his thumb over the rim of the cup and inhaled the concentrated scent of roasting meat with delicate spices. He looked into Fatima's wide eyes. "How did you get to be so wise, *cara?*"

She grinned. "You taught me, Maestro."

Magda slapped the damp newspaper on the bar, prompting the two officers to flinch. "Chiara! I told you! I told you the developers were coming!"

Chiara sighed inwardly, before checking herself. Magda was like a shark. She couldn't control her combative tone. "What's happened now?"

"The developers! Did you not read this?" Magda pushed the paper toward Chiara with the edges of her fingers, as if she couldn't bear to be contaminated with this filth.

"I didn't read the *giornale* yet, not today. What does it say?"

Magda rolled her eyes at the ceiling and grumbled. "Jesus, Chiara. I have a busy vacation rental and many people who require my expertise, and I somehow managed to read the paper by evening. What's wrong with you?"

"Just lazy, I suppose."

Magda glared at Chiara, wondering if she was mocking her. The corners of Chiara's lips twitched. Magda tried to hold her glower, but it was impossible in the face of Chiara's determined cheer. At the seal-like barking laugh that finally got the better of Magda, Edo looked over curiously. He returned to buffing the water spots out of the glassware.

"Okay, okay, Chiara. So let me tell you what the article says. A developer is coming from Rome to scope out the swamp land where the falls meet the river. To pour concrete over the marsh and build a shopping center! A *shopping* center!"

Chiara's face fell. "Let me see that." She reached for the paper with her left hand while she pulled her glasses suspended on a chain around her neck to the bridge of her nose with her right. Snapping the paper open, she read quietly, her lips moving. After a few minutes while Magda loudly stirred the sugar into her coffee and sniped at Edoardo for not making hers with enough foam, Chiara smoothed the paper back on the bar and dropped her glasses back to rest top of her ample chest. "I don't see a reason for panic."

"What? Did you read the right article?" Magda snatched back the paper and scanned the headlines to see if it was possible that Chiara had read the wrong one.

"Yes, yes, I read the right one. But it says it's a proposal. You should know by now, this idea comes up every three or four years. Someone realizes that there is a beautiful space for building, within walking distance of the station in Girona and surrounded by picturesque mountains. But once people start investigating, they realize it won't work."

"Won't work? Why won't work? It could work! It's a special piece of land! Those falls are famous!"

Chiara leaned forward and spoke softly, looking earnestly into Magda's eyes, which were darting from the paper to Chiara's face. "Of course they are," Chiara soothed. "But every time the engineers come and start poking about in the swamp, all of a sudden, everyone disappears, and the idea is abandoned for another couple of years."

Edoardo, whose attention was caught, brought his *espresso* over to stand by Chiara. "Why is that, Zia?"

Chiara smiled at her nephew, he so rarely called her "aunt."

"I'm not sure. But there are townspeople, I won't say which ones, who speculate that it's because of all the dead bodies in the swamp."

Magda let out an involuntary shriek of alarm and then covered her mouth quickly while furtively gawking at the officers. She leaned toward Chiara, while Edoardo smiled and thoughtfully sipped his coffee, one thumb hooked on his apron.

In a strangled whisper, Magda said, "Chiara. You can't be serious."

"Well, I'm not saying I believe there are bodies in there. I'm just telling you what I've heard. Seems as good a reason as any, and far more interesting than there's a rare kind of frog in the marsh. You must have heard that one."

"Frog? What are you talking about? You go from dead bodies to frogs?"

Chiara laughed easily and began wiping the fingerprints from the bar with the towel looped through the apron around her waist.

At the sound of the bell over the door, all heads turned. Luciano stood planted, twisting his hat in his hands. At the assembled blank looks, Luciano sagged and retreated into the dusk.

Edo and Chiara communicated wordlessly, was Luciano drunk? He didn't seem so, what with the lack of bellowing that usually accompanied his wine consumption.

Magda caught the eye of one of the officers. "You should put that man away. He's a disgrace."

The taller officer shrugged. "He's not hurting anyone. Not illegal to be drunk. I checked before joining." He smiled at Chiara and gestured toward the case displaying a lone piece of bread threaded with wine must and raisins. "Can I have that last piece of *pane di mosto*, Chiara?"

Chiara replied, "*Con piacere*, Marcello. How is Laura?" She plucked the aromatic bread out of the case and placed it on a saucer, settling it in front of the officer.

Marcello smiled, "Much better. She'll be home soon."

"Good, I'm glad."

Magda shook her head. "Still. I mean, he's threatening."

Chiara was confused, and then realized Magda was still talking about Luciano, "To whom? Massimo? You can hardly blame him."

Magda leaned forward, pleased to have engaged Chiara in debate, "What? Because of Giulia? You think Luciano blames Massimo for Giulia's death." It was more a statement than a question.

"I didn't say that." Chiara traded a knowing look with Edo, who offered her a smile of support. How did she get embroiled in this conversation? "Just . . . losing his daughter was heartbreaking for Luciano. I'm sure the sight of her husband is a constant irritant. He doesn't know what he's saying."

"Doesn't he?"

The shorter officer, Alessandro, chimed in, "Plus, Luciano's wife dying so soon afterward. Of course he hasn't recovered."

Magda harrumphed, "Well, he's never going to recover if he drowns his sorrows in drink all the time. People should at least stop selling it to him. Luciano needs to face reality."

Wiping his mouth with the napkin, Marcello offered, "I'm not actually sure how he gets by. A retired school teacher, right? He can't get that much pension, and with the amount of wine I've seen him drink."

Magda shook her finger in triumph, "See? Someone needs to stop him."

Chiara bit her lip before returning to buffing the bar to a high gleam. "Let him be, Magda. No one can imagine what that kind of devastation can do to a person."

Magda face stiffened. Her eyes were hooded and suspicious as she stared at Chiara.

Edoardo shook his head and stepped away from Magda and Chiara. He didn't understand their relationship. His aunt was the only person he knew who could endure Magda. Yet somehow, with Chiara, Magda was . . . tolerable. Chiara knew how to throw Magda off just enough to keep her need to criticize and micromanage at bay. Usually. Tonight, though, she was in rare form. You will unquestionably consider it a blessing to focus on the newcomer sauntering into the bar.

Edo moved to the open end of the counter to greet the man as the police officers strolled out into the evening. "*Buona sera,*" he offered, "What can I get you?"

The man wasn't dressed like a local. His muscled legs were wrapped in tight black jeans, and his black t-shirt strained across his powerfully built chest. His styled-to-the-point-of-shine hair was cut short, and his almond-shaped eyes shone brightly in his tanned face. He fanned his fingers over the bar, considering, while pursing his lips. He leaned toward Edoardo to ask, "What do you recommend?"

"A *caffè?* A glass of wine? What are you in the mood for?"

The man's eyes widened briefly before he smiled and replied, "I'm in the mood for something different."

Edoardo, unsure of his meaning, decided to take him at the literal. "Like a martini? I'm afraid this bar is a bit too old school for modern cocktails. I can make you a *negroni.*"

Chuckling, the man said, "Why would I want a martini? But yes, a *negroni* sounds perfect." He held onto the bar and leaned back, unaware of how the tension made his biceps pop into full relief. Or perhaps he was very aware. In any case, he looked around the bar appreciatively, as Edoardo reached for the bottles of Campari, vermouth, and gin. His back to the man in black, he began mixing the *negroni.*

The hair on Edoardo's neck began to tingle, and he wondered if the stranger was watching him. He could practically feel the heat of the man's gaze. Briefly his eyes flitted to the mirrored wall in front of him. Indeed, those almond-eyes were contemplating his back. Unapologetically. In fact, when Edoardo caught his eye in the mirror, the man smiled a slow smile.

Edoardo's lips tightened into a thin line, before he turned with the finished *aperitivo,* efficiently taking a cocktail napkin to slide under the glass as he set it down. The man reached for the drink and allowed his finger to run along Edoardo's as he smiled that same slow smile.

Edoardo snatched his hand back and shot a look at Chiara laughing and wagging a finger at Magda. Magda was holding her hands up as if claiming innocence. He stepped beside Chiara and put a hand on her arm. She turned to him, still laughing, "*Sì?*"

"Chiara. Can I take off? It's dead and I need to go."

"Sure, of course." She noticed the unknown man for the first time and asked, "What did he have?"

"Um. A *negroni*. Oh, he still needs peanuts and chips. I . . . didn't get to it."

"Didn't get to it?" A shadow passed over Chiara's face, and she looked back at the man for a moment. She turned back to Edoardo with a firm smile. "Okay, no problem, I'll take care of it. Go. Have fun."

Edoardo nodded in thanks before striding to the door that led upstairs, avoiding eye contact with the man.

Once the door was closed firmly behind him, he breathed a sigh of relief. Leaning against the wall of the stairwell, he listened to the sound of Chiara rustling in the bins of snacks and prattling with the stranger. After a few beats, Edo climbed the stairs to his room.

He showered, sudsing a day's worth of *espresso* off his lean body. He toweled off, and with the towel tucked around his waist, he blow dried his hair, carefully arranging each glossy lock. Once satisfied, he selected a purple silk shirt from his closet and pulled it on, delighting in the way the material slid over his skin with fingertip softness. He pulled on his dark blue jeans with carefully ripped patches, and turned to the mirror to admire the effect. He checked the time. There was no way the man could still be in the bar. Just to be safe, he stepped down the steps on tiptoe, and pushed the door open just a hair. Chiara was humming to the radio while she washed dishes, and the bar was empty.

Edoardo flung the door open. "*Ciao*, Chiara! Don't wait up."

"*Ciao*, Edo. I never do," Chiara smiled.

Edoardo walked out the door, and inhaled the breeze's subtle spice of rosemary before slipping into the night.

Elisa walked slowly, her eyes raking the ground weakly lit by the mid-afternoon sun. Her head cocked at a flash of light winking between cobblestones. Pouncing, she came up with a coin pinched between her fingers. Her face fell into a scowl. It was only a five cent coin, not the 50 cent coin it had appeared to be while glittering in the street.

She didn't have near enough. Still.

And Luciano tutoring her was not going to work. Fatima had been forced to admit that though she'd tried to talk to him, he was too foggy to understand. So that was a dead end. As were the couch cushions, the fountain, and the tourists' pockets that she'd dared to reach into. There were no coins, and she wasn't going to get her grades up, even with Fatima's daily efforts to plan Elisa's evenings. She was doing better at not losing and forgetting things, but no better at understanding. And time was running out.

Elisa spied movement ahead at the park. Stefano. Stefano and his friends. She wanted to run, but she knew that would only delay what was bound to happen.

The one-eyed dog brushed past her. She wished she could dash here and there, without a care in the world. It would be worth having one eye and salami rinds in her fur to be able to avoid this.

Walking in a slow serpentine fashion, she approached Stefano, who leaned against the battered metal slide, smoking with his friends.

"Stefano?"

"Ah, Elisa! My favorite and youngest customer. Got the money?"

Elisa's eyes flew from one teenage boy face to another. Stefano nodded and said, "Hey, I'm conducting business here! You all, scram!"

The boys drifted to the other end of the playground, sitting on the *ciambella*, donut, shaped spinning wheel that always made Elisa feel like throwing up.

"Now, Elisa. Having trouble in school again?"

Elisa chewed her lip and nodded.

"Well, you're in luck. I've raised my price, but I'm giving you the pretty girl discount. Because you are, you know. A pretty girl." Stefano lifted Elisa's face up to pass his eyes over her face and down her body. "A little on the scrawny side, but not too bad."

Elisa backed away from Stefano, her breath torn with anxiety. "So, twenty euros? And you'll do it like before?"

Stefano laughed easily, "Relax, *cara*. I wouldn't take anything not offered to me. To be honest, I prefer my girls to beg."

"Twenty? Like before?"

"Sure, *cara*, sure. Twenty. Fork it over."

"I don't have it."

"You don't have it? What do you mean?"

"I mean I don't have it!" Elisa said, wildly.

Stefano's eyes narrowed, "Then what are you doing here? Are you spying? Going to rat me out?"

"No! Never! I have some of it. I can give you some of it. I just need more time to get all of it."

"So you think you can come here with less than my price, and I'll just, what? Fix your report card for nothing?"

"No! I'll pay for all of it, I promise! I'll work harder to get it all."

Stefano pressed closer to Elisa, until she could smell the stale smoke on his breath. "You better have it all by report card time, Elisa. Otherwise, you'll be begging me. Just like I like."

Isotta blinked at the burnished copper air as Massimo's car pulled into the parking lot outside the walls of Santa Lucia. "Is the light always like this?"

"Like what?"

"So . . . full. Like . . . like . . . the crescendo of an opera."

Massimo laughed. "I think you were on that dark train for too long. But I like how poetical you are. You'll fit right into Santa Lucia."

Stopping the car, he leapt out and jogged around the car while Isotta gathered her purse and sunglasses. He opened her door with a small bow. Isotta smiled into his eyes, charmed. Massimo held out his hand, and when she took it, he guided her out of the car, where he wrapped his arms around her and pressed her head against his chest. "I'm so glad you are here," he said softly. "It's felt like months since I've seen you. I almost started to believe I made up that smell of orange flower where your hair meets your neck. But no," he inhaled dramatically, "here you stand, sweet and lovely." Gently he dropped his face until he was almost kissing her, almost. He gazed searchingly into her eyes, and Isotta lips tingled at the anticipated touch. He whispered, "Aren't you glad you came?"

"Yes, oh, yes. Massimo. I was stupid to hesitate." She stretched to kiss him. Massimo pulled back, teasingly, before slowly bringing his lips to hers. Isotta trembled at his touch, warm and full. Massimo brushed her hair behind her back and kissed her exposed neck.

"It's always foolish to question me, Isotta." He kissed the other side of her neck softly, and then burrowed a little, tasting the salt on her skin. His lips moved back to her mouth, where Isotta met him with a quiver. He kissed her as a thirsty man drinks from a street fountain. His hands drifted down her back, resting in the curve of her hips, lifting her up slightly. Isotta wound her arms around him and kissed him deeply. Massimo's hands traveled back up, brushing the sides of her chest, before they cupped her chin as he pulled away and then rested his forehead against hers.

"*Sei pronta*, Isotta? Are you ready?" At her silent nod, eyes naked with longing, Massimo smiled and said, "Then let's go." He plucked Isotta's purse out of her seat, and then popped open the trunk to heft out her overnight bag. All the while, Isotta stood transfixed. Hardly able to believe she was here, with him, in his town with its saturated light.

Massimo laughed and reached for her hand to tug her out of the parking lot. "I think you'll like Santa Lucia. It's not Florence, of course, but it doesn't pretend to be. Do you know about the falls?"

She shook her head.

"Ah, you can't see them from this side of the mountain, but I'll take you to see them later. They are spectacular," a note of pride rang in his words.

Isotta nodded and gestured toward the olive groves flanking the town's entrance. "Those trees are enormous. They look like they are going to twist right out of the ground."

Massimo smiled again at Isotta's phrasing. "Yes, they are ancient, planted long before the Romans thought to put a town at this outpost. Not all of those old trees are still here." Massimo's sweeping gesture took in the trees stretching into the hill above the street. "But just about all of us have at least one ancient tree in our plots. We believe that's what makes our olive oil so particular."

"Plots?"

"Oh, yes. You wouldn't have this in Florence. Here, most of us own a section of the groves. Soon we'll all harvest and send our olives to the mill we passed on the way up the road. Then we each get a bit of the oil and sell the rest to tourists. I'll send you home with a bottle. No offense, but Tuscan olive oil leaves much to be desired. Too gentle and Americanized. Ours is strong, like these Apennine mountains."

Isotta thought about the oil her family got each year from their distant cousins. How its fruity butteriness perfumed the air when sprinkled on hot vegetables or meat or pasta. Instead of answering, she pointed her chin toward the long-hair white cat sleeping in a flowerpot. "How sweet."

"Yes, Santa Lucia is lousy with cats. During the summer when everyone escapes to the water, some joke there are more cats in Santa Lucia than people." He grinned at Isotta as they walked and she beamed in return.

"I like cats."

"So do I. Or at least I like how rat-free they keep the town. We never need traps."

"So do they belong to anyone?"

"Some, but they're mostly strays that the old ladies have taken to feeding. The town pays for almost all of them to be fixed so we don't replace a rat problem with a cat problem. Now, look! Through this break in the buildings you can see across the valley."

Isotta lifted her hand to her eyes to shield her vision from the glare, and squinted down at what at first blush appeared to be another alley. But this one was framed not just by buildings, but an arch made of single stones draped between the creamy, rough-hewn walls. The effect reminded Isotta of the photo she'd seen of a landscape as viewed through a keyhole. A black cat picked its way to the top of the arch, turned once, and curled into itself. "It's beautiful." And it was. Olive trees glimmered, sending a confetti of light into the top of the mountain covered with trees so deeply green they appeared indigo. Behind the mountain, the sky sighed overhead, the blue of an angel's eyes.

Chiara checked her watch. If Edo wasn't down in the next thirty minutes, she'd have to go up and look in on him. She wondered if she should dash upstairs in the next break between customers. Just a real quick check. He'd gotten home later than usual last night, and seemed to struggle to put the key in the lock. She hoped he remembered that she needed to go to the park later with Patrizia. There wasn't anything she could do for her friend, she knew, but she looked forward to sitting together in the park with gelato, letting the last of the summer sunshine warm their faces while Marco went around and around the spinning disk like he liked to do. It would be restorative for both of them.

She was dragged from her imagining by the entrance of the mayor.

"*Ciao*, Dante, *un caffè?*"

"*Sì, grazie.*"

Dante paraded to the bar and repeatedly turned a business card over on the bar. Each click of card on stone was a small explosion.

Chiara's eyes flickered toward him, thinking about Stella.

Placing the cup on the saucer, Chiara handed the coffee to Dante. "Would you like anything to eat?"

Dante was staring outside the door and still turning the business card to rap each edge on the bar.

"Dante? *Vuoi qualcosa da mangiare?*" Chiara repeated.

The mayor startled. "Oh! No. I apologize, Chiara. I was thinking."

"You seem distracted."

He sighed importantly. "Yes, it appears I am. Sometimes I wish this town would run itself for a little while."

It seemed to Chiara that he hitched his shoulders back a touch as he made his pronouncement.

Chiara answered with a smile, "The demands of the wooden-spoon-waving grandmothers and *gelato*-eating children a bit too much for you?"

"You're mocking me, Chiara. It's hardly appreciated."

The grin disappeared from Chiara's face. "I apologize, Dante."

He sighed. "I shouldn't snap at you, it's not your fault. But it seems like no one is ever happy. Half the town wants me to preserve their old ways of living. Subsidize the oil mill so they can press their oil as they have for generations. While the other half of the town wants to modernize. 'Why can't we get faster Wi-Fi? Recycling? Email at school?' I swear, Chiara. There is no way of pleasing them all."

She nodded thoughtfully. "It's true, I hear all of that here."

"Yes, but no one expects you to do anything about it."

This was also true.

"Whereas for me, people are always angry because I'm not fixing their exact problem. Like I'm God as well as mayor! I swear, every time I see that German, Magda, I duck into an alley. She's the worst! 'Why don't you make a city website that features my special rentals? The Del Fiacco family moved to Lazio, why can't I have their *uliveto?* Why can't you change the angle of the sunrise so my rooms don't get so hot in the morning?' Jesus."

"Now, Dante, that's unfair."

"Maybe a little," he conceded. "She doesn't actually order me to fix the sunrise. Just complains about it." He smiled, wearily.

An idea bubbled into Chiara's consciousness. "Have you thought of stepping down? Let someone else be mayor? Might be nice for you to have a break. And I'm sure it would do you and Stella good to have time together without the children or the town making demands."

"Stella? What does she have to do with this?"

"Nothing really. I was just thinking, if it's hard to be mayor, it's probably hard to be the mayor's wife. You two can't have much time together. Maybe a vacation?"

Dante waved off her words. "Stella's fine. She knew what she was getting into when she married me. I'm civic minded. When I'm no longer mayor, you know I'll still be involved."

"But wouldn't it be nice—"

"I'm fine, Chiara. Thank you for the coffee and for listening to me carp, but I just needed to blow off steam. Everything is fine."

Chiara wished she could believe it.

The walk through Santa Lucia passed in a blur. Sooner than Isotta expected, Massimo stopped at a wooden door set into a rock arch, bushes of hydrangeas under the adjacent windows. When they burst forth in a riot of blue and purple, they would be spectacular.

The door was apparently kept unlocked because Massimo turned the handle and it immediately gave. Isotta brushed her hair with her hands, worried that the drive and the parking lot embrace made her look less than presentable to Massimo's mother. Massimo grinned and leaned to kiss her. "You look perfect. They'll love you."

Isotta wondered who the "they" could refer to. Perhaps there was more family in Santa Lucia to meet? She attempted a smile and then followed

Massimo into the house. "*Ciao!*" he called, "I brought my visitor!"

The sound of an oven door closing preceded the appearance of what could only be Massimo's mother. As the woman walked out of the kitchen wiping her hands, Isotta noted that Massimo had inherited his mother's height. And also the proud expression, which creased into a forced smile as she moved to greet Isotta. Other than that, Massimo and his mother didn't really resemble each other. Massimo must have gotten his strong and chiseled features from his father.

Before Anna was halfway across the room, Isotta was startled by the sound of fluttering footsteps. A child, no more than two years old, careened around the corner and flung her arms around Massimo's legs. Massimo ran his fingers through the child's tangled black curls. "Isotta," he began, "This is Margherita." Isotta waited to hear him explain the relationship. Was this a visiting niece, daughter to a sibling waiting in the kitchen? The child herself was far too young to be Massimo's sister. Besides, his mother's dyed black hair did nothing to disguise the fact that her child-bearing days ended before Berlusconi was prime minister. Isotta looked at Massimo, waiting.

His lip nudged upward into a smile as he softly added, "Margherita is my daughter."

Isotta took an involuntary step away. Massimo's eyes narrowed before he hooked his hands under Margherita's arms and pulled her up against him. The child curled against her father and her thumb crept into her mouth. Instantly, her eyelids started to droop.

"Your . . . daughter?"

"Yes, my daughter. And this is my mother, Anna." The acidity in Massimo's voice pushed Isotta out of her confused stupor.

"Ah, yes. Anna, it is a pleasure to meet you."

Anna's face lost some of its stiffness. "And I you. Massimo has told me much about you. It seems the connection between you was lightening fast. Like fate." Isotta couldn't tell if Anna's tone was bemused or sardonic.

Isotta tried to smile. She looked at Massimo, who was swaying a bit while whispering what sounded like a lullaby to his daughter. The image was beautiful, and Isotta lost some of her panic in the very domesticity of the scene. She moved a little closer to Massimo and touched Margherita lightly on the arm. The child's drowsy eyes flew open, but then she smiled around her thumb still lodged in her mouth. "*Ciao*, Margherita, *come sei bella.* How beautiful you are."

Margherita lunged her head forward to rest on Isotta's shoulder and Isotta was surprised by the sudden rush of affection she felt for this little person.

Massimo looked over the top of his daughter's head, resting on his lover's shoulder and shot a look at his mother as if to say, "Didn't I tell you?"

Anna imperceptibly tensed, but she nodded, with a scrape of a smile. "I have coffee ready, and I baked a *torta*. Come into the kitchen."

At the mention of sweets, Margherita's head bolted upright. "*Torta?*"

Anna said, "Yes, *torta*, you sure love your *dolci*. Put her in her seat, Massimo, I'll serve. Sit down, Isotta, sit down! You will be part of this family, you mustn't wait to be invited in."

Massimo put his hand on the small of Isotta's back and guided her ahead of him into the kitchen. Isotta attempted a level of cheeriness that her awkwardness scrambled. "What a lovely kitchen! Do you share it?"

Isotta felt silly asking the question, sure that given the fact that she and Massimo were presumed to be getting married, she should know about the structure and function of his household. No one else seemed to find the question odd, though. Massimo nodded as he settled Margherita into her high chair, and said, "Yes, a few years ago I toyed with the idea of moving into Girona. But with Mamma's intermittent heart condition, we decided instead to make the family home more comfortable for sharing."

Anna's voice was laced with flint. "Massimo, you make me sound like an old woman. I'm hardly falling apart."

Massimo soothed, "Of course you're not, Mamma." He turned to

Isotta, "Mamma is very strong and healthy. I just didn't want to take any chances. Plus, there are many advantages to sharing a home."

Anna chimed in, "My quarters are on one side of the house, my son's are on the other. They connect through Margherita's room and the kitchen. Since Massimo can hardly boil water for pasta, and I spend my days with Margherita, it has been a good arrangement." She poured thick coffee from the aged silver *moka* into three identical white cups rimmed with bold navy stripes, and then set the coffees in front of each adult.

Isotta ventured, "Is there anything I can help with?"

Anna said, "Absolutely not." She waved Isotta toward an empty chair before turning back to the range. Anna peered into the oven while reaching for a pot-holder hung in arm's reach. Nodding in satisfaction, Anna pulled the cake from the oven and rested it on the stovetop. Deftly, Anna plucked the cake server out of the jug of gleaming cooking implements and brought the plum-spangled *torta* to the table.

Margherita banged her high chair in approval and then ducked her head and looked over at Isotta through lowered lashes. At Isotta's smile, Margherita banged again and chortled.

The adults laughed in unison, which broke the remaining tension. Isotta let her confusion about why Massimo didn't tell her about his daughter fade into the auburn light streaming into the kitchen. He probably had a good reason. Maybe his behavior wasn't typical, but he had yet to be wrong. He was clearly one of those people whose hands were on the reins, utterly in control of his life. As a person who constantly felt like her own life was on the edges of slipping out from underneath her, it was probably good that she had this steady and clear-eyed man beside he. So why not get married? It's not like waiting years would change what Massimo seemed to know was inevitable. Plus, she had to admit to herself, she was eager to slip into bed beside Massimo every night. Her cheeks flushed at the thought, and then flushed further when she realized that Massimo and Anna were both looking at her.

"Isotta?" prompted Massimo.

"Oh, yes, sorry!" Isotta tried to laugh off her distraction.

"Mamma was asking you a question. It's rude not to pay attention."

Isotta flushed in shame. Her mother often said the same thing when Isotta's thoughts wavered.

Anna said, "Oh, Massimo, lighten up. The poor child spent the day traveling, she just met your family. Give her a moment to take it in." Isotta sucked in her breath, sure that Massimo would bark at his mother. Instead his face relaxed into its softer lines and he took his mother's hand and then her own and said, "Of course. I apologize, Isotta."

Isotta smiled weakly.

Massimo went on. "So, darling, mother and I were just wondering about timing for the wedding. I would love to do it next month, but that's probably not enough time. What about November?"

Isotta's smile shook briefly, but then steadied. "Of course. Whatever you think, Massimo."

Massimo shot Anna a triumphant smile. Anna gave a begrudging nod before clasping Massimo's hand in hers. Isotta, touched that her agreement would mean so much to Massimo, beamed.

It was as if her life—her family, her schooling, her career, her understanding of the serpentine streets that spiraled out from the Duomo—were being erased. It felt scary, but at the same time, Isotta wasn't sure why she'd hang onto that life, when life here included Massimo, his solicitous mother, and little Margherita. A family ready to love her.

Glancing at the clock, Edo calculated he'd be able to duck out in an hour. Less than that, if the bar continued to be this quiet. His pulse quickened.

"Got an appointment?" Chiara asked with a smile.

"What?" Edo startled.

"You've been checking the clock just about every minute and a half."

"Oh," Edo tried to laugh casually, but he felt too irritable. Instead he turned away to refill the cocoa container.

"So, you heading out again tonight?"

Edo bit his lip and considered. It wasn't any of her business. He could just sneak out when she was sleeping, save the questions. It worked with his parents. Only, upon further reflection, it didn't. Not really. Just put more space between them.

"I was planning to."

"That's fine, Edo. You're a big boy." Chiara fought down the mix of innate curiosity and concern to avoid asking where he was going. She was worried about how brittle he'd been lately, and started wondering if maybe her brother had been right about Edo's need for a "firm hand." But, she had seen Edo when people asked him even innocent questions. His expressive eyes turned stony, and his full lips grew taught. Too much of that and he became unreachable. She wanted to simply enjoy his gentle presence. You can debate whether or not Chiara should exert some authority—certainly the villagers found much to discuss here—but ultimately, Chiara couldn't be other than what she was. She added, "But maybe if you come in late, watch the third step? The creaking wouldn't normally bother me, but I haven't been sleeping."

"Not sleeping? Why?" Was she staying up to monitor him? That seemed unlikely, but maybe his father was putting her up to it. Not for the first time, he wondered if they'd bugged his phone.

Chiara wondered how to answer her nephew. She couldn't tell him about the loneliness that crept in, the feeling that her days were slipping by and she was unable to hold onto them. "Oh, the usual. The bar, the apartments, the customers. I think we may need to buy more cups before the festival. Last year we almost ran out during the rush, and I know we've broken some since."

Edo didn't look like he believed her, but he nodded and looked back at the clock.

"Go," Chiara prompted.

"What?"

"It's quiet. You're young. Go. Have fun. You deserve it."

Edo stopped himself from impulsively saying that Chiara deserved fun too. He couldn't figure out what would prompt him to say such a thing. She seemed perfectly content with her life of running the bar and occasionally playing cards in the evening at a table pushed into the center of the room, or walking with her friends. He hated it when people pried into his personal life, so he avoided doing the same. Instead, he stifled his irritation and gave Chiara a quick hug on his way up the stairs. "Look, Zia! I'm practicing! Skipped the third step!"

Chiara laughed and then, as the bell above the door tinkled, she called out, "*Buona sera, come stai*, Stella?"

The women's chattering and laughing nagged at Edo as he rounded the top of the steps and entered his room. Not quite his, yet, perhaps. He had yet to unpack his CD collection, and some of his socks were still in the suitcase.

As he pulled off his vest and green shirt, he noticed a headache forming behind his eyes. Now that he stopped to pay attention to it, his stomach was also upset. He felt almost motion sick, and a little dizzy. Deciding it was nothing, he started the water running for his shower. That would perk him up.

Toweling off, Edo shrugged on the crisp plum-colored shirt he'd ironed last night and added a dab of product to revive the angle in his hair. His mind was already buzzing in anticipation. So was his heart. In fact it was beating sort of erratically. Probably just excitement. Hurriedly, he swept up his wallet, his leather jacket, and with one nod at his reflection he bounded out of the room and down the stairs.

"*A dopo!*" he called, dashing out into the darkness.

Massimo softly closed Margherita's bedroom door. He whispered to Isotta, "She's asleep. Let's go to dinner."

"But what if she needs you while you're gone?"

"She knows to get her grandmother in the night. It has always been this way. Well, at least since . . ." His voice trailed off.

"Oh, I'm sorry Massimo. I didn't mean to . . ."

Massimo shook his head and replaced his surly expression with a light one. "No matter. Shall we?" He crooked his arm toward her and waggled his eyebrows suggestively. Isotta laughed and took his arm. She was glad that his wife's memory caused not more than a blip in his mood.

They bid Anna, who was watching TV while her dinner reheated in the oven, goodnight.

As they closed the door, Isotta asked, "Does she mind that I'm staying here? Before we're married, I mean?" She felt her cheeks warm a bit at the word "married." She could hardly believe this was serious. Not a pretend wedding like she and her sisters staged as children.

"Of course not. Why would she?"

"I don't know. If we did this at my parents' house, they'd need to debate whether to first kill me or disown me." Massimo squeezed Isotta's hand. She continued, "Which is strange, now that I think about it. It's not like they think my sisters are chaste. All of them have had . . . have had . . ." Her voice trailed, shyly.

Massimo offered Isotta his broad grin, the one that jellied her legs, "If you can do it, you should be able to say it, darling."

Isotta nodded. "Sex," she whispered. "They've had sex," she added, more strongly. The words rang out between the stones of the ancient buildings, ricocheting until they landed into the alley where a group of old women were seated, each with a bowl of greens in her lap. The women cackled merrily at the unexpected plop of ribaldry. They ducked their heads together as they continued sorting their leaves into piles for salad, piles for *frittata*, and a wilted pile for Bea's chickens.

Massimo's laugh boomed over the top of her embarrassment. He pulled Isotta to him and hugged her with one arm as he directed her steps to the *piazza*.

"I'm sorry for laughing, *cara mia*. You were saying?"

Isotta, warm with Massimo's arm wrapped around her, said, "Well, you know. They are all active. That way. Our parents must know. My sisters' excuses border on the ridiculous. Who spends all night cleaning the train station as a public service? Sometimes I think my sisters vie for who can tell the most outlandish story to explain their absence. But my parents just turn a blind eye and pretend they are raising virgins."

Massimo thought about this. "I suppose it's a parent's prerogative to ignore what can't be helped and would only aggravate."

They walked for a few moments in silence.

Then Massimo continued, "Soon you won't have to worry about your parents' displeasure, Isotta. I promise to make an honest woman out of you. And which of your sisters can say that? Now look, see here? That is the *macelleria*, where Giuseppe the butcher cuts the most perfect pork chop and has a secret for making chicken sausages more flavorful than you can imagine."

Isotta peered into the window, still lit against the gathering darkness. "It's so busy!"

"Yes, the population of Santa Lucia may not break a thousand people, but since this is the only butcher shop, and thank the Madonna Giuseppe doesn't take advantage of this as he might, everyone comes here. You will too."

Isotta tried to imagine standing with these locals, leaning over the counter to chat with the butcher about how the beef was raised. She was struck with gratitude that she knew how to cook. Her mother's fascination with dressing up her more beautiful daughters and parading them down the banks of the Arno had left her little time for cookery. Through trial and error and the internet, and watching her grandmother who lived in the countryside outside of Greve in Chianti, Isotta had learned to roll pasta, simmer a *ragù*, and pound a pesto. It wasn't fancy, but it was serviceable enough for her family. She shivered at the thought that she'd be cooking for a new family soon.

Smitten as she was, it didn't occur to her to wonder about Anna's proprietary control over her domain. Those further removed from Massimo's magnetic smile will more easily guess the truth—Isotta would never cook in that kitchen.

"Now, over here," Massimo continued, breaking her reverie, "is the *forno*. It has been in this spot since before my family arrived in Santa Lucia in the late 1800's. The *cornetti* are not quite sweet enough for me, so I get plain ones and fill them with my mother's jam. My mother's jam is simply the best."

Isotta smiled at how boyish Massimo sounded, praising his mother's cooking. "I'm sure it is, if her *torta* is any indication."

Massimo kissed her hand, still wrapped in his own. "Her secret is that she always knows what's missing. Always." He leaned down to brush his lips over Isotta's, before tugging her forward, down the street.

Isotta found his enthusiasm infectious, a change from his usual imposing air. "And here on the left is Bar Birbo. *Aspetta*, let's go through. I must show you the falls."

She followed him, laughing, until she caught sight of the Madonna in her azure niche. Isotta stopped, her hand slipping from Massimo's to step closer to the glowing figure. Florence had instilled an appreciation for religious iconography, but this Madonna invited observation for more than artistic reasons. There was an expression of consummate adoration and tender compassion on Mary's face.

Long ago, Isotta had lost her childhood upswell of warmth at the sight of Mary, the mother of God. The Madonna had become more of an intellectual figure, to compare the talent of artists and the depth of art historians. But this Mary . . . Perhaps she lacked the sophistication of her later Renaissance cousins, but she utterly captured the purity, the simplicity of Mary's love. Her love for her son and her love for the world. Her hands reached out in gentle blessing, and Isotta wanted to answer the unspoken call, to touch the ethereal figure, but Massimo pulled her hand. Isotta cast one last glance at the Madonna before allowing herself to be catapulted into the bar. Immediately, the burble of voices stalled.

Massimo called out, "Chiara! Edoardo! I'm just going to show her the falls!"

Chiara was startled out of pouring a glass of wine for a man with a burgundy velvet smoking jacket. The man was paused mid-gesture. Isotta noticed Chiara's eyes widen as she took a step back, bumping into a thin young man, who must be Edoardo, behind her. The younger man didn't react to the contact. He was standing stock still, staring.

Isotta squeezed Massimo's hand in confusion, but he was focused on striding out the back door and ignored her mute entreaty. Once outside, he drew her to the end of the *terrazza*, where there was a clear view to the falls.

"Isn't it beautiful? Its hard to appreciate its full impact at night, of course, but the lights they have inset between the boulders allow you to get a sense of the falls at least."

Isotta was momentarily distracted from the scene at the bar by the enchanting play of light over the dancing water, the music made by eddies tapping and rustling around the rocks. The water sprang free about 20 meters below them into a free-fall down to the bottom of the mountain. She inhaled the scent of the water, like a frozen forest floor. She felt Massimo wrap his arms around her, his chin on the crown of her head. "Beautiful isn't it?"

"*Sì*," Isotta sighed. She relaxed against Massimo's chest and breathed in both the light and the airy play of the water cascading where it was loosed from spaces in the stones at the level of Bar Birbo, and the crashing power of the falls as they struck shelves of boulders on their rush down the mountain. After a few moments of companionable silence, Isotta whispered, "Massimo?"

"Hmm?"

"When we walked into the bar, the people looked . . . surprised."

"They did?"

"*Sì*. Why would that be?"

Massimo thought for a moment. "I guess they aren't used to seeing me with anyone. They probably thought I'd be single forever. I know I did. Until I met you." Gently, Massimo turned Isotta until she faced him. He lifted her chin up and leaned to press his full lips against hers. He whispered again, "Until I met you."

OCTOBER

"Your teacher called."

Elisa froze at the sound of Concetta's voice from the kitchen. Her mother was rarely up when she got home from school. But there she was, sitting at the table. A stream of smoke sailed toward the dusty light fixture. Elisa suddenly noticed that only one of the four bulbs was giving light. The rest were dull, without even the memory of warmth.

"Elisa!"

"*Sì*, Mamma?"

"I said your teacher called."

"Which one?"

Her mother snorted. "You expect me to remember the names of your teachers? The man, the math teacher."

"Oh."

"Oh? Is that all you can say? Oh?" Her mother stood and moved toward her. Elisa backed away. "Where are you going? You stay right here! Sit down!"

Elisa scuttled around her mother to the kitchen chair and dropped into it, hugging her backpack to her chest. Her head dropped to the heavy nylon that still smelled a little musty from the last rain.

"Your teacher says you are failing. Failing! Do you know what your father will do if he finds out? What am I supposed to do?" Her mother's voice quavered and she dropped into the seat across from Elisa. "What am I supposed to do? He'll blame me."

Elisa's voice was tight, "I'm trying, Mamma. I really am. I just can't . . ."

Her mother's voice hardened again. "So this is my fault?"

"What? No!"

"You are trying and failing, so it must be that I'm not providing enough 'parental support'?"

"What do you mean?"

"Because that's what your teacher said, Elisa. That I should be looking over your shoulder. Double checking your work. Apparently you are making too much work for him, and so I'm supposed to pick up his slack? Believe me, Elisa, your brothers' teachers never told me I had to provide more 'parental support'. So this is *not* my fault!"

"No, of course it's not. I . . . I can't make my brain work right."

"Oh, I see. And that's my fault too, is it? Well, I can tell you, Elisa, your waste of a brain didn't come from me—"

"No! I didn't mean, I didn't . . ."

Elisa's mother leaned forward. "Well, you better figure it out. I don't have time to coddle you like a two year old."

Elisa quickly wondered if her mother ever coddled her when she was two. She did have a dim memory of spooning tomatoes on bruschetta to the sound of her mother's singing. Did she make this up? See it in a movie? Or did that happen? She blinked hard, trying to focus.

"I will, Mamma. I'll do better."

"You better. Because if your report card comes and you fail a class, your father . . ." Once again, her voice shook.

Elisa reached for her mother's hand. "I know. I will. I promise."

Buona sera, **Isotta.**

Isotta gripped the phone. Finally!

Isotta

Buona sera, **Massimo.**

She hesitated, and then typed:

I missed talking to you yesterday.

Yes that's true.

I called

Yes I saw.

Ok

It was a busy day at the bank and in the evening my mother had a dinner with family in Perugia. It is too hard to make calls with Margherita.

Isotta swallowed her sigh of relief.

How is Margherita?

> She's well she misses you.

:) How can that be?

> Why would you doubt it?

She just met me

Isotta briefly wondered if she should call him instead. His tone was so hard to read. But then her sisters would hear her, and it would draw attention to the fact that she was locked in the closet.

> Be that as it may she's attached as
> I knew she would be.

Isotta paused, thinking.

> Isotta?

Yes, I'm here

> What did your parents say?

About what sorry?

> What do you think?

The wedding

You haven't told them

Not yet

Jesus Isotta. It's not like you're marrying into the mafia. I'm a normal man, a banker. It's not complicated.

I know. It's not you.

When Massimo didn't respond, Isotta added

It's personal.

There's something you won't tell me?

Isotta tried not to read an edge of threat into Massimo's words:

I'd tell you anything!

Isotta's fingers slipped as she tried to explain:

I don't have a close relationship with my family. We never talk. About anything.

Isotta drew in a shaking breath. No dots from Massimo, so she went on:

I don't want to share this with them. I don't want their opinions. I want this for myself, a little longer.

A pause.

Isotta tapped her fingers on her teeth and exhaled as the three rolling circles indicated Massimo typing his response:

> I see that. But until you tell them, we can't spend another night together.

I don't understand. Why?

> I can't let you sneak around behind your parents' backs.

But last weekend?

> Now that we are getting married, I can't see you without them knowing. And I can't bed you until I have a ring on your finger.

You're serious?

> Do I often lack sincerity?

You want to wait until we are married to spend another night together?

> No, I do not. I can't think of those nights without

Isotta waited, *without what? Without what?*

Massimo typed again:

> This can't turn into one of those calls.

Isotta typed before she could talk herself out of it:

> Why not? I like those calls.

> So do I. But we have business to attend to. I don't want to be sexual with you again until we're married.

Isotta, her daring increasing, typed:

> But what if I want to be sexual with you?

A pause.

A longer pause.

> Isotta, that's not attractive.

> I'm sorry.

> Listen until you are my wife

> Okay I understand.

> Is that right?

Not really. But I trust you. I'll tell them soon

Good. And when you talk to them, you can also tell them that I spoke with Don Alfonso and he can do the ceremony later this month. We can have an October wedding after all, as long as we do it on a weekday.

This month? I thought you said that would be impossible.

I believed it would be, but it's amazing what a nice contribution to the church will get you.

That's so soon.

Is that a problem?

No! Of course not. It's just a lot to do. Isn't there a lot of planning?

It's my second wedding. It shouldn't be elaborate. You find a nice dress, we'll arrange a lunch afterwards. That's it.

Something about this seemed wrong to Isotta. She typed dully:

That's it

And then we can sleep together again. As man and wife. I can hardly wait.

Me either. But Massimo?

Yes?

Isn't it typical for the wedding to be at the bride's church?

You said your family hardly go to church. Wouldn't it make more sense for you to get married in the community of people that will be your neighbors and friends?

I suppose so.

Of course. Now, call me when you've told your parents, so we can plan our next visit.

Okay. Buona notte, Massimo.

Buona notte, cara.

"Zia? Can you hear me?"

Chiara clutched the phone with both hands and turned from the bar. "Edo? What is it? Where are you? I thought you would be home hours ago."

"I . . . there's been an, an accident." Edo's voice was slurred, but careful. "I don't know what happened. Can you get me?"

Breathless, Chiara asked, "Where are you?"

Silence.

"Edo? Edo? Are you there?" Chiara was having a hard time containing the panic in her voice so that it didn't spill out over the bar.

A crackle and then, "Yeah, sorry, I was looking at the signs. I'm close to . . . I think the Autogrill outside of Terni?"

"Why is your voice so strange?"

"Zia? Please, just come get me? Before the cops do?"

"I'm on my way."

Magda propelled her guest by the arm as townspeople hugged the side of the street, avoiding eye contact. She stopped outside the *alimentari* and gestured toward the *cinghiali* heads perched on either side of the doorway, like porcine gaslights. "Now this is our famous grocery store. It's the best in the region. Truly, people come from Rome just to shop here!"

At the tourist's incredulous expression, Magda went on, "It's true! There are special *salumi* here that you just can't find anywhere else, even Norcia. Giovanni, the owner, goes to little farms to get the very best, most particular kinds of foods. My guests always tell me this is their favorite shop in all of Umbria. Maybe all of Italy!"

The tourist peeked her head into the darkened shop. It didn't look like much. It's true that the shop is a bit on the underwhelming side at first blush, but those who take their time to root through the crowded shelves are amply rewarded by finds almost deserving of Magda's hyperbole.

Before the tourist could discover for herself the gems tucked alongside the oil-packed tuna, she was pulled out by Magda who had likewise grabbed the arm of a man walking by in an apron. "Oh! Now this is Giuseppe! We call Giuseppe the mayor of Santa Lucia! He's not the mayor, of course. The mayor is too busy to talk to the people who live and pay taxes in this community. Giuseppe is the butcher. The best in Umbria or Le Marche."

Giuseppe offered a watery smile and nodded at the tourist, who nodded faintly back. To which Giuseppe grinned more broadly.

"It's true! People are always sending me postcards from around the world to tell me how much they love Giuseppe's pork stuffed with sausage, *mortadella*, and cheese. It's one of the advantages of renting my apartment, you get to cook with all of our famous local specialties. It is too bad you won't be here for the *sagra* next month." Magda pursed her lips as she launched into her contribution to the tourist's education. "*Sagra* means sacred, you see, so ours is a sacred festival celebrating wild boar. You won't have had boar, of course, as Germans have such limited palates. At the *sagra*, Giuseppe will roast many *cinghiali*, plus oversee the making of a stew that is famous throughout this region. You should come back! Better yet, you can write about it on the internet."

Giuseppe gently removed his arm from Magda's grip, murmuring that he needed to pick up arugula and get back to the shop.

"Okay, *ciao*, Giuseppe! *Ciao! Salutami a Patrizia*, send my greetings to your wife!" Magda turned back to the tourist and added with a chuckle, "His wife is very adorable. I don't get to see them as much as I'd like because, you know, I'm always so busy, but whenever I do, she tells me about how grateful she is for all the business I bring to Santa Lucia and to their shop. She sometimes works in the shop, of course, but she's often gone visiting her daughter. Her daughter's son is retarded or something. I can't remember."

The tourist flinched at the word. Magda shot a worried glance at her and asked, "Wait, am I speaking Italian or German? Sometimes I can't tell anymore."

"Italian, but that's fine, I studied in Italy and my sister married an Italian."

"She did! From where?"

"From Bologna."

"Ach. Terrible city. So much traffic. Do your sister and her husband live there?"

"She does. They're not married anymore."

"Then why doesn't she go back to Germany? Your family is from Berlin, isn't that what your documentation said? That's a rather grim city, but it has plenty of attractions for a young divorcée."

The tourist pulled her arm away from Magda and wrinkled her nose at a sudden foul odor. She began walking back to the apartment, muttering that she wanted to get her camera.

Magda followed. "Well? Why is she still here?"

"If you must know, they had a son, and the court won't let her take him out of Italy, so she's stuck here."

Magda's face went white. "Oh, I'm so sorry."

"Well, there's nothing to be done."

"Do you need the name of a lawyer? I know several famous ones in both Italy and Germany that owe me favors."

"No, but thank you." The tourist gave Magda a more genuine smile. But kept walking.

"Are you sure?" Magda hurried her pace to keep up. "I have family that's rather high up in Germany. They have power." The box under the bed flashed in her mind, but she blinked rapidly and tossed her hair off her face, and the image faded.

"Yes, I'm sure. We've consulted with multiple lawyers. There's no chance of getting her and her son out. Now we're just trying to help her enjoy her time here. Which is complicated since she hates Italians at the moment." The tourist tried to laugh but the sound got caught in her throat.

"Well. Italians can be difficult." Magda thought about all the Italians she knew that never took her up on her offers to sit in her garden and gather cherries from her trees, that kick she felt in her chest at every rejection. "But! Your sister will need to look on the bright side! She has a child! She is living in a famous, if overly trafficked, city! She must learn to make the best of every situation."

The tourist stalled and considered Magda who stopped alongside her. After a pause, she began walking, but more slowly, "Yes, I suppose that's true."

The light blared through Edoardo's eyelids. A visual foghorn that sent him pressing the covers over his eyes. Until his own rank breath forced him to whip the sheets away from his face as he panted to catch a full swallow of air. It wasn't just his breath, his whole body stank. Edoardo looked down at his bare chest. Was it his imagination or was his skin coated in a thick layer of something shiny and slick? He rubbed his eyes and thought, what happened last night?

Sketchy images danced across the screen of his mind. Pounding music. Strobe lights skittering across bare skin. Foreign-sounding drinks. Pills people kept pressing into his hands. And the drive home in the morning. The car, the crunching shock.

Oh, *Madonna*, his head hurt.

Gingerly, Edoardo shifted his legs over the side of the bed and planted his feet on the floor. Where was this pain in his legs coming from? The accident? But the airbag had inflated, he remembered the flying wall of white. He didn't even have any scratches except along his forearm when he winched himself out of the car and scraped himself along the road. His left big toe though, that was oddly swollen. And purple. He sucked in his breath as he remembered a large man, possibly Spanish, reeling backward and stomping on his foot as he windmilled over a table, crashing in a heap. The left toe throbbed helpfully, as if in confirmation. It was discolored and a bit swollen, but other than that, didn't look terrible.

Nothing really looked too terrible. But the inside of his head seemed to have been filled with mildewy cotton batting. His left hand gripping the headboard, he pulled himself to standing.

Whew. Mission accomplished.

The contents of his stomach lurched dangerously, and Edoardo lunged for the bathroom, barely making it to the toilet in time to void the liquid contents of his belly.

Shower, he needed a shower. But first, he waved his hand through the medicine cabinet until he clutched the packet of pain reliever.

As he swallowed the powder with warm water gulped from the faucet, he wondered what possessed him to go so overboard. He knew how to pace himself, how to eat and drink so that he never got carried away. Something prompted him to attempt oblivion. Edoardo decided he didn't want to remember what it was.

He stumbled to the shower and turned it on. Gripping the side of the stall he waited for a fresh bout of nausea to pass. Would he need the toilet? No, this one passed with only a twisting of his stomach. Pulling off his underwear, he stepped into the shower and sat down, letting the water rain on his head and run down his shoulders. He hugged his legs to his chest and rested his chin on his knees.

How was he going to get through this day? He moaned aloud at the image of himself in the bar, with the acrid coffee and cigarette smells, the relentless chatter of the customers, and the infernal binging of the register, and the relentless sound of jackhammers slamming into the *piazza's* concrete.

Please, please, start working, he begged the pain reliever.

This wasn't his first hangover, but he couldn't remember a worse one.

What was he doing?

This wasn't living, this was procrastinating.

It scared him that last night was so hazy. He couldn't remember who he danced with, what chest his fingers lingered over in the dark, who he kissed. There was someone, that he knew. He had a clear memory of lips pressed against his in the darkness, a tongue searching his mouth as the music pounded. But the eyes connected to those lips? The body? It was a mystery. A hollow, scorched-out, iridescent mystery.

The more he tried to remember what happened after the club, the more his memory became pockmarked. A haze of driving home, like a flip book with pages missing. The car crumpled against a wall more solid than anything he ever imagined. The white balloon around his face, the smell of asphalt against his nose, the sudden blackness, the relief at finding his phone in his pocket, his shuddering fingers as he called his aunt.

Chiara.

Oh, God, what would she think of him now? She'd probably kick him out. No good, he was never any good.

He wondered what shape his life would take if he were a worthy person.

It seemed he wasn't ever to know.

His future wasn't the wide open door he'd imagined as a child. Rather his unceasing string of tomorrows was rumpled, dingy. The days and years ahead filled with emptiness.

Luciano was out of breath. He tired so easily. It was discouraging, and he had to keep reminding himself that he was able to walk farther today than yesterday, and that had to be worth something. It had been a week or more since Fatima had sat with him as he recovered from his rage in Giovanni's *alimentari.* Was it the next day that he had caught sight of himself in the mirror? It must have been the next day, or perhaps the day after. All he really remembered as he pulled himself out of the muck was the sight of his face, his eyes set in ravaged sockets, the lines etching his cheeks into gristly patterns, spittle crusting around his mouth. A monster. He looked like a monster. His wife, his daughter, they would never have recognized him.

He reckoned he must have sat there for fully ten minutes, staring aghast at what he had done to himself, to his life.

To be frank, it was closer to an hour. Time is a blurry thing when one is emerging from a liquor-laced existence.

He leaned back and let the sun warm his face. Closing his eyes, he breathed in the scent of the groves behind him and the fog flowing across the valley, caught in ragged pieces in the clustered trees. He imagined that fog's journey from sea mist on the Le Marche coast, creeping and mingling with the smoke from snapping fires roasting chestnuts and meat. To land here, in this valley that had seen footsteps of man since the ancient Umbri roamed in search of their next meal. And here he was, a teacher, a man. More than a little flawed, and yet still a part of this divine play, this humanity.

Startled, Luciano noticed that he had followed a complete idea, one thought to another.

He closed his eyes and breathed the fog-laced breeze deep into his lungs. He coughed spastically, then sat tall and tried again. He felt the air fill his ribcage like a balloon, before falling into his legs and swirling around his toes. He smiled.

Stretching, Luciano hoisted himself to standing. Noticing that he was less reliant on his cane, he ambled through the streets of Santa Lucia to the park, hoping to catch a glimpse of his granddaughter. He'd avoided her face for a year. It had been too painful to see that little smile follow her mother's familiar pathway. But now, the despair was less insistent, heard as if behind a door. Giving him a breath of freedom to seek out those dark curls.

The park was empty, but as he paused, Patrizia passed him holding hands with her little grandson. He watched her settle the boy onto the swing. Her face was pinched with worry as she adjusted his jacket which had bunched around his armpits. From where Luciano stood, the boy's eyes looked distant, gazing through his grandmother. When the swing began moving his focus cleared. The boy cackled and then laughed.

Patrizia's shoulders dropped from their position around her ears, and her face relaxed. As Luciano stood beyond the cypress trees, he heard the twining laughter of grandmother and grandson rise into the air. He smiled, glad to witness this moment.

He ambled to the *rosticceria* and stepped in. How could he have forgotten about the homey smell of cheese melting into a savory tomato sauce? Luciano ran his tongue over his upper lip, deliberating over his choice. Strange to notice his hunger.

Finally he selected a slice with mushrooms and eggplant. The girl, Bea's granddaughter, he was fairly certain, slipped the pizza into a square of wax paper and handed it to him in exchange for a euro. He walked out of the shop, nibbling a corner of the pizza, wanting to make it last.

Luciano considered returning to the park to eat, but then decided to head back to the center of Santa Lucia.

Passing the *alimentari,* he heard the footfalls of goblins persuading him to enter this place where there was wine. His mind lurched into a ghostland inhabited by his wife and daughter shaming him for his half-life. They taunted him to join them, they mocked the cowardice that kept him rooted to the earthly plane. Luciano shuddered, and took a step toward the *alimentari* door. He still had some money from his October pension. He wouldn't have to steal or beg. He could purchase his wine like anybody else. Other people bought wine and it wasn't a problem, why should it be a problem for him? He deserved this. After all he'd been through, after the week—almost two weeks!—of abstaining, how could one bottle hurt?

He heard a giggle behind him and turned to see Stella, the mayor's wife. He was surprised, the laugh had been unexpectedly girlish from this staid housewife. Then again, she didn't look like a staid housewife. She'd exchanged her usual navy polyester smock for a fitted, patterned dress in vivid colors. And she was engaged in eager conversation with Vale, the town handyman.

They passed, their whispered conversation peppered with chuckles, and Luciano was fairly certain that they trailed the scent of perfume.

He smiled to himself, watching them drift up the street as he finished his pizza.

Luciano wanted to follow them, to take the long way home and perhaps check on Bea's chickens.

But the roar of wine was too loud to resist.

Luciano turned into the *alimentari*. One glass at dinner. Only one glass. He'd done so well today, after all. He needed the wine to beat away the shadows that were sure to come at night.

Even days after the accident, Chiara noticed that Edo still winced at the sound of the register. He walked gingerly, like a dog waiting to be thwacked on the snout with a rolled up *giornale*. She kept hoping he'd say something, but his attempt at conversation had been limited to periodically asking if the new credit card machine was causing any problems. It wasn't at all. Mostly because no one paid her with anything other than euro coins.

When Bea and Ava left the bar, pausing to talk to Elisa on her way to the park with Carosello at her side, Chiara took a breath. Before she could say anything, Edo turned and said, "I'm sorry. I know this isn't what you hoped for you when you took me in. I understand if you need me to go."

"Go? Go where?"

"I don't know. Get another job, another apartment. I didn't show up for work, you had to close the bar and get me from the side of the road, you had to arrange to have my car towed. I have no idea when I'll have enough money to pay you back. I blew it. I know I blew it."

"Edo . . ."

"No, I get it. I wouldn't want me around either."

"Edo! Seriously, what's with all the self-flagellation? Yes, the accident was terrible, and avoidable. But wearing a hair shirt now is hardly going to change that."

He hung his head and repeated, "I blew it."

"Yes, you did."

Edo's wounded eyes met hers. Chiara added, "You did, Edo. No use pretending otherwise."

"I *know!* I know."

"The question is, Edo, why?"

"I don't know."

"Look, it's not my job to push you, but I think you can do better than that. I think you deserve better than that."

Edo turned and began dropping spoons in the canister.

"Edo?"

"Yes, I heard you. I'm thinking." He turned back. "I don't know. When I party . . . all my walls come down. I feel part of something."

Chiara frowned, "What do you mean?"

"I don't know if I can explain it. I just . . . I feel like me. Not like . . . this."

"Edo."

"No, I get it, Chiara, I do. That's on me, too. Sometimes I just feel a million miles from everything. Separate. Different. Going to clubs, with the music, and the, well the drinking, and, and—"

"Drugs," Chiara prompted.

Edo looked at her with surprise. "You knew?"

"I figured."

"I didn't—"

"I'm not that oblivious, Edo."

"I know, it's just hard to say even to myself. Anyway, you wouldn't get it. You fit in everywhere."

"Ha!"

"What?"

"You heard me. That's ridiculous. What gives you the idea that I fit in everywhere?"

"But ... well, because I see you. Everyone loves you. You can talk to anyone. I'm not like that. I never was."

"Edo, I hate to shatter your illusions, but I hardly fit in. Look at me. Look at my life."

"But you've gotten past all that."

"Maybe I'm just better at pretending."

Edo rubbed the pile on his towel back and forth while he mulled over her words.

Chiara added, "And maybe I've realized that we're all pretending. Just a bit. So I don't know, I accept people. Life can be rotten, the best we can do is hold each other up when the weight of that pushes us down. In that way, I guess I figure we all sort of fit in."

Edo scratched his cheek. "Does this mean you forgive me?"

"I do. But I think the important piece is that you need to forgive yourself."

Edo face twisted in confusion. "For crashing the car?"

Chiara stroked her nephew's cheek and sought something in his eyes, "For whatever it is that's haunting you."

"*Ciao*, Elisa!"

"*Ciao*, Fatima! *Come va?*"

"Good, thanks. Are you hungry?"

"I just ate," Elisa lied. Her brothers were gone all day at a soccer game, so there had been no reason for her mother to leave her bedroom to restock their bare cupboards. Elisa wasn't worried about being hungry so much as dreading the eruption that was likely to take place if her father came home to nothing to eat.

Fatima chewed on her lower lip as she regarded Elisa. "Well, I'm starving, I'm going to get a piece of pizza at the *rosticceria*. Will you share it with me?"

"Sure!"

Fatima linked arms with Elisa, and they walked from the park to the shop. The smell of browning cheese filled Elisa, and she stopped to breathe it in. Fatima tugged on her arm, "What kind? I usually get the potato kind, with *rosmarino*."

"Okay." Elisa gazed off beyond the walls.

"Elisa? Where'd you go?"

"I was just remembering. A long time ago we went on a field trip to a castle. I don't even remember where or what it looked like because I found a giant rosemary bush and hid inside it the whole time. I pretended it was my house and I was a wood sprite."

Fatima smiled and said, "I bet it smelled good in there."

Elisa said, "It did. The teacher was so mad, though."

Fatima took Elisa's hand and squeezed. She considered the slices of pizza in the case, then turned to her friend and whispered. "I think today I want to get sausage."

Elisa shrugged. "Sure, *perchè no?*"

Fatima ordered and then picked up two plastic containers of peach tea and added them to the square piece of pizza on the counter. Digging in her pockets she pulled out a five euro note, swept the change into her hand, and led Elisa back out to the park. Elisa's eyes lingered on the change. Could she take money from Fatima now? Now that they were real friends?

The girls found a bench and sat down. They speared the tops of the tea with the thin straws, and then Fatima pulled back the waxed paper of the pizza and took a bite, before handing it to Elisa. As Elisa accepted the pizza with both hands, Fatima closed her eyes and chewed slowly.

"Wow," she said.

"What is it?"

Fatima paused. "Sausage. Sausage doesn't taste at all like I expected. It is so good. "

"Of course it is." Elisa frowned. "Wait, this is your first time eating sausage?"

Fatima nodded.

"Oh! It's pork, isn't it? I never think about it." Fatima had told Elisa last week that her family didn't eat pigs, so she had never tasted cured pork. She'd breathed the confession after she had traded one of the girls her *cornetto* for a *panino* with *prosciutto*. They had laughed because after the first bite, Fatima had said that it tasted like salty soap that she wanted to eat forever. Elisa had never thought about it, but when she took the bite Fatima offered, she could see what she meant.

Fatima nodded again.

"I still don't get why you can't eat pork."

Fatima accepted the pizza that Elisa handed back. "I don't really understand either. It seems like a silly rule." They chewed in companionable silence for a few minutes, watching the breeze swoop up sun-warmed leaves before tossing them up and over the fence and down the hill.

Elisa asked, "Will you tell your parents?"

Fatima coughed on her pizza. "No! They are already worried that I will forget how to be a good Moroccan girl. If they knew I ate pork . . ." Fatima paused, considering, before saying, "And have a crush."

Elisa's face whipped toward her friend. "You like a boy? Who?"

Fatima blushed. "I don't want to say."

Elisa was bewildered, "Why? Who can it be?" She thought about the boys in their class. "It's Mario, isn't it?"

Fatima's open mouth confirmed Elisa's hunch. Fatima gasped, "How did you guess?"

Elisa shrugged. "You look at him a lot, but you never say anything to him."

Fatima ventured, "Do you think he likes me too?"

Elisa sat back and closed her eyes, scanning her memory. Opening her eyes she said, "Yes."

Fatima beamed, "Really? Why?"

Elisa grinned at her friend and shrugged again. "He smiles a lot when he sees you."

Fatima beamed and sat back, staring without seeing over the distant hills.

Elisa was glad her friend was happy, but she did not understand why Fatima would care about boys. Her thoughts darted to Stefano's hand brushing her behind as she walked away. She shivered. Boys were awful. And a little scary.

Fatima drained the last of her tea and handed the pizza back to Elisa, "Mamma will kill me if I don't eat my whole dinner. She says I'm so thin I'll blow away. Can you finish it?"

"Sure. Okay," Elisa took the last quarter of the pizza and concentrated on not wolfing it down. She finished, and licked her fingers before using the napkins to wipe her hands clean.

Fatima leapt up, "C'mon! Do you think we could play in those trees and pretend they are rosemary? I want to be a wood princess with a crown of leaves."

"I'll be a traveling mushroom seller! And I come with my mushrooms and you aren't sure to trust me or not. Too bad there aren't any *porcini* around, but look! I see some moss, we can use that!"

The playground was empty, as it often was when there was a nip in the air. Pork and boys and money and grades were left behind as the girls filled the park with their laughter. They chased each other around the pomegranate tree, then used the fruit to stain their lips. They stood on the swings, pretending to be flying goddesses. Elisa was showing Fatima how to do a cartwheel on the small patch of grass, rubbed almost to dirt by the attempts of small boys to play soccer, when their conversation was cut off by a yell.

"Elisa!"

They both looked up.

A woman hurried into the park, oily hanks of hair escaping the scarf she'd tossed over her head, a coat buttoned haphazardly over her loose flower print dress. Elisa's face went white against the pomegranate juice smeared across her mouth. She backed up like a crab.

The woman grabbed Elisa by the arm and yanked her to standing.

"What do you think you are doing? I wake up and you are gone with this ... this *note!* What do you think your father would say if he came home and found it?"

"I'm sorry, Mamma, I'm sorry! I didn't think about him finding it, I thought you would find it."

"You thought! *You* thought! If you thought for a moment it would be a miracle worthy of Santa Lucia herself. How *dare* you! How dare you *leave!* After everything we've done for you!"

The woman's hand flung across space and time, connecting to Elisa's face with a cracking sound. Elisa's hand cupped her cheek and she sobbed, "I'm sorry, Mamma! I'm so sorry! Is he home?"

The woman looked at her child, and sagged. "No, not yet. I found your note as I got up to go shopping. I panicked. Oh, Elisa. I hurt you." She reached out her hand to touch Elisa's face.

"It's okay, Mamma. We'll go shopping now. We'll go shopping together. It will be okay."

But the woman stopped moving, she was staring at the angry welt on her daughter's face. "Elisa?"

"Come on, Mamma, let's go. Quickly, now." Elisa pulled her mother forward, out of the park. She didn't look back to see Fatima, arms wrapped around her skinny knees, watching, as Elisa and her mother stumbled out of the park.

Fatima rubbed the red from her lips, finally using her arm to wipe across her mouth. She stood up, brushed the seat of her pants free of dirt, and slowly walked home.

"Chiara! Did you hear?" Arturo blew into the bar, his cheeks flushed from the wind and his news.

Chiara wiped the bar free of a scattering of sugar from the teenage boys that just left. "About what?" She hoped it wasn't fresh evidence against his gorgeous wife, who was, truth be told, probably having an affair. But Chiara hated to see Arturo spinning like a decapitated chicken rather than making a move to extricate himself from the situation.

"Massimo is getting married!"

"Ah, yes."

"You knew?" Arturo's face fell. He'd been sure he held the keys to this news. Anna, Massimo's mother, had proudly told him just this morning.

"Anna came in this morning."

"Oh, well. Can you believe it? Giulia died, what? A year ago?"

Chiara measured her response. It didn't seem like Arturo knew the juiciest part of this gossip, and on the off-chance that it was all in her head, Chiara wasn't daring to say anything. "Not exactly a year." She ducked to check the number of bottles of water on the shelf.

"Well, I say it's not normal."

"What's not normal?" asked Patrizia, unwinding the scarf from her head as she walked in the door.

Arturo whipped toward Patrizia, and before Chiara could rise, he said, "Massimo is getting married!"

"Yes, I heard."

Arturo was crestfallen. "How did *you* find out?"

"I saw him with Margherita at the park when I was there with my grandson. He told me."

"He did? He told you? Did he say anything about his *fidanzata?*"

"The usual. She's wonderful, smart, beautiful." At this Chiara stood, a confused expression furrowing her eyebrows. She swallowed, then crouched down below the counter again as Patrizia continued. "Oh! I think he said she's from Florence. A city girl. I wonder how she'll cope with the quiet here."

"Florence! I didn't know that part. I wonder how he met her?"

"Met who?" said Edoardo, entering the bar from the door behind the counter.

Chiara turned and faced her nephew with a carefully neutral expression on her face, "Arturo and Patrizia were talking about Massimo getting married."

Edoardo felt a hook pulling him into the conversation, but one look at Chiara's still face and he stalled. He took his time closing the door, then latched it softly before turning to the bar. "Ah, yes. Wonderful news." He glanced over at Chiara and saw her nod in approval. Edo ran his teeth over his lower lip, and then passed his aunt with a pat on her shoulder before opening the drawer to pull out his apron.

"*Wonderful?*" shouted Arturo. "Isn't anyone else shocked that he'd be getting married with his wife hardly cold in the ground?"

All heads turned. Chiara murmured, "Now, Arturo . . ."

Arturo looked chastened, "*None* of you think it's strange? *Un caffè*, by the way, Chiara."

"Sure, *un attimo*." Chiara washed her hands, and when she turned to dry them, everyone was studying different corners of the bar, not speaking. "You want one, Edo?"

"Yes, thanks, Zia."

The bar was quiet as Chiara prepared the coffee. All heads faced the door as Bea swept in, "*Fa un freddo cane!* It's so cold out there!" She removed her coat and hung it by the door. "Did you hear? Massimo is getting married!"

Arturo's eyes narrowed. "Don't you think that's a little soon?"

"Yes! Giulia, bless her heart, died just a year ago! And we all thought he was pining for her. Ha! He was making moves on another woman. Maybe loads of women, for all we know."

Chiara set Arturo's coffee in front of him and gestured toward it to Bea. Bea nodded, and then said, "Wait, no make it *un cappuccino*." She reached for a sugar packet and started shaking it by the corner as she looked around, "It's disturbing, no?"

Arturo nodded, "Yes! That's just what I was saying!"

Chiara, Patrizia, and Edoardo tried not to look at each other—Chiara pulling shots for Edo and Bea, Edo retying his apron, Patrizia studying the drink menu she'd no doubt memorized since it had rarely changed in her lifetime.

Bea shook her head. "Poor Giulia must be rolling over in her grave."

Arturo shot a look at Chiara, but she focused on filling the metal pitcher with milk. He pressed on firmly, "*Esatto*. What do you know about the woman he's marrying?"

Bea sighed as she ripped open her sugar packet. "Only what the men were saying in the *piazza*. She works at the bank. I think she has a big family in Florence, though no one recognized her surname."

Chiara handed the *espresso* to Edoardo and the *cappuccino* to Bea, who thanked her before asking, "Chiara, you must know something. *Dai*, come on, tell us!"

Chiara shook her head, "No, that's more than I knew."

"Ha! What a crock," snickered Bea. "You forget, I dated your uncle before he married your aunt. I know this bar is *the* hotbed of gossip. The stories he told me! It's one of the reasons I refused to marry him, you know. I would hate to hold everybody's secrets. I don't know how you do it, Chiara."

Chiara smiled and began stacking cups in the dishwasher.

Arturo groaned, "Oh, no, here comes the German."

Bea rolled her eyes. "I wonder what we're doing wrong today. Last week she told me I should be feeding my chickens leftover potato peels like they do in Germany. How many potatoes does the woman think I eat?"

The door swung open and Magda strode in. "Did you hear about Massimo? He's getting married!"

To the silence that greeted her pronouncement, Magda added, "To a woman who is the spitting image of his dead wife."

This had the desired effect. All faces swiveled to her like sunflowers. She smiled roundly at everyone, looking for all the world like the cat that got the cream. She stepped between Arturo and Bea and announced, "I'll have my usual, Chiara."

Finally, the parade of customers ran out of ways to recycle their limited facts about Massimo and his betrothed. One by one, they filed out into the hastening dusk.

The stranger looked up from his paper and caught Chiara's glance. "Pardon me, but if you don't mind my asking—that woman who just left, where is she from? I can't place her accent." He gestured with his chin towards Magda's back, receding down the street.

"Magda? She moved here from Germany, oh, twenty years ago? Now she lives around the corner. She owns 'Villa Tramonte.' I assumed you were staying there. You're not?" Chiara couldn't figure out why she added that last part. She only knew she wanted the conversation to continue.

"Ah, no."

Chiara bit her lip to keep from asking where he was staying. She looked up from putting Magda's coffee cup into the dishwasher and saw that the stranger was watching her. A smile crept across his face until he was chuckling.

"What?" Chiara asked, smiling too, despite herself.

"You want to ask where I'm staying, don't you?"

Chiara set down her towel. "And why would I want to know that?"

"Oh, Chiara, even with just the couple of weeks I have been in Santa

Lucia, I can see that you are at the center of everything. No problem is too great or too small for people not to come in here and lay it at your feet. For there to be information you don't have, it must kill you, no?"

Chiara toyed with indignation and protest. But there was something about this man that made her not want to adopt any artifice. Instead, she leaned forward on her elbows and grinned. "It is true that you are a bit of a mystery. We don't get many mysteries around here. I'm afraid I'm out of practice."

The man chuckled and folded his newspaper along the creases. "What do you want to know?"

"We could begin with your name. It's rather unfair that you know mine."

"It would be impossible not to know yours. But mine is Fabrizio," and with this the man gave a mock bow, which was more of a flirtatious head tilt.

"All right then, Fabrizio. Where are you staying, if not at Magda's?"

"At the apartment of a friend of a friend, on the edge of town."

"Do you know what family owns the apartment?"

"Yes, Benito di Pasqua. Do you know him?"

"A little. I knew his grandparents when I was small, before they moved. Now the family rarely visits. Sometimes at Ferragosto or when it's hot in Rome."

"Yes, that sounds about right."

Chiara leaned back and debated asking another question.

Fabrizio smiled his slow grin again. He said quietly, "Go ahead, Chiara."

"So why are you here? With your notebooks and papers. Some people have said—oh, never mind."

"What have they said, Chiara?"

Chiara shook her head and turned her back. She began polishing the flawlessly shiny La Pavoni.

Fabrizio hazarded, "I bet I know at least two theories. They think I'm either a private investigator hired by Arturo to see if his French wife is in fact cheating on him or a government agent sent to check to see if properties match what they pay in taxes."

Chiara whirled around, her face confused, "How . . ."

Fabrizio stood and tucked his paper under his arm. "It's a small town, Chiara. That everything is public is Santa Lucia's worst kept secret. You should know that better than anyone. But I'll let you in on a little truth." He walked to the bar.

Chiara leaned toward him, eyes drawn to his.

Fabrizio rested his arms on the bar and let his face drift down to Chiara's, until his warm breath bushed against her cheekbones. Fabrizio touched her hand with his forefinger and murmured, "I'm not sure how sinister this will seem to you, Chiara, but . . ."

"*Ciao!* Chiara!" A voice hailed from the doorway. Chiara reflexively stepped back from Fabrizio who immediately straightened, dropped a two euro coin in the copper plate and nodded his goodbye to her, stepping briskly out the door.

Chiara gaze lingered after him. When they drifted to the counter she noticed the uniformed figure before her. "Ah, *ciao,* Marcello. How is your mother?"

Marcello's scowled. "Improving. She just returned home Thursday. What was that?"

"What was what?" Chiara widened her eyes and shrugged.

"That man. Why were you so close to him Chiara? You looked like you were kissing."

Chiara attempted to laugh this off while she ground *espresso* beans.

"I'm serious, Chiara. That man is dangerous, I don't even think you should be alone with him."

"What are you talking about?"

"Were you kissing him?"

"Mind your place, Marcé." Chiara chided. The effect of the statement would have been stronger if both she and Marcello hadn't noticed the blush beginning at the base of her neck. She swept on, "I am your elder, one of your mother's oldest friends, not your peer. But to avoid fanning flames of gossip, I'll tell you that no, I wasn't."

Marcello scratched his chin and approached the bar. "Chiara, no disrespect, but you looked awfully friendly. I'm telling you, you need to watch yourself. I know it's your nature to be welcoming, but that stranger is no good for you."

Chiara pretended a level of nonchalance she did not feel. "Oh, really? Why?"

"*Ma dai*, I can hardly discuss that with you."

"Has he done something illegal?"

"Not exactly. He's perfectly polite. Too polite if you ask me. Like he has something to hide. Chiara, trust me. Between the two of us, who is the more trained to spot derelicts? Stay away from that man."

Chiara let her eyes drift out the door. She wasn't sure she wanted to stay away, and the foreignness of that feeling concerned her more than Marcello's warning.

The morning sun hung weakly in the mid-October sky when Fatima stepped onto the cobblestone streets of Santa Lucia, money for couscous pushed deep into her pocket. She trailed her fingers along the walls, letting them wind into the greenery that erupted from the mortar. The stones had warmed a bit in the afternoon sun, and she enjoyed the emanating heat against the coolness of the tickling fronds.

She hoped the *alimentari* had couscous. Time was they never did, but after a few months of her family living in Santa Lucia and asking for it periodically, Giovanni had begun stocking it. Not a lot, and sometimes it disappeared from the shelves just when her family was craving a taste of home, but Fatima appreciated the effort. She'd even been inveigled into conversations about how her family prepared the dish. She liked it topped with good Umbrian lamb, which her tastebuds insisted (as much as her parents vociferously denied) was even tastier than what they ate in Morocco.

Her mouth watered in anticipation of dinner. The smell of the sauce had wafted out with her, and still clung to her sweater. As she was wondering what shape pasta she would choose if the *alimentari* was out of couscous, she caught sight of Luciano walking out of San Nicola. He raised his head and blinked at the sudden sunshine. Fatima noted that he wasn't listing to the side as did on bad days, and his cane was nowhere in sight. She ran up to him and tugged at his coat as he walked to the *piazza*.

"Ah, Fatima, *buon pomeriggio.*" Was it her imagination, or was Luciano's voice rusty from disuse? How long had it been since he'd talked to anyone?

"*Ciao*, Maestro. *Come va?*"

"I'm well, Fatima."

"You were in church?"

"I was."

"For services?" Fatima could never keep track of Catholics' praying schedule, even though she snuck into the church often enough to study the paintings. Those saints were enigmatic, she wished she knew their stories. She debated coming out from the safety of the wall's obscurity and asking the priest to explain the Catholic cast of characters to her. He had been so nice and engaging that time he saw her staring at the Madonna in her niche, she knew he would be happy to share his knowledge. But the thought of what her parents would say if they found out she'd even set foot in a Catholic church kept her tucked in the shadows.

"No services today, *cara*," Luciano chuckled at Fatima's creased forehead. "But sometimes it's nice to go in and pray."

"You can do that?"

"Of course."

"You don't pray at home?"

"Well, yes, I do." Luciano considered Fatima's question. "I suppose I prefer praying surrounded by reminders of my faith. In church, the rest of the world falls away and I can hear God, the pope, or, I don't know. Maybe just myself." Not for the first time, Luciano regarded this child with a mixture of amusement and wonder. "I don't know Fatima," he added, forestalling her question. "I'm not sure what it is. It's strange though, how much you always make me question what I've always assumed to be beyond questioning."

Fatima ducked her head and frowned, "I'm sorry, Maestro."

He chuckled again, "No need to apologize. Today it's nice to be prompted to think a bit more. Not everyday, mind you, but today . . ." His voice trailed off.

Fatima walked beside her teacher, thinking about what he'd said.

Luciano put his hand on Fatima's voluminous black hair, wrestled neatly into two braids. "So, where are you off to?"

"Oh! The *alimentari*. Mamma ran out of couscous."

"Mmm, your mother's couscous. With lamb sauce, I presume?"

Fatima laughed. "Yes, my favorite. But Maestro, I have a favor to ask."

"Yes?"

Fatima took a breath. "I have a friend at school, Elisa. Do you know her?"

"*Allora*, is she the one you hold hands with on the way out of school?"

Fatima stopped walking. He'd noticed?

Luciano slowed his steps until Fatima caught up. She said, "Yes, that's her. Her parents sort of forget about her, and her brothers, I think maybe they do, too. She's not stuck to life very well."

Luciano smiled.

Fatima paused to make sure Luciano was still paying attention. He nodded for her to continue. "She also gets in trouble a lot at school. She's not bad or anything! It's only that she loses papers a lot and math is really hard for her. Anyway, I was thinking, maybe you can help her? I remember how well you taught me the conditional tense."

Luciano said, "I wish I could take credit, but that wasn't me. You are born to learn."

Fatima tipped her head up to grin at Maestro. "Okay, then, you taught my siblings. And my parents. I still can't get my parents to remember how *ziti* and *penne* are different, so . . ."

Luciano rubbed his forehead and sighed, "Fatima, I'm afraid my teaching days are finished. They were finished long ago."

The girl hung her head. Luciano said, "I wish I could help, I do, but it's a useless endeavor. I can't teach her, or anyone."

Fatima's lip trembled. "You won't try? Maestro, I don't know what else to do. Some days it looks like she's going to melt away. Like *gelato* left in the *piazza*."

The thought of having another tether on life, no, it was impossible. Even if Luciano's heart quivered at the thought of a struggling child. He said, "The math teacher. It is part of a teacher's job to stay after school to support those students—"

"The math teacher hits her."

Luciano stopped walking, agape. "The teacher does what?"

"Hits her. Not often, at least I heard that it used to be more last year. Mostly now he puts Elisa in the corner and makes fun of her."

His mouth worked as his thoughts raced in many directions, "But this is unacceptable. Why isn't someone putting a stop to this?"

Fatima snorted. "Like who? I told you about her family."

Luciano wanted to shrug away this responsibility to insist it wasn't his problem, but the thought of this little girl trapped by her life with no way out. He took Fatima's hand and started walking again, "Let's say once and see how it goes."

Massimo would be calling soon, Isotta chided herself. She had to tell her parents about him, despite the dread roiling in her gut. At least two of her sisters were ostensibly at Florence's storied Pitti Palace for a concert of Mozart music, but more probably in their boyfriend's beds listening to American rap. In any event, there were fewer opportunities for interruption. It was now or never.

"Mamma, do you want some help?" Isotta asked, wringing her hands behind her back.

Her mother, Caterina, sighed and handed the celery she was mincing to Isotta. "Yes, thank you. I don't know why your sisters wait until the last possible moment to tell me they are bringing their boyfriends home for dinner after the concert. Of course I'm happy to feed them, but how am I going to make this pasta sauce serve ten people?" She opened a cupboard and pulled out another can of tomatoes. "Thank the *Madonna* we have this. The meat will be sparse, but that can't be helped." She sat on a dining room chair with a sigh, and picked up a magazine.

"Um, Mamma? There's something I've been wanting to tell you."

"*Madonna mia*, you're not bringing someone to dinner are you?"

"No, no."

"Good. Then again," Caterina let out a screech of laughter, "who would you bring? That's one thing we can say about our Isotta, she doesn't exactly have suitors beating down our door."

Isotta flinched. Her mother rolled her eyes, "God, Isotta. Don't be so sensitive. You'll find someone. It'll take a little longer, what with the weak chin you got from your father and the bulging eyes you got from my mother, but you are a nice enough girl, with steady work. And since you are the youngest, you'll eventually meet the friends of all your sisters' boyfriends." She chuckled and flipped the pages of her magazine.

"Well, Mamma. That's sort of what I wanted to talk to you about. I did find someone."

Caterina looked up from her reading, all the tension of her raised eyebrows leaving her mouth hanging open.

Isotta turned and scraped the chopped celery into the waiting bowl of diced carrots. Wiping her hands, she ventured, "Mamma?"

Her mother blinked, and shook her head. "What do you mean? You have a crush on a boy? It's about time. Your father and I often wondered if perhaps you were . . . never mind, it doesn't bear mentioning. Wait, it is a man, isn't it?"

Isotta was glad her back was to her mother. The heat was creeping up her cheeks, as she conjured images of Massimo and his thorough maleness. She pressed her cool hands against her face, steadied herself, and pivoted back toward her mother, a few cloves of garlic in her hand. She focused on peeling them steadily while she answered, "Yes. It's a man. But it's not just a 'crush'. I'm . . . I'm seeing him."

Catarina sat up straighter. "Well! You are seeing a man. A man you've never introduced to your family?" Her voice tripped from confusion to iciness. "Who is he?"

Isotta waited to answer until she'd pounded each clove of garlic to dislodge the papery skin. "His name is Massimo."

"He's from Florence."

Isotta squirmed. "Um . . ."

"Tuscan? Please tell me he's Tuscan."

"Actually, no. He's from Santa Lucia."

"*Sicily?*"

"No, Umbria."

"Well, thank the Madonna for that." She paused, "There's a Santa Lucia in Umbria?"

"Yes, south, past Perugia, on the border of Le Marche."

"Never heard of it. Then again, why would I?"

Isotta finished mincing the garlic and selected an onion from the basket. Holding it out toward her mother, Isotta waited for Caterina's nod that she should chop it before crackling the peel off in shards.

"How would you meet an Umbrian?"

"He works for the bank." Isotta faltered. If she said she met Massimo in Rome, her mother, less predisposed to turn a blind eye to her than to her sisters, was likely to put two and two together and realize that the overnight she had in Rome was not because of food poisoning, but because of something far more dire. If pressed, she decided to say that she met him here, in Florence.

Caterina's eyes were still furrowed, as she slowly processed her daughter's words.

"So you are seeing a man, an Umbrian man, whom you haven't introduced to your family." She smoothed her dress over her knees. "What's wrong with him?"

Isotta, cutting the onion from pole to pole, looked up at her mother with wide eyes.

"Don't look at me like that, Isotta. It's a fair question. What's wrong with him?" It *is* a fair question. Those familiar with the story of Massimo and Isotta will have wondered the same.

Isotta sighed, and began slicing through the halved onion. "Nothing, Mamma. Nothing is wrong with him."

"Well, when will you bring him to meet us?"

"Next week?"

"Okay, then." Caterina leaned back and began flipping the pages of her magazine again. She guffawed, "Looks like our little bird is puffing out, eh? Your father will be amused. And your sisters!"

Isotta scraped the diced onion into the bowl with the back of her knife. She set down the knife and pressed her hands on the counter to steady herself.

"Mamma?"

"*Sì?*"

"There's more."

"More?"

"Yes . . ."

The color drained from Caterina's face. "Oh, my God, you're pregnant."

"No! No, I'm not pregnant. It's just that . . ."

"Isotta! Tell me! What is it?"

"It's just that," Isotta closed her eyes and breathed deeply, gathering her courage. "We are getting married."

Luciano stood in the *piazza* ticking off his internal checklist. The tea kettle was filled from the spigot in the alley. He would usher everyone quickly to the garden so he wouldn't need to explain the lack of power. He calculated that with a few weeks of careful spending he would have enough to contact the utilities and start a payment program to regain water and electricity. He thanked the Madonna that the gas—despite the warning letter he'd gotten in the mail—was still flowing. Especially with the colder months coming on.

He smiled when he saw Fatima appear at the edge of the *piazza*. She straightened and beamed at him with a mixture of relief and excitement. Tugging Elisa's hand she said, "There he is!"

Elisa wanted to pull back a bit. Meeting people was always awkward for her, she'd had to do it so rarely. Besides, Luciano seemed so . . . unpredictable. And sometimes he smelled weird. Like vinegar and ashes. But he looked better than usual now—his candyfloss hair was combed and his outfit looked clean, if a little rumpled.

The girls arrived in front of Luciano.

"*Ciao*, you must be Elisa. I'm delighted to meet you," said Luciano, leaning forward to drop a polite kiss on each of Elisa's cheeks.

"*Ciao*, Maestro. *Piacere*, it's nice to meet you, too."

Fatima stood and grinned.

Luciano gestured up the street, "Fatima tells me that math is a puzzle for you?"

Elisa nodded, "Yes. It feels like everything I learn just falls out of my head."

Luciano chuckled, "Yes, numbers have a tendency to do that. Slippery rascals."

Elisa searched Luciano's face to see if he was making fun of her, but he was grinning easily. She decided she was being jumpy.

Fatima stopped her friends, "I'm just going to run into the *forno* before they close. Focaccia? Or Maestro would you prefer *biscotti?*" She asked with a knowing smile.

Luciano chuckled again, "With *albicocche.*" To Elisa he added, "Fatima knows my weakness for apricot cookies. All sweets, if I'm to be honest."

Fatima smiled and said, "You two go ahead, I'll catch up." Fatima squeezed Elisa's hand in reassurance and then skipped backward, waving.

Luciano nodded, "So how old are you, Elisa?"

"Eleven."

"Ah, a good age. I remember it well."

"You do?"

"Well, not really," Luciano admitted, with a smile. "It's just one of those annoying things old people say to sound important. And you live in Santa Lucia?"

"Yes, at the other end, by the park, a little outside the gates."

"Your parents' surnames?"

"Lucarelli and Bruno."

"Hmm. Those names don't sound familiar. Did they go to school in Santa Lucia?"

"No, they are from Foligno, but moved here because my father got a job at power plant in Girona."

Luciano nodded, "Do you get to see your extended family often?"

"No, my father isn't close to his family, and my mother was an only child, and her parents died."

Elisa kicked herself for using the word. When Fatima had told her about Luciano's double loss, she warned Elisa not to remind him by mentioning death. He was being so nice, why did she have to go and ruin it? But though Maestro blanched a little, he didn't look angry. He simply answered, "*Allora*, it is difficult to be without family."

Luciano turned into a doorway and said, "Ah, we've arrived, *eccociqua*."

As he jiggled the doorknob, Fatima's footsteps hurried up to them. "Here I am! They didn't have them with *albicocche,* so I got *prugne*. I hope that's okay."

Elisa said simply, "I love prune."

Luciano grinned his agreement.

Fatima smiled. "Good. Oh, *ciao,* Degas!"

A black cat with white on its chest, face, and feet had flung itself on Fatima's legs. "Elisa, this is Degas, Maestro's cat."

Elisa got down on the floor cross-legged and whispered to Degas, "*Ciao, micio, ciao* kitty." Degas leapt lightly into her lap and curled into a tight ball, purring.

Fatima laughed, "Trapped by a cat."

Luciano peered around the corner from where he'd started the kettle for his favorite *camomilla* tea, and smiled. "It appears he approves of you, Elisa. Do you have pets?"

Elisa scratched the top of Degas's head and said, "No. My parents never let me. Sometimes I make friends with one of the Santa Lucia cats. But when it starts following me home my brothers chase it off. Or my father does." A cloud marred Elisa's bright features.

Luciano nodded before heading back into the kitchen. He called over his shoulder, "That is unfortunate. You clearly have a gift with animals. Or at least my animal. Bring him some *mortadella* sometime and he'll cling to you like a caper berry."

Winking at Elisa, Fatima rubbed her belly. She had just tried *mortadella* the day before and loved it almost as much as *prosciutto*. Fatima turned and followed Luciano to the kitchen, "Maestro? Are capers actually sticky? Do you know how to make them?" Elisa wondered if perhaps Fatima was less caper-curious and perhaps just making sure her teacher wasn't taking out wine. As Elisa stroked the white patch behind the cat's ear, admiring how such a thin beast could create such a loud rumble of satisfaction, she heard Luciano's chuckle and response of, "I don't know, Fatima, to own the truth, I never picked a caper in my life. But they look like they should be sticky, don't they?" The voices muted to a low burble and then Fatima returned with a broad smile. "Luciano says we can have our snack in the garden, his house is a little . . . cluttered."

Elisa scanned the room. Her own house was rarely orderly, but this was something else entirely. Teetering stacks of papers and books trampled every available surface. Nothing seemed to have been touched in months. The dust had settled everywhere, cramming crevices. Elisa felt invisible particles clogging her lungs.

This was stupid, ridiculous even! What was she doing in this crazy drunk's house? Yes, Fatima said he was nice and everything, but Fatima was too trusting, as that dumb coin still weighing down her pocket proved. Even if he wasn't crazy, how could this help? She couldn't *do* school, and was better off figuring out ways to get money. It was almost report card time. *Report card time.* Elisa couldn't catch her breath, she pushed the cat off her lap and bolted up.

Fatima furrowed her brows at Elisa. She mouthed, "What's wrong?"

Elisa just shook her head. She had to get out of here. Fatima took her hand and pulled her toward the back door. Elisa shot one more glance over her shoulder at her escape, but as she couldn't think of a way to explain her leaving, she allowed herself to be guided out the door. She'd just stay for ten minutes. And then she'd figure out an excuse to go. That would be better, if she left while the others were still outside, she'd be able to pluck something on her way out. It didn't look like Maestro's house would have any money, but there were a few brass knickknacks she might be able to pocket. Maybe Stefano would take those in lieu of money.

Once outside, she gasped.

Fatima smiled, "Yes, that's how I felt the first time, too."

The view was different from what Elisa was used to. From here, the mountains across the valley didn't look so far away, in fact, they seemed to fold greenly against Santa Lucia. She could hear the waterfall from around the mountain, and the birds swooped and dove, carving lines into the startlingly turquoise sky. The garden itself was overgrown with weeds, but Elisa could tell it would be a restful space with just a little work. Round concrete benches surrounded several fruit trees, and there was an olive tree in the corner of the garden, hanging heavy with darkening fruit, and a line of bay bushes against the back of the garden wall. Rosemary lined the iron fence facing out over the valley. The grass was too long and dry, or scraped bare in places, but still gave the garden a stretched-out, welcoming appearance.

Fatima sat at the stone table, unpacking the treats from the *forno* onto waxy paper napkins. Luciano appeared with a tray and three teacups. Elisa sat down with a sigh. "This is just beautiful."

"I'm glad you like it. I'm not out here as often as I should be. Some days it's easiest to stay in the dark of the house. But you are always welcome."

Elisa blinked back tears of surprise.

"Okay," Luciano said gently. "Let's talk math."

It was late.

Chiara knew she should close the bar, but last week Fabrizio had come in for a glass of wine right at closing time. She hadn't been able to talk to him because the bar had been full of neighbors swapping theories about

Massimo. After greeting the bar patrons in his customary formal way, he'd asked for a glass of Sagrantino and taken it outside. Probably to watch the falls while enjoying his red wine and the fennel seed rings she nestled next to the glass. But maybe he had been waiting for her? To join him? To have a word in private? She couldn't decide.

At times it seemed like Fabrizio was interested, and sometimes he seemed so remote. It was aggravating. Her impatience to know if he liked her was even more aggravating. What was she, some errant school girl with a crush on a handsome college boy? It was ridiculous. The more ridiculous because even if he did like her, it wasn't like she was in a position to pursue a relationship. Even if he wasn't a stranger, and Santa Lucia's newest source of suspicion.

And yet, here she was, wiping down counters that were already clean and polishing the faucet that was already so reflective she couldn't escape the sight of her wistful face.

She heard Edo step softly down the stairs and open the landing door. "Need help closing up, Chiara?"

"No, thanks, I've got it."

"Okay, goodnight."

"Goodnight, *caro*."

She turned out the light.

Florence's train station wasn't all that hot, and yet Isotta wiped her hands on her pants. Again. Why did her body choose today of all days to start manifesting anxiety as sweat? She longed for the familiar jerking of her gut. And this wasn't just any sweat, it was a prodigious sweat. An old woman in a blue cardigan cast Isotta a curious look as the younger woman fanned her chest with her light silk shirt. Isotta dropped her hand.

If only it were summer so she could pass off this sweat as heat related.

She was betrayed by the cool October breeze. No, it wasn't heat, but rather the threat of her secret Massimo-world colliding with her family reality. She couldn't decide if she was more nervous about her family rejecting Massimo, or Massimo seeing her through her family's eyes and rejecting her. She landed on the latter. Partly because she couldn't imagine anyone rejecting Massimo, he was far too ... "grand" was the only word that sprang to mind. But also partly because she nursed a shred of doubt about what Massimo saw in her. Isotta had enough self-awareness to know that she was intelligent and could even be witty if circumstances allowed her to feel comfortable, but with Massimo she was often tongue-tied, and spent more time listening. Maybe that was what he liked about her. Her ability to listen, which friends had often told her was a gift, though it seemed to Isotta the most basic of functions.

The train from Perugia had another ten minutes before its slated arrival. Isotta added an extra ten minutes to account for predictable delays. She was too jittery to stand on the platform for twenty minutes, or even ten, and decided to go into the station bar. The coffee was dreadful, but she didn't think caffeine would be helpful anyway. Walking into the bar, she chose a post at the end of the counter, and in answer to the barista's inquiring expression, ordered an *orzo*, a toasted barley drink. She could never decide if she liked *orzo*, but she couldn't wait for tea to steep, and it would give her hands something to do. She smoothed her hair with her still-damp hands. Memories of her talk with her mother intruded into her attempts to still her nerves.

News of the engagement had not gone over well. Her mother had let out an involuntary scream, which brought the rest of the family running. Pointing at her daughter, Caterina had garbled out the words that Isotta was getting married to a man none of them knew, who wasn't Florentine, or even Tuscan. Her sisters and father shot a look of disbelief at Isotta as they gathered around her mother. Their shock turned to outrage. Who was this man? How could he propose to her without asking her family first? She tried to explain that Massimo was a decisive person, strong and used to making decisions, after all he had a daughter to care for—*bedlam*.

He had been married already?

What in God's name was she thinking accepting the advances of a strange man who had already been married?

Isotta checked the time and realized that Massimo's train was due to arrive any minute, if it actually arrived on time. She paid at the register and tried to release the lingering memories of her family's outrage. She tried to hope that once they met him … but deeper fears outpaced her nascent optimism.

She rushed to the platform, and saw the train just arriving. Isotta exhaled with relief. If she had been late, Massimo would have been justly furious. She wiped her hands on her pants again and smoothed her cream shirt over her chest, so the opening was centered, revealing what Massimo had murmured were her best assets. She toyed with opening one more button, but decided against it.

There! There he was! Stepping off the train, his crisp blue shirt stark against the black train and billowing steam. He stood on the step, surveying the assembled crowd. Isotta stood breathless, her old impulse to hide behind something taking over. It was implausible that this man was searching for her. But he was. When his eyes met hers he smiled that slow perfect smile. Lightly, he leapt down the steps. Looking neither right nor left, he kept his gaze on her as he walked purposely through the crowd. Isotta noticed that the faint lines around his eyes made him, if anything, more handsome. Suddenly, he was in front of her, his hand stroking her arm, as he leaned down and kissed her lightly, just once. Isotta smiled at him, and felt, for the first time in her life, beautiful.

Clasping her hand, they walked out of the station. Past the chaos of passengers arriving and departing, she asked, "How is Margherita, and your mother?"

"Both fine, looking forward to the wedding and having you there."

Isotta nodded. "Me too."

Massimo smiled and they continued walking. "Nervous?" He asked.

"Well, yes, actually. Thanks for coming earlier than we planned. The tension in my house is awful."

"Of course. It's right that your parents be worried. You are their precious baby, after all."

Isotta snorted. "I think it has more to do with what the neighbors will say. My family seems certain you'll have two heads or a putrid skin condition."

Massimo frowned. "Why?"

Isotta licked her bottom lip before saying, lightly. "Well, because you chose me, actually. It must mean there is something wrong with you."

Massimo stopped and took Isotta's other hand, gazing down into her eyes. "Now why would they think that?"

"Oh, Massimo. You know."

"I don't. Tell me. Is there something wrong with you I should know about? Do *you* have a putrid skin condition?" He grinned and tucked a strand of her blond hair behind her ear before stroking her cheek and leaning forward to kiss the tip of her nose. "Because you seem pretty okay to me."

"You haven't met my sisters." It struck Isotta that perhaps this was the cause of her sweat. Her sisters, unbeknownst to their parents, were terrible flirts. It wouldn't be out of the range of possibility for one of them to come on to Massimo, and the thought of him flirting back . . .

It was so painful no wonder she'd pushed that fear down so deeply. She regarded the ground, frowning. Massimo tucked his finger under her chin and lifted it until he was searching her eyes again.

"Hey," he said. "I love you. You love me. Your family will see that, and they'll understand why this happened so quickly. I promise." Isotta's lower lip twitched down, but she tried to smile at his reassurance. "Anyway, I left my second head behind in Santa Lucia, so we should be fine." Isotta looked confused for a moment before the planes of her face relaxed, and she laughed in earnest.

Massimo squeezed her hand and started walking again. Isotta noticed that the breeze caressed her skin, which was no longer sweating. She squeezed Massimo's hand in return. "This way, we're just past Santa Maria Novella."

The meeting of the parents could be an entertaining, if predictable, scene. But not nearly as compelling as what would be happening at nightfall back in Santa Lucia.

The bell over the door tinkled and Chiara turned, ready to tell the late-arriving customer that she was closing. She stalled, damp cloth clutched in her hand, when she saw it was Fabrizio.

He nodded at Chiara, swallowed, and then turned to carefully close the door behind him, even though they both knew perfectly well the door shut on its own. He turned back to Chiara and watched her silent face as he moved to stand opposite her, the gleaming bar between them.

"Chiara?"

"*Sì*," she breathed.

"I am aware that it is late. You must be closing."

"*Sì* . . . I am, I was."

"But you see, I was interrupted the other day, and then, what with all the people, I've been unable to finish what I was saying."

"Finish?"

Fabrizio's sideways smile rose to his eyes.

"Finish, yes. But Chiara, without my saying anything at all, you must know . . . you must at least suspect . . ."

Chiara bit her lower lip and looked down at the counter, "I don't know you at all. You're a riddle."

Fabrizio nodded, "I'm afraid it's true, I haven't been completely forthcoming. And yet, you must have guessed how I feel." His words floundered into a whisper.

Chiara felt a magnet behind her heart draw her forward, she wanted to reach across the bar and lean her forehead against Fabrizio's and drown in the gold flecks of his eyes.

Fabrizio licked his lower lip. His breath seemed to shallow. The air between them fairly hummed, tumbling the gears of Chiara's thoughts. Hesitating for only a moment longer, Fabrizio took up Chiara's hand and slowly drew it to his lips. The kiss was soft, and then raising his head, his other hand closed over Chiara's and he gently pulled her closer to his chest. A jolt of energy coursed down her ribcage and loosed the tendons behind her knees. Chiara's mind flooded with warmth and confusion. She couldn't, she just couldn't let this happen, but *oddio*, she felt drawn to Fabrizio in a way she hadn't to anyone in years. She wanted to trace the lines on his face and talk to him about the statue newly unearthed in Rome and how she was the only person in her family to not adore snail stew. She wanted to feel his arms around her, she wanted to lean into his shoulders and feel his strength, and smell the fabric softener deep in his shirt material.

His voice thick with gravity, Fabrizio asked, "May I join you behind the counter?"

"Fabrizio, I hardly know you, I'm not sure—"

"You know enough. I know you feel it too. There is something between us. Please, Chiara, let me come back there. I want to talk to you without this bar between us."

Chiara checked the racing of her brain. Her life had been so even for so many years, which was just how she wanted it. She'd had enough drama for a lifetime. She couldn't, she *couldn't* invite the possibility of unrest into her gently rhythmic days. And yet, she couldn't deny the delicious fluttering in her chest. Yes, he was a stranger here for reasons unknown, but somehow, that only seemed to add to this feeling of twinkling possibility.

A road had suddenly opened. She couldn't bear the thought of turning back now.

She untied her apron, "No, you can't come back here."

Fabrizio sagged, "I can't?"

She turned back with a grin, "The health department would never let me live it down. Let's get out of here."

Fabrizio's eyes searched hers, looking for teasing or jest.

Chiara grinned, and stepped down and around the counter to stand in front of Fabrizio. He moved to place his hands on her shoulders, cautious as butterflies. Finally he lightly slid his hands down her arms to hold her hands. He raised them to his lips and kissed one, and then the other. Chiara's breath grew uneven and her face tingled in an unfamiliar craving to rest against his. Gazing at Chiara, Fabrizio's smiled rakishly. "I don't suppose you would fancy a walk?"

Chiara nodded, "I would, as a matter of fact." She pushed away the sirens going off in her mind, jangling that this was ridiculous and short-sighted. She concentrated instead on the warmth of Fabrizio's crooked smile, the humming of her arm clasped in his. She wanted to feel this feeling a little longer.

He ran a finger over her cheek as she smiled, probably like an idiot, she thought, up at him. She was suddenly aware of the difference in their heights.

His brow furrowed, "But you'll be cold."

Still smiling, Chiara answered, "I have a coat, up on the hook."

Fabrizio nodded and strode to the jacket rack, plucked the only covering still hanging, and held it out for Chiara to shrug on. Looking up from zipping the jacket to her neck, she asked, "Would you like a nighttime tour of the groves?"

"The groves? Won't it be too dark to navigate?"

"I know those groves like I know the patterns in the stone of this counter. I'll lead you."

Fabrizio chuckled and placed a hand over Chiara's snug in the crook of his arm. "I put my life in your hands." As they moved to the door, Fabrizio added, "I bet those groves have quite a history."

Chiara nodded, serious now. "They do. Those olive branches look like any others, perhaps, but I promise you, their gnarled knobs have born witness to some spectacular stories."

"I want to hear them all."

"Maestro!"

Luciano's gaze broke away from the Madonna in her niche.

He smiled, "*Ciao*, Edoardo." Turning back to the statue, he continued, "It's so strange, I feel like I haven't seen this Madonna in years. Look how the color of her niche exactly matches the color of the sky. And see here? The hem of her robe is glossy from our ancestors brushing their fingertips across it."

He turned to Edo in time to see the young man put his hand on his forehead to ward off a dizzy spell.

"Edo? Are you quite well?"

The dizzy spells were less frequent now, but still popped up when Edo moved suddenly, as he had when he'd spotted Luciano outside the bar. "*Mi dispiace*, Maestro, I'm out of shape."

"I'm familiar with the feeling."

Edo smiled and straightened.

"I'm okay now."

"Ah, to be young and resilient."

"I'm not sure about that, but I wanted to ask you something."

"Fire away."

"Well, I was thinking about how you used to tell me about the immigrant families that you tutored. I wondered if you thought I could do something like that."

A wide smile lit Luciano's face. "Indeed! How marvelous!"

"Really? I wasn't sure if you'd think I was suitable. Didn't get past high school, and I'm not exactly a pillar of the community."

"Neither of those matters in this work. Only patience and a willingness to reach outside your sphere of comfort."

"Hmm. I'm not sure I'm good at either of those."

Luciano narrowed one eye and peered closely at Edoardo. Edo nervously wiped his face and fluffed his hair. It'd been two weeks since the accident. Luciano couldn't possibly sense the darkness that lingered around Edo's edges like a stubborn stain, could he?

As if silently agreeing with himself, Luciano nodded. "You'll do just fine."

"Really, but I said—"

"I heard what you said. But I suspect that it is not that you fundamentally lack skills in patience and moving beyond your barriers, but you haven't had much modeling or practice."

"Maybe," conceded Edo.

"Yes, I feel sure. I myself have been out of the tutoring world for some time, as perhaps you may have noticed."

Edo, not knowing what to say, said nothing. Luciano nodded again, "But this is a good reminder. Giovanni at the *alimentari* was just telling me about a young man right outside of Santa Lucia, newly arrived from Morocco. He may be hard to track down, since he's making his money in the usual newcomer way, returning carts at the Girona SuperConti for the euro deposit and selling tissue packets and tube socks door to door. But perhaps some evening you and I can pay him a visit?"

Edo shifted uncomfortably. "It would be okay for us to just drop in, unannounced?"

Luciano smiled, "I believe you'll find that Santa Lucia's rules about propriety are less shared than we assume."

"Dante! Dante! *Signore Sindaco!*" Magda rushed to Dante, waving frantically.

Dante rolled his eyes and shoved his hands in his pockets. Ignoring her was not going to work. He turned around and stretched his mouth into a smile. "*Sì*, Magda?"

"I've been calling you all down Via Romana! You really should get your hearing checked. It's annoying to have to chase after you." Magda leaned over and huffed, her hands on her knees.

Dante took advantage of the moment by rolling his eyes at the bracingly blue sky again. "I apologize. Deep in thought. What can I do for you?"

"Ah," Magda announced, straightening, "It's not what you can do for me, it is what I can do for you!"

From anyone else, this might have been welcome news, but Dante knew that Magda's ideas of what she could do for him always involved some sacrifice on his part. He adjusted his scarf to better cover his throat and a bit of his mouth to avoid the unpleasant airs that often emanated from the German woman. He aimed for a tone of nonchalance, "Oh? What's on your mind?"

"The *Sagra del Cinghiale*. The pipe-laying begins on the *piazza*, what, next week?" Magda didn't wait for Dante's nod, but went on. "And it won't be completed in time for the festival. I know because I've been calling the service authority, and after several rounds of them ignoring my calls or pretending they didn't understand my accent, I finally spoke with a supervisor who said that they don't expect to be finished before January. And you know Italians, that means March."

Magda snickered knowingly while Dante scowled. She went on, "Anyway, even in the best of circumstances, it means we can't hold the festival in the *piazza*."

"Yes, I know. My office is looking into other options."

"Like what?"

"Like roasting the *cinghiali* on Chiara's *terrazza* and setting the tables down the street."

"Won't work."

"What do you mean it won't work? You may not be aware of this but towns up and down the Italian peninsula hold their *feste* in the street."

"I know that." Magda replied, tartly. "I mean roasting the *cinghiali* at Bar Birbo won't work. I talked to Chiara and she agreed that there isn't enough room on the *terrazza* for the fire and all the people who like to stand around the roast. Plus, the dripping fat would stain the stones of her *terrazza*, and you know how much of your 'famous'," Magda mimed quotes around the word, "olive oil we go through that night, too. It would be a mess. Besides, the smoke would no doubt invade the bar, and her apartment. Getting out the smell of *cinghiale* is all but impossible."

Dante sighed. No doubt Magda had forced this "agreement" for her own ends. His own fault. He should have secured Chiara's approval earlier. But every time he came in lately she looked at him with a stiff expression on her face, and it did not bode welcoming for favors.

"And you have an alternative."

"I do, as a matter of fact." Magda took a breath and smiled broadly. "The *castello*."

"The castle?"

"Yes! Isn't that perfect?"

Dante chuckled, "If we could track down the owner and ask permission perhaps."

"Oh, *pshh*," Magda said with a wave of her hand. "What does that matter?"

"Quite a bit actually, if we want to stay within the confines of the law."

"Dante, how long has it been since anybody has heard anything, I mean *anything*, about the owners?"

"*Allora*, at least thirty years, but—"

"*Esatto!* What are the odds that he'll return to Santa Lucia on that specific weekend?"

"Low, of course, but still—"

"Yes! And there's no place else we can do it! We can't lose the revenue that the festival brings in. Shops and restaurants make more that weekend than they do the rest of the winter. I myself have had tourists booked in the rental apartment for six months. What do you think will happen if they find out there is no festival?"

"Maybe I can call the service authority again and ask them to put off the work."

"I've tried. Believe me, I've spoken with everyone there. They have already started, they aren't going to back out now. Especially since they say that now that they've exposed the line, it's in danger of freezing. They either have to bury what they've done, or move forward. What do you think they'll choose?"

"True," Dante bit his lip. "There's the park, I suppose. We could do it there."

"What are you, insane? With all those overhanging trees? Hardly the place to build a large enough fire to roast multiple *cinghiali*, not to mention the fire for cooking the sausages and the one under the pot of *cinghiale* stew."

As much as he hated to admit it, Magda was probably right.

He ventured, "I'll consider it."

"Good," Magda grinned broadly.

"We'd have to get town approval to use the castle."

"Once everyone understands that it's that or no *sagra*, I'm sure they'll be on board. No, it's not ideal, but just from an ownership standpoint. From the perspective of the festival, it is marvelous. The view from up there is top-notch, and having a ruined castle as a backdrop, well, that will be a celebration to remember." Magda beamed, clasping her hands in front of her heart. The lines of bitterness etched in her face blurred into softness as a stray filigree of light caught the glow in her eyes.

You must forgive Dante for the step backward he took at this shift in Magda.

He wondered at the unpleasantness she wore like a cheap sweater. He was tempted to blame it on her husband's disappearance, in Thailand of all places! But he actually thought she'd mellowed a bit since then. When she first arrived, she'd been thoroughly insufferable. Now she was just a nuisance. But she might very well be the nuisance that saved the *sagra*.

Luciano set a cup of *camomilla* beside Elisa. "Having trouble?"

"I got a little lost," Elisa answered, tensing.

"Do you need help finding your way?"

Elisa looked up, startled. And then smiled. She should have remembered by now, Luciano didn't get angry with her when she spaced out in the middle of working or couldn't remember the next step. This was her first time here without Fatima, and perhaps she felt a little vulnerable without her anchor.

Elisa shook her head. "No, let me just look at the beginning and see if I can retrace my steps."

"That's right, Elisa. If you can't, what's your strategy?"

"To say it out loud."

"Good girl. Your words are your riches. Talk yourself through it to streamline your thinking."

Elisa nodded and chewed the end of her pen while she avoided looking at the russet grapevines whispering across the valley. She stared instead at the problem. Whispering under her breath she ran her pen under the words as Maestro had taught her to keep her focused. A light crept into her mind, and the answer gradually illuminated. Suddenly, Elisa cried, "Oh!" and her pen flew across the page. She held the paper out to Maestro with a smile.

Luciano took the page and nodded as he followed her work. He laughed aloud as he wrote, "*10 e lode,*" Ten and praise, across the top of the paper. Elisa's breath caught.

"*Davvero*, Maestro?"

"*Davvero*. Nicely done. Now you are all ready for class tomorrow."

"*Grazie, mille grazie!*"

"It is my pleasure, Elisa. You are a smart girl, you merely lack faith in yourself."

"That's because I can't do anything right."

"But Elisa, do you not see? Your brain merely works in a slightly different way. Your teachers at school are too busy, and possibly uninterested, to teach you to how to use your skills. That poor mind of yours has been lying dormant, ready for action. Now look what it can do."

Elisa blushed and grinned.

Luciano went on, "Did you get your paper back yet? The one on The Great Schism?"

"Yes."

"And?"

Elisa ran her fingers over the grooves in the wooden table. She hesitated before saying, "*Maestra* read it aloud to the class. She told the class my work was well-reasoned and made good connections."

"Ah."

"Yes, I know you said the same thing, Maestro. But it's hard to believe it. And besides, you helped me with that paper."

"Just in organizing, Elisa. The ideas were all yours. Next time, you will require even less of my help. Soon you will fly."

Elisa took a sip of her tea to hide her embarrassment.

Luciano said, "Okay! And now it is my turn."

"Your turn for what?"

"I want you to teach me."

Elisa sputtered. "Teach you what?"

"Art."

"Art? What do you mean?"

"Elisa," Luciano continued, gently, "I've seen your drawings. On the backs of your schoolwork, and on the sides of your papers when you are thinking. You've been hiding a gift from me, and it's time you share it."

"What? My doodles? My doodles are nothing special. My art teacher says I'm terrible."

"Isn't your art teacher the same as your math teacher?"

"Yes."

"And haven't we already established that perhaps he isn't particularly suited to seeing your strengths?"

"He's strict, if that's what you mean."

"*Allora*, Elisa. He's not simply strict. He completely misses your abilities and lacks the skills to bring them forward. From what I've seen, your drawings are unusual and I can see that he would dismiss them. But to me they seem unusual in a way that indicates talent and a mind freed from conventional norms and ideas."

Elisa furrowed her brow in concentration before asking, "What?"

"I'm sorry, I was thinking aloud. He's wrong, Elisa. I know this. Here, show me a drawing."

"No."

"No?"

"I . . . I can't, Maestro."

"But why ever not?"

Elisa hung her head. "I don't want to talk about this anymore. Can we just do math?"

"Absolutely. But I would like to understand this resistance."

Elisa said nothing.

"Elisa?" Luciano ached at how the child cringed at the sound of her name.

"I don't know what to say."

"Elisa, this isn't a test and you aren't in trouble."

"But you are angry with me."

"Do I look angry with you?"

Elisa hesitated before looking up into her teacher's warm eyes. "No."

"Elisa, you don't have to show me your drawings. Of course you don't. But I want you to remember one thing. I'm your friend. And I'm asking to see your drawings because I think they are important to you, and thus, they are important to me. I hope one day you'll feel comfortable enough with me, to trust me enough to share them."

Elisa blinked, unsure of what to say. "You won't laugh?"

"Not for the wide world."

"Okay. Maybe I can show you one today. If you *promise* not to laugh."

"No promise has been so easily granted."

"Which one?"

"No matter, any from that stack of papers from your backpack. I see Fatima has not succeeded in getting you to keep your papers organized."

"It's Friday! I do well at the beginning of the week, and then . . ."

"Perfectly understandable. Once in a while I enjoy taking the liberty of teasing a bit. Ah, here we are." Luciano sat back as Elisa pulled out her geography worksheet and flipped it over to reveal the back.

In sure strokes, Elisa had drawn a bird flying high over terraced olive groves. With delicate and meticulous crosshatching, Elisa had suggested that the bird's shadow darkened roughly half the trees. Luciano's heartbeat quickened as his eyes raked over the drawing. He murmured, "Look at how alive, how vital, your olive trees are. With just variations in how you cluster lines, you've somehow managed to suggest the contorted quality of ancient trunks, and you've used the darkness as a foil to illuminate the olive leaves out of reach of the bird's shadow, while suggesting that the leaves themselves embody both darkness on one side, and light on the other. All at once your drawing celebrates contrasts—dark and light, rigid and flexible, mourning and joy." He brought the drawing closer to his eyes and then held it at arm's length.

Elisa peered over Luciano's shoulder and appraised the drawing with eyes squinted in effort. "But it doesn't look like a real olive grove, or a real bird, or even a real shadow. Shadows aren't that big."

"Exactly, Elisa. It is not a realist drawing, it's surrealist. Do you know that what means?"

"No."

"It's a style of art that moves beyond the real to express the world in distorted and discordant ways."

"I don't understand." But she did. Or at least, she was beginning to. She had considered this drawing garbage because it failed to accurately represent what she saw. But the drawing of it had pleased her. Every crosshatch calmed her as she filled the paper, because it captured the slightly askew way she saw the world.

"I think you do. Elisa, I don't want to praise you, because I know that makes you uncomfortable. You have had far too little acknowledgment in your life, but I have to tell you—this drawing flirts with brilliance."

Isotta was surprised by how much more comfortable she felt rounding up the mountain to Santa Lucia this time. Maybe because she knew what to expect. Also, the last time she made this trip, she didn't know that Massimo was gearing up to introduce her to his daughter. She had very likely picked up on his secrecy. Or maybe her new increased comfort was due to the ring on her finger. A ring he'd given her in front of her family, who had been utterly charmed by him. Indeed her sisters had cast her sidelong glances and made remarks under their breath about how she must be a wildcat in bed to have landed a man like Massimo. The fact that he had been married before, that he had a daughter, paled next to his insistence on setting the table, his speaking knowledgeably on the euro crisis, and his asking protective questions about her sisters' boyfriends. Charmed was probably not a strong enough word.

In any case, with all the secrets out, Isotta felt, for the first time, at ease. Not completely, she wouldn't lie to herself. But truly, she couldn't imagine ever being completely relaxed around Massimo. He set her insides fluttering in a way that didn't feel entirely safe. In fact, it sometimes seemed almost dangerous. And thrilling. Her skin was constantly alert for the brush of his fingers. Her soul was ever hungering for a soft word. Wasn't that titillating feeling the stuff of romance? Didn't she want the opposite of her parent's marriage, the way her mother bossed Isotta's father around, nagging him incessantly about his ragged bedroom slippers? That wasn't romance.

So no, she wasn't completely relaxed, as she peeped over at Massimo's eyes trained to the road. There was a slight trill of danger. But rather than be scared of that, now she relished it, as part of a relationship that she couldn't believe she was lucky enough to have.

"It's a beautiful day," she said, breaking the silence. Massimo gave her a slight glance and raised his eyebrows above the rims of his sunglasses before turning his attention back to the hairpin turn ahead of him. Isotta gestured out to the undulating hills all around them, Santa Lucia sitting above like a crown. Or a like a queen. Indeed, the town pulsated with a rather human emotion. Maybe it was that afternoon light that seemed effervescent when tossed about in the arms of the olive branches, and heavy when bent under the evergreens.

Massimo said nothing.

The tires of the Fiat screeched as they turned into the parking lot, rending the quiet of a sleepy Saturday afternoon. Remembering her last visit, Isotta took her time gathering her sunglasses and purse, smiling in anticipation of Massimo's opening her door and holding out his hand. But even after she gathered all of her belongings, the door remained closed.

She peered out from lowered lashes, and realized he was standing outside the driver side door, his back to her. She gingerly opened her door and stepped out. He glanced over, "Ready?"

He began walking.

"Massimo?"

"*Sì.*"

"Is anything wrong? You're not . . . you're not saying much."

"Why should anything be wrong?"

"I don't know."

"Then don't be ridiculous."

"Okay. I . . . I'm sorry."

Massimo said nothing, and Isotta jogged to keep up with his long stride.

Desperate to fill a silence that was rapidly passing awkward, she began chattering about her assistant at the bank.

He cut her off. "That won't matter for much longer."

"Oh! Wait. What? Why won't it matter?"

"C'mon, it's not like you'll have that assistant a month from now."

"Why? Is she moving branches? How could you know that and I wouldn't know that?" Isotta frowned, her right eyebrow tilting downward. "Though come to think of it, that does explain why she's so scattered in scheduling my December meetings. I suppose she doesn't feel like she has a stake in them."

Massimo snorted, "No, that's not it. How would I know if your assistant is transferring, and indeed, why should I care?"

"Oh. I don't know. Then what do you mean?"

"Please, Isotta. Don't be dense. It's not like you'll be working there in two weeks."

"I won't? Why won't I?"

Massimo stopped and faced her, drawing his sunglasses to rest on his head so that he could study her face. He gentled his voice as if speaking to a child, "Because you're quitting when we get married. Don't tell me you haven't yet given your notice? That's hardly professional."

"I'm quitting? Why am I quitting? I hadn't planned on quitting."

"You really plan to commute across Umbria on a daily basis?"

"Well, no, of course not, but I thought I'd transfer to your branch. I've already talked to my boss, I mean I know it'll mean a demotion . . ."

Massimo shoved his hands in his pockets and glared down at Isotta. Her heart chilled. He frowned and said, "That was presumptuous."

"I . . . I'm sorry . . . I didn't mean . . ."

Massimo rubbed his forehead and tipped his head back as if to gain sustenance from the sky.

"Massimo, I'm sorry, but . . . why shouldn't I work here?"

"Are you serious? Can you imagine the speculation if you worked? The gossip about how I can't support my wife? Besides, how can you be Margherita's mother if you are gone eight hours a day?"

Isotta bit her lip. "I hadn't considered that."

"Isotta . . . you are going to have to start thinking like a mother."

"But, I'm not her mother, Massimo."

"Yes, you are."

Luciano pulled his rolling cart up the street. It was heavy, not with bottles of wine, but with cans of tomatoes and packages of yogurt and pasta and a few links of Giuseppe's chicken *salsiccia*. He found himself looking forward to eating a Saturday dinner he took time to prepare. It felt good to hunger for something, and feel capable of providing it for himself. He waved at Edo serving coffee to Patrizia, while Chiara stood beside her friend. Edo grinned, and, waving, called out, "*Ciao!* Maestro!"

Luciano smiled. He knew what Edo must have thought about him, what they all thought about him. That he was a drunk, an embarrassment to the town. It was a point of pride among his countrymen that they never became the gibbering drunks they saw in so many American films. That shame and ridicule at his fall into drink, none of it had touched him. There had been an ocean of pain between him and the rest of the world and everything that mattered to him lay within that ocean.

Well, almost everything. Once in awhile something had seemed to glide over the vastness into his heart. Like Fatima. Her uncomplicated trust and curiosity somehow reminded him of who he was even when the wine obliterated everything else. Many times the thought of Fatima's expression if she saw him stumbling in the street kept him from reaching for the bottle until past dark. Some of those days he saw her, and some of those days he didn't. But the times when he resisted the siren call of the wine and then saw her, and they shared a few moments of gentle conversation, those times made it easier and easier to wait longer and longer periods before popping open a bottle. Once it was popped, he would leave it dry. That was a surety.

Now there was also Elisa. His heart moved in pain. She was a quicksilver—sometimes her eyes were wide and earnest as she followed his pencil scribing formulas. Sometimes they were shuttered. He knew from teaching children for more than thirty years that skittishness was often a sign of trauma. Probably constant trauma.

He heard a car squeal into the parking lot at the edge of town, just past his house. He chuckled. Teenagers. Always in a hurry. They'd pass him in a few moments, shoving each other while making sure their hair remained meticulously styled. Unless they were headed into the groves for a spot of unsupervised fun. He hoped they avoided his plot. He hated finding the leavings of revelry in the form of trampled grass and crippled boughs.

His thoughts drifted back to Elisa. Whenever he saw her now, his eyes scanned her limbs for bruises. He never found any. Whoever was hurting the child was either calculated in the injury or left internal scars. Probably the latter. From talking to Elisa, it was clear that she saw herself as stupid.

But she wasn't. Math wasn't her gift, but she made leaps of logic and connection when he spoke of the Via Flaminia that were advanced for a child much older than herself. Plus, there was her artistic talent. He wondered how to get her to trust him enough to let him keep one of her sketches. He wanted to show it to old friends who worked at a gallery in Spoleto. Of course, that would necessitate calling people he hadn't spoken to in more than a year. But he was sure to get his phone turned back on within a month or so, and the thought of dialing now caused no more than a ripple of discomfort.

Lost in his thoughts, he was brought up short by shadows coming toward him. Probably those teenagers. He squinted into the streaming light and realized that two people were approaching in a more reserved fashion than adolescents prone to careening and swaggering. He moved to the side of the street to allow the couple to pass unimpeded.

As they came nearer, they were no longer silhouetted. He realized it was Massimo. Massimo with Giulia.

His breath caught. It was Giulia! It was! His girl! With her head glowing like an angel!

His hand went to his heart and then tentatively reached for the apparition.

But as she neared, he realized it wasn't his daughter. Of course not, only a foolish old man would imagine it. This woman was blond, hence the crown of light he confused with a halo. And her features were watery, only her luminous eyes stood out from her plain face. Not Giulia. Who was she?

Her eyes met his as she passed him. He stepped back further, aghast. No, she wasn't his beloved, but what was this faded copy of his daughter doing with Massimo? Their gaze broke, and he heard the woman murmur a question to Massimo, who responded, his voices ringing clearly through the dissolving sunshine, "Don't mind him. Just the town drunk."

Elisa shifted restlessly at the rickety table in her room. She was supposed to be doing her math homework. Not what was assigned for Monday—that she had already completed with Maestro. These were extra problems, written out in Luciano's precise plumed handwriting. When he pulled out the sheet, she had shuddered, but grew easier when Luciano assured her that she knew how to work each problem, and the extra practice at home would be like armor going into the next week's lessons.

Now she smiled to see large boxes of whitespace where Maestro had noted that she was to doodle something for him. A quick glance at the problems comforted her too. Not only were they manageable after Maestro's lesson, but included questions about how to divide cookies. The work came more fluidly than she could ever remember.

Then her father came home.

She tensed when she heard the door slam and the tight sound of something small crashing in the kitchen. Her hands flew to her ears, but then she couldn't write, which left her mind too free to imagine what was happening outside her door. She tried covering only one ear so she could still write, or even filling in the doodle box with her other hand, but she couldn't focus enough to work the fractions and the drawing that had begun as a dancing pomegranate tree was quickly crosshatched into unrecognizability. Her pen tore a hole in the paper, and she startled and threw the pen across the room. It's a shame, it would have been a lovely drawing.

Her older brother, Guido, popped his head into her room. "We're going to the park, do you want to come?"

Elisa leapt up, "Yes!"

The three children slid past their parents' bedroom door, out of which they heard the too familiar sounds of barking insults, and the sickening sound of skin being struck. Grabbing their coats from the pole by the door, they quietly opened the door and stepped into the brisk evening air.

Guido closed the door behind them. The shouts muted. He put his hand against the door and muttered, "I hate leaving her like this."

Matteo answered, "You say that every time."

Guido sighed while Elisa turned her gaze to follow this conversation, the first time she'd been allowed in. "I mean it every time."

Matteo started walking down the road. "Bastard. He clearly hates her. Why doesn't he go? For good?"

Guido nodded curtly and said nothing.

Elisa ventured, her hands shoved deep into her pocket, "But . . . I don't understand."

Matteo rolled his eyes, "Well, that's a surprise."

Guido shoved Matteo's shoulder, "Hey, c'mon. Don't take it out on her."

"Please. She never knows what's going on. She's in her own world, like, all the time. You know how ridiculous she is, she—"

Elisa's hands flung up to cover her ears. "Shut up! Just shut the hell up!"

Matteo stopped and stared at his sister. "What?"

Elisa forced herself to pull her arms back down. "I thought you finally included me because you care about me, but you don't! I don't belong in that house. I don't belong anywhere! Just leave me alone!"

She stormed down the street, away from the park, desperately hoping the tears wouldn't break before she got out of hearing range.

Matteo's voice softened and he ran to catch his sister. "Hey, I'm sorry, Elisa. I didn't mean it that way."

Elisa pulled away. "Leave me alone! You sound just like them."

Guido nodded, "She's right, Matteo. They are always on her. Is it any wonder she's dreamy?" He put his arm around his sister, "I bet the world in your head is better than the one you wake up to each day."

Elisa looked up at her brother, stunned. She nodded.

Guido went on, "We were so busy trying to protect Mamma, we sort of forgot about protecting you."

Matteo bit his lip and added, "Okay, okay. That wasn't fair, Elisa. At all. I *am* sorry, really sorry. I didn't realize I was talking like Papà. He doesn't see us at all."

Elisa's words escaped her before she could pull them back, "He sees you plenty. Both of you."

Guido and Matteo looked at each other. Guido hesitated before saying, "Yes, that's true. At least he sees our grades and how many goals we save or score."

Matteo thought for a moment. "Why is he so hard on Elisa?"

Guido shrugged. "Maybe he just doesn't like women. I mean, he's horrible to Mamma, right?"

Elisa whispered, "He told me I was a mistake."

Guido's head whipped toward her. "*What?*"

"Once, when he was yelling at me because I failed a test and he had to sign it. He said I was a mistake."

Matteo asked, "You must have misunderstood."

Silence.

Matteo said, "I'm sorry. Of course you didn't misunderstand."

Guido wondered aloud, "What a strange thing to say."

Elisa just sighed. "Well, it's probably true. I'm so much younger than you two. Mamma got upset and tried to shush him, but you know how he is when she tries to step in."

Matteo hugged his sister and asked, "What are we going to do?"

Guido sighed. "I don't know. It's not like any of us have an instruction manual to tell us how to fix this toaster. All I know is that we can't let Elisa bear the brunt of our father's cruelty and our mother's fear anymore. That ends now."

As Chiara caught the last of the sugar granules scattered across the bar with her damp towel, she spotted Stella outside, talking to Vale. Again. Chiara wasn't sure if it was her imagination, or if Stella's hand bumped against Vale's side a bit more often than strictly necessary, even with the uneven terrain of the ancient cobblestones to discombobulate a walker. Certainly Vale's hand lingered a little long on Stella's arm or back as he reached to steady her. As Chiara watched, Stella smiled up into Vale's face. No, this was not her imagination. Stella's expression was awestruck, rapt, full of wonder. Not the way one looks at one's handyman, no matter what plumbing or electric service he's sorted. And Vale was looking at Stella in a way that Dante never did.

Chiara bit her lip. Part of her was relieved to see her oldest friend's face rinsed of the aggrieved lines that had taken up shop around her eyes. But more of her was worried. The mayor's wife couldn't play around. Shenanigans would be too easily spotted. Especially in a town as small as Santa Lucia. True, the children were grown and safe from the mud that would no doubt be splattered if Stella wasn't more careful. But Chiara knew that being the subject of waggling tongues would kill Stella. She was already self-conscious of her position and her weight.

Though now, as Stella spoke earnestly to Vale while he steadily regarded her, Chiara could see that the weight settled around her friend differently. Rather than being an anchor of heaviness, it seemed a conduit to glow in a round, luscious sort of way. Certainly, Vale's eyes moved appreciatively from Stella's animated face to the curves moving intriguingly under her dress.

As Chiara watched, Vale plucked a loose strand of hair from the front of Stella's dress, his fingers brushing and lingering for a scant moment before he twined the hair in his fingers and tucked it into his breast pocket. Stella laughed and placed her hand on Vale's chest. Playfully, Chiara thought, but also familiarly. The two ducked their heads in conference for a moment before they straightened and adopted a pose of nonchalance. They kissed each other's cheeks perfunctorily, then separated with just the barest suggestion of lingering hands. Vale called out "*Ciao!*" and then walked away, catching Chiara's eye to wave before sauntering to the *piazza*.

Stella walked into the bar. She noted Chiara considering her before hurriedly moving to make coffee. Stella swallowed and said good morning with determined cheerfulness. Chiara knew her "*buongiorno*" was on the muted side.

Silence.

Chiara cleared her throat and asked, "*Un caffè o un cappuccino stamattina?*"

"I don't know, Chiara. If you are going to be strange, I'll just have *un caffè*. But if you'll be normal, then I'd like to have *un cappuccino* and talk. It's been awhile."

"I'm sorry, Stella. I was just caught off guard. I'll make your *cappuccino*. I'd like to catch up."

Stella scraped her top lip against her bottom teeth and thought for a minute. Finally she said, "How's Edo?"

"Okay, I think. He's not going out anymore. Well, he goes out, but just to run or bike. So he looks healthy, getting a lot of exercise and fresh air, which makes him eat more. You know I like that. But I don't know . . . he still looks like he's about to cave in on himself." Chiara set the *cappuccino* in front of Stella.

Stella reached for a sugar packet, "What do you mean?"

"I don't know. Something is troubling him. He seems like a fruit with a small bruise, and that bruise is darkening and spreading. I'm probably making too much of it. But before when he was partying, he at least had some joy. He's really quiet."

Stella stirred her coffee thoughtfully. "Strange that he won't talk to you."

"That part doesn't surprise me. He never really talks to anybody. I think he used to talk to Luciano, before Luciano went off the rails."

"Oh! That reminds me. Have you seen Luciano lately? He was looking sober for awhile, but now he's as deep as he's ever been."

Chiara nodded. "I know. I think he saw Isotta, Massimo's fiancée. Earlier this week I saw him leave the *macelleria* looking normal. Then a few minutes later, I saw Massimo with Isotta. It stopped my heart, I can only imagine what it did to Luciano. They must have passed in the street."

"That situation is so weird. Do you think the girl knows?"

"That she's a dead woman's *doppelgänger?* I doubt it."

Stella sipped her coffee while Chiara emptied the tiny dishwasher.

"Stella?"

"Hmm?"

"You know I love you."

"Yes, of course. I love you, too."

"So, please hear this in the right spirit. Be careful."

Stella furrowed her brow. "I don't know what you mean."

"Just that. Be careful."

Luciano stumbled toward the door. The rapping was like a knife digging into the area behind his eyes. He had to make the rapping stop. He flung open the door.

In front of him were two strange little people. Not so little, maybe. And no, they weren't strangers. An insistent voice within him assured him that they were his friends. Sources of happiness. But how could sources of happiness make such a racket and cause him so much pain?

"What?" he bellowed at them, and tried to ignore the twisting of his heart as the fairer girl cringed. The darker one—why couldn't he remember her name?—reached for the other one's hand to stay her.

That same one murmured, "Maestro? It's Fatima. Remember? And here is Elisa. We were supposed to come today. Elisa finally agreed to show us her whole collection of drawings." Fatima peered around Luciano into the dimness of the house. She could see chairs tumbled over and papers scattered across the floor. A photograph that usually had pride of place in the entryway was smashed against the corner.

Luciano muttered incomprehensibly.

Elisa pleaded, "Fatima, let's go. Maestro isn't . . . well."

Fatima reached a hand to touch Luciano's arm. He flinched and made a low growling sound in his throat. She withdrew her hand but took a small step toward him to whisper, her voice settling into a receptive part of his brain, quiet and soothing like a cat's purr. Come to think of it, where was his cat? He wasn't sure he had seen it. A dim memory of an angry moment. Did he swipe at Degas? Throw something at him when he meowed for food? Luciano groaned and tripped backward.

"Maestro!" Fatima clutched his arm. She steadied him and started to lead him to the couch. "Elisa! Help me! He's too heavy!"

"I . . . I can't . . ."

"Elisa! Maestro needs our help!" Elisa swallowed and rubbed her arms to quell the trembling. As Luciano's knees began to give out, she darted forward and took his other arm. He put his weight on the girls, who helped him walk to the couch, and then lowered him down. "Elisa, go get a bowl of cool water and a towel."

"But, is it okay if—"

"Go! And put on water for coffee."

Elisa nodded tightly and sprinted into the kitchen.

It was a disaster. Ants surrounded crumbs on the table, the dishes look like they hadn't been done since their last visit. Yes, there were bits of Fatima's Moroccan cookies growing green and sodden in the sink. Elisa focused on the task at hand. Pay attention! She ordered herself. She flung open cabinets until she found a green plastic bowl. She turned the knob on the faucet with a creak, but nothing happened. She tried the other knob. Still nothing.

But she did spy a half-bottle of mineral water on the table. She poured it into a bowl, and then opened drawers, looking for a clean towel. There weren't any, but she found a napkin shoved in the back of the utensil drawer. She fluttered it open by waving it jerkily, then folded it into crisp lines. She brought the bowl and napkin to the living room, preparing her apologies for not finding a towel. But Fatima simply accepted the offering with a nod, turning her attention to Luciano.

As Fatima began dipping the napkin in water and dabbing Luciano's face, Elisa whispered, "Fatima? I don't think he has water."

Fatima rounded toward her, "What? What do you mean?"

"There's no water."

"That makes sense, actually," Fatima sighed. She dipped the napkin back in the water.

Elisa returned to the kitchen. She found a bag of coffee in a shopping bag filled with rancid parcels of what must be meat, judging from the butcher paper. She shook the coffee into the *moka*, filled the bottom of the coffee maker with the rest of the bottled water, screwed the base on the top and set it to heat, grateful for the first time that her home life had necessitated learning to make coffee for her mother at an early age.

While she waited for the water in the *moka* to boil, she found a garbage bag under the sink. She shook it open with a pang of worry that the noise would bother Maestro. But no sound came from the living room other than Fatima's soothing drone as she whispered words of comfort while washing Luciano's face and hands over and over. Elisa inspected the contents of the shopping cart and tossed all the rotting parcels into the garbage bag, setting the jar of jam on the counter. She moved through the kitchen adding the stale bread, salami rinds, and half-empty bottle of rancid milk to the growing collection of trash in the bag. Tying the top, she set the bag by the kitchen door, mindful that the water in the *moka* was beginning to bang against the metal sides of the coffeemaker. With a paper towel she found, she wiped down the table and counters with a cleaner she'd located behind the garbage bags.

Elisa located a cup and filled it with dark, nutty coffee, adding a spoon of sugar before bringing it out to Fatima. As she handed it she asked, her voice pitched low, "Are you okay with him? I want to keep cleaning the kitchen, I think there must be a faucet in the alley where I can get some water."

Fatima bowed her head in thanks as she took the cup. "Great idea. I'm so glad you're here."

Elisa swallowed. "Is he okay?"

"I don't know. He was so confused when we got here. He's never not recognized me before. Now he's a little better. Calmer, anyway. But he keeps talking about Giulia and Margherita."

"Margherita?"

"Yes, his granddaughter. He used to talk about her all the time before Giulia died. I haven't heard him mention her in ages."

Fatima blew on the surface of the coffee, sending the dots of oil swirling across the surface of the cup. Elisa studied Luciano as he moaned and tossed his head. She startled at a sudden realization. "Wait, is his daughter's husband Massimo the same Massimo that's getting married next week?"

"Is there a Massimo getting married next week?"

"Yes, I heard it announced at church."

"It could be."

"*Madonna*, just as he was starting to seem happy."

Elisa reached for Fatima's hand. Fatima took it and squeezed, then reached for Luciano's hand. The three of them stood in the dim living room, inhaling the warm scent of coffee, the sharp odor of cleanser that Elisa had sprayed in the kitchen, and the soft childlike sound of Luciano, beginning to weep.

Edo's bike skirted the edge of the dirt path as he pumped harder to the top of the mountain. Standing, he cranked the pedals with all his weight, relishing the feeling of single-mindedness. There was no space in his brain or his heart for anything other than determination. With a final groan, Edo reached the summit. He planted his feet on either side of the pedals to catch his breath. Panting heavily, he leaned the bike against a tree and walked to the drop-off, his eyes drinking in the view. The hills below him resembled a child's finger-painting—the silvery green of the olive trees blurred with streaks of golds and reds from the grapevines turning in the autumnal chill. Sometimes he forgot how beautiful the world was, or at least his corner of it.

Spying a stone bench, Edoardo seated himself, stretching his legs with a groan. He tipped his face up to the sun and felt the toxins stored in his body leaching out to evaporate into the crisp air. Sobriety was feeling pretty good. At least right now.

Staying clean was a lot harder when he felt his body itch for the high of the clubs. Looking back at his last few weeks, though he definitely experienced periods of mourning for the sweet oblivion of the dance floor—fingers reaching toward him in the dark, the beat of the music thumping through his core—mostly he found himself relieved. There was so much about clubbing that felt wrong and shameful, not the least of which was how horrible the mornings-after were.

Now, he woke up clearheaded. And that felt good. Good enough to mostly override the sense that something was missing. From his days, from his life—something was just missing. He tried filling it by throwing himself into the bar. That worked during the day. In the evenings, he tried filling the void with books. But though he enjoyed reading, particularly the memoirs that made him feel close to the writer, he still felt restless. He'd tried to center himself by tracking down the Moroccan immigrant and pushing himself past his fears of rejection to pantomime his willingness to help the man learn Italian. It was a heartwarming distraction, at least for now. But at times he still couldn't help begrudging his two-dimensional life.

Edoardo's breath lost some of its scorching exhaustion, and he inhaled deeply, filling his lungs with clean air. As a tendril of breeze drifted across his face, he watched the leaves of the trees trip across the achingly blue sky. For right now, this was enough.

From a distance, he heard the sound of approaching cyclists. Faster than he anticipated, the voices drew near, cheering their arrival at the tallest peak in the region's hills. He heard the smacking of high-fives and laughter and hoots as the cyclists squirted water at each other. Edoardo closed his eyes and offered a prayer that his oasis wouldn't be breached. The last thing he wanted was to play the smalltalk introduction game with a bunch of strangers.

But like most of Edoardo's fervent prayers, this one went unanswered and the group fanned out around the peak looking for resting spots. A young man in professional-looking royal-blue bike shorts and jersey startled at the sight of Edoardo sitting tensely on the bench. "Oh!" said the biker, "I didn't see you there. Beautiful day for a ride, isn't it?"

Edoardo nodded.

The biker didn't seem to notice Edoardo's reluctance to engage and went on, "Did you ride up from Girona?"

Edoardo shook his head, "No. Santa Lucia."

"Santa Lucia?"

Edoardo sighed lightly, "Yes, it's a few kilometers into the hills from Girona."

"Ah! Right! That's where the *Sagra del Cinghiale* is, right?"

"Yes, that's right."

The biker nodded and then gestured to the bench.

Edoardo sighed inwardly once again before nodding and then scooting over to make room for the cyclist.

"I saw signs for the *sagra* in the Girona shops. We're here from Rome, my friends and I, just for a weekend of biking. Is the festival worth coming back for?"

Edoardo turned his head to look at the cyclist, trying to convey his reluctance to talk right now. He wanted to sit in the quiet and enjoy the feeling of his heart rate slowing down and his muscles shivering out of their clenched position. But the man was smiling and leaning toward him. His light brown eyes were framed with dark lashes and in those eyes Edoardo saw true interest. He warmed to the openness on the biker's face, the dimples framing his easy smile.

"Well, we call it the *Sagra del Cinghiale*, but the real star is the olive oil. We've been growing it from these trees for a thousand years." Edo's expression came to life as he told the cyclist about how the festival always opened the olive harvest season, and the subsequent pressing of the oil. The man leaned forward and asked, "Is there another *sagra* for the oil like in other towns?"

"No," Edo furrowed his brow at the question. "I never thought about it, but the pressing of the oil is just for us."

The man nodded in understanding, and asked, "So then, what happens at the *Sagra del Cinghiale?*"

Surprised by how much he was enjoying a conversation he never wanted to have, Edo went on, telling him about the *sagra*'s giant fire, how the smell of roasting *cinghiale* drifted all through Santa Lucia, and how old ladies surreptitiously shoved their potatoes into the ashes for their own *contorni*. The biker smiled when Edoardo described how the next day's clean up would invariably dislodge several forgotten and charred potatoes, along with small items poked into the ashes by children. The chuckles turned to laughter when Edoardo confessed that as a child he had once stuck a plastic pig in the fire, in his quest to be like the men.

The biker held out his right hand, "I'm Arnaldo, by the way."

"*Ciao*, Arnaldo, I'm Edoardo . . . Edo. *Ciao*."

"*Ciao*."

A voice called out from the groves, "You alright there, Arnaldo?"

"Yes, yes, I'm fine. Come meet a new friend."

Edoardo was surprised to find that his irritation at having his silence intruded on had vanished, and smiled in greeting as one by one the men stepped forward to introduce themselves.

Two arrived holding hands, one tucking in his shirt with his free hand. This set off a titter from the assembled cyclists, one clucking, "Really, guys. You couldn't wait till we're back at the hotel?"

The taller of the two raised his eyebrows and mugged, "And miss an *al fresco* situation? Not a chance."

Arnaldo turned to Edoardo and smiled, "I apologize for my friends' lack of chasteness. They really are a stand-up group of guys. Not always entirely . . . seemly . . . but good guys."

Edoardo fought down a confusing mixture of panic and intrigue. "Are you all . . . together?"

The men laughed before settling down on the ground to lean back and stretch out their legs. Arnaldo frowned in confusion, "Together? No. Just those two are together."

A voice from the group rang out, "He's asking if we're all gay, Arnaldo. How thick can you be?"

Edo shook his head and stammered, "No, really—"

Arnaldo smiled and touched Edo's hand lightly, "It's okay. We are. Well, except Silvio there, who insists he's straight but hangs with us rather than go on dates with the girls his mother keeps flinging at him."

A man, presumably Silvio, tossed his head back to add, "You've seen the girls my mom wants me to date. Toads, all of them. I'd rather hang with you guys. At least you all are easy on the eyes."

Arnaldo gave Edoardo a meaningful look as if to say, "See?"

Then he nudged Edoardo's elbow with his own. "So where are you headed next?"

"Me?"

Arnoldo ducked his head and grinned, his dimples deepening. "Sure. Why don't you join us? We can loop back to Santa Lucia this evening."

"Oh!" Edoardo stood up and brushed off his shorts. "Oh, that's nice. But I can't. I have to get back to work."

"That's not what I . . ."

"Yes, I know. I know. But I . . . can't."

Arnaldo nodded, "Okay, I get it. I'll walk you to your bike." Edo waved goodbye to the assembled cyclists, now unpacking *panini* and bottles of water while unfolding a large map of the surrounding mountains. They responded with calls to stay and join them, which turned to farewells when Edo insisted he needed to leave.

Once Edo reached his bike, he turned to find Arnaldo closer behind him than he expected. Arnaldo grinned. "Well, if you change your mind and want to join us for a glass of wine later, we're the only biking group from Rome staying at Hotel del Lago."

Edo nodded, distracted by the golden streaks in Arnaldo's wind-tousled hair, scattering light like the olive groves all around them. That maddening dimple fluttered in Arnaldo's left cheek as he leaned forward and took Edo's hand. Edo could smell Arnaldo's shaving cream, like *limoncello*. Arnaldo pressed his cheek against Edo's and whispered, "I'd love to see you again."

Arnaldo slowly pulled back and regarded Edo levelly for a moment, their faces inches apart. Arnaldo hesitated, then leaned forward and lightly pressed his lips against Edo's.

There was an explosion in Edo's ribcage, sending a pulse of warmth throughout his body. Arnaldo sighed into the kiss before breaking contact. Another wink of that dimple, and Arnaldo turned back to the groves.

Edo watched him stroll away, mesmerized. Arnaldo looked over his shoulder and ran his gaze up over Edo's lean form, lingering at his eyes.

Simultaneously, the men lifted their hands in parting.

Turning, Edo stumbled to mount his bike. He pushed off, and arced his path to head down the hill to Santa Lucia. But a whispering voice within him murmured that he'd left something behind amongst the olive trees. Something that'd he'd never be able to get back.

"Wow, Isotta, this place is incredible." Isotta's sister, Isabella, murmured as they began their ascent up the hill to Santa Lucia. "Are we at a higher elevation or something? The light is vivid."

"Not by much. But I know what you mean, it reminds me of the light on an island, like there's more water in the air or something. It's always like this. I don't think Massimo even notices."

"Hmm." Isabella nodded. "Nervous?" She asked, as Isotta plucked up the creases of her lilac dress.

"No. Yes. A little."

Isabella checked her rear-view mirror, "Everyone is right behind us, so we didn't get separated like you were stressed about."

"I know."

"And Massimo seems like a great guy."

"He is."

"And so dreamy."

Isotta turned to glare at her sister.

"What? What did I say? Should I say he's painful to look at? Well he is in a way, he causes all sorts of pain in my—"

"*Basta!* That's enough."

"*Ai*, Isotta. I was only teasing. It's good that he's so handsome. I like them better that way." She turned and archly raised her eyebrows.

"Just watch the road, Isabella."

Isabella did just that, following the hairpin turns to the top of the mountain, where she parked.

"Will we have to walk to the church?"

"Yes. No cars in Santa Lucia. Unless you want to sit in the back of an Ape."

"Ha! That would hardly be dignified for the wedding of the first of the Fabbro girls to get hitched."

Isotta bit her lip.

"Hey. What is it?"

"Well, I hardly thought I'd be the first. I didn't think this would ever happen for me."

"Oh, Isotta, you've always been so hard on yourself."

"You try being the youngest and drabbest of four beautiful sisters."

"Well, the implied compliment aside, Isotta, you've always sold yourself short. Just because you are some sort of genetic throwback with your blond hair and light eyes."

"It's not just that."

"I know . . . you don't look like the rest of us, but on days like this, when you hold yourself up high and are blushing with excitement, well, I can see why Massimo fell for you."

"Really?"

"Yes, of course, really." Isotta looked out over the valley, waiting for the rest of her family to pull into the lot. Unlike her sister who had raced up the mountain, they had slowed to a crawl at the unfamiliar turns.

At her silence, Isabella asked, "What is it now?"

"Nothing."

"*Ma dai*, the others will be here in a minute. Don't make me have to pull it out of you."

You can hardly blame Isotta for being evasive. This wasn't exactly an easy topic to broach.

Isotta inhaled deeply and then said all in a breath, "Sometimes I just don't understand why Massimo is marrying me."

Isabella rolled her eyes. "I thought we already covered this. You're beautiful and intelligent and *blah blah blah*. Stop with the insecurity already. It clashes with your wedding dress."

Isotta shook her head. "No, that's not what I mean."

"What then?"

"It's hard to explain."

"Well, try. And hurry. They're almost here."

"Okay. And I know this sounds weird. But sometimes it feels like Massimo is looking through me, not at me. Like I'm an item on a list he needs to check off. Not all the time, sometimes when he touches me it's like I'm the only woman in the world. But others . . ."

"Wedding jitters. He's smitten with you, anybody with eyes can see that."

"Sometimes. And then other times, he's . . . distant. In a world of his own. And I start wondering if he's actually over his dead wife."

"Oh, God, Isotta. That's enough. Nobody invited the dead wife to the wedding."

"But it's just so odd. He clams up whenever Giulia comes up. Not like he's sad. Like . . . there's more to it. His mom, too. She actually sounds bitter or something. And they both change the subject really quickly. It makes me think neither of them is over her death. And why would they be? It was tragic. Isn't it too soon to start over?"

"Seriously, Isotta. Stop it. How is a man—or his mother, even—supposed to act when he's talking about his former wife in front of his bride? And so he's moody. You just haven't been with enough men to know. They are all that way. It's like they have one gear. If they are happy, they can't remember feeling otherwise, and when they are down, they take that on like their permanent personality. It's enough to give a woman whiplash, and make us feel like we're delusional for remembering all the other gears. That's just men, Isotta. Don't worry."

"Really? Because sometimes . . ."

"Really. I promise. Why do you think it's so hard to find one we like? Because they are different Monday than they were Thursday. Seriously, if they didn't have all the right equipment for getting me off, I'm not sure they'd be worth the bother."

Isotta looked quickly at her sister, worried she was having her leg pulled.

"Yes, I'm joking, but just a little. Relax. Massimo loves you. Mamma and Papà would never let you marry him otherwise. And they know. Remember they wouldn't allow Ilaria to marry that foot doctor? The guy seemed nice enough, but then he ended up getting busted for embezzlement. They are our clearer minds. And they approve."

"Yes, that's true."

"Of course it is. Now put on a happy face, you're getting married! I can't wait to meet your step-daughter."

Isotta smiled at the thought of Margherita. "You'll love her."

"I already do." The eight cars filed into the parking lot and out poured Isotta's family—sisters, father, mother, aunts, grandparents. She blinked back tears. She couldn't believe this was happening. She was getting married, becoming a mother, and here was her family, beautifully dressed and arrayed, here to support her, surround her.

Her mother hurried over. "Too fast! Isabella, you drove too fast! We almost lost you. You could have gotten in an accident!"

Isabella sighed. Then she took Isotta's hand. "Ready?"

"Ready."

"That's my girl."

A voice called from the farther car. "Isotta! Do we go straight to the church? We have an hour before the wedding. Should we get a coffee?"

Isotta laughed, "I can't, Zio, I need to get to church. But if you want to stop on the way, there's time."

Her uncle nodded and conferred with his wife.

The group began making its way through town, filling the quiet streets with their excited chatter. Isotta's grandmother took her arm, "It's so peaceful here, *cara*, but is there enough for a young woman to do? You've been raised at the heartbeat of the world, will you be okay here?"

"*Sì*, Nonna. I like it. And I can't be bored, I'll have Margherita."

"*Sì, sì*," her nonna muttered.

"What?" Isotta asked, yanking her arm back a bit.

"Nothing, dear. Just . . . so much has changed so quickly."

"Yes, that is definitely true."

They walked amicably, nodding at the townspeople they passed.

"Isotta? Why is everyone staring at you?"

Isabella had just joined them, "Ai, Nonna, what do you think? She's a bride!"

Isotta nodded, slowly. It was surely that. Soon she'd be a regular fixture in Santa Lucia and wouldn't get such disarming stares. After a lifetime spent shrugging away from notice, it was oddly disquieting to be the focus of so many intent eyes.

Isotta pointed out Bar Birbo to her uncle, and the men stopped with him, while the women continued to the church. They stepped through the giant wooden doors, pausing to allow their eyes to adjust. The smell of incense filled their bodies, a scent of familiarity in an unfamiliar place. From an alcove a priest bustled toward them.

"Isotta! How lovely you look!" He caught her hands and beamed at her. She blushed and nodded her thanks before introducing her family. Don Alfonso greeted each of them before turning back to Isotta, "Dear one, let's get you settled, I have a room prepared."

Isotta took his proffered elbow and allowed herself to be led deeper into the shadows of the church.

Magda stalked out of the *alimentari*, her bag heavy with pasta, packages of Ementhal and würstel to make rice salad for her supper, and a tin of the olive oil that was cheaper than the one locals tried to pass off as superior just because it was pressed in their precious mill, but wasn't all that special. As she stepped outside, she sneered at the two women arguing by the *salumi*. They were debating if Laura should take one or two tablespoons of olive oil a day to ward off another heart attack. Such superstitious fools.

In the *piazza* she stopped to gawk at Patrizia on her knees by the bushes.

Patrizia didn't see her. She was focused on her grandson. Magda could never remember his name. The boy was sitting on the ground, calling one of the cats who resided permanently under the bushes.

Magda stopped and watched Patrizia try to cajole her grandson, wheedling him to get up off the ground, pointing at the bakery, no doubt offering the child a treat for doing what he should be doing anyway, which was minding his grandmother.

Not for the first time, Magda regretted that she never had offspring. She saw so many children growing up without a tight rein. She was sure she would have made an excellent mother. The best, really. Because what did children need more in life than strict adherence to guiding principles? An image blew across the canvas of her mind—a girl huddled behind the couch while her mother smacked a ruler impatiently against her palm. Magda shook it away. Never mind, never mind. Anyway, children had never been in the cards for her. By the time she had been at a point in her marriage where she considered bringing an unruly baby into her ordered world, her marriage had become sexless.

Magda repeatedly tucked her hair behind her ears, lost in thought. Was it Gustav who decided that he no longer wanted to share a bed with her, or had that come from her? It seemed to just happen, and she couldn't remember what had been the catalyst. Perhaps there hadn't been one. She remembered her wedding night—it hadn't hurt as much as she'd expected, but she just couldn't see what all the fuss was about. It seemed like smelly, sticky calisthenics.

Gustav had seemed to enjoy it, though. At least at first. But when he attempted to stretch out their lovemaking, to include caressing and lingering, she just got impatient.

No, she never could see what all the fuss was about.

In any case, that brief spate of sex at the start of their marriage never did lead to children. If it had, she would no doubt be more capable than Patrizia, now trying to distract her grandson with a fan, to no avail. The boy determinedly crouched, peering under the bushes.

Patrizia sighed and looked heavenward, the pleading etched in her eyes.

That was enough. Magda stormed over to the boy and yanked him up by his arm. His mingled shriek of surprise coiled into Patrizia's yelp of protest. Above their raised voices, Magda shouted, "Your nonna told you to get up!"

Patrizia snatched her grandson's forearm out of Magda's grip. "Magda! Stop! What are you doing?"

"I'm teaching your grandson some manners."

Over the child's wailing, Patrizia glared and said bitingly, "This is none of your business. He is on his own timetable. It is not your concern."

"Well, if you don't make him mind you, how will he ever mind his teacher or his boss? He'll assume that the world will bend to his will."

Patrizia paused and caressed her grandson's head, smoothing his hair. Her eyes narrowed at Magda. "Traumatizing him won't teach him anything, Magda, except how to fear adults."

Magda recoiled. Traumatizing?

She regarded the boy hiccuping and using his grandmother's dress to wipe his tears.

"Well, I didn't mean to scare him. I just wanted him to listen to you. He *does* need to listen to you. He can't assume that he can do whatever he wants, always."

Patrizia shook her head and then got down on her knees. "Marco? Are you ready for your *biscotto* now?"

Marco sniffled and nodded. Docilely, he took his grandmother's hand and followed her out of the *piazza*. Patrizia threw a glance over her shoulder at Magda as if to say, "See? Kindness works."

Magda wasn't convinced. She muttered, "If I hadn't come along, she'd still be trying to get him off the ground. I made him mind her. It's the only reason he is being good now."

She grumbled to herself, "Not sure why I bother. No one is ever grateful."   Insight was never Magda's strong suit.

Picking up her bag she walked up the hill and into Bar Birbo.

That stranger was in the corner, with his newspaper and now a little notebook. Magda got the distinct feeling that there had been conversation the moment before she walked in, but now the man was furiously writing, and Chiara was polishing the display case glass with more than usual attention. As Magda approached the bar, the sight of a crumpled sugar packet on the floor cued her memory. She started peering around the edges of the bar, where it met the floor.

"Magda? Can I help you with something?" Chiara asked.

"Oh, no . . . I just . . . thought I may have left something."

"Just now?"

"No. It was . . . never mind."

Fatima moved slowly through the street, clutching her jacket tighter around herself. She shivered and tried to think warm thoughts—for instance, how her heart had lightened when Mario described *The Simpsons*, an American TV show he liked. At her intrigued expression, he had offered to stay after school later in the week and bring his big sister's iPad so they could watch it at the playground.

The memory failed to overcome her internal chilliness. Maybe because seeing Mario after school would mean outright lying to her parents about who she was with. She was able to justify her deviations from Islam in the name of allowing herself to experience her new home, but a violation of this magnitude . . . she couldn't do it.

Fatima considered going home and pulling the magazine out from under her mattress. Reading about American singers and French fashion models often served as a delicious escape. She shook her head. She wanted to be out as long as possible before her mother came home.

She supposed she would just keep walking, and play her game of trying to notice details she had never seen before. Like the Roman inscription on that wall. Had she really missed that every time she walked past the church? What was it doing here? What did it mean? Fatima drew closer, trying to see if the remains were decipherable, and similar to modern Italian.

"Fatima!" She heard Elisa's voice hailing her. She turned around to wait for her friend, who was running hard to catch up. Eyes bright from the quick sprint through the cold streets, Elisa panted, "Are you sick? You weren't at school today."

"No, I'm okay," Fatima traced the cobblestone with her toe.

"Oh. Well, then where were you?"

Fatima hesitated.

"Fatima? What is it?"

"I'm just surprised you haven't figured it out."

"Figured what out?"

"You must have heard about the bombing at the French embassy in Germany yesterday."

"Oh. Yes, I did hear about that. But why would you not be in school . . . oh, *Madonna mia!* Was someone in your family there? Oh, Fatima, I'm so sorry, I didn't think—"

"No," Fatima put a hand on Elisa's arm, then drew her hand around her friend's elbow and started walking to the park. "No, I didn't know anybody there. But those bad guys who killed all those people. They were Muslim."

Elisa looked at her friend, confused.

"Elisa. I, I'm Muslim." Fatima waited for a sharp intake of breath at this news.

"I know that."

"You knew I was Muslim?"

"Well, yes. You leave the room during religion class, so I knew you must not be Catholic. I looked up what religions are common in Morocco, and the book said most people are Muslim. It also said Muslims don't eat pork, so I just figured . . ."

"But you never said anything."

"What would I say?"

They walked in silence.

Finally Elisa ventured, "I'm sorry, Fatima, but I still don't get why you didn't come to school."

"Oh, well, when something like this happens, it becomes dangerous for people like me. My brother . . ." Fatima's voice rose an octave as she tightened her voice around her tears, "he was beat up last night."

"What! Which brother?"

"Ahmed. He's a dishwasher at a restaurant in Girona. Some guys saw him dumping the trash in the alley, and they . . . and they . . ."

"*Madonna*, I'm so, so sorry. Is he okay?"

"Well, he's no longer the pretty one, at least until the swelling goes down. But he'll be okay. Anyway, my parents wouldn't let me come to school today. Mamma took Papà to work this afternoon, so I left. I know I shouldn't, but I had to get out."

"I won't let anything happen to you!"

Fatima smiled weakly. "I don't think anyone would hurt me here. This happens every time. They keep me out of school until people forget. And they do. So far anyway."

Elisa considered Fatima's words. "This isn't fair."

"I guess." Fatima sighed. "I thought if you found out I was Muslim, you might not want to be my friend."

"That's weird."

"I guess."

"Why would it matter?"

"It doesn't."

"Anyway, you've seen how awful my family is. You're still my friend."

"We never talked about that—"

"I don't want to talk about it."

The girls climbed on the swings and set their legs to pumping.

Fatima said, "I wish it was easier for you."

Elisa countered, "I wish it was easier for you, too."

Fatima added, "And for Luciano."

"How is he?"

Fatima shook her head.

Elisa nodded and fingered the few gathered coins in her pocket. "I hate this. It's so unfair."

"I know. But we can help Maestro. We can be with him and show him that the world isn't all bad."

"Isn't it?"

Fatima tried to smile. "You know it's not."

Elisa wasn't so sure. "I'm so mad at Massimo. What an awful man. I always knew he was awful, walking around like he owns this town, giving mean looks when I only accidentally wander into him. Acting like I'm Carosello making pee on his leg."

Fatima smiled this time for real. "I know, he's not exactly friendly. But we can't know what lies beneath."

Elisa nodded again. She looked over at her friend placidly swinging, eyes fixed on the horizon. Elisa thought about the fact that others who saw Fatima would just see darker skin, exotic eyes, no cross around her neck. If they saw her, and didn't know her, would they miss the kindness that shone in her face? How could anyone confuse Fatima with a crazy attacker? It was impossible.

But Fatima knew, and she was scared. Was it just because of what happened to her brother, or was Fatima actually in any danger?

The door of Bar Birbo opened and Fabrizio slipped in. Stella and Patrizia, who had been laughing with Chiara, suddenly grew grave at his entrance. They silently stirred their already stirred coffee while darting looks at him.

Fabrizio raised a finger to ask for his customary coffee. Chiara nodded and blushed a little as she ground the beans. She hoped the whirring sound would prevent Fabrizio from noticing Stella and Patrizia's whispered conferencing, but a quick glance in the mirrored wall showed her that his head was cocked in their direction.

As she handed Fabrizio the coffee, he looked into her eyes with teasing warmth. He thanked her quietly and took his coffee to the table, picking up a newspaper on a wooden spool. He laid the paper down and started shaking his sugar packet as he scanned the headlines.

Chiara stepped back to her friends, wondering if she could play it as cool as Fabrizio. He was so nonplussed, she wondered if she'd imagined the night they'd spent in the groves. But no, it had taken a quarter hour to get the dust off the seat of her pants and the back of her jacket. And the way he'd touched her, softly, reverently, questioningly, no. She couldn't have made that up. But now, in the cold light of day, why was he so removed?

Stella picked up where she'd left off, but now her voice had an unfamiliar hushed quality. "So anyway, I think the wedding dress looked just like Giulia's, but Chiara said no."

Chiara countered, "I didn't say that. How would I remember Giulia's wedding dress? How would you? That was a decade ago. I said I didn't think that *she* looked just like Giulia."

Patrizia nodded, "I agree."

Stella slapped the back of her hand against the front of her other hand and then cringed as the loud smacking sound reverberating through the quiet bar. Fabrizio placidly looked up. Returning his gaze to the paper, he continued to stir sugar into his *espresso*. Chiara noticed a small smile playing about his lips. She slid her gaze away, back to her friends.

Stella huddled forward, "What? Do you not have eyes? Are you so totally hoodwinked by the hair? Make the new girl a brunette, and you have a carbon copy of his dead wife!"

Chiara watched as Fabrizio "read" the same headline repeatedly, his head angled toward the clutch of women. She wiped the bar and stayed silent, wishing he was less interested in their conversation.

Patrizia said, "There is a resemblance, of course, anyone can see that, but I'd never say she was identical." She paused. "But I get it, don't you? I mean, Giulia's death was so sudden, so awful, don't you think he'd be drawn to someone like the wife he adored?"

Stella snorted. "Well, 'adored' is too strong a word in my opinion. Remember that period of time, what was it, like five years? Ten? After they got married but before she had Margherita? He was a miserable husband to her. Treated her like some annoying *zanzara*, mosquito. And his mother! Giulia just couldn't do anything right by her. At one point I thought for sure she'd move back to her parents' house to get away from Massimo's devotion to Anna."

Patrizia demurred, "All Italian men are like that. If I had a euro for each time Giuseppe grieved that my *ragù* wasn't as good as his mother's . . ." Patrizia chuckled. "It's true though. I don't know what she puts in it, but mine has yet to come close," she mused, stirring the dregs of her coffee thoughtfully.

Stella shook her head emphatically. "Of course Italian men are all more or less *mammoni*, that's no surprise. But please, Massimo? Those apron strings tie like a noose. Anna resented Giulia, you can't deny it. And Massimo always followed his mother."

Chiara had heard this before, of course. Massimo and Anna's entangled relationship was a source of some whispered hilarity, but Chiara herself had never found it particularly amusing. In fact, whenever she witnessed Anna trying to hold hands with her young adult son, or saw the naked longing in Anna's eyes as she droned on and on about what a perfect father and husband Massimo was, Chiara just felt queasy. Perhaps you feel the same.

Patrizia wondered aloud, "I always thought that was the stress of trying to have a baby for so long. That can make people irritable and anxious. I mean, it took Giuseppe and me a year, and it was the hardest year of our marriage."

Stella conceded, "Once Giulia got pregnant with Margherita, it's true Massimo treated her like a queen. For awhile anyway."

Patrizia reminisced, "Being a mother brought her so much joy. Remember? She and Margherita were always together. Poor little dove, losing her Mamma so young. What was she, a year old? Less?"

Stella nodded, "And the *way* she died . . ."

The eyes of all three women looked over at Fabrizio who studiously turned the page of the paper while taking a noisy sip of his coffee. Stella ducked her head closer to her friends. "I mean, really. Suddenly dying in the shallow waters of the Adriatic? That never happens."

Patrizia looked horrified. "Stella, what are you implying?"

"Nothing I haven't said before. And I'm not alone, loads of people agree with me. The match was always a strange one. Everyone seemed unhappy, and then poof! She's dead. Dead from drowning in two feet of calm water. Don't tell me that's not bizarre."

Chiara couldn't help herself, "But remember right before they left for the sea? Massimo was so tender toward Giulia. The two of them were happy, really happy. Always touching each other like they shared a secret. Stella, I remember you yourself said that it looked like Massimo's restless youth was over and he was finally settling down as a husband and father."

Stella scowled, but nodded in agreement. She did remember Giulia and Massimo walking down the street, hand in hand like newlyweds, Margherita perched high on her father's shoulder. That was only a week or two before Giulia's death, but it had been such a change, seeing Giulia radiant after months of her growing more and more ashen. She hadn't been able to forget it.

Chiara went on, "Anyway, seriously think about what you're saying. A husband killing his wife? For what? A world where that can happen—I can't stomach it. Massimo has always been a bit . . . aloof, it's true, but we've known him since he was a child. He's not a villain. It's much easier to believe that there was some sort of freak accident than to assume he had a hand in Giulia's death."

Stella looked chastened. "You could be right. But it doesn't change the fact that he found a new wife a year from his old wife's death who looks just like her, down to the worshipful infatuation."

Patrizia reluctantly murmured agreement.

The door opened.

Vale entered, jingling his keys. "*Buongiorno!*" He caught sight of Stella, and his face split into a grin that reminded Chiara of a child being offered his first *cioccolata calda* of the season. Stella blushed and stammered a good morning before turning to hunch over her coffee. Vale took up a spot beside her and leaned over the counter to ask for *un cappuccino*. Chiara nodded.

Patrizia watched with curiosity as the red in her friend's cheeks flushed and receded. "*Tutto a posto*, Stella?"

"*Sì, sì*, why shouldn't everything be okay? Oh! Chiara! What do you think about holding the *sagra* up at the castle?"

Vale and Patrizia looked at her quizzically. Patrizia said, "Is it? How do you know?"

Stella began, "Dante, last night, told . . ." but her voice trailed off. Vale flinched and leaned a hair away. He focused on his right thumb rubbing the area of his left hand between his thumb and forefinger.

Chiara broke in, feeling Fabrizio's eyes on her, "Yes, I heard. At first I thought it was a terrible idea, but it's growing on me. It's about time we reclaim that castle. It's been sitting there in disrepair since before I was born." She watched Fabrizio lean back to peer out the window at the steps of the castle. He ran his tongue over his teeth as he pondered the street, before returning his attention to the newspaper.

Stella added in a rush, "Yes, Magda's idea. Which means, of course, we'll never hear the end of it."

They all chuckled, but Chiara was glad to note that the tenor wasn't mean spirited. Stella braved a glance at Vale, who caught her gaze and held it, his thumb momentarily pausing its worrying path over his hand. Stella leaned against Vale, almost imperceptibly. Chiara's eyebrows flew up. She turned to wash the dishes.

Isotta hesitated before stepping into the *alimentari*. It couldn't be her imagination that every single time she'd entered the shop, the voices had stopped like a TV suddenly switched off. And heads had turned suddenly away as if the packaged *biscotti* were suddenly deeply intriguing. She knew small towns were known for being closed to outsiders, but this sort of scrutiny and awkwardness was unlike anything she'd imagined.

This time, she'd brought Margherita, her first outing with the child. She hoped that the presence of the little girl would soften the silence, or at the very least give her something to focus on rather than how long her arms suddenly felt.

Margherita sprinted in her funny, rolling gait toward the shop's entrance. Obviously she'd learned to equate the shop with a treat. Indeed she ran into the dimly lit shop, rounded the shelves, and stopped in front of the candy. Isotta followed, smiling bravely at the customers that, as expected, had grown stiff.

She murmured to Margherita, grateful to have discovered that small town notions of health food were not the same as Florentine ones. She had initially been shocked at the snack cakes that her husband (husband!) and mother-in-law (mother-in-law!) gave Margherita for breakfast. Just this morning, she had bit her lip before suggesting maybe some *pane* with *marmellata*. But she hadn't spoken loudly, and it was easy for everyone to ignore her. Everyone except Margherita who had toddled over to her and rested her hand on Isotta's knee before patting her face softly and tottering to fetch her snack cake. So she didn't fear crossing a line by treating Margherita to some candy. At least there was one aspect of her new life that didn't feel like she was teetering on a precipice.

Isotta sank to her knees next to Margherita and pulled her close. Margherita selected a Lion bar and clutched it to her chest before taking another and trying to feed it to Isotta, wrapper and all. Isotta laughed, "Not for me darling. You're all the sweet I need." Isotta stood up and brushed off her knees to find the cashier, his friend, and an old lady with her hand gripping an orange staring at her.

You might empathize with the villagers, certainly, but it would have been nice if they had adopted a bit of artifice. This was an awful lot for Isotta to take.

Pressing her lips into a smile, she guided Margherita through the rest of the shop, picking out a pack of yogurt, a box of *ditalini* pasta for the soup Anna was making for lunch, and a bottle of pureed tomatoes. Placing the items on the counter, she looked the cashier directly in the eyes before saying with more firmness than she planned, "*Buongiorno.*"

"*Buongiorno, signora,*" he answered, his voice laced with softness.

Unexpected softness. Isotta looked around, and noticed for the first time, that the people in the shop weren't holding themselves distant in the way of people unaccustomed to strangers. They looked like they were in mourning.

But why? She felt like there was a puzzle in front of her, missing too many pieces for her to make sense of the whole design. She pushed the money to the cashier who returned her change with a sorrowful smile. Isotta smiled back, more confused than ever.

She followed Margherita's tiny, pumping legs back up the hill and into the alley that led to her new home.

It still felt strange to open the door and barge in. But of course, she couldn't exactly knock either. She split the difference and allowed Margherita to proceed her, and called out, "We're home!"

Anna called from the kitchen. "Ah, you're back."

Margherita barreled into her grandmother's legs, and Anna hoisted her up as she continued to stir the soup. Isotta dropped the bag on the kitchen table and started unloading. She wanted to help cook, but she knew from experience that Anna might trust her with Margherita, but she definitely didn't trust her with lunch.

"Anna?"

"*Sì*," Anna answered, blowing on a spoonful of soup before tipping it into her granddaughter's mouth.

"I want to ask you something difficult but I'm not sure how."

Anna blanched. Isotta wondered if her mother-in-law feared being asked something bedroom-related. The fear of making Anna uncomfortable propelled Isotta to blurt out her question. "People keep looking at me like I'm a deformed animal. Like they pity me and find me disturbing at the same time. Is that normally how locals treat a newcomer? Or could I be doing something wrong, wearing something wrong?"

Isotta gazed down at her cream sweater. It was a little form-fitting perhaps, but didn't seem provocative. At least not by Florentine standards. She missed the look of relief that flashed across her mother-in-law's face.

By the time Isotta looked back up, Anna had turned back to her soup, hitching Margherita higher as the child tried to stick her finger into the burbling liquid. "Wrong? What can you mean?"

"I don't know. Like just now, I handed money to the guy at the *alimentari,* and he looked like his pet rabbit had been mauled by a fox."

A quick intake of breath, and then Anna answered, eyes firmly on the broth, "You are reading into things. People here are not like they are in Florence. They are just trying to figure out if they should invest time getting to know you if you'll just be doing your shopping in Girona."

"You think so?"

"I'm sure of it. Anyway, I happen to know that Giovanni, the man who owns the *alimentari,* is in love with his first cousin, so he always looks depressed. Stop worrying so much."

"Okay. I'll try."

"I'm telling you, Chiara. That stranger is up to something."

"What do you mean, Stella?"

"Look, the other day when I was walking with Vale—"

"You were walking with Vale? Stella—"

"Nice try, Chiara, but this isn't the time to talk about my relationship with Vale. No time is the right time, actually. I'm a grown woman and I can do what I want. Anyway, that's beside the point. We saw him following the *vigili . . . taking notes.*"

Chiara tried not to laugh aloud. "Taking notes? Really, Stella, that's hardly a behavior worthy of all this cloak and dagger, *sottovoce* suspicion."

Stella blinked theatrically. "Chiara, don't be dense. Why is he taking notes? In fact, every time I see the man, he's taking notes. What is he up to?"

Chiara pushed back the memory of Fabrizio's hands tracing the neckline of her shirt, his cheek nuzzled against her neck inhaling her scent. Why hadn't he acknowledged that night? Not once, beyond that unreadable expression. Wasn't that odd? Yes, it definitely seemed odd. She answered Stella lightly, "Okay, I'll play along. What do you think he's up to?"

"I'm sure I don't know. But a man doesn't just move to an out-of-the-way place like Santa Lucia without a reason, and I think that reason has something to do with why he's always writing in that damn notebook. And why you seem to be the only person he speaks to."

"Can't a man just move here for a change of scenery? We get plenty of tourists this time of year—"

"Tourists! He's not a tourist, and you know it."

"Stella, what in the world do you think he's doing?"

"To tell you the truth? I think he's a spy."

This time Chiara couldn't keep from laughing. "A spy? For whom? Who cares what the *vigili* in Santa Lucia are talking about? Or the coffee drinkers?"

Stella sniffed, "You know as well as I do that this country was founded on layers upon layers of ruthlessness. For all I know he's a spy for the mafia, and there is someone in Santa Lucia who has crossed them. There are definitely shifty characters in town. Magda for one. Hasn't she been acting strangely lately? Or! Maybe he's spying for a development company. Maybe they are trying to develop the swamp again. Chiara, you know that would ruin Santa Lucia."

Chiara opened a drawer and took out a fresh white cloth. Reaching below the counter she grabbed a spray bottle, and began spritzing the counter. Silently, she buffed the stone.

"Chiara? What is it?"

"I don't know what to say. Now, not only is Fabrizio—"

"Oh, you know his name?"

Chiara sighed and said, "Yes, I know his name. Not only is Fabrizio guilty of some vague crime, but Magda is too?"

"I didn't say that for sure, I just said it was possible."

"Please. She's guilty of nothing more than being different. Doesn't mean she's in league with the mafia."

"I never said she was in *league* with them."

"Hiding from them, then. Or that there is some catastrophe around the corner. I happen to think that Magda has a good heart, she's just . . . complicated."

Stella rolled her eyes. "I'll say."

"I don't understand your desire to manufacture danger. Aren't our lives full enough as it is? Especially you, Stella."

"And what is that supposed to mean?"

Chiara put down the spray. "You know what I mean. You're so busy assuming Magda is wrapped up with the mafia or Fabrizio is spying for some nefarious corporation or that Massimo killed his first wife and has designs on doing in his second, that you can't see the mess that's brewing at your feet."

Stella's voice was chilly, "Don't say it, Chiara. Don't say what can't be unsaid."

"I will say it, because it's time to attend to the fact that your own house is on fire. You are married to the mayor. Do you think you can have an affair with the town handyman and not have it blow up in your face?"

Stella plucked her coat from the chair and began putting it on, glaring at Chiara. "I won't stay here to be schooled like a child."

"You're blinded! I love you, and if you get branded as an adulteress, you won't be able to show your face around here. I can't have that happen to you. Because I love you." She repeated, lamely.

"This isn't love, Chiara. This is nosiness. You think just because you're privy to everyone else's secrets and gossip, you're entitled to know about my life. Nosy, yes. Nosy and vindictive. Trying to ruin the first bit of happiness I've had in a good long while. Vale makes me happy, okay? He makes me feel alive. He makes me feel important. He wants to know what I'm thinking and pays attention when I speak. How dare you take that and stomp all over it?"

Chiara's voice softened. "I didn't know you felt all that about him, Stella. Even so, can't you see? Can't you see what'll happen?"

Stella snatched up her purse and hitched it over her shoulder. "All I see is that you're jealous. Yes! Jealous. I have someone to love me and you . . . well, the less said about that the better. You're lonely and spiteful and just want to spit on my relationship. Instead of warning me of my house on fire, Chiara, maybe you should look to your own."

Chiara drew back as if slapped.

Stella went on, "Yes! Your own house! You're a lonely aging woman who seems to have a crush on a suspicious man and your nephew isn't . . . *right*. He isn't right, Chiara! So maybe you should deal with that instead of stirring up dirt in other people's gardens!"

And with that, she swirled her coat around her shoulders and swept out the door. A little melodramatic, perhaps, but it had the desired effect. Chiara slumped against the counter and pressed her hands against her eyes.

It was a week since Edoardo met the group of gay cyclists. He tried not to think about it. But it was hard. Much harder since the interaction hadn't been hazed over with liquor and drugs. He realized now—all those nights of firm hands moving over his hips, all those nights plunging his own hands down the muscular stomachs of men whose faces were obscured in darkness. All those nights were in a venomous shade. Coated with confusion, they were easy to push aside, to forget.

But the way he felt when Arnaldo had put his hand on his arm and leaned forward to kiss him goodbye. The way Edo's heart had dropped. The way he'd felt a hook around his navel that propelled him closer to Arnaldo, while at the same time he had yearned for the ride home. How he'd needed the escape of a punishing hill to block out the echoing thoughts that reverberated in his head.

"Gay . . . gay . . . gay . . ."

The problem with starting at the top of the hill was that down was the only recourse. Edoardo had forced his eyes to watch the terrain, his brain to make sense of every curve to keep his memory from wandering back to that sunlit hill, surrounded by those cyclists, so comfortable and relaxed, leaning back on each other's legs, sharing bottles of water.

Somehow, he'd made it home.

But the thoughts hadn't left.

And what was dim was now clear.

He was gay.

Gay . . . gay . . . gay . . . gay.

Of course he'd known that. Not always clearly, perhaps, but he'd always known. So had everyone else. He could duck his head in the sand and pretend he didn't know why he was always the last kid picked for sports teams and why he was held at a distance from other men. But he knew. That part of him that he let out only in low-light conditions was always there, humming its knowledge that he was damaged. Sinful.

He didn't need the church to tell him. He had only to see how people looked at him suspiciously. He hated that separation and had tried to be normal. Hadn't he taken out that girl in high school? Somehow he had managed to have sex with her, by both invoking and rejecting the image of a man underneath him. He broke up with her soon after, and she had frankly seemed relieved. He supposed it hadn't been all that good for her.

After high school, he continued to date, sure. There was that girl he had met through his cousin. He remembered her with some affection now. She was more experienced, more forward, and had come onto him from the moment she met him in a way that he, who didn't get women, perfectly understood. She had been demanding in bed, which was at first freeing, as it kept his mind from wandering into images of broader chests and different appendages. Though after awhile, she tired of the work it took to arouse him and called it off with a jovial boxing of his shoulder. She was married now, with a child. He was glad she was happy.

The clubs. Those began as a joke, a dare by his friends. Then, it was an addiction. An addiction far stronger than the liquor and drugs that were in constant supply on the edge of the dance floor.

All those nights. How could he have denied the truth? No matter how many substances clouded his judgment and memory?

He supposed it was willful self-delusion. He didn't want to be what he feared he was. Being gay meant resigning to residing in liminal space, where he never wanted to be. He wanted to be in the thick of life, not on the margins.

For a day or two after the revelation on the top of the mountain, Edoardo toyed with the idea of trying to find Arnaldo. He got the feeling that Armando saw the demons and the desire in Edoardo, and didn't judge either.

In spare moments, Edo allowed himself to relive the electricity of that kiss. He treasured the memory of getting lost in a man's eyes. He preserved the image of Arnaldo's smiling face lit by the sun. That dimple, unbridled.

Edoardo felt the shame seep from him, like the last of the toxins he'd been harboring.

Chiara tensed as the door opened. She wanted to close the bar and be done with this damnable day.

"*Ciao*, Chiara," she heard the modulated voice of Patrizia.

With a sigh of relief, Chiara turned and smiled at her friend. "*Ciao*, Patrizia. What will you have this evening?"

"*Il solito.*"

Chiara tucked a fall of hair behind her ear and turned to prepare the *latte caldo.*

Patrizia shook out her coat, damp from the intensifying mist filling the streets. "*Tutto bene*, Chiara?"

"*Sì, sì*, everything is fine." Chiara flicked the wand down into the metal pitcher. The homey sound of frothing milk filled the quiet bar.

Chiara set the warm milk in front of her friend, sprinkled it with a blur of cocoa powder, then leaned forward. "How is everything, Patrizia? How are Filamena and Marco?"

Patrizia reached for a sugar packet and, shaking it, said, "*Piano, piano* . . . things seem to be improving. Maybe slower than we'd like, but still . . . improving. The school switched Marco's teacher to someone that has experience with kids like Marco."

"Hmm. What does that mean?"

"I don't know. Someone who can help him with his work, I suppose. I think they said they're going to try lots of rewards when he does what he's asked to do. Anyway, it is helping. Some." Her eyes welled with tears and her voice shook.

"That must be a relief."

"It is. It really is."

Patrizia sipped her milk, and Chiara reached into the refrigerator for a green glass bottle of *frizzante.* She poured the bubbly mineral water and added a splash of orange juice. Stirring with a long-handled spoon, she enjoyed the moment of quiet, and the noticeably more relaxed features of her friend.

Chiara took a sip and then said, "And how is Giuseppe?"

"Good, good. Gearing up for the *sagra.* It's so strange to think of not celebrating in the *piazza.*"

"Well, it's a change, but I think it—" her voice cut off at the sound of the door opening.

Fabrizio stepped in and nodded to the women before holding his finger aloft and asking, "*Un caffè lungo, per favore.*"

Chiara's cheeks flushed as she turned to grind the beans.

Patrizia looked from Chiara to the man, now standing at the edge of the bar, examining the display of candy. She turned back to Chiara with one eyebrow raised in question. Chiara avoided her eye contact as she plunked the coffee on the counter. Fabrizio nodded his thanks and carried his coffee to the table.

Patrizia ran her tongue over her teeth, before staring into her *latte caldo*. She swallowed the rest in one gulp, coughed, and moved to get her purse. Placing some coins in the tray next to the register, she said goodbye. Chiara waved, and placed the cup into the sink.

Fabrizio followed Patrizia's exit with his eyes and then stood and crossed the bar to the counter. "Chiara?"

Chiara turned up the water and began humming.

Fabrizio stood up and moved to the bar. "Chiara?"

Chiara stiffened and washed the cup more thoroughly than was strictly necessary given that she'd overspent for a dishwasher with scouring capabilities.

"Chiara!"

She jumped and turned off the water. Chiara dried her hands on the towel before facing Fabrizio. "Yes? Can I get you something to eat?"

"No. But something is bothering you. I'd like to know what it is."

"There's nothing to tell."

"Chiara."

"Really! It's nothing, I just got in a fight with a friend earlier, and I guess I'm not really feeling right since then."

"What did you fight about?"

Chiara flushed and concentrated on drying the counter.

Fabrizio went on. "I know it's not my place. But something is clearly bothering you, and I thought it might help to talk about it."

Chiara shook out the towel and then, tucking it back into her apron, she blurted, "Okay, if you must know, you, actually."

Fabrizio rubbed his thumbnail. "Me?"

Biting her lip, Chiara said, "Look, you know people are suspicious, and you aren't exactly candid, plus we haven't even talked since—"

"Ah."

"Ah? What is that supposed to mean?"

"It seems that perhaps that's the problem."

"Well, maybe. I mean, it's not exactly normal. We had that one night talking and . . . well, mostly talking. And since then, you've been closed tight as an Adriatic clam. Maybe you regret it, or—"

"Regret it? Chiara, why would you think that? We agreed to take it slow. I was respecting that. Respecting you."

"I know. But I guess when we're not talking, and then there's all these wild theories about why you're here, it makes me second guess everything."

"That doesn't sound like you."

Chiara smiled. "It doesn't feel like me either, but there you have it."

Fabrizio leaned across the bar and said, "If it helps, I haven't been able to stop thinking about you."

Chiara closed her eyes and focused on catching her breath. "You haven't?"

"Mmm . . . At night, I've had the most delicious dreams. I even came by at one in the morning the other night, hoping I'd see a light on."

"Why didn't you tell me?"

"Honestly? I didn't want to scare you off. That night, Chiara. It was beautiful . . . magical. I was afraid if I was too close to you you'd see my hunger to be with you again and you'd feel pressured. I won't break this delicate thing between us."

Chiara swallowed, her skin prickling in anticipation of his touch.

As if in answer, Fabrizio ran his finger over her cheek and pulled her chin across the bar to softly press his lips against hers.

He pulled back and smiled. "Besides, there's always some blasted person in here. Getting you alone takes actual stalking."

Chiara shivered at the word, but shook it off. She looked around the empty bar. "I'm alone now."

"I see that."

"It's a little cold for a walk though."

Fabrizio flushed, saying "Could we go upstairs?"

"Edo. I'm not ready yet to explain . . ."

"Understood. Well, I've always enjoyed the brisk night air. At least it's clear. It's supposed to rain tomorrow."

"I'll get a blanket."

Fatima did a double take. Was that someone huddled on the playground bench? It was too drizzly and cold to be sitting outside. In fact, she had her umbrella fixed over her head as she hurried home with a bag of *mandarini* and a head of lettuce. Wait, was that Elisa? The hat looked familiar.

Fatima ventured closer. "Elisa?"

Elisa's head jerked up. She gasped before registering that the person standing in front of her in the half-light was Fatima. "Oh, Fatima. You scared me."

"What are you doing out here?"

Elisa drew her knees up to under her chin and her chin trembled. "I can't go home."

Fatima thought about asking why, but she knew why. Instead she sat down on the bench and drew her arm through Elisa's, holding the umbrella above them both. She said, "He's in a bad mood?"

Elisa thought about expressing surprise at Fatima's question, but she also didn't have the energy to pretend. "Yes."

"Worse than usual?"

"Yes." She leaned her head on Fatima's.

"Oh, Elisa, I'm so sorry."

Elisa nodded, then said, "It had gotten better. Or, not better exactly, but easier because my brothers have let me go with them when they leave. We talk about other things, and I've shown them my drawings. It would be a nice time if we didn't have to wonder ..."

Fatima nodded, then asked, "But tonight?"

"Oh, right. No, my brothers are both at a soccer tournament. It's just me. I tried to get out like I do when I'm with them, but it doesn't work alone. I hate it, Fatima. I *hate* him."

"I know."

Elisa drew in a shaky breath. "And this time, when my father was yelling at her, he kept saying my name. Like I am her fault." Elisa's voice shook and the tears she'd been choking back sprung free.

Fatima wrapped her arms around her friend, "Hey, it's okay. You're going to be okay."

"How?"

Fatima stroked Elisa's hair and thought about the question. "I have no idea."

Elisa moaned. "And what's going to happen when my brothers go to university?"

Shaking her head, Fatima said, "I don't know. But by then, you'll be in high school. So you'll be gone more. And maybe you can come to my house."

"Your house?"

"Yes. I've been thinking about this. With Maestro the way he is nowadays, and the weather not so good. I can't go to your house unless my parents meet your parents—"

Elisa said, "Which can't ever happen."

Fatima nodded, "Right. But you can come to mine. I hadn't thought of it before, because we never have guests. My parents are suspicious about locals looking down on us because we're *stranieri*, and not just any foreigners, but from Morocco. Anyway, it might be awkward. At least at first. But we always had a houseful of people in Morocco. It would be good to bring people into our quiet house."

"I can't even imagine what a quiet house is like."

Fatima unwound her arm from Elisa's shoulder and squeezed her hand. "Anyway, maybe you coming can change our habit. Of being only us."

"But what if I do something wrong?"

"Don't worry. Just don't say anything about my eating pork or the shirts you made me or the . . . oh, you know. All the stuff they can't know. They'll worry too much. *Ascolta*, why don't you come home with me now?"

"Really?"

"Really. At least to come in out of the rain. Stay for a few minutes to dry, which will get my mother used to the idea."

Elisa wiped her eyes. "If you're sure it's okay."

The girls rose and Fatima situated the umbrella over their heads. Their shoulders adhered together, they dashed through the streets, giggling. They moved through the town, into the edge of Santa Lucia. "Here we are," Fatima said as they stood in front of a blue front door, the streetlight full and resonant as it reflected the sheer raindrops. Fatima shook out her umbrella and then opened the door. Elisa grabbed her hand, "Fatima! I'm scared."

"It'll be okay. I promise. Better than being out in the rain, right?"

Fatima pulled Elisa into the house and took off her shoes, gesturing for Elisa to do the same. Elisa cocked her head in question, but then followed suit. Calling out in a language Elisa couldn't understand, Fatima took off her coat. An answering voice echoed from what must be the kitchen, given the sizzling noises and curious smells. Fatima whispered, "Good so far, Mamma seems to be in a good mood." She held out her hand to take Elisa's thin, sodden jacket. Elisa was pulling her arms out of the sleeves, when she remembered the Moroccan coin, still in the inside pocket. She hadn't yet found a way to get it back, and if Fatima noticed it . . . if Fatima took her friendship away . . .

Fatima grinned and snatched the coat away. "Slowpoke! I'll take it."

Elisa held her breath, watching Fatima's hands as they brushed over the coat to remove the raindrops and hang it straight. Her hands paused momentarily at the lining, and Elisa thought she might faint. Fatima hung the coat and looked at her friend with concern. "Elisa? Are you okay?"

Elisa nodded, her stomach pinched. Fatima led her friend into the kitchen. In slow Italian, she said to her mother, a short stocky woman with her black frizzy hair escaping from its bun, "I brought my friend here to meet you. This is Elisa."

Fatima's mother looked up from grinding spices. Her gaze raked over the thin girl. Elisa's overlarge eyes were still red-rimmed and drops of water fell from the ends of her hair. "*Buona sera*, Elisa. *Piacere*. I'm Salma."

"*Piacere*," Elisa managed to say, and gave a hesitant smile and what may have been a slight curtsy.

"Mamma, can Elisa stay for a little bit?"

"That depends."

"On what?"

"Can she peel carrots?"

Chiara ran her thumb along the edges of the envelope in her pocket. The hum in her fingers skipped up her arm until she was smiling again. She seemed to be unable to stop smiling.

As Arturo and Sauro entered the bar, she called out merrily, "*Buongiorno, signori!* Isn't it a beautiful day?"

Arturo and Sauro glanced at each other before squinting back out over their shoulder at the sodden sky. Arturo answered, "Actually, we were just saying how *brutto* it is. Last night's rain has left everything slippery."

"Yes, well, the clouds are leaving now. The sky is clearing. You can tell today will be glorious."

Arturo narrowed his eyes at Chiara and smiled, "Okay, Chiara whatever you say. *Un cappuccino*, please."

Sauro raised his index finger, "For me, too, Chiara."

Edo opened the landing door and stepped into the bar, greeting Arturo and Sauro before dropping a kiss on his aunt's cheek. "Sleep well?" he asked her.

"I did, actually."

Was she blushing?

Chiara turned away to grind the beans.

The bell chimed again and Ava entered, smiling her shy smile at Edo, who welcomed her warmly. "*Ciao*, Ava. I hear you've been working hard at the castle."

Ava nodded, clearly pleased at the notice. "Yes. It's looking good, though the hedges aren't cooperating."

She rested her hands on the bar, and everyone gathered to cluck over the scratches lining her arms.

"You should've worn a long-sleeve shirt," Edo chided with a frown, as he picked up Ava's hand to peer more closely at the scrapes on her wrist.

Ava took a shuddering breath. "I did. Ruined the shirt. Those thorns . . ."

Arturo said, "Rub olive oil into the cuts. That'll clear it right up."

Sauro nodded, "Yes, that's a good idea. I got a burn from the bread oven last week, rubbed olive oil into it after the pain subsided, and the mark healed in no time."

Ava and Edo rolled their eyes lightly. Smiling, Ava said, "Sure, I'll try that. My Mamma said the same."

Chiara shook her head and turned away, dipping her hand into her apron pocket to touch the letter again. "*My dear, Chiara . . .*" She had memorized it already.

She calculated when she could see Fabrizio again. Tonight, maybe? Edo had offered to help her with a make-over, to get her style out of the dark ages, as he'd said with a teasing smile. He was still unaccountably quiet lately, but he was smiling more. Yes, maybe tonight, after the make-over. Fabrizio might come by late, as he'd been doing lately. She'd have on that sweater he said he liked, just in case—

The door flew open.

Luciano stood, feet planted wide and pointed at Edo. "You! You think you can come around with your nice words and your offers to . . . to . . . purify my house. I don't need you! I don't need any of you! Just stay away! All you lousy blights. Stay . . . *away!*" Luciano thrust his finger at each person standing, open-mouthed, at the bar before he took a deep intake of breath and shouted, "None of this is normal! You act like it's normal, but it's not! *You're* not! You're not normal!" He glared at Edo and then grumbled and turned, stumbling a little, and then shambled down the street.

Sauro mumbled, "What was that?"

Ava peeked at Edo through lowered lashes.

Edo answered, "I don't know. I saw him yesterday and I did offer to come by and help. He didn't answer, I didn't even think he heard me."

Chiara put her hand on Edo's arm, "He doesn't mean it, Edo. He loves you, always has."

Edo shook his head, "Maybe. I clearly did something wrong. I'm clearly 'not normal'."

Ava bit her lip and ventured, "It's not you that did something wrong. It's Massimo. It's just made Luciano so angry and sad that he's confused."

Chiara leaned toward Ava. The girl seemed to be trying not to cry.

The bar was quiet.

Sauro cleared his throat, "Dante says we're finally getting recycling bins."

Edo darted his eyes at Ava. She blinked and then turned to Sauro. "Really? And only ten years after Perugia got theirs."

Everyone visibly relaxed. Arturo added, "My prediction is that Carosello will use those recycling bins more than everyone else put together."

Edo laughed and said, "At first maybe. But people will catch on. Northern Italy has been doing it forever, and it works. Santa Lucia will figure it out."

Talk turned to the gossip about Rosetta, the principal, and her trip to the Dolomiti. Her son had had a narrow miss with a drunk Russian man careening down the ski slope. The child was fine, but Rosetta had come home hopping mad. Who were these Russians to come to their country and act like it was their playground? Ordering the most expensive food and eating it all with sides of vodka and the wrong wines (selected purely because they were the priciest)? And then drunk skiing with no regard for Italian children.

Soon the bar was full of laughter again, and Chiara returned to the business of making coffee, her hand ducking into her pocket one more time to touch the corner of the envelope.

Magda stormed into Bar Birbo moments before the end of the morning rush, her head swiveling from side to side, as if she were watching an invisible, aggravating game of tennis. Chiara smiled and greeted her while flipping on the La Pavoni to make Magda her *cappuccino*.

"*Tutto a posto*, Magda?"

"*Sì, sì* . . ." Magda took a breath, "Only, um."

Chiara glanced over her shoulder at Magda still standing in the center of the bar. "Are you okay?"

"Yes! Of course! I mean, well why . . . I mean . . . I just wanted to see. It's probably not anyway," Magda stammered.

You can't be familiar with this side of Magda. It is so rarely on display.

Chiara poured the milk into the cup with the coffee and handed it to Magda with an expression of concern. She must be having the same thought. "Seriously Magda, I've never seen you not be able to get a sentence out. What's wrong?" Ah, yes, exactly.

"Nothing! Well, I mean, not really it's just a strange thing, and I . . ." her voice trailed off.

"Oh, *Madonna mia!* Did you hear something about your husband? Did they find him? Is he alive?"

Magda clucked, "Chiara, why on earth would I care what that scumbag does? I have no idea if he's alive or dead and I don't even have a preference as long as he stays away from me."

"Okay. What is it then?"

Magda hesitated before straightening her shoulders, "It's not a big deal, Chiara, so don't turn it into one. It's simply that I keep forgetting to ask you if you found my amulet in the bar."

"Amulet? Like for *malocchio?*"

"No, no, nothing to do with warding off the evil eye, just an amulet. I think it slipped off of my necklace some weeks ago."

"It did? Why didn't you ask me sooner?" Chiara pulled out a box under the register and began extracting items. Sunglasses, a scarf, a keychain, a faded photograph, a child's tiny doll.

"Maybe I would have, but there are always people in here. I didn't want a lot of questions. 'Oh, Magda! What are you looking for? Oh, Magda, you mean you *dropped* something? What is it? Where does it come from? Why is it special?' This town is full of interfering gossips."

Chiara smothered a smile. "Well, it's not here."

Magda sighed. "I didn't think so. And you clean regularly on the edges of the shop? Could it have been kicked against a wall and gone unnoticed?" Magda began frowning at the place where the wall, covered with signs for the *sagra*, met the floor.

Laughing, Chiara said, "I'll go ahead and ignore the implicit accusation that I'm slovenly when it comes to cleaning my bar and just say . . .

oh! Wait a minute." Chiara hit a button on the register so that the drawer popped open. "I just remembered, Edo found a little golden something on the floor a month ago. It was small, and looked like it could be important, so we put it in the register rather than in the lost box." Chiara fished through a small well in the drawer, extracting coins from other countries that she'd accidentally accepted and keys to her *grappa* cases, while Magda hurried over to watch.

Chiara pulled out a golden 'Y' shape with an extra prong, like a trimmed down representation of a broom, and held it up with triumph, "Here it is! Actually, is it? I don't really know what it is."

Magda snatched it from Chiara's fingers and barked. "Yes! That's it!"

"Oh, good. I wish you had mentioned it sooner. Or that I remembered it when you said you lost an amulet. I think of amulets as stones or shells."

"It's probably an error in translation from German. Regardless, thank you."

"Glad I could help. What is it anyway?"

Magda shot a glowering stare at Chiara, who held up her hands, "Okay, okay, I don't mean to pry. It's unusual, that's all."

Twitching her hair back over her shoulder, Magda mumbled, "My mother gave it to me as a child."

"Ah, so it has sentimental value."

Magda shuddered before guffawing, "Ha! No, not at all. In fact, it's quite the opposite."

With that, Magda dropped coins in the copper plate, turned on her heel, and, leaving her *cappuccino* untasted, walked with stately purpose out the door. Chiara watched as the door closing behind Magda spurred her steps, and she fairly flew down the street, away from Bar Birbo.

Magda turned left out of Bar Birbo, tears clouding her vision. She didn't know where she was going, she just knew she had to move, to escape the images crowding her head.

But the voices only got louder the farther she got from Chiara's gentle bewilderment.

"Magda! You idiot! What will the Gestapo say when they see you here with your hair all untidy like a Jew!"

"Magda! What is this I hear about you whispering during the prayer for our Führer at school? Didn't you think for a moment of the shame you were bringing on your family?"

"Magda! You don't need second helpings, you fat cow!"

Her mother's voice chased her down the street, her father added the icy undertone.

"Magda, get in here. I heard about you speaking to a Jew on the street outside the bakery."

"Magda, if only you had never been born. Then I wouldn't have this shame of a daughter who is an idiot."

The cries threatened to erupt out of her, she had to get home, she had to get home! She couldn't shame herself by collapsing in the street. Furiously, Magda wiped her eyes and gulped for breath. Where was she? Where was she? Ah, in the *piazza*. Stop! Think! She ordered herself. Turn right, then at the end of the alley, a left and then she could rush to her door. Magda narrowly avoided banging into Luciano sitting on the bench. *"Scusi. Entschuldigen sie."*

Luciano looked up. "Hey! What the—Magda?" His voice wavered with drink.

"Leave me alone!"

Luciano pressed down on his cane to reach out to Magda, but she batted away his arm as she hurried away. He plopped back onto the bench and tried to corral his blurry thoughts into order. What was the matter with Magda?

Meanwhile, Magda stumbled over a loose cobblestone dashing down the alley, then careened around the corner.

Her hand curled tightly around the amulet, until she could feel the cold metal biting into her skin, a familiar sensation which helped clear her mind. "It doesn't matter, it doesn't matter, it doesn't matter," she chanted under her breath.

Her parents were dead. Long dead. Buried in a Nazi graveyard somewhere in Germany. They couldn't hurt her anymore.

But those voices lacerated her soul. She had to quiet the voices. They had only haunted her when she thought about the box under her bed. Now they were unleashed, and more clamorous than ever.

Fumbling, Magda removed her key from her pocket and stabbed the lock several times before she was able to pop it open and rush inside. As if chased, Magda pivoted around the door and slammed it shut with all her weight, turning the lock.

She sighed.

But who was she keeping out?

The voices, the voices were still with her. Taunting her. The voices jeered while Magda sank to the floor, head on her knees, and sobbed.

Luciano continued to sit, planted, long after Magda's back receded down the alley. He tried in vain to process her hunched posture. Even his sluggish brain registered her shape as uncharacteristic. She wasn't a pleasant person to interact with, but she had admirable posture—erect and confident. Imperious, at times.

An hour later, his mind kept returning to the puzzle that was Magda, running sloppily, practically falling into the rosebushes.

Another hour later, and the clawing hunger was stronger than the remaining drink in his brain. He needed to move, but exhaustion settled like a mantle over his body. His mind was still stuck on Magda.

A far off feeling within him flickered in sympathy. She was clearly cowed by pain. And pain was something Luciano understood. His eyes welled with tears at the thought of so much pain in the world. This world that was so evil, that delighted in tormenting those with open hearts. Though frankly, he'd never before considered Magda someone with an open heart.

Luciano tipped his face into the sun, which aggravated those easy tears. The numbness was wearing off. He needed more wine. He'd move in a minute, he just needed to see if she appeared, so he could watch her from a distance. No, she wasn't his beloved daughter, but something about her slid into a place within him. It's what kept him coming back to this bench, to see her crossing the *piazza*, her eyes wary and her shoulders curved inward. Yes, one thing she shared with Giulia was a lack of comfort with her space in this world. A lack of surety. He wondered where that had come from in Giulia. He and his wife had doted on her as a child, a teenager, a woman. They could never believe they made something so precious. He blamed Massimo for turning his daughter into a walking apology.

In any case, though seeing Massimo's new wife grated against the wound in his heart, he also felt compelled to seek her out, to seek out this pain, again and again. He found himself saving the bulk of his wine for the late afternoons, so that he could have the chance to see her less foggy from drink.

Luciano closed his eyes and leaned back, relishing the sounds of swallows, joyous in the absence of the construction work that filled the weekdays.

A shadow fell across his closed lids, and he opened his eyes to see Elisa standing in front of him.

"Elisa."

Elisa bit her lip and sat down beside Luciano. She said nothing.

"Elisa?"

Elisa shook her head, and put her head in her hands.

"What is it?"

Elisa just shook her head again.

Luciano watched her, wondering what to do. He remembered now, Elisa's skittishness, her tendency to leap out of her seat at the sound of anything hitting the floor, even a spoon. Her stream of apologies at what she deemed an infraction against himself or Fatima, that would leave the two of them looking bewildered at each other while Elisa ran to a darkened corner to catch her breath.

She had grown less edgy in their time together. Now? There was an air of her old brittleness. What had been happening?

"Maestro?"

Luciano startled, Elisa was regarding him, her face strained.

"Sì, cara?"

"Are you okay?"

Ah, so this was no fresh insult at home that was causing her pain. It was him.

He sagged against the solid safety of the ancient wooden bench. Felt it prodding against his bones, perhaps more brittle with age, but still solid. Luciano breathed heavily.

He opened his eyes and saw that Elisa was still watching him, chewing her lower lip as she did when they worked out math problems together. That lip was red and chapped.

"I'll be honest, cara. It's been a difficult time. And I've let it get the better of me."

Elisa was silent.

The two of them watched the pigeons and cats argue over a scrap of food in the piazza. The bell tolled the hour and at the fifth sonorous bong, Luciano stood up. Elisa startled slightly before smiling at him in a fleeting way.

Luciano nodded to himself and whispered, "Allora."

Isotta felt Margherita's head tip onto her shoulder. The curls, frizzy from a day of playing at the park and chasing Isotta though the streets, tickled Isotta's chin. Hardly daring to breathe, Isotta laid the child into her crib. Margherita twitched and sighed, freezing Isotta as she removed her hands. But then the little girl rolled onto her side, popped her thumb into her mouth and sank into slumber.

Isotta sighed in relief. Lately Margherita had fought sleep. Always wanting one more game of hide and seek, or one more drink of water, or one more story read aloud. Isotta could never refuse her, particularly when it came to books. In fact, even now, the end of Margherita's crib was stacked with books. Perhaps they would keep her occupied if she woke again at five in the morning.

Tiptoeing out, Isotta followed the sound of the soccer game into the living room. She sat on the arm of the chair to lean against her husband, whose vision was trained on the television. "How's the game?" she asked.

Massimo glared at her. "Fine. Trying to watch."

Rebuked, Isotta got up and went to the kitchen, where Anna was washing dishes. "Can I help?"

"No, no. I'm about done. Is she sleeping?"

"Yes, finally. She ran me ragged today. It's a wonder she didn't use her plate of sausage as a pillow and nod off at the table."

Anna placed the last dish in the rack above the sink and reached for a towel.

"Are you sure there's nothing I can do?"

"I said I'm fine! Go watch the game with Massimo."

Isotta adjusted her blouse before answering in a measured tone, "Oh, I think Massimo would prefer to watch it alone."

Anna smiled, tightly. "Men. Always hypnotized by a moving ball."

Drumming her hands on the table, Isotta noted a rising level of irritation. She was getting tired of gender being used as an explanation for violating social conventions. First her sister, now this. Plus, there was that awkward conversation with her mother that she never wanted to think about again. So much for relying on a mother's wisdom for advice on how to broach the subject of birth control with Massimo.

Did she get any special passes just by virtue of being a woman? Or was that grace only extended to people with penises?

The bluntness of her thoughts rattled her. But in retrospect, Isotta realized that she had spent her life muting herself in order to be seen as attractive. It was this whirlwind of her new life that made her value concise honesty. At least in her own reasoning process.

Anna carefully placed a wineglass in the cabinet. At Isotta's lack of response she turned toward her and said, "Isotta, it is not your place to be offended."

Isotta flinched. "I'm not offended."

"Then stop acting like a child."

"How am I acting like a child?" Isotta fought back the tears rising in her throat at the sudden criticism from a woman she had started to feel safe with.

"Sulking in the kitchen? Come on, Isotta. Go be with your husband."

"But he doesn't want me there."

"Just because he's not fawning all over you doesn't mean he doesn't want you there. You can't expect it to be your honeymoon forever."

That was true, but the words might have been easier to swallow if there had actually been a honeymoon. Instead, she went from her wedding day straight into instant motherhood. Isotta's thoughts battled between wondering if perhaps it was unreasonable to expect affection from her husband after a month of marriage and countering that a smile or a kind word weren't too much to ask.

"Look, Isotta, I speak my mind when it comes to my household. Massimo works hard during the day to provide for the family. Is it too much to ask that we make his evenings pleasant? He likes a good meal, so I cook a full dinner every night. The least you can do is allow him room to unwind. If you pout, he'll find you unpleasant. That's how affairs happen."

The logic of this didn't sit well with Isotta, but maybe it was one more way her lack of experience didn't prepare her for marriage. She nodded and stood to go back to the living room.

"That's better," Anna grumbled.

Isotta sat on the couch and tucked her bare feet underneath her. Massimo and Anna had teased her relentlessly about her preference for bare feet, even as the weather shifted to the chill of November, but her baby habits died hard. She smiled thinking about how Margherita had started flinging off her shoes and socks.

That child. She was amazed how smitten she was with a child not of her blood. Isotta would never say it aloud, but she marveled at how Margherita resembled a more attractive version of herself. Like all her traits and been smudged and redrawn just a hair to make them more appealing. She wondered what Giulia had looked like, but her perfunctory efforts at snooping hadn't revealed any photographs. Which, she supposed, made sense. Massimo would not choose to be reminded of the tragedy of his wife's loss. Or maybe it was in deference to her? The thought softened Isotta's resentment. She leaned back into the couch.

Looking around, Isotta realized that there was actually only one framed photograph in the house, of Massimo as a toddler in his mother's arms. In the photo, Anna smiled at her son, only a sliver of her face turned toward the camera. Even with her features only partially revealed, Isotta could see how besotted Anna was with her little boy. Isotta plucked the photo off the side table and examined it more carefully.

Interesting.

Anna had the same rounded chin that Isotta did. And Margherita. Well, that explained why Margherita looked a little like her, she and Anna both had small chins. It wasn't exactly an unusual feature, Isotta was embarrassed that she had internally relished the vague similarity between her and Margherita, when the resemblance came down to something as basic as one kind of chin over another just as common. Isotta suddenly understood that she had been looking for a similarity between her and Margherita, to match the increasing bond she felt with the child.

Isotta peered more closely at the photograph in her hands. Anna's eye shape was round, like her own. She wondered why she hadn't noticed it before, but she supposed age and gravity shifted a face's edges.

Not for the first time, Isotta wondered about Massimo's father. Massimo and Anna never mentioned him, and when Isotta asked when he'd died, they both grew tight lipped. Anna finally said that he'd had a heart attack during Massimo's final year at university. The response didn't encourage Isotta to ask further questions, though she couldn't contain her curiosity. She gathered from the tenor of that one conversation that he wasn't a well-loved man, at least in this household. Did he know that? Did he regret it? Did he deserve it?

She wished at least one photograph remained so she could chart the family resemblance. Massimo looked so little like his mother beyond height and expression, Isotta wondered how much he took after his father. As an aside, if Isotta could have seen a photograph of Massimo's father, she would have been gobsmacked by the resemblance. It is unfortunate that Isotta never found the photograph that revealed the father-and-son likeness. Well, to be more precise, she did find it, but by that point, she was far too frantic to note something as mundane as the inheritance of intense eyelashes. But one mustn't get ahead of oneself.

Isotta rested the picture back on the table. Funny that that was the only photo on display. Isotta made a mental note to charge her camera battery overnight. If tomorrow was a pretty day, maybe she could take photos of Margherita in the groves. Framed, they would make charming gifts for Massimo and Anna. And frankly a few whimsical photographs would cheer up a house that was a bit prone toward dark stuffiness.

Massimo cheered at the TV, breaking through Isotta's rambling thoughts. She startled, and he looked over at her and laughed. A loud voice and tinny jingle began, signaling the start of the halftime commercial break. Massimo came and sat on the couch next to her, pulling her close. "Are you going to watch the game with me?"

"Yes, of course, if you'd like me to."

"I would. And then after the game . . ." Massimo leaned over and kissed the base of her neck. Once, twice, and then nibbling a little before sliding his lips up to kiss the place where her ear met her jawbone. Isotta felt the familiar flutter at her core, which irritated her for reasons she couldn't fathom.

Bang, bang, bang!

Magda stirred under her heavy blankets.

Bang, bang, bang!

Groaning, she reached a hand out to grab her aged clock with its cheerful round face and brass cap, but inadvertently shoved it off the nightstand. Its clattering surprised her into sitting up.

Bang, bang, bang!

"*Gottverdammt,*" Magda muttered. She cleared her throat and then called out, "*Arrivo!*"

The banging continued.

Magda found her robe in a heap on the floor and clumsily worked it over her arms and shoulders, tying it around her waist while she called out, more loudly this time, "*Arrivo!*"

The banging stopped. Magda located her slippers and shoved her feet into them, wondering who could be at the door this early. Or was it early? She seemed to remember collapsing into bed, just last night. Or was it last night? Now that she thought about it, she remembered waking up to both sun and starlight, punctuated with trips to the bathroom. How long had it been? Her eyes were at least dry now, though a quick pass with her hand told her they were crusted with sleep. She wondered if she had time to wash her face and teeth.

The thought of the banging propelled her to the door. She flung it open to see Chiara glowing in the sunlight. Chiara smiled broadly. "There you are!"

"Yes. Where else would I be?" Magda gestured faintly toward the living room, and walked backward, allowing Chiara in.

"*Permesso*," Chiara murmured as she stepped through the doorway.

Magda noticed that Chiara carried a *cesta*, which she heaved onto the dining room table. As Chiara opened the basket and took out baked goods and what looked like a small styrofoam cup of coffee, she chattered brightly, "I can't remember the last time I went a few days without seeing you. I asked around, and nobody had seen you anywhere. And anyway, it wouldn't be like you to go away this close to the *sagra*. I started worrying that you were ill."

"I'm not ill," though the way she slumped into the tall back chair belied her words.

"Hmm. I can't say you look well."

"Well, Chiara. That's awfully rude."

"Not rude. Just honest. Can I air this place out? It's . . . well, it's none too fresh smelling in here."

Magda nodded mutely while Chiara threw open the shutters and opened the windows, allowing the air, scented with mint that grew close to the ground in Magda's yard, to enter the dimness of the room. Turning to Magda, Chiara asked, "What's going on? You left the bar all in a huff, and then Luciano said you almost collided with him in the *piazza* before racing down an alley, and then you seem to have not left the house in days. Days which, by the look of it, have not found you deep in kitchen projects." Or hygiene, Chiara added to herself, silently.

"Luciano said that? I'm surprised he'd noticed. Drunk as a monkey, that one."

Chiara rolled her eyes as she turned her back to Magda to flutter open a cloth to lay the food on.

"Yes well, it's been a trying time for him."

"You mean because of Isotta and how she's a dead ringer for Giulia?" Magda's eyes brightened, and she leaned forward eagerly.

"Mmm," Chiara answered noncommittally. "In any case, he's been sober when he's come in the bar the past couple of days."

Magda waved the words away with sound of impatience. "Come on, Chiara, we've seen him fall on and off the wagon with dizzying speed."

"Yes, well, as far as I can see, the best predictor of success is how many times one tries. If that's true, this time may well stick."

Magda rolled her eyes. "Oh, Chiara, you really do insist on seeing the best in people don't you?"

Chiara smiled and put the basket away without comment.

Magda seemed to recollect herself and tightened her robe around her, lifting her chin. It is challenging to be haughty in a bathrobe, but Magda was doing an admirable job.

Chiara sighed. "Anyway, I was worried about you. When you ran out—"

"I was fine." Magda answered, tightly.

Chiara narrowed her eyes. Then, food set out, she sat down.

Magda mumbled, "Well, I was."

"Magda. Seriously. I've known you for a lot of years. I don't think I have ever seen you lose your composure, even when your husband disappeared. You bolted out of my bar like someone set your hair on fire."

Magda shuddered, the smell of burning hair suddenly filling her nostrils. She shook her head, forcing herself to stay present.

"Well, Chiara, we may not be what you'd call 'close' but I'd say you know me better than anyone in this closed up backwater of a town."

Chiara stiffened involuntarily. "*Ma dai*, Magda. Santa Lucia is no bustling metropolis, but really . . ."

"There's certainly no value in welcoming strangers, you have to admit that."

Chiara pushed a *cornetto* towards Magda and then took one for herself, pulling off the tip with a satisfying stretch. "Well, that may be true," she conceded. "But you haven't exactly embraced the townspeople either."

"What? How can you say that? You know how hard I work to get people to better themselves and their businesses!"

Chiara pulled off another piece of *cornetto*, revealing the cream within. "I'm not sure I'd exactly call that ingratiating yourself with the townspeople. In any case, my point is, something rattled you in my bar, and I want to make sure there's nothing I can do."

"Oh, yes. Well." Magda cleared her throat. "The amulet, and what you said about mothers. It brought back some memories."

"Where is the amulet? I thought it would be on a chain around your neck or something. You didn't lose it again, did you?"

"No, it's right here." Magda opened her hand to lay the amulet on the table.

Chiara's sharp intake of breath drew Magda's notice to her own hand. The amulet was stuck to her hand by a series of cuts. The blood had welded the metal to her palm and she shook her hand irritably.

"Magda. What is it about that amulet?"

Isotta walked out of the *alimentari*. Luciano breathed to gentle his instinctual stutter at the sight of the woman who looked so like the child he lost. But he had noticed, in watching her, that her eyes, unlike Giulia's, were constantly wary.

He had so wanted to hate her.

Hate the woman who took the place of his daughter. How could she have slid into the spot once reserved for his beautiful girl? Living in the house she once tidied, bedding the man she once cherished, mothering the child she once coddled. It was this last that was the most painful. Every time he saw Isotta with Margherita, a pain clawed his chest so furiously it took all of his prayers for intercession, all of his self-command, to keep from turning toward a bottle of wine for solace.

Margherita herself didn't remember him. The last time he'd held her had been at her mother's funeral, when she'd been barely a year old. She hadn't understood what was happening. She had kept turning toward the back of the church, no doubt waiting for her mother. But her mother was gone. Along with the baby brother or sister that had just taken hold in this world.

He remembered Giulia's face when she told him and his wife about the pregnancy. If her mother hadn't been so ill, Giulia probably would have guarded her secret a bit longer. There had been so many disappointments. But that was Giulia. She wanted to give her mother a lift, and so she shared the news of the pregnancy earlier than she otherwise would have.

She'd been wan with morning sickness and a little daunted at the prospect of mothering a toddler and a newborn, but two children was far more than she had dared hope for just a few years before, so she waved off her discomfort with her usual grace and cheer. He'd wanted to make her a bowl of pasta with olive oil to help with the nausea, but she'd laughed that Anna had forced her to keep a cup of tea in her hand for the same purpose. Luciano had startled at this. To own the truth, he'd always suspected Massimo's mother resented the presence of another woman in her home.

Massimo had at times seemed to harbor that same resentment, but when the couple sat on the sofa, hands clasped, and shared their news, he, too, had been thrilled. Massimo treated Giulia like she was the Madonna herself. Careful, tender, his hand always on her to steady her. Her first pregnancy he'd been the same, but this time seemed more striking.

Boy or girl, they never found out. Giulia drowned the very afternoon she shared the news with her parents.

Now there was this stranger walking through Santa Lucia with Margherita on her hip and a proprietary smile of affection for Luciano's granddaughter.

Yes, Luciano wanted to hate her.

But watching her as he had, soberly, he'd realized that she wasn't a bad person. She had a ready, if shy, smile for everyone. When Margherita misbehaved, she didn't lose her temper; rather she got on her knees and spoke firmly but lovingly to the child. When they went to the park, Isotta's laughter as she pushed Margherita on the swing was as light and joyous as his granddaughter's. Luciano had seen Isotta rush to catch up with Bea stumbling on the cobblestones. He'd watched her hand over money for her groceries, down to the cent, even before Giovanni had finished ringing up her purchases. He'd seen her pause and smile in pleasure at the sight of Edo strolling beside his student Kamal, pointing out objects and naming them slowly in Italian.

Through all this watching, he learned enough about Isotta to wonder—did she have any idea at all about the role she had slipped into?

Their lingering goodnight kiss was interrupted when Chiara realized they were being watched.

She jerked back and looked down the alley with a gasp.

Fabrizio startled, "What is it?"

Laughing Chiara said, "Sorry, nothing, it's just Carosello."

"Carosello?"

"You haven't met Carosello? I'd call him over to introduce you, but he's either deaf or utterly unbiddable. See? Down there?" Chiara pointed and Fabrizio peered into the darkness and saw a dim beige shape.

"That dog?"

"Yes, sorry. I guess I felt his stare. It's okay, look he's leaving now." With a resigned wave of his tail, the dog was trotting into the darkness.

Fabrizio turned her head with his fingertips, "Hey, so, as we were?" He leaned toward her.

Chiara ducked her chin and said, "No, I actually better get back. I open tomorrow early and there's a lot to do before the *sagra* on Friday."

Fabrizio pulled her closer, "At the *sagra*, do you think we can take this thing—you and me—out for a spin in the open?"

Chiara shifted her weight, "You mean—"

"Yes," he breathed.

"Oh, I don't know about that."

"C'mon, Chiara, I know you don't care what people think about us. And anyway, we're not doing anything wrong."

Chiara looked away.

"Chiara?"

"I don't think that's a good idea."

"Why?"

"I just don't feel like inviting a lot of conversation."

"Chiara, if you feel even a little bit of what I feel when we're together, you know this is going to have to come out sooner or later."

"Look, you have to know what people say about you. Nobody knows who you are. I don't even know who you are."

"Yes. You do."

"Fabrizio, what are you doing here? Why the secrecy?"

"I'm not ready—"

"Well, then, neither am I."

"Listen, I could lie about it, Chiara, but I don't want to do that. And what I'm doing here has nothing to do with who I am. Not really."

Chiara laughed mirthlessly. "Look, there's no sense in being open about our relationship or whatever you want to call it—"

"Relationship works for me."

"—If we can't be open about who we are to each other."

"I promise, there's not much I haven't told you."

"Well, maybe there are things I haven't told you."

"Like what?" Fabrizio asked, frowning.

"Never mind. Forget it."

"No, tell me."

"You tell me. Why are you here?"

Fabrizio stared at the wall above Chiara's head.

She sighed. "Look, this was futile. I never should have pretended I could do this. I can't. I'm sorry."

Chiara stepped away from the wall under the Madonna, nestled in her blue niche. Chiara's hand instinctively reached to touch the hem of the stone gown, but she focused on walking away, into the darkened bar. Prayers would wait until tomorrow.

"Chiara, please. What are you doing?"

"Not this, I can't do this anymore. It was fun, it was. But it's not going to work. I knew it wouldn't. I was a fool to try."

"Chiara!"

She walked into Bar Birbo and locked the door.

Isotta entered the bedroom, and paused to ask Massimo, "Shall I turn off the lights?"

Massimo didn't look up from the magazine he was flipping through. "No, I want to read a bit longer."

Isotta bit her lip, her hand hesitating around the light switch, before climbing into the bed. She lay on top of the covers and darted a look at Massimo.

He turned the page with a crackling sound.

Isotta considered getting under the covers. After all, the room was chilly and her arms were speckled with goosebumps (hardly sexy). But she needed Massimo to see her.

Or at least what she was wearing.

How they had fought about that negligee.

He had given it to her a few days ago, wrapped with a large bow. The grin when he handed it to her had made her hopes soar.

"What's this for?" she asked.

"I saw it and thought of you." Massimo answered.

Isotta felt a rush of warmth released in her chest, and the tears she hadn't even known were building rise to behind her eyes. It wasn't until that moment that she realized she had begun to doubt Massimo's love for her. When she spoke, she often noticed him gritting his teeth, as if he found her voice grating.

Wasn't this gift proof of his adoration, though perhaps mercurial, had not evaporated? Her relief had wilted the tension in her shoulders.

"What is it?" Massimo asked, frowning.

"Nothing! Nothing! Just . . . I'm really touched."

Massimo had grinned. "Well, open it then, darling."

Isotta had carefully unwrapped the box, taking as long as she could to savor the feeling of expectation. She'd lifted the lid of the box, folded back the sheer tissue paper to reveal a black negligee.

Unsure of how to respond, Isotta simply took it out of the box and held it up by the straps. The style was dated and the color was wrong. When did she ever, *ever* wear black? Hadn't she even told Massimo, during one of their voluble conversations over heady wine at l'Ora Durata that her mother, who always wore black, was so dour, that as a child, Isotta had decided that her mother's bitterness was a direct result of wearing black? And that she'd resolved to never wear it herself? Yes, she had told him that because then he'd asked how she'd gotten a job, never wearing black, and she'd grinned and told him that that's why God made brown tweed. They'd laughed, she remembered, and she'd admitted that even after she learned about superstition and realized that nothing bad would happen to her if she wore black, she just couldn't bring herself to wear it.

Isotta had wondered what to say, as she'd continued holding up the negligee. It even smelled odd. Musty. Scrabbling to find a place to land her voice, she ventured, "Massimo, I don't know what to say."

"It's beautiful isn't it? I thought it would really shape your body. Put it on, I want to see it on you."

Without meaning to, Isotta quickly shook her head.

Massimo narrowed his eyes. "What's the problem? Margherita is sound asleep. I checked on her myself."

"It's not that."

"Then what is it, pray tell." Massimo's voice hardened.

Isottta grabbed his hand and brought it to her chest. "Don't be mad, please. I just . . . It's just . . . it's black."

"So? Black is sexy."

"Not to me." The words had shot out of her, and instantly Isotta wished she could recall them.

"If black is good enough for other women, why shouldn't it be good enough for you?"

Isotta whispered, "I told you why. Remember?"

Massimo shook his hand free of Isotta's and waved her off. "Oh, come off it, Isotta. Don't be so neurotic."

The tears sprang to Isotta's eyes. Massimo sneered, "And being a crybaby won't help. Jesus."

Isotta's breath constricted and she stumbled to answer, "I don't like it."

Massimo let loose a string of invectives, and soon Isotta found herself apologizing, crying, kissing his hands, and promising that she'd wear it. Just not that night. It was too late. Massimo claimed not to care, she was too blotchy and sniffly.

Now here she was, all decked out in this garment that didn't feel like it could ever belong to her. And he was absorbed in his magazine.

Isotta wriggled a little.

Nothing.

Finally, she noticed her lotion on his nightstand. She leaned over him, muttering an apology for reaching. She moved back to her side of the bed, lotion in hand. Without looking to see if he'd noticed, Isotta uncapped the bottle and poured a little of the lotion onto her hands. She rubbed her hands together to warm the cream before bringing her knee up to her chin and smoothing it over her calf in sure, solid strokes. Noticing that Massimo hadn't turned the page, Isotta dared a glance at him from below her lashes. He was staring at her, immobile. She grinned slightly before offering Massimo the bottle, "Would you mind putting some on my shoulders?"

Massimo took the bottle and put a dab on his palm. He moved her hair off of her back with one hand, and started etching the lotion along her shoulder blades with the other. Soon both hands were sliding down her arms, his fingers brushing the sides of her breasts. He kissed the back of her neck and breathed, "You're wearing it."

"Yes."

"You've never looked lovelier. Turn around."

Isotta got on her knees and pivoted toward Massimo, feeling suddenly exposed. He ran a finger down the plunging neckline, loitering at the deepest part. He placed his hands on either side of her face and pulled her toward him, kissing her gently on the lips. But before Isotta could lean into the kiss, Massimo pulled back slightly. Smiling he said, "There's one more thing."

NOVEMBER BEGINS

*M*idnight, and the gibbous moon bloomed over Santa Lucia. The air was flush with pearly light from millions of olive leaves. A soft *pad-pad-pad* echoed as Carosello jogged up the hill, trailing the scent of mint, dust, and pine.

Passing underneath the arch that marked the entry into the village, the dog ignored the ancient stonework stretching high above him. Instead, his steps propelled him onward, past the row of homes standing between the cobblestone street and the valley spread below. He barely glanced at Degas, asleep in a neighbor's pot of hosta. The cat had missed Luciano's call for dinner, and would produce the most wounded of wails in the morning when summoned for breakfast. Pitiful bawling could on occasion produce *mortadella*. Poor Degas would stalk out the door when Luciano, spent from a night of tossing and turning—didn't Isotta deserve more than to be cast as an understudy for a ghost? Was it his job to tell her the truth? Or could he in good conscience stay away from the inevitable debacle—irritably reminded Degas that without electricity, there was no *mortadella* chilling in the refrigerator.

After a few more minutes of languid jogging, Carosello slowed his step at the opening into an alley. He paused, seeming to weigh the advantage of continuing straight or turning right into the narrow lane that led to Via Romana. A sudden peal of laughter pulled him into the alley, where a few old ladies remained on their white plastic chairs, crocheting as they gossiped about romantic beginnings and sensational endings. Their talk stilled for a moment as the dog passed, sniffing for abandoned food leavings. The walls above the old women were checkered with blue windows, where husbands dozed in front of televisions, and dark windows, where grandchildren slept, their thumbs falling out of gaping mouths with gentle overbites.

Carosello exited the alley and turned left down Via Romana. He trotted past classrooms, festooned with drawings of olive trees and wildflowers and grapes taped carefully to the windows. He passed the art studio, shuttered against the night. He passed the butcher shop. Here, the dog snuffled the ground, as Giuseppe often left a little bit of this or that in a styrofoam dish outside the door as an evening treat for the aged dog. There! A tasty morsel. Or what was left after Santa Lucia's wandering cat population had enjoyed their share.

The dog licked his chops, hoping for more down the road. The *rosticceria* often offered a nice variety of delicacies—a bit of mozzarella or even breaded meat cutlets that had gone a bit off.

There was a right hand turn just past the *macelleria*, but Carosello ignored it and kept trotting forward. Had he gone down that cobblestone lane that wound around to shoulder the terraced groves, he would have passed Massimo and Isotta's home. Where Margherita slept the sleep of the blameless, Anna slept the sleep of the vicious, Massimo slept the sleep of the twisted, and Isotta slept not at all. She sat in bed, arms wrapped tightly around her legs, staring out at the sky. Staring without seeing, her turbulent thoughts more magnetic than the moon.

The dog rejected the next turn as well. Those steps led to the deserted castle, where there was so rarely anything to eat. Instead, Carosello pressed on past the *comune*'s salmon-colored walls, bleached now to gray in the starlight. Within those walls stacks of paper, some which had been shuttled from one desk to another for fifty years, patiently waited to be ignored for one day more.

Just past the *comune*, Carosello approached the Madonna, tucked high and out of sight of the one-eyed dog. Even so, as he passed her outstretched hand his steps slowed and his fur prickled. The Madonna's eyes gazed past and through and beyond the dog's journey, radiating an expression of deep love and boundless adoration.

Chiara observed Carosello's stride slow from her window in the apartment above Bar Birbo. She wiped her eyes with a soft handkerchief fringed with threads loosened by years of washing. She sniffed and choked back a sob. By the time she peered back out the window, the dog had jogged out of sight.

He loped through the *piazza* with its trees standing sentinel behind each bench. The rustling leaves of those trees shaded the faces of the old men who gathered here daily to discuss the same things they discussed yesterday. The dog scarcely spared a head turn for the mini-excavator parked at the edge of the *piazza*, finally quiet after a day of sending the sound of breaking concrete throughout the town.

Almost to the edge of Santa Lucia now, Carosello picked up speed. The streets were narrower on this side of town. They stretched and tangled into a warren of pathways. One such stone-lined alley hosted yet another group of old women clustered under a tall arbor of drying grape branches. A larger alley wound back past Bea's chicken yard to the gates that lead up into the terraced *uliveti*, the olive groves, and the walking paths around Santa Lucia.

Another *piazza*, this one smaller, more of a bit of breathing space within the hodgepodge of lanes. At one end stood the Church of San Nicola, where a lone organ player practiced music for Sunday's service before a fresco of the archangel Gabriele kneeling before Mary. His entire audience comprising one grey kitten curled tightly on the front pew. The music swelled, drifting out into the street, where it hushed in reverence.

Carosello arrived at the *rosticceria*, where a tart chalk scent signaled the rising pizza dough. He nosed along the wall until he met with a windfall—a styrofoam tray of meat-stuffed olives, breaded and fried. The dog practically inhaled the *Ascolana* olives. They were a bit stale perhaps, but for his canine sensibilities the aging process enhanced the treat. He licked the tray clean and stood straight, his single eye bright.

He cocked his head toward the groves and without a backward glance, he wound his way through the playground encircled by umbrella pines. The swings danced to unknown music as, down the hill, Elisa counted and recounted her coins. Almost enough. Almost.

Carosello loped through the opening in the playground wall, skirting the cemetery perched in a crevice of the mountain where the wind sings to the ancestors that once walked the streets of Santa Lucia.

As for him, his day had drawn to a close. Nose to the ground, he sniffed until he found his favorite tree. So old the roots lifted out of the soil, creating a hideaway perfect for a satiated, if filthy, dog. Carosello crawled on his belly until he exactly fit his den of root and earth. Turning tightly, he rested his black snout on the stringy buff-colored fur of his haunches.

Lulled by the playful wind murmuring between the leaves and ripening fruit of the olive tree, Carosello drifted to sleep.

Though it was undoubtedly going to be a long day, Isotta was pleased Massimo had suggested heading to the Tuscan coast after their visit with her family. It would decrease the time she had to cope with the prying eyes and cutting remarks of her parents and sisters, and anyway, she was eager to have a jaunt for just her, Massimo, and Margherita.

Anna had been perfectly civil since her callous words in the kitchen, yet Isotta still felt tentative around her. Besides, Isotta hoped, irrelevantly, if this foreshadowing is any indication, that some bonding time might encourage Massimo to forget his unsettling request from the other night. She had told him she would think about it, afraid to spur his displeasure, but she'd spent an alarming amount of time trying not to think about it.

Isotta took heart in watching how Massimo relished this day together. He had turned up the charm with her family, and it seemed to have lingered. While Margherita slumbered strapped into her carseat, he reached for Isotta's hand each time he finished shifting. His thumb ran over her knuckles, smoothing away the anxiety from the last few hours.

As it turned out, nobody had actually criticized her, even tacitly, but she had grown tense waiting for a remark about how worn she looked or how unstylish her dress was or how Margherita didn't respect her as a mother. Well, there they had nothing to remark on. Margherita had her father's capacity for charm and had made the rounds, pausing at each knee in turn, to lean in and babble seriously. Plus, her love for Isotta was readily apparent. In fact, the most satisfying moment from the interminably long lunch was when Isotta returned to the dining room after escaping to catch her breath in the bathroom, and Margherita, shouting in wonder and glee, ran to throw her thin arms around Isotta's knees. Isotta had lifted Margherita up and tucked her into her chest, nuzzling those silky curls. Looking up, she'd seen the surprised faces of her family, and Massimo beaming.

It still caught her off guard, how easily Margherita accepted her as if Isotta were really her mother. But it surprised Isotta just as much how thoroughly the child had melded into her heart—as if they belonged to each other.

Isotta peered back to check on the child.

"She's fine," said Massimo, with a smile.

"I know. It's been a long day, I want her to get a good nap."

"She will. Listen to her breathe, that's a deep sleep."

Isotta placed her right hand over Massimo's, and used her hands to bring his fingers to her lips to kiss them. He grinned, easily.

Isotta impulsively shared her thoughts, "I can't believe how much I love her."

Massimo stiffened. "What do you mean? Why wouldn't you?"

Isotta, suddenly wary at Massimo's change in tone, affected a laugh to sound more casual than she felt. "Well, a few months ago I didn't know she existed and now I can't picture my life without her."

Massimo gritted his teeth before placing his hand back on the gear-shift.

Isotta looked out the window and watched the familiar scenery flash by, wondering what she had said to make Massimo withdraw. Wondering how to fix it.

He seemed to recover his spirits as they pulled into the parking lot. Margherita stretched and murmured, "*Eccoci!*" here we are. She held out her arms for Massimo to unstrap her and once he pulled her out of the car, she lunged at Isotta. Isotta moved swiftly, until the three of them were huddled together, locked in place by the force of Margherita's love. "Mmm," breathed Margherita before shouting at the sight of the ocean and squirming to get down.

Massimo leaned down to let his daughter toddle to the low wall. Though they had no schedule, he drew his arm up to check the time before reaching for Isotta and pulling her to his chest. Slowly, deliberately, he ran his hand up and down her back. He kissed her ear and then lifted her chin with his forefinger to force her to look at him. Her eyes searched his, looking for a key to understand if he'd forgiven her for her inadvertent transgression. Maybe it was reminding him of the loss of Margherita's mother? He smiled and kissed her nose, before taking her hand and moving to help Margherita, who was struggling to throw her little leg over the wall.

Massimo guided his daughter back down and walked her to the opening in the wall that lead to the rustling sea. Yelping, the child chased a lizard into the sea grasses that bordered the wall.

Isotta wanted to ask how long it had been since Margherita had been to the sea, but then realized the last time could well have been the day her mother died, and she loathed to raise the memory. Anyway, she wasn't clear enough on the story to be sure if Margherita was even there that day.

She leaned into Massimo as they followed the child's tiny footprints. He put his arm around her, and let his hand fall to her hip. Isotta felt her heart sink into a place of warmth, the way her body always reacted to her husband's touch. She sighed and put her head on his shoulder, allowing herself to forget the strangeness in the car, and instead focused on the pleasure of his hand sliding up and down her side, his fingers floating to the places he knew made her tremble.

A shriek from Margherita as her feet touched the cold water startled her into alertness.

She rushed to Margherita, urging her to step back from the water, but Massimo pulled her back. "So her shoes get wet. Come here."

Isotta cast one more worried glance at Margherita. Was she fine? The ocean looked calm, and damp shoes could be remedied, as long as Anna never saw them. Her mother-in-law rankled at the oddest things. Like last week, when Isotta wondered aloud if essential oils might soothe Margherita's bug bites. Isotta had spent an hour cleaning up the dry beans Anna had dropped as a spasm seemed to grip her. Isotta hadn't bothered telling Massimo about the incident. She had learned that he did not like to talk about his mother, unless it was to praise her exemplary cooking or grandmotherly skills.

Margherita apparently decided that the water was unpleasant, as she raced back into the bleached grass to search for more lizards.

Massimo drew Isotta down onto the sand beside him, breaking her reverie. "Off season is nice because was have the beach to ourselves, though I do miss the chairs."

"But, Margherita . . ."

"She's fine," Massimo said firmly. He pulled her face toward his own, kissing her lightly, then more firmly. Isotta fought a rising sense of panic. Her mind screamed, "Watch the child!" but Massimo's tongue was nudging her lips open to receive him, and she knew he'd be livid if she didn't allow him to exert his authority. Still, she couldn't quell the feeling that any child needed to be watched near water, especially this one.

Though her thoughts scratched at her heart like a mouse clawing at a wall, her fear of Massimo's reaction kept her silent. He pressed her back against the sand, his hand roaming over her shirt, before sliding underneath it.

What was Massimo thinking? He couldn't possibly be thinking of having sex here? Outside? With his daughter so near the water's edge?

As if hearing her thoughts, Massimo murmured, "Relax, I'm not going to take you here. I just want a taste." Massimo began enumerating where he was going to touch her and where he wanted her hands, his breath getting short and his hands sliding under the waistband of Isotta's jeans until she was worried that he wouldn't wait until they got home.

She ventured, kissing him along the cords of his neck, "Oh, darling, I want you too . . . but Margherita . . . let's just check if she's okay."

Massimo pulled back and said, sharply, "I said she's fine!" He leaned forward again and began to kiss the swell of her breasts, "Now, please, just stop worrying." His mouth became more insistent as his hands moved from stroking her to cupping and practically pinching her, as if he wanted to prove she was real. Isotta opened her eyes, unable to feel aroused. Massimo's face was roving over and under her shirt, oblivious to her lack of response. He shuddered, moaning, as his hands became frenzied and he murmured, "It'll be okay. Let me. Let me make it right, Giulia."

Isotta leapt to her feet. She sputtered, unable to form thoughts, let alone sentences. Massimo scowled and then as the reality of his words hit him, his face collapsed and he turned away from her. Isotta stormed away, scanning the shore. Margherita was no longer among the grasses. Isotta ordered herself to stay focused, to stay upright, as her knees began buckling and her heart skidded recklessly in her ribcage. Margherita, where was Margherita? Isotta forced her jumpy eyes to smoothly scan the water.

There! Margherita's head, surrounded by her favorite pink sweater billowing around her. She'd wandered too far in, or perhaps stumbled on trying to escape the cold water, and unable to find her footing was growing frantic, her mouth filling with water. Isotta rushed into the sea, her eyes fixed on the bobbing splash of rose. The icy coldness of the November Mediterranean created merely a momentary sensation of curiosity as she flung herself forward. A few more leaps and she snatched Margherita out of the water, clutching her firmly against her chest.

Margherita clung to Isotta, the two of them crying as they left a dripping trail out of the water.

Massimo ran to them, his mouth a dark O, his forehead creased with worry. He reached for his daughter, but Isotta twisted her body away from him, holding her more tightly. She whipped her head around to give Massimo a glare of pure steel.

Massimo, for perhaps the first time in his life, blanched.

Magda bustled into Bar Birbo, ignoring Chiara's searching expression.

She'd already admitted too much to that bar-owning busybody. The final straw was Chiara pressing her on the amulet. Next she'd be asking about the box under the bed! No, this was far enough by half. Magda was only glad she had been able to plead a headache and get Chiara out of the house that day. If only the woman would stop looking at her like she was damaged. She wasn't! If anyone was damaged, it was Chiara.

Magda's husband may have gotten himself declared missing in Thailand, but at least the shame wasn't directed at her. No matter what the whispers suggested. No, she was fine. Gustav was an idiot. It was that simple.

Steadfastly examining the bottles of liquor lining the wall, Magda successfully avoided making eye contact with Chiara. Who, frankly, looked distracted anyway. Probably brooding over that gangster. He didn't look like a gangster to her, he moved far too dreamily through town to be a *mafioso*. If he was really involved in organized crime, shouldn't he swagger or at least strut? Then again, who knew? Germans were too civilized a lot to have to wrestle with such questions, and she was no different.

The *espresso* cup clattered down to the saucer and Magda pushed back from the bar to drop a euro onto the copper plate before hustling out and to the *macelleria*.

She pushed the door open with a whoosh, practically colliding with Stella, who was walking out with her bag of paper-wrapped meat. Irritably, Magda waited for Ava, who was asking far too many questions about the provenance of the pork chops. Then the annoying woman—she didn't even have a husband did she? Who was she cooking for?—had the con-summate gall to equivocate for a staggeringly long time between the ages of *pecorino*. It was all Magda could do not to push forward and order for Ava. Finally Ava left, tremulously offering an apologetic smile to Magda who rolled her eyes in response. Come to think of it, why was Ava single? She was attractive enough, at least for an Italian.

No mind, there was work to do.

She sailed up to the counter. "Giuseppe!"

The butcher, who had been rinsing his hands, turned slowly, carefully drying each finger on the towel hung around his waist. Magda could sense him gathering his reserve before he smiled kindly and asked what he could do for her.

Collecting herself, Magda stretched her lips over her teeth in an approximation of a smile before demanding two chicken sausages, a con-tainer of *tartufata* sauce, and her favorite shaved beef mixed with fresh arugula. "Is it fresh?" she asked, as always.

"Of course," Giuseppe answered, as always.

Lifting her jacket from the post by the door, Isotta whispered to Anna, who was washing the lunch dishes, "I'm going to go get those light bulbs before the *ferramenta* closes for *pranzo*. Anything else we need?"

Anna turned off the water, "Margherita's sleeping?"

"Yes, that's why I thought I'd go now. She's hard to follow in the store."

Anna nodded, "Yes, she's become quite a climber. I'll have to get Massimo to bolt back that bookcase." She thought for a moment, "Can you pick up cookies for when she wakes up? The chocolate kind with stars?"

"Sure," Isotta nodded and slipped out the door. She was grateful that the stiff patch between them had dissolved.

You're wondering, of course, how in the world that happened, how the fight between Isotta and Massimo resolved, or if it resolved at all.

Massimo had spent the drive to Santa Lucia apologizing, attempting his native charm by rakishly owning that he couldn't help himself when she was near. Isotta ignored his justification. He added that maybe she shouldn't have worn that green shirt with the plunging neckline. It wasn't all that appropriate for a family lunch anyway.

At this, she'd grown only stonier and kept her vision fixed to the horizon the rest of the drive home. Once they returned to Santa Lucia, and Margherita was bathed and fed and tucked snug into her bed, Massimo had pulled Isotta into the bedroom, ignoring Anna's quizzical stares at the prickliness between the couple. He'd held her hands and apologized in earnest for letting himself get distracted at the water's edge.

Isotta's removed her hands from his. "I heard what you said."

"What did I say?" he smiled weakly.

"You called me Giulia."

"I did not."

"You did."

"That's not true, you misheard."

"You were the one unhinged, not me. I heard you quite clearly."

Massimo silently rubbed his eyes with his fists. He looked so forlorn and childlike, Isotta felt something like pity for him. She turned her head away, staring out the window.

Massimo began speaking slowly. "Okay, you're right, I probably did. There have been many times I have almost said her name and caught myself, so I suppose it should not be a surprise that her name came out when I was least guarded."

Isotta bit her lip and stared at the floor.

Massimo went on, "Look, it's not easy to suddenly have her name be forbidden, when she was part of my life since I was a child. The harder I try not to say her name, the stronger the impulse is to say it. As today would indicate."

Massimo tentatively reached for Isotta's hand. She offered no resistance and he threaded her fingers through his.

Softly, she asked, "Why did you think you couldn't talk about her?"

Massimo thought for a moment. "I judged that it would be in poor taste. That you would be offended."

Isotta sighed. "Why would I be offended? I'm not your first love, it would be ridiculous to pretend I am. She was a huge part of your life. Huge. It actually concerned me that you never mentioned her."

"I thought that was the right thing to do."

"No, being honest is the right thing to do."

"Okay. I'll remember that."

They hadn't spoken any more about it, but he'd held her tenderly the whole night through, like she was made of glass, and when she rose in the morning, Massimo had left her a love note on her pillow. When she had come downstairs for breakfast, Anna, too, had been particularly conciliatory.

She supposed these were the hurdles people had to overcome in any marriage, and her marriage was no doubt complicated by Massimo's loss and their impetuous union. There was bound to be a rocky adjustment period. The air felt so much clearer between them now that she couldn't help an upswell in optimism. It would all be okay. Better than okay.

Door closed gently behind her, Isotta faced the olive groves rising to her right and breathed for a moment, before turning around and walking to Via Romana. Now that the townspeople had grown accustomed to her, Isotta looked forward to her daily outings. Yes, there was still a bit of awkwardness at times, but for the most part, she found the warmth of people whose names she was still learning to be charming. She knew that Fabio, the friendly man who owned the *ferramenta* where she bought oil for the squeaky door and today's light bulbs played the tuba in the local band, and she planned to ask him if there were any upcoming performances she could bring Margherita to. The child loved music.

"*Ciao, micio!*" She greeted a calico cat who yawned and stretched on the neighboring step. The cat purred at the notice and trotted to lunge his head at Isotta's knee. Isotta laughed and scratched him behind his ears. The cat looked up at her with dewy eyes. "Such a sweet kitty," Isotta murmured, before straightening.

"Okay, *micio*, I have to go now."

The cat meowed, as if in assent.

Isotta walked down the alley to Via Romana, the cat trotting at her heels. As she turned the corner, the one-eyed dog loped down the street. The cat hissed and tore away, darting between the legs of an old man Isotta recognized as the one who often sat alone in the *piazza*. Knocked off center, the man lost his balance, and Isotta reached to steady him. He began to thank her and then catching sight of her face, he gasped and pushed her hand off of his arm.

As he backed away, he tripped over an uneven spot in the street, and Isotta once again tried to offer her hand. He regained his balance, but was still staring at her, eyes wide.

"Are you okay, *signore?*"

Th man's mouth worked like a fish gasping for breath.

"*Signore?*"

The man's breath slowed and his face eased. "Yes, yes, I'm sorry. You just startled me there for a moment. That and the cat. And the dog."

"Yes, that was a lot of commotion."

"Well, not just that, but . . . I mean, *allora*, just a temporary startle. I'm fine. I'm more worried about the cat. Yours?"

"No, my neighbor's. But don't worry, he's fine. See there? He's cleaning himself in the *piazza*." Isotta gestured down the street.

The man followed her finger to locate the cat, who was indeed furiously cleaning his tail while steadfastly glaring at the dog who turned down an alley as if on a mission. The man laughed, coughing a little.

"Are you sure you're okay?"

"Yes, yes, I'm an old man, but my heart is good." He thumped on his chest for emphasis.

Isotta studied his eyes, warm and alive, and nodded.

"I'm Isotta," she announced, offering her hand, then instantly regretting this big city gesture in a town where cheek kissing was a more customary first time greeting.

But the man smiled without suspicion and reached easily for her hand.

"I'm Luciano."

Chiara watched as Fabrizio peered into Bar Birbo before nodding in approval at its emptiness. Her mouth compressed into a faltering line as she turned toward the glasses marching predictably across the shelf. She willed him to keep walking.

The door opened. "Chiara, can I speak with you? Privately?"

She sighed. "Edo could back any minute. And I have work to do, besides."

"As I can't ever get you alone, I'll have to take my chances."

Chiara turned away and started unloading clean cups from the dishwasher.

"Chiara? Why can't you look at me?"

"What do you mean?" she answered, carefully stacking the saucers.

Fabrizio grinned despite himself. "Well, for starters. You aren't looking at me."

Chiara sighed and turned around. "What do you want, Fabrizio?" She chided herself for the way her heart skipped a bit as she looked levelly at Fabrizio's face, his eyes pleasantly creased with years spent finding humor in dark corners.

Before she could turn back, Fabrizio clasped her hand. Chiara felt betrayed by the catch in her breath. Why couldn't her body get the message? This was over.

This was over before it started.

"Please, Chiara. Talk to me. How did I offend you? Let me make it up to you?"

"You didn't offend me. But it's no use pretending we can be something when we can't."

Fabrizio absently stroked her clasped hand. "Your words say we can't be something, but your eyes say otherwise."

Chiara breathed deeply, letting her fingers untangle from Fabrizio's before resting them lightly on his chest and returning them to the counter. "There's something I should have told you from the beginning. I don't know, I guess I just thought somebody else would, and I wouldn't have to say the words aloud. Every time you walked in, I searched your face, wondering, does he know? I guess we can thank your natural standoffishness for the little time we had. But it's not fair to you. Whatever secrets you're keeping from me, I should have been honest with you about mine."

"Hey, you're scaring me. You don't have a dead body back there do you?"

Chiara smiled wanly at Fabrizio's attempt to lighten the mood. "No.

But, in some ways that would be easier to explain. And I know I need to—"

The stillness was broken by the opening of the door. Stella strolled in.

Chiara was pleased to see her. Maybe she was as ready as Chiara was to forgive and forget? All the same, Stella's timing couldn't be worse. She approached the bar and stood beside Fabrizio. "*Salve*," she said to him with a languid smile.

Fabrizio startled a bit at this unexpected bit of friendliness, but hesitated for only a moment before he said, "*Salve, signora, come sta?*"

"Oh, you don't need to be so formal with me," Stella assured him before leaning toward Chiara, elbows resting on the bar. "I can't stay, Chiara, Dante needs me. You know, a mayor's wife has so many duties for the *sagra*. I just wanted to pop in and ask if you've heard from your husband lately?"

The door was shoved open again, as Dante ushered in a delegation of visitors. He waved his hand over the group and called to Chiara, "Coffee for everyone, Chiara. *Siamo in fretta*, please hurry, we have a castle garden to organize!"

Elisa slipped the paper underneath her math at the sound of Maestro's footsteps.

He chuckled, "Elisa, you know you are welcome to draw here."

Elisa startled, and then giggled. "Sorry, Maestro. I forgot. It's been awhile since I was here and . . ."

Her voice trailed off, afraid she'd offended her teacher.

Luciano patted her shoulder before sliding the tray of *biscotti* onto the table. "It's okay, Elisa. I know I haven't been—goodness, this is a challenge. I haven't been exactly reasonable lately." Luciano shook his head in mute annoyance at his inability to express himself. "Oh, hang it. I was drinking, and I know that made your life challenging, and I'm sorry."

Elisa blinked, unable to respond.

"Elisa?"

"Oh, yes, sorry Maestro. It's just . . . I don't think I've ever heard an adult apologize before."

Luciano regarded her for a moment before shaking his head. "That, my dear, is a shame. None of us is perfect. We all transgress, no matter our age."

Elisa nodded and dared to add, "It was harder on Fatima than me."

Elisa paused as Fatima herself stepped into the garden, carrying a tray with a teapot and three cups. A beam of light played across the shine of her hair.

"I suspect it was challenging on each of you in your own way. Fatima certainly feels some responsibility for me. But you, I think, need this time even more than she does?"

Luciano didn't elaborate, as Elisa's chewing her lower lip alerted him that he was treading dangerous waters. Instead he called out, "Fatima, dear! Thank you for bringing the tea."

"No trouble."

"I was just apologizing to Elisa for my absence in the last month or so. I imagine it must've been very difficult."

Fatima looked over at Elisa who was nibbling a cookie and cross-hatching a drawing of a persimmon tree, heavy with fruit. Fatima sighed, like a world-weary old woman. Then she began pouring the tea. "Yes, that wasn't so good."

Luciano nodded, chastened. "I really am sorry."

"I know. I'm glad you are better now. I hope . . ."

"You hope, what?"

Fatima handed out the cups and then sat down across from Elisa and Maestro. "I don't want it to happen again."

"It won't."

Elisa looked up. "It won't?"

Maestro's mouth formed a grim line and he repeated, firmly, "It won't."

"How do you know?" Both girls asked in unison, their brown eyes beseeching him in a way that pulled his heart.

"I lit a candle."

The girls looked at each other, was this code for something? What did he mean?

Luciano sighed. How could he explain it? The walks in the groves, once a day, sometimes twice. His thinking sharpening, his memories losing some of their old shame and taking on the patina of silver and sage green. His realization that there was more path open ahead of him.

Fatima queried, "Maestro?"

He shrugged, "I suppose I realized I'm not useless."

"You were never useless!" Fatima countered, hotly.

Luciano reached to wrap her small fist in his hand. "I know that now."

Elisa, nose pressed to paper, asked as she returned to her drawing, carefully scribing another heavy orb, "Luciano?"

"Yes?"

Elisa sat up, regarded her art with a skeptical gaze before putting it down to look at Fatima, helplessly.

Fatima rolled her eyes at her friend. "What Elisa can't say is that we saw you with Massimo's new wife. And we kind of worried that it would make you drink again."

Maestro nodded and pulled the plate toward himself, selecting his favorite cookie filled with apricot. "Yes, I've talked to her several times. And no, it hasn't made me want to drink. That's actually why I'm fairly certain I'm on the other side."

Fatima leaned forward. "What's she like?"

Luciano took a noisy sip of his hot tea, wondering how to answer.

"Maestro?" Elisa ventured.

"*Allora*, when I first saw her, I thought she was my daughter."

Both girls shook their heads, appalled.

"She looks just like her. Actually, now that I know her I don't see it quite as much, but at first . . . it was uncanny."

Fatima chewed a cookie thoughtfully, while Elisa began to crosshatch shadows of the persimmons against the glowing tree.

Finally, Fatima asked, "Maestro? I hope you don't mind my asking . . ."

"Anything, *cara.*"

"What about Margherita?"

Elisa looked up suddenly from her drawing, amazed at her friend's daring.

But Maestro just selected another cookie before answering, "Well, Isotta often has Margherita with her. I was able to play with her at the park yesterday for the first time since Giulia . . . died."

"It's okay," he added in a rush at the matching set of furrowed eyebrows. "I'm okay. It's probably better that I accept this as having happened. Talking about it as if it's real keeps me from feeling the tug of wanting to numb away my life. Anyway, Margherita doesn't remember me, but to play with her again, even as just another old man . . . to help her on the swing, and hear her laugh. Oh, girls, that was something."

Fatima broke off a corner of the cookie and tossed it to a sparrow eyeing her on the fence. "But, Maestro? Does Isotta know who you are? Who your daughter was?"

Elisa added, "And who your granddaughter is?"

Luciano pushed his glasses further onto his nose and took a deep breath. "No. She doesn't. But think it's time she found out."

Massimo

Mamma says she's going to take M to visit her sister in Perugia next week for a few days.

Isotta

Okay. That sounds fine. I'll miss her though.

:)

Will they be back in time for the sagra?

Of course

Good, I'm looking forward to it.

You headed home soon?

Yes, just wrapping things up here.

Did you do it?

Isotta?

???

I'm here. No. Not yet.

We decided

I'm just waiting for the right time.

I don't like waiting.

I know. I'm sorry. Maybe I'll do it when your mom takes M. So I have the house to myself.

It's not like you can keep it a secret.

I know.

So?

It'll just be easier.

For who?

I don't know.

I don't believe you'll really do it

I will I promise.

I'm impatient. Just thinking about it makes me want to leave work now and get into bed with you. You can't even imagine what this will do for us

I get it. I have to go to the store first anyway, so I promise. Within the next couple of days.

That's my girl

...

...

I love you.

Isotta waved merrily as Luciano approached.

"*Ciao*, Luciano!"

"*Ciao, bella*," Luciano wished he'd brought his cane. His balance was better, but the uneven ground was difficult.

Isotta placed her hand on the old man's shoulder, "Are you okay?"

"*Sì, sì*. I've been under the weather for some time. I'm trying to increase my stamina, but it seems like old bodies don't rebound like young bodies do."

Isotta grinned, "Oh, you are still young."

Luciano put his hand to his heart and staggered backward, as Isotta laughed.

Isotta slowed her footsteps to match Luciano's slower pace, "Looks like we had the same idea. These warm days are a call to the mountains, aren't they?"

Luciano smiled, saving his breath.

Brushing a stray olive branch out of their way, Isotta went on, "That's one advantage Santa Lucia has over Firenze. In a city it is such work to breathe clean air."

Luciano asked, "Do you miss Firenze, *cara*?"

"Only when it rains."

Luciano stopped walking in confusion. Isotta hooked her arm through his to continue strolling down the path, "Santa Lucia shuts down when it rains. Everyone stays indoors, there's just nothing to do. In Firenze . . ." Isotta sighed, "the city is always humming. Rainy days are an excuse to duck into a museum or to see a show or, I don't know—explore a cathedral. I've lived in Firenze all my life, and still, every day, I could find something new."

"How about your family. Do you miss them?"

Isotta's arm jerked a little. "Would you judge me terribly if I said not really?"

Luciano clucked, and shook his head before responding, "Not everyone is lucky enough to have a family that deserves to be missed."

Isotta nodded. The two of them walked quietly until she said, "I miss my sisters sometimes. We started getting closer before my marriage. Before that, they were merely the meter stick my mother used to find fault with me."

"Hmm . . . You have a lot of sisters?"

"Four."

"And you weren't close with any of them growing up?"

"No. There is an age difference, and anyway, my sisters are gorgeous."

To Luciano's furrowed eyebrows, Isotta went on, "It's hard to be the shy, plain one in a family of socially gifted, beautiful girls."

"You don't seem plain to me. Or shy."

Isotta pulled his arm closer as she picked her way around a loose scattering of stones. "Well, it's easy to talk to you."

Luciano snorted.

"No, it's true! And anyway, I'm probably less shy nowadays because of Margherita."

"Margherita?"

"Yes. She is so outrageous and engaged with everyone and everything, she keeps me from hiding."

Luciano whispered, "She sounds wonderful."

Isotta grinned, "Oh, she is. I can't believe how much I love her."

Noticing how pale Luciano was, Isotta gestured to a bench up ahead. Luciano nodded, grateful. He said, "I don't mean to keep you from your exercise. You don't need to keep pace with an old man. You are welcome to go ahead."

Patting his hand, Isotta said, "I'm just fine. My mother-in-law took Margherita to visit relatives for a few days. It's nice to be able to sit for no reason."

The two of them surveyed the rooftops below, people passing on the street and clustered in the *piazza*. At the castle, workmen were building a pit for the *cinghiale* roast.

Isotta tipped her face toward the sun and breathed deeply.

Luciano bit his lip, coughed, then was quiet.

Isotta turned to him, "You know what, I've been going on and on, but I don't know anything about you. Do you have children?"

Luciano pulled in a deep breath to quiet his racing heart. Was now the time? He looked directly into Isotta's ethereal eyes. "I had one daughter."

"Had?"

Luciano pushed his glasses back onto his nose before looking away. No, he just couldn't do it.

"It's a story for another time."

As they picked their way along the path, Isotta trailing her fingers through the shimmering olive leaves, Luciano wondered if he could ever tell her. She seemed happy with her life. Was it really his job to ruin that for her? To lay devastation on her doorstep?

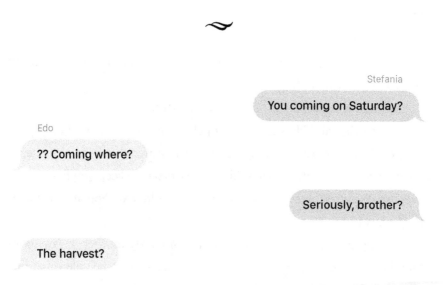

Of course the harvest.

You know you're not being fair to Mamma and Papà.

I'm not being fair? Do you know what they said to me?

Yes, they were angry, but that was months ago and anyway you sure seem to LOVE living with Chiara.

Bitter much?

Look, I had my stint with Chiara too and it was fun, but I moved on, when will you?

Ladies and gentleman, she wonders why I'm not enthusiastic about family time

Okay, Edo, I'm sorry. We just miss you

Seems to me you just miss your scapegoat.

That's not fair

It's certainly not

Not what I meant

I know

Look, I'm figuring stuff out, and I can't do that when I'm constantly being told I'm doing everything wrong.

So that's why you won't leave the bar? Because Chiara is too soft-hearted to ever say a harsh/true word?

she says plenty of harsh and true words. But it's different. Maybe because she believes in me.

And we don't?

Not so I can tell, no

Maybe when you mature a bit you'll understand.

Once again case in point.

...

...

Okay I get that.

Look, I just need some time to feel surer that I'm good enough.

I never meant you're not good enough. I love you.

I know. But you/them-it's always about my hair my music how I don't want to go to college or the right career, how I spend my money, who I'm with

We just want what's best for you.

But how can you know what that is?
I don't even know what that is yet

So what am I supposed to tell them? And you know Angelo is coming up from Naples. He'll want to see his brother, too

Just say I'm working. Or better yet, I'll tell them. That's the truth anyway.

Chiara isn't picking Saturday?

Right after the *sagra?* No way, the bar will still be packed and she'll be wiped, I'll be wiped. We're harvesting her plot next weekend.

Okay. But I do miss you brother.

I miss you, too. I do. I'll call you soon. Maybe by the time the oil is all pressed

You think you'll be ready by then?

Maybe. I think so. I hope so.

Chiara stepped outside into the strengthening morning light. Thank the Madonna the weather was clear and looked to stay that way. A faint breeze brought the scent of bay leaves from a nearby garden, and the swallows were scribing invisible sonnets to the endless blue sky. She smiled. At least it was a perfect day for the *sagra*.

Hefting her boxes higher onto her arms, she ran through her mental list of tasks to prepare the bar for the influx of people who would start trickling in soon, though the festival wouldn't really begin until evening.

As she placed her foot on the first step, she heard a clattering behind her.

"Chiara!"

She was afraid of this. She'd been able to successfully avoid Fabrizio since the day in the bar when she finally revealed her marital status. It had been difficult. Luckily the swelling of Santa Lucia's population in anticipation of the festival meant that Edo didn't wonder why she required his presence beside her so often at the bar.

She paused. Fabrizio caught up and said, "I'm so glad I caught you."

"Yes, well, I have to get this box to the castle and then get back to the bar."

Before Fabrizio could respond, Marcello, gussied up in his dress-day police uniform, jogged down the steps with uncharacteristic lightness. He paused to narrow his eyes at Fabrizio before greeting Chiara, "Beautiful day for the *sagra!*"

"It is. Is Laura well enough?"

"Not quite yet. But I'll fetch her a plate. The medicine must be doing something odd to her digestion, she has an insatiable craving for boar ear. Giuseppe just promised to save one for her. "

Chiara chuckled, "How funny, I seem to remember she was always pestering Giuseppe to save the ear from the *porchetta* when she was pregnant with you. I'm glad she's feeling better."

Marcello nodded and rocked up on the balls of his feet a few times while jingling the keys in his pocket. He looked from Chiara to Fabrizio who gazed levelly at the brass buttons on the police officer's uniform. After a beat, Marcello leaned forward and asked in a lowered voice, "Anything I can help you with here, Chiara?"

"No, I'm fine. Just send my regards to Laura and tell her I'll be by to visit tomorrow."

"Okay, then." After another searching pause, Marcello hurried down the stairs and turned right down Via Romana to the police station in the *piazza*.

Chiara followed him with her eyes before turning to Fabrizio, "Okay, so I hope you enjoy the *sagra*—"

"What? No! Chiara, we have to talk about—"

"We don't have to talk about anything, actually. I've already said too much."

"Here, let me carry some of the boxes. Where are we taking them?"

"To the castle gate."

"Oh, they're light. What is it?" Fabrizio asked as he fell in step beside Chiara.

"*Torta al testo.* I ordered extra from my supplier to serve with the *cinghiale*. It's my contribution to the *sagra*. Sauro at the *forno* can't manage the flatbread, what with all the other bread he has to make."

"That's nice of you."

Chiara shrugged. "You can just put them here."

Fabrizio placed his boxes on top of hers and the two of them straightened to watch the activity in the garden. Men fussed with the fire pit, calling to Giuseppe who was supervising the placement of the *cinghiale* on the spit. Clutches of people bustled about setting up tables with an air of importance. Chiara smiled.

She felt Fabrizio slip his hand into hers and she shook it off, turning away. "I have to get back to the bar. There will be a *sacco di gente* here before we know it."

Fabrizio moved his body in front of Chiara's. Resting his hands on her shoulders he said, softly. "Please. We need to talk."

"So, talk, but quickly. I need to get this over with and move on." She ignored the wounded look in Fabrizio's eyes.

"Chiara, how can you be married?"

She ducked her head, "The usual way I suppose. Fall in love, go to church, say some words."

"You know what I mean. I've never seen you with a man. I asked around. There hasn't been a man around you in years."

"You asked around?" Chiara frowned.

"Casually, Chiara. Not in a way to spread gossip, I promise."

Chiara sighed. "My husband. I haven't seen him in years."

"Where is he?"

"Jail."

"Jail? What happened?"

"I don't want to talk about it. Though I'm surprised people didn't leap to tell you every sordid detail."

"This town loves you, Chiara. They want to keep you safe, from outsiders, from me particularly." His laugh was a short bark. "But I need to know what happened."

"You need to know? But what gives you the right? It's not like you've been so open."

"You're right, I'm sorry. I misspoke. I just want to understand."

"The only thing you need to understand is that there can't be anything between us. We're finished. So drop it. It's not your concern. You're just passing through anyway, and I should've known better than—"

Her voice broke. Fabrizio asked softly, "Known better than what, Chiara?"

Chiara stared at the ground.

Gently, Fabrizio lifted her chin to look in her eyes. "*Cara*, what is it? Why won't you tell me?"

Voice cracking, Chiara said, "I can't. I just can't do . . . any of this. I can't fall for . . . I can't *be* with anyone, and I just can't. It was stupid to pretend." She pressed her hands into her eyes to push back the tears that threatened to rise.

"Hey," Fabrizio soothed, pulling her to him. "It's okay. I know it's okay. I know you well enough to know, if you are married, that marriage must be over. In your heart if not on paper. And if you feel something for me . . . you *do* feel something for me?"

Chiara nodded and pressed her cheek against Fabrizio's chest.

"Then that feeling is good and right."

"But I don't know why you are here, or for how long, and Fabrizio, I don't want to talk about what happened with my husband, but I will tell you that I lived in the dark for too many years. I don't want any more secrets. I want my life lived out loud."

Fabrizio's arms tightened around Chiara and he breathed in her scent of earthy coffee grounds and caramelizing sugar. "I don't want secrets either."

Ava and the other volunteer gardeners had clipped and primped to exhaustion. As a structure, you might find the castle a touch windswept and desolate, with the slumbering vines creeping up the walls, pockmarked with crumbling corners. But somehow the grey and somber edifice rose as a worthy backdrop to Santa Lucia's trademark festival. It elevated the colors in the stands set up throughout the day, and the dour presence of the ancient monolith served as a foil to the musical laughter and drumming cadence of shouted greetings.

The smoke curling into the watery blue sky carried a rich scent, with a touch of crackle. The fire beneath the turning wild pig flickered steadily, and farmers hauled more wood to light under massive black kettles, into which their wives poured wine and sautéed herbed onions and cubed *cinghiale* meat. As the afternoon progressed, countrymen arrived with the iron grills. They loaded the backs of the grills with dry wood that they lit to merry resonance, raking the coals forward to cook the sausages. The snap of the sausages added another layer of scent and sound to the quickening afternoon.

Tables filled. The farmer above town arrived with toys whittled from olive wood. The couple that lived in the plains at the base of Santa Lucia set out their collection of slow-cooked apricot preserves and cherry wine. A group of laughing men arranged literature about the Santa Lucia arm of the communist party. A weathered man from nearby Abruzzo came, as he did every year, with his collection of honey from lime and chestnut trees. A spectacled old woman with a festive shawl settled herself in her seat, her granddaughter beside her, weaving softened branches into baskets. A sprightly young man arrived with his truffle dogs and slabs of *pecorino* flecked with the pungent fungus.

Table after table filled with scarves, tea-colored postcards, rusted cooking implements, baked goods splashed with red liquor and scattered with sugar, bottles of beer flavored with elderflower from the new brewery in Girona, and a display of photographs from festivals past.

As the men and women gossiped and laughed under an amiable ultramarine sky, surrounded on one side by the ancient castle and on the other three sides by their treasured olive groves, not one of them guessed the terror that awaited them.

Elisa sprinted down Via Romana. She couldn't wait to tell Fatima about her math score. A ten! She'd never gotten a *dieci* on a math test before! She pictured her friend's eyes widening in surprise like Luciano's just did.

Plus, it was uncharacteristically warm, a San Martino's summer, and she felt so lucky, she was sure she'd finally be able to get the Moroccan coin into Fatima's pocket when they put their coats on a bench to fetch a square of pizza. As long as she remembered this time, and she felt sure she would.

As Elisa took off her coat in anticipation, she caught sight of the Madonna in the niche. She rushed to it and pressed her fingertips against the stone feet in thanks, breathing a small prayer.

She noticed her heart was as light as her feet. Things were getting better, they really were. Luciano was Luciano again, with the tourists in town she'd nicked enough money to pay Stefano—and this might be last time she needed it, her brothers were talking about taking her with them to their next soccer game, and her mother had found less to criticize. Yes, her life was no longer feeling like a Sunday dress long outgrown.

She rounded the corner to the park. Suddenly, her heart stopped. Fatima was already there. And she was talking to Stefano. Or at least, Stefano was talking to her. Would he tell her friend about their arrangement?

Elisa ran up to Fatima and tried to avoid making eye contact with Stefano. "*Ciao*! Did you just get here? Are you hungry? Getting pizza maybe? Today I'll buy."

Elisa noticed that Fatima had to drag her eyes away from Stefano.

Stefano whooped, "It's little Elisa! Is this *muliana* your friend?"

Elisa glared, "Don't call her that!"

"Why not?" Stefano grinned easily. "She's as dark as an eggplant, aren't you, *marocchina?*"

Elisa put herself between Fatima and Stefano. She lowered her voice, "You stay away from her, Stefano, I mean it."

"Or you'll do what? Tell me, I'm dying to know."

"I'll . . . I'll . . . bite you!"

"Oh, Elisa, don't tease me, I'm likely to take you up on that offer . . ."

Fatima pulled Elisa's hand. "C'mon, Elisa, let's go."

"No! I won't let him talk to you like that."

Stefano leaned toward the girls. "Are you worried I'll like her better than you, Elisa? You don't have to worry. I don't mind skinny girls like you, but I would never touch a muddy one."

Elisa gasped. "How . . . how dare you!"

"It's pretty easy actually. But, I don't have all day. Where's the money?"

Fatima turned toward her friend, her face wrinkled in confusion.

Stefano leered, "Elisa didn't tell you she owes me money? You see I perform certain 'favors' for her. For which she pays me. Not enough, but I'm a charitable guy. So where is it?"

Elisa glared and to Fatima's still face she whispered, "It's okay, I'll explain later."

Her heart beating madly, she plunged her hands into the pockets of her coat, still draped over her arm. She pulled out the fistful of coins. "Here, I counted, that's the rest."

"Like I'd trust you to count correctly, even if you didn't plan to lie to me." Stefano counted out the coins and nodded. "Okay then. Bring me the report card when it comes, and I'll have it back to you the next day. In the meantime, a bit of advice? I wouldn't play with foreigners, Elisa. Their kind hates Catholics. I've heard her family is plotting to blow up the town." Stefano's laugh followed him as he moved up the street.

Elisa collapsed onto the ground, her head in her hands.

Fatima leaned down, "What is it?"

Elisa sobbed into her knees and shook her head.

"Elisa, what did you give him money for?"

Elisa struggled to get the words out between crying breaths, "For . . . failing . . . report . . . cards. He . . . fixes them so my parents don't punish me."

Fatima frowned, "Report cards? But those came today."

Elisa's hands grew icy. "Today, what do you mean today?"

"I mean today. You didn't get yours?"

"I haven't been home, I went to show Maestro my quiz. Today? Are you sure? I thought it would be Friday!"

"It *is* Friday."

"Oh, *noooooooo*," Elisa keened.

Suddenly she bolted up and whipped her arms through the sleeves of her coat, "I have to get home. Maybe she won't have gotten it yet. Maybe she didn't check the mail or maybe she's at the store, yes! I think she said she was going to the store! I'll explain later, Fatima."

"Slow down, Elisa! I don't understand, and anyway, you're dropping things, look here's a coin—"

Fatima held out the coin and then pulled it back and looked more closely at it. Her face grew still. "This is my coin."

Elisa breath was shallow as she closed her eyes and prayed for divine intervention. Where was Santa Maria when she needed her? She opened her eyes, but all the angles were unchanged. And there was no time. If her mother didn't get the report card yet, she was sure to be finding it soon, she had to get there first.

Fatima looked up slowly from the coin clutched in her fingers. Her face was ashen. "I see." She turned and began walking away.

Elisa grabbed Fatima's hand and kissed it. Her face wet with tears, she cried, "I'm sorry, I'm so sorry, Fatima."

Fatima shook her head. "You lied to me. You stole from me."

"Yes . . . no! I didn't know, I didn't mean to, *please*, I'll explain at the *sagra* tonight." She ran off to the edge of town, her colorless hair flying behind her, her treadless sneakers slipping on the cobblestones.

It was strange not to have Margherita swinging on her hand. Though

Isotta missed the prattle of nonsense, she did have to admit she was enjoying the quiet. Her daughter—when would she be able to form her mouth around this word as easily as Massimo did?—would be back later this afternoon for the *sagra*, but in the meantime, Isotta strolled alone through Santa Lucia, watching the town prepare.

She paused at the darkened window of the *macelleria* and the *forno*, closed today in preparation for the celebration. Isotta lingered in front of a poster advertising the *sagra*. Her family back home would no doubt find such goings on unbearably provincial, but she felt proud of Santa Lucia. She knew she hadn't been here that long, and it was only recently that townspeople had stopped staring and instead chatting to her about ordinary things, like the chance of rain and the upcoming U.S. election, but she felt like Santa Lucia belonged to her somehow. She valued the strength she got from those casual exchanges.

Detouring a touch to walk through the *piazza*, Isotta ran her hands against the stone walls, worn smooth by time. She paused to touch the Madonna in the sky-blue niche across from Bar Birbo. Turning, she used the bar's window as a mirror to smooth her hair, fiddling with the front. Since she'd dyed it, it hung differently. She wondered how long it would take to get used to.

As Massimo predicted, it did make her look more sophisticated, but she'd always secretly prided herself on her blond hair. It wasn't common in Italy and was one of her few features she'd never found fault with. But she'd had to concede Massimo's point—she didn't have to look at it as much as he did, and he found her much more attractive with dark hair. It was true that he'd been much more enthusiastic about their lovemaking again. He was tender and joyful, touching her with a reverence she hadn't felt since their first night together in Rome. She just wished she could trust it. His moods darted like dandelion fluff in a windy valley, and she couldn't remember why she ever found that charming.

She shook her head and ignored the ends of her black hair scratching against her cheek. She reminded herself, as her sister extolled, that marriage was about compromise, and that she and Massimo were still so newly one that of course they were still navigating the waters of how to meld together.

A soft voice within her wheedled that maybe what *she* wanted should matter more? Massimo was authoritative, but did that really mean he was always right? It had been her instinct to keep her eye on Margherita on that disastrous day at the beach, her instinct which she'd choked back in favor of Massimo's confident assurances. And who had been right? She had.

The whole scenario made her queasy whenever she thought about it, which was more often than she wished. Beyond the bone-chilling memory of being called by his dead wife's name, how could a man who lost his wife to the ocean be cavalier with his daughter anywhere close to the water?

The swings in her thinking were alarming.

She knew she was lucky to have Massimo. She *knew* it. Her mother told her so, her sisters told her so, and besides, it seemed empirically obvious. When had any man given her the time of day before Massimo? She was lucky, unbearably lucky. She couldn't—*shouldn't!*—question him. His approval was everything.

The push and pull within her was increasingly unbearable. Which was why she'd finally capitulated and dyed her hair.

Unfortunately, the change didn't quiet her doubts. And she hated how alarmed the townspeople were by her dark hair. A new hush followed her as she walked, and even Luciano had looked aghast at the change. Eventually, holding onto a stone wall for support, he'd been gallant and complimentary, but it hadn't escaped her that even though he casually invited her over for coffee in his garden, his eyes hadn't left her hair.

She hoped he'd be used to it by now. She was looking forward to visiting with him. Isotta had heard from the nice lady, Chiara, at Bar Birbo that Luciano had once taught in the elementary school. Isotta wanted to ask him if he knew who to contact about volunteering at the *scuola dell'infanzia*. Being with Margherita had made her realize how much she enjoyed children and she liked the idea of being there when Margherita started next year.

Isotta continued down the street, and angled toward the edge of Santa Lucia, to the light-grained door surrounded by wisteria that Luciano had described. She knocked and heard within his quiet response of "*Arrivo!*"

Though Luciano's eyes did travel spontaneously to her hairline, he otherwise greeted her without a trace of astonishment.

She kissed his weathered cheeks and followed him to the garden, where a *moka*, cups, and a cloth-covered tray waited on the table. Such a gentleman, she thought, glad again of their burgeoning friendship.

"What a lovely view you have!" Isotta said, gesturing to the expanse stretching before her, edged with verdant hills and a lacework of distant snow-covered mountains. Luciano smiled, "Yes, I enjoy it even on chilly days, like today. I hope you don't mind sitting outside. My house is rather dim, and I prefer sunshine, even when it's cold."

Isotta smiled, and patted her jacket. "I'm the same. Anyway, I've got the *sangue bollente*, hot blood, you know."

Luciano gestured for Isotta to sit down and then he took a seat across from her. He poured coffee into each of the two cups, and when Isotta didn't immediately reach for hers he said, "It's not as good as Chiara's, I'm afraid. I have never really gotten the knack."

Isotta said, "I'm sure it's delicious. But my stomach is feeling off today. I drank milk to finish the bottle this morning, and milk never agrees with me."

Luciano's silver-threaded eyebrows bent in concern, "Would you prefer *orzo?* I have some. I often take it when I have indigestion."

"No, please, this is fine. I'm sure I'll drink the coffee in a little bit."

Luciano smiled slightly, looking as if the effort pained him. Isotta's eyes moved to the tray, wondering if Luciano was going to offer her a *cornetto* from under the napkin. She hoped not. The idea of any pastry made her queasy, and she didn't want to reject anything else. Instead, he closed his eyes and kneaded his forehead.

"Luciano? Are you okay?"

"Yes. I'm just ... no, actually. I'm afraid I have something to tell you that will pain the both of us."

"What do you mean, what is it?" Isotta sat up straighter, and felt her breath catch.

"It is hard to begin." Luciano closed his eyes and drew a deep intake of breath. He ran his hands over the tablecloth until his fingertips buzzed, and then he nodded and looked searchingly into Isotta's eyes. "You know that Massimo has been married before?"

"Yes, of course. To Margherita's mother." Isotta sighed in relief. It was very sweet and protective of the old man to be worried about her not knowing this. But—that couldn't be the painful news, could it? Obviously she'd have to have known that she wasn't Massimo's first wife.

"Yes, to Giulia." Luciano chewed his lower lip and then continued, "Giulia was my daughter."

"She was? Oh, I'm so sorry you lost your daughter. I can't imagine how hard that must be."

Luciano watched Isotta, an expression of gentle sadness in his eyes.

She frowned. "But, *aspetta.* That means you are Margherita's grandfather."

Luciano slowly nodded.

Eyes narrowing Isotta asked, "How could I not know this? Why did no one tell me? Why didn't *you* tell me? I've been going on and on about my family, and you are a part of that family?"

"*Allora*, when Giulia died, my grief ... it was an abyss both impossible and uninteresting to explain. Then, soon after I lost my daughter, my wife passed away. A double loss. I didn't deal with it well. I shut myself away. Truth be told, I drank. Too much."

The chokehold around Isotta's heart loosened, as she remembered her first glimpses of Luciano, his lost eyes and his rumpled suit. "I understand. I mean, I can't really understand, that much sadness is hard to even imagine. But of course, grief would create a wall between you and the family. I'm happy to build a relationship back, I'm sure Margherita would love to know you as her grandfather and—"

"No." Luciano held out a hand to forestall her. "I apologize, I don't mean to be short. But I'm not asking anything of you. Quite the opposite, I fear."

He took a breath, trying not to look at Isotta's face, devoid of color now as she waited.

"Have you by chance seen any photos of Giulia?"

"No. Why?"

Luciano took the towel off the tray to reveal a picture frame. Slowly he picked up the frame and handed it to Isotta. "I believe it is time you see this."

Isotta, her face twisted in confusion, took the photo. It was scratched and there was no glass in the frame. "But, that's me. That's me and Massimo, when was this taken?"

"No, *cara*," Luciano said gently, "That's my daughter. That's Giulia."

At the ringing shut of the empty mailbox, the front door flew open. Elisa's hands shielded her face. Her mother scanned the street to see who was watching, nodded at the lack of neighbors, and then yanked Elisa indoors by the shirt.

"WHAT IS THIS?" Concetta began, snapping a piece of paper that Elisa assumed was her report card.

Elisa closed her eyes and cried, wildly shaking her head back and forth and moaning, "*Noooooooo . . .*"

"I TOLD you, Elisa! I TOLD YOU. But you are such a DIMWIT apparently you didn't even understand my very simple 'YOU MUST NOT FAIL'!"

Elisa crumpled onto the floor as Guido ran into the room. "What's going on? I have a test tomorrow I need to study for—"

"Tell that to your waste of a sister who can't even pass her idiotic classes! She FAILED. FAILED MATH." Concetta collapsed onto the couch across from Elisa. Arms clasped between her legs she raised her eyes to her son. "What are we going to do . . . your father . . . I can't, Guido, I can't . . ."

Guido crouched beside Elisa and put his arm around her, which only made her howl harder. "I'm sorry, Mamma! I'm sorry! I'm doing better, I am! Look!" She clutched at her backpack, her sweaty fingers flying off the zipper until she wiped her hand on her shirt and tried again. "*Guarda*, Mamma? See? *Dieci!* I got full marks, and the one before this I got an eight! It's getting better. I'm working, I'm trying!"

Guido took the test from Elisa. "Wow, nice job Elisa. Is this what you were studying for all weekend?"

Elisa sniffed and nodded.

"And no doodles! You must have been very focused."

Elisa knew her brother was teasing her to make her smile, she only sagged against him. "I just needed help. I have help now, I'm doing better."

Concetta narrowed her eyes. "Help? What do you mean, 'help'?"

"A tutor, I was getting tutored, I told you . . ."

"You never did."

"I did! I did!"

"We have no money for a tutor. How are you paying this miracle worker?"

Guido interrupted. "Mamma, stop talking to Elisa like that. If her grades are improving, she won't be held back."

"But *now*, Guido. What do I tell your father?"

"What do you tell me about what?" The square of draining light behind the figure at the threshold disappeared as Elisa's father shut the door.

Isotta ran through the street, desperate to get back to her house.

She hadn't been able to stay at Luciano's for even a minute after he had shown her the photograph. One look at Massimo gazing adoringly at a woman who looked like she could be Isotta's twin had been enough to turn her insides to water. Everything about the last two months clicked into a new pattern. Massimo's sudden interest, his insistence on their rapid marriage and her taking up the mantle of Margherita's mother. Margherita . . . is this why the child bonded with her so quickly? Did Massimo marry her just to give his daughter back the mother she'd lost too early? So that they could both avoid grieving a past that couldn't ever be changed?

She couldn't think, she couldn't think. He had to be wrong—that photo, it must have been manipulated. Luciano seemed like a befuddled, harmless man, but maybe this was all some scam, some trick. Someone helped him, doctored the photo. Maybe he was angry that she was with Margherita when his own stupid drinking had denied him that privilege.

Finally, her front door. She wrenched the doorknob and shoved the door open, slamming it behind her and rushing to her room.

But it didn't feel like her room. It felt like the room of a fiction, a story. A story that was distorted and grainy, and only getting more so as the minutes ticked by. There was nothing here. And Anna could be home with Margherita at any moment.

She spun on her heel and strode down the hallway into Anna's room. Flicking on the light, her eyes cast around for a likely place in which to hide . . . there! A chest, covered with a blanket. Shaking off propriety, Isotta flung off the blanket and flipped up the metal clasps on either side of the trunk. The lid was heavy, but she flung it upward.

Inside, scrapbooks, photographs, pieces of paper. Isotta lifted out a photo album and quickly turned the pages, scanning for an image of herself. Nothing, these were of Massimo's youth. So was the next. And the next. And the next. How many homages did one boy need? Isotta lifted out a stack of Massimo's old schoolwork and a box of awards. Yes, yes, her husband was a shining star. Her stomach lurched in anger.

Isotta's fingers brushed bare wood and she scooped up a final handful of report cards. Could this be all? She'd been so sure she'd find something here. The house was small and Massimo could hardly hide anything in their room or the living room. Did he destroy all evidence of Giulia?

Sitting back on her ankles, Isotta noticed that the inside base of the chest was almost a foot higher than the ancient wood floor she sat on.

A false bottom?

She dug her fingers in the crevice between the wood and the sides of the trunk and began to tug. The floor of the trunk lifted slightly before slamming back down. Isotta spent the next few minutes moving her fingers around the edge of the panel of wood. She mindlessly ripped off a snagged nail, and was heedless of her fingertips now scraped raw.

Isotta panted in frustration. Each side of the panel moved, but not enough. She cast her eyes around the room, looking for a tool. The fireplace! She leapt up and raced to the kitchen, snatching up the iron poker. At first she tried to use it to lever the side of the panel upwards, but then in a fit of fury, she slammed the poker down into the wood. It splintered.

Isotta whooped, and continued slamming the poker down into the place of give on the left hand side of the trunk. The wood split, then broke. She pulled at the pieces, snapping them where necessary, until she was able to get a hold of the panel from the sides of the hole she'd made and lift straight up. She threw the wood across the room and kneeled back down.

What was that sound? Anna and Margherita returning? How would she explain . . .

No, it was just neighbors passing, talking loudly. Quickly now, aware of the danger of being interrupted, Isotta brushed the debris off the top album and lifted it out of the chest. She breathed in and out, trying to slow her heart which seemed in danger of beating a path right out of her body. Isotta sat cross-legged and opened the cover. Instantly, she lost all the breath she'd fought to regain. It was a photo of Massimo and Giulia on their wedding day. The clear plastic page made a screaming sound as Isotta opened it to unstick the photo. She held it up close, staring at the woman's features. No, not quite the same face. Not exactly. But enough to be eerie. And the look on Giulia's face, she was sure she herself looked that besotted with Massimo on her wedding day.

An image, a memory, loomed—of the townspeople's faces as she walked to the church. Of course. It's not that they were ignorant country dwellers who couldn't tolerate a stranger. They thought the dead had risen. Isotta reached up to shove her hair back from her forehead. With her fingers on the shadow-hued lock, she started to moan. Clutching the photograph to her chest she rolled on the floor and unleashed the sobbing that had been waiting for release.

Isotta's stomach lurched, and she ran for the bathroom.

At the knock on the door, Luciano looked up from the spread of papers he was using to make a worksheet for Elisa.

He called, "*Arrivo.*" His limbs were creaking, probably from the stress of the day. He couldn't get Isotta's shattered face out of his mind—how it looked like a collapsed shell of a balloon that let go of all its air and all its color.

He opened the door to find Isotta.

Quickly, he held the door wider and moved to the side to allow her entry.

She strode in, suitcase in hand. "I can't stay there any longer, Luciano, I just can't. Massimo will be getting home from work soon, and Anna will be back with Margherita and the thought of seeing them both after this."

Isotta dropped her suitcase and then let her head fall into her hands,

"I don't know what to do. I'm sorry I ran out. I just didn't want to believe it was all a lie."

Luciano put his arm around Isotta and led her to the couch. He said nothing while she sobbed against his shoulder.

Minutes passed. Finally, the sobs subsided and she sniffed, "I'm sorry."

"Believe me, of all the things you could be feeling right now, apologetic should not be one of them."

"I hate dumping my problems on you."

"Considering I'm the reason you are in this condition, I can think of no better place for you to 'dump' your problems, as you so eloquently put it."

Isotta pulled back and wiped her eyes. "No. You didn't cause this. It was Massimo." Her lip shook and she dropped her head in her hands, "Plus, of course how stupid I am. Stupid! I should have known he couldn't love me unless there was something wrong with him." Isotta began crying again, but this time, Luciano shook her shoulder.

"*Allora.* Please, listen to me. This is not about you. Massimo is charming. I happen to know, he also charmed my daughter. Many was the time I found him repugnant, the way he treated her, the way he talked to her like she was an annoying child, rather than a light on this earth . . ." Luciano shook his head to clear it of the memories, "but Giulia, she could never see anything but good in him. As you were charmed, so was she. He can be hard to resist."

"Luciano, do you think . . . ? Massimo always acted so strange when he talked about Giulia's death." Isotta's thoughts darted back to the water's edge. "Not just sad but . . . something else. Sometimes cold, sometimes angry, and sometimes . . . well . . . almost ashamed." Isotta couldn't believe she was even asking this, so she hurried forward to finish the thought. "Do you think? Could he have had anything to do with Giulia's death?"

It is quite probable that you, like many in Santa Lucia, have been wondering the same.

He sighed, "Oh, *dolcezza,* my sweet. What a question. The thought occurred to me, I admit. I pored over the lab report that found nothing but a few elevated chemicals in her bloodstream. But I just can't believe that of him. Even snakes have their limits. And I do think he loved her in his way. She certainly worked hard to never disappoint or anger him, it's hard to imagine what would prompt him to violate his humanity."

Perhaps this quells your curiosity, and perhaps not.

Isotta nodded. "Luciano? Can I stay here tonight? The last train to Florence has already left Girona, and anyway, I need time to figure out what to tell my parents. I don't have a place to go."

"Of course. Of course. As long as you like. Does Massimo know you're here?"

"No. He doesn't even know I know you, so he won't come looking for me here. And I turned the ringer off my phone. I can't think about him right now. He'll figure out I left when he sees the mess of photographs all over the floor."

They fell silent.

"All right then. But before you decide to stay, I'm afraid there is one little snag I must mention." Luciano said carefully. "I should tell you that I don't have electricity, so it will be a bit like camping, I'm afraid."

"No power? But why? I have my mobile, I can call the power company for you. I don't know the name because Massimo and Anna always kept me away from the mail, but you probably have the number on an old bill."

"Thank you, *cara*. That's very kind, but I'm afraid the loss of electricity is entirely my own doing. I . . . it's not particularly flattering, but there was quite a period of time where I was unable, or at least, I didn't make myself able, to pay my bills. Power, water, luckily the house has been in my family for generations, or I could have lost my home. I was able to negotiate getting the power back on last month for a bit, but understandably lost the grace of the power company when I failed to honor our agreement."

Luciano turned his head away from Isotta's puzzled expression. She rested a hand on his and said, "I love camping."

"You do?"

"I do. Always have. My parents never took me, but I had aunts in the country that would go several times a year. I'll tell you about it over dinner."

Luciano's smile spread across his face. "*Va bene!* One more thing, I don't have any wine. I find it best not to keep it in the house. The only beverage I can offer you is water from the spigot in the alley."

Isotta waved her hand carelessly, "It's been a trying afternoon. I don't even think I could handle wine. Maybe just some simple pasta?"

"That I can do. Not well, I'm afraid, but I can boil water. Unless you'd like to cook?"

Isotta grinned, "Yes, as a matter of fact. I would love to cook."

"Well?" Carlo tossed his wallet and keys to the sideboard with a loud jangle. "I'm waiting."

Elisa gasped like a fish, and looked from her mother to her father.

Concetta faltered, "Elisa was just telling us about one of her teachers. It's not important. Good day, Carlo? What did your boss say about your taking next weekend off for the boys' soccer game?"

Carlo unfastened the buttons on his cuffs and rolled his sleeves up to the elbows.

Elisa scooted backward and ducked her head against her brother.

Carlo's voice was even as he asked, "Do I look like an idiot? What are you keeping from me?"

Concetta stood and smoothed down the skirt of her dress before gesturing Carlo to follow her into the kitchen. "Here, I'll get you something to eat. Elisa, Guido, why don't the two of you go to the *alimentari* for some *pancetta?* The butcher will be at the *sagra*, but Giovanni should be open a little longer—"

"No. They'll stay here until I know what's going on."

Concetta came back from the kitchen and stood in front of her children. "It's not really a big deal, I just was thrown off guard for a moment right when you walked in."

"Tell me." Carlo moved towards his family who winced in unison.

Elisa took a breath and then said, louder than she meant, "It's my fault, Papà . . . I got a bad grade on my report card, but I'm getting better—"

Guido and Concetta rushed forward in unison, "She is!"

"—And I won't fail now! I figured out how, you see—"

"Fail? You are in danger of failing? Even though you know what shame that will bring to our family?"

Silence.

"Where is this report card?"

Nobody answered, but Carlo caught his wife's defensive glance at the TV. He strode forward and plucked the folded piece of paper to his wife's sharp intake of breath.

"She did fail. She failed math. And her other subjects are awful." He glared accusingly at Concetta, "You were going to keep this from me? So that I could become the laughingstock of the factory?"

"Carlo—"

"Quiet! I'm done with the embarrassment of this child."

"Carlo, please, don't, let's go for a walk before—"

"I'll do what I please, woman. You've had your way for far too long. If it wasn't for your whining, we wouldn't have had this stupid girl in the first place."

"No, please . . ." Concetta collapsed with her arms around her children, crying, "Please, Carlo, don't—"

"I said, SHUT UP! Why don't you ever listen to me? I work all day, and then you think you can tell me when to speak and when to keep silent?"

"I don't, I'm sorry, please, just let the children go out, and then you can say what you want. Do what you want—"

"What I want is this thorn out of my side."

"No! Please! Please, I beg you!"

Carlo turned the report card over and over in his hands, running his fingers along its edge. Elisa tried madly to process what was happening. Her muscles strained to run out of the room. To Fatima's—but no, Fatima wouldn't want her after what happened. To Luciano's. He'd accept her. She had to get out of there, anywhere, even the threshold of San Nicola chapel.

Carlo said softly, "It's time for her to leave."

Elisa recoiled. Could her father read her thoughts?

Concetta stammered, "Leave? Leave where? This is her home, we're her family. She'll do better, show him your math test, Elisa, the one you got a perfect score on. He'll be so proud of you, he will, show him, *show him*, your father will be so proud . . ."

"You'll have to find her father first. Check the *sagra*, he may be there. I never did learn who he was, but maybe you can find him by looking for the man with the same blank expression as this one." He gestured at Elisa.

More silence.

Then a deep keening sound sprung from Concetta's throat, a sound unlike any Elisa had ever heard. Guido pulled Elisa closer. A beat later, Elisa blinked. He . . . wasn't her father?

Concetta sobbed, "You promised! You promised you'd never say anything to her, to anyone . . ."

"You promised raising a third baby would make you happy. Would make you a better wife. Promises can be broken. And I'm tired of raising someone's bastard."

"She's ours, she ours as surely as she was born to us. As surely as our sons."

"Our sons bring us credit."

Elisa pulled her brother's arm, "I don't understand—"

Carlo laughed, "See? A moron. She's an embarrassment. It's time for her to go back where she came from."

"We can't do that! You know that, her mother—"

Guido stopped stroking Elisa's hair away from her forehead. He shot a look at his mother.

Carlo snickered again. "What? Did you think your mother found someone to sleep with when I was at work, and Elisa is the product of an affair? Don't be dense, Guido, I expected more from you. Elisa isn't your sister, not your full sister, not your half-sister. She's nothing to us. You really never figured out why your mother had to go away to have the new baby?"

"You said the baby was twisted and Mamma had to be on bed rest in a special hospital—"

Carlo shook his head in disappointment. "I seriously never thought you believed that. I figured you knew. Your mother couldn't have more children after Matteo and when a man at the factory told us about this pregnant teenage girl, your mother insisted that taking her in would fill the hole we needed in this family. Turns out, she's been nothing but a drain."

Concetta pulled Elisa to her and glared up at Carlo. "Just go, Carlo. You've done enough damage."

"Don't you think we should tell Elisa who her mother is? The father, of course, we'll never know since her mother likely spread her legs for every man in a 100 kilometer range of Santa Lucia. But Elisa can live with her mother—"

Concetta stood up. "Elisa does live with her mother. I *am* her mother, the only mother she knows. It's you that doesn't live here anymore. Get the hell out of this house."

"You can't be serious. We'll get rid of the girl and then we'll have dinner and our lives will go back to normal. When my income only has to stretch to a family of four, and we only have children who bring us honor, we can finally have a happy life. You'll have time to keep the house clean for a change. You'll remember to brush you hair before I get home, put on some make-up. Look like someone worth coming home to. Once she's gone, we won't fight so much because you'll be able to do your wifely duty."

"No! Elisa, Guido, go to the *questura*, tell the police your father is beating your mother."

"I haven't laid a finger on you—"

"Yet. But you will. Now, go Guido, take Elisa, keep her safe. Get Matteo from the playground on your way. I don't want him here for this."

Guido pulled Elisa to standing and they cowered around Carlo, still gritting his teeth as he stared levelly at his wife.

Massimo

WHERE ARE YOU??? 17:35

WHAT DID YOU DO TO MY MOTHER'S ROOM? 17:45

YOU NEED TO COME HOME. NOW. 17:48

Please, Isotta. 17:51

WHERE ARE YOU??? 18:20

Edo skirted away from the table of jeering men. The wine had raised their voices and distorted their manners, and he wanted to stop the rush of shouted insults before it could mar the evening. Which had, up until now, been quite pleasant. It was a warmer day than could usually be counted on in November, a boon since the festival wasn't protected by the walls of the *piazza*.

Everyone appeared to be enjoying the *sagra* more than usual. Edo himself noticed aspects of the festival brought vividly into the foreground. Had the light always been this slanted? Was the scent of popping herb-infused fat always this pervasive? Did the laughter of the townspeople arm in arm with the tourists always ripple into the softening twilight? He wasn't sure, but he had to concede that a festival presided over by a crumbling castle was an inspired idea.

In an effort to preserve this overflowing feeling of good will, Edo went the long way around the tables to refill his plate with wild, earthy, roasted *cinghiale* meat. As he passed a group of tourists, he slowed his steps, playing his favorite game of guessing where the guests were from. He heard one of the women call, "Scott, you've got to try this!" and he chuckled. English. Or Australian? He slowed his steps even more. One of the young men, clean shaven and wearing a blue and white striped sweater that fit snugly over his thin frame was glaring at the table Edo had just passed. A woman in a blue down vest leaned across the table and asked, "What are they saying, Trevor?"

The man, Trevor apparently, shook his head. "I can't catch all of it, the dialect is different than the Roman one, but the men at that table are making fun of someone."

"For what?" The woman craned her neck, looking for someone doing something ridiculous and worth mocking.

"For being gay, as far as I can tell."

"What? You're kidding."

"Nope, not kidding. This is why I couldn't live in a small town like this, no matter how beautiful it is. Full of blooming idiots."

Edo gasped aloud.

Trevor looked up and grinned, "*Salve! Buona sera!*"

Edo looked around to be sure the man was talking to him. He blinked rapidly then muttered, "*Salve.*"

Trevor continued in almost flawless Italian, "Are you from Santa Lucia? Or just passing through?"

Edo took a step out of the darkness, closer to the table lit with candles and the smiling faces of the guests who felt lucky to have stumbled upon this one-of-a-kind traveling experience. He looked around and managed to smile, "I've lived here all my life."

Trevor scooted to the side, making room for Edo. He tucked his chin at the empty seat. "Please, join us."

"Oh, that's okay, I was just getting another plate." He considered, then asked in halting English, "I bring a person something? Some . . . wine maybe?"

The table sighed appreciatively, "Oh, he's so nice! Italians are *so nice!*"

It's true, Edo was quite welcoming, but you must know that to English speakers, anything said in an Italian accent receives bonus points.

Someone piped up, "Can you imagine a Londoner asking a tourist if he could get him anything?" The table roared with laughter.

Edo, who hadn't quite caught the words smiled awkwardly. Trevor touched Edo's hand lightly before saying in Italian. "It's okay. They're just surprised that you would be so welcoming. We live in London, and being welcoming isn't part of our DNA."

Edo nodded, trying to ignore the way his heart flickered as a line of electricity snaked from his hand at the stranger's touch. He started to mutter good evening before moving away, but Trevor reached out again, "Please, we'd love for you to join us."

Edo scanned the faces looking up at him expectantly with a mixture of curiosity and welcome. Definitely no hostility. He smiled at Trevor and nodded. "*Sì,* I'll be right back."

"Luciano! *Luciano!*"

Luciano sighed deeply before turning around to face Massimo.

"*Sì*, Massimo?"

"Where is my wife?"

"Excuse me?"

"My wife! My wife!"

When Luciano didn't answer quickly enough, Massimo moved closer to him, forcing the old man to take a step backward. "She's gone, and I've talked to two different people who said they saw her on your doorstep."

Luciano sighed. The busybodies of Santa Lucia. Even when the alleyways seemed clear, there was always an old woman who may pretend blindness but could spot a hair out of place from across the street and through gauze curtains. Leave it to them to find a way to tell Massimo that his wife had sought refuge at the home of the town drunk.

Only Luciano was not drunk.

And for that he was grateful, because this situation required great facility of mind.

"If you want to speak to Isotta, why not call her?"

Massimo made a low, growling sound. "I tried, she's not answering her phone."

"How odd." Luciano smiled and moved away.

Massimo grabbed his arm. "Look, there may have been a little . . . quarrel . . . that perhaps she took more personally than she should have. You know women, always going off half-cocked at the tiniest problem."

"Actually that's not at all how I would describe my wife. Or my daughter."

Massimo took a half-step back at the mention of his dead wife. "Well, no, Giulia wasn't like that."

"Hmm . . . no. One wonders from what well you draw your ideas about women."

"Oh, come on. Everyone knows how moody and unpredictable women are. I'm hardly making that up."

"As is your privilege," Luciano started to turn away again, but Massimo's hand stayed him.

"Not so fast old man. I want to know where Isotta is now."

"I thought you said you knew?"

"Yes! But I went by your house. No one answered the door!"

"Well, then. That must have been some 'quarrel'."

Massimo's grabbed Luciano's arm. "Stop being coy. I must speak with her."

Luciano's gaze darted around, but the pocket of darkness shielded them from notice. No one even glanced in their direction. "Due respect, Massimo. But if she's not answering your calls or your knock, it sounds like she doesn't want to speak to you."

"Well, like it or not, she's going to have to."

"The thing is, Massimo, she doesn't *have* to do anything. I think that's the place where you've been confused. She's not your puppet, and she's not your toy."

Through clenched teeth, Massimo sneered, "Just what are you implying?"

"Nothing. Forget it." Luciano lifted his arm in an attempt to disentangle it from Massimo's grip. Then he stopped. "Actually, you know what, Massimo? I am going to tell you the thing nobody seems to have the courage to tell you. You are sick. A sick, sick man."

Massimo jeered, "You'll forgive me if I don't take the words of a drunk loser too much to heart. You are hardly the man to judge me, you chose wine over your own granddaughter. What kind of deadbeat does that?"

Luciano's eyes shuttered. "Yes. I did wrong by her, and in that way, I did wrong by my daughter. But here's what I know: At least I am honest with myself about my mistakes, and I evolve and want to make amends to

Margherita. Whereas you seem to think that replacing a dead wife with her physical twin is a perfectly reasonable way to cope. You don't know Isotta. You don't know her at all. Which is too bad, because somehow you happened to convince another wonderful woman to marry you, and now you've destroyed any chance you had to be happy together."

Massimo moved closer to Luciano, his towering physical presence shadowing the smaller man. "First of all, you will never, ever get within ten meters of my daughter. And second of all, how dare you speak to me that way?"

Luciano sighed. "You are stuck, Massimo. You are so stuck you can't even see how stuck you are. How stuck we all know that you are."

Massimo pulled back his right arm, clenching it into a fist just as a spark from the fire landed on a particularly dry patch of hanging wisteria. Fanned by a passing breeze, the vine caught.

Luciano tried to duck, but his reflexes lagged. Massimo's punch landed squarely on his temple. At the impact, Luciano spun wildly, arms flailing, and flew to the ground. His face skidded against the gravel walkway with a sound like tearing cardboard. Luciano struggled to roll over, to protect his face from another blow. An explosion of pain as Massimo kicked the fallen man's thigh. Luciano grunted and tensed for another blow, but none came. He heard Massimo's footsteps moving away, a crunching that faded into the crowd.

Gingerly, Luciano lifted his hand to his head. His fingers came away wet, and he realized the ground beside him was damp with his blood. He staggered into a standing position, wishing for his cane. Meanwhile, a small flame popped and spread, hungrily consuming the deadened vines that laced the castle.

The fire flickered momentarily. Perhaps it would have died out without ever being noticed, as fires so often do, if there'd been even a slight bit of grace. But grace was in short supply in Santa Lucia just then.

A bracing breeze freed yet more sparks from the flames prattling around the roasting *cinghiale*, and they provided reinforcements for the lagging tendrils of fire.

Up above the heads of the chattering crowd, nobody noticed the gathering glow, the heat that was now cackling, gaining momentum, racing up the curlicues of vine and catching on the weathered wood of the arbor. From here it was a simple matter to leap to the straw wine holders arrayed on the table of local wares. It was at this point that the greedy flames were finally noticed.

It was Fabrizio who first spied the flames licking the dry plywood. He had come to the *sagra* impatient to find Chiara, but instead discovered a conflagration that could bring Santa Lucia to her knees.

His gaze held, spellbound, as he choked out the words, "Fire ... *fire* ..."

With herculean effort, he broke the magnetic thrall of the flames consuming the pamphlets. A spray of embers shot into the intensifying breeze. He ripped his vision away and faced the crowd, "Fire! There's a fire! Where is the fire department? Someone call them! Everyone down the steps! Orderly, people, orderly!" He shouted as various screams sounded through the clotted gathering.

The irrelevant part of Fabrizio's brain mulled that this hysteria was probably akin to the pandemonium that chased the people of Pompeii to their deaths. And that one exit would create a bottleneck of people pushing forward to escape. He offered a prayer to the God he had thought he no longer believed in, begging please, please, get everyone out safely. *Where was Chiara?*

Even as he had the thought, the wind whipped the fire into a demonic rainbow above the crowd. It leapt across the castle, into the vines that tethered the rock wall, and fell like a shower onto the dry grass that stretched along the olive groves.

"The trees!" Someone in the crowd shrieked, "The trees!" Whipping off coats, several of the townspeople rushed forward to try to smother the flames even now racing along the hidden roots to the beloved olive groves.

"Ai! It burns! *Help!* My hand!"

"I can't get closer, the fire—"

"There's—oh my God! More, help!"

"Oh, *Madonna!* Another tree! I can't stop it!"

"Help me! HELP!"

"The arbor, watch out! MOVE, everyone, the *arbor!*"

With a snap and a creak the arbor—engulfed now in flames—plunged forward, cleaving the darkness with a trail of fire. It crashed to the ground, the blaze exploding upward. Fabrizio felt a burst of heat on his face. A shriek beside him. Sauro was on fire, tongues of flame spreading up his arm. The baker flung himself to the ground, rolling madly.

All around, people fell like trees or crumpled like paper. Rolling and yelling for water.

Beneath the high-pitched wailing, a bass of footfalls as people scrambled to the stairs.

The townspeople ran erratically around the walls of flames that now created dead ends along the festival grounds.

Fabrizio took off his own coat and rushed toward the rosemary hedge nearest him, already smoldering. "Ah!" He shouted as the fire catapulted to burn his leg. The olive tree burst into flame. No coat could put out this inferno. The groves were in danger of complete annihilation. Was Chiara out there?

"Chiara!" he bellowed, *"Chiara!"*

Magda had left the *sagra* early. Seeing the stupid tourists gabbing with the residents of Santa Lucia when nobody would give her the time of day was too galling. She had stayed long enough to make sure the setup matched her expectations, and to get a heaping plate of *cinghiale*. When she had turned with her plate to face the humming crowds, she suddenly felt ridiculous. Alone, with a plate garishly piled with too much food for one person. Vale, the town handyman, stood and shouted, gesturing for her to join him, a grin lighting his face. Immediately Magda's heartbeat concentrated. She was wanted, valued finally for her tireless work for this wreck of a town. Her smile wavered, but she stood straight and began walking to join him, when she felt Stella brush by her. Stella's plate held mostly pasta with shreds of *porcini* mushrooms, and just a suggestion of *cinghiale*. She practically shimmied as she approached Vale, his smile gaining in warmth as Stella moved close enough for him to casually pull her in by her elbow. Magda stood another moment, unsure. Willing Vale to see her and realize he'd meant for her to join them. But no, his head was lowered with Stella's in conference.

It was indecent.

If she were Dante, she would not put up with it.

Her head whipped around to find the mayor. There he was, standing with Giuseppe slicing one of the *cinghiale*. Dante should be warned. His wife's shameful behavior should be exposed! The mayor was a cuckold! But a soft voice, more of a footfall, really, whispered that being the author of someone's misery would hardly make her feel better. The thought smarted, like a slap. She turned on her heel, and marched down the stairs, tossing her full plate into the trash can.

Back at home, she'd thrown together a can of tuna with a handful of rice salad and parked herself on her garden bench with her plate and a half-glass of wine.

She listened to the sounds of a giddy crowd. Someone had brought an accordion. Cheers greeted the first full notes of music. No one noticed that the person who had been the savior of this whole festival was absent. Nobody. She may as well be invisible.

"Magda?"

A voice called from her garden gate. Magda wiped the stupid tear that was threatening to spill over her lower eyelid.

"Chiara? What is it?"

"There you are! I was looking around the festival for you, but didn't see you, and wondered if you were okay."

"Oh. That was nice of you. But I don't want to take you away from all your millions of fans."

Chiara laughed bitterly. "Can I join you?"

"Sure. No, wait, let me get the wine and bring it out."

"No, no . . . you look so settled and comfortable. I'll grab it. In the kitchen?"

"Yes. Glasses to the left of the sink."

"Okay. I'll be right back."

Magda looked out over the valley, the lights of Girona winking in the distance, not unlike the flickering of firelight. A soft breeze moved the hair curling against the nape of her neck. The gate creaked, announcing Chiara's presence.

"I brought the bottle. In case you needed another glass."

"I'm still on this one, but thank you."

"Of course." Chiara sat down next to Magda with a sigh. Even in the half-light of the garden lamp, Magda thought Chiara looked beautiful. She wished it didn't make her irritable. It was considerate of Chiara to come visit.

"So Magda, you didn't feel up for the *sagra?*"

"No."

"Me neither."

"Why?"

"I don't know. Well, that's a lie. Something . . . happened today. And it brought back a lot of memories. Of my husband."

"You never talk about that."

"What is there to say?"

"I don't know. I'd be furious."

"Are you furious at your husband?"

"Of course I am. When I'm not feeling relieved that I don't have to pretend I care what he thinks anymore. In any case, for all I know he's dead."

Chiara snorted. "Well, I guess our circumstances are different. After all, Francesco didn't disappear in a foreign country. He went to jail for having sex with a prostitute."

"A 13-year-old prostitute."

"Thank you, Magda. I was on the verge of forgetting. How helpful to have that reminder."

"I'm sorry, I didn't mean it as a barb, just that the man was clearly trash. What kind of man lusts after little girls? Who pays those mothers for the privilege of rutting on whores-in-training who want to buy the latest cell phone? Really, I see it as a blessing that that man is out of your life."

"Do you?" Chiara took a breath, and continued, "Because I see it as there must be something deeply wrong with me that my husband would do that."

Magda turned toward Chiara. "Chiara. You can't be serious. You can't possibly see this as your fault?"

"Sometimes I do. I guess when I'm lonely."

"That's just crazy," Magda huffed, conveniently forgetting that in weaker moments, she herself had implicated Chiara. "So all the wives of the other men who got caught as part of that sting, they are all complicit, too?"

"Well, I never thought of that."

"Think about it then."

Chiara mulled quietly, swirling her wine before taking a sip. "No, I would never blame those wives."

"*Esatto!*" Magda said, triumphantly.

A scream cut through the thickening night air.

Magda and Chiara looked at each other, their expressions suddenly twin-like with furrowed eyebrows and gaping mouths.

Chiara stood, "What was that? Somebody excited?"

Magda stood beside her, "No, it can't be. I know what that scream means."

Chiara's head tipped to the side, but before she could ask, Magda answered, steel in her voice, "I grew up in a household that cherished that sound. Someone is terrified."

Magda's heart leapt into her throat and she began bolting toward the sound, repeated now, over and over by more voices, in heightening volumes. Chiara took a moment to grasp what Magda had just revealed and put it together with what she knew of Magda's background and the episode with the amulet. Then she ran, hard on Magda's heels.

As small shouts of surprise gurgled like soap bubbles, popping in the increasing heat, Edo leapt up and addressed the table of tourists. "Don't panic! Everyone form a line. Let's go, now!"

Edo assisted an older woman, disentangling her from the bench and table that were suddenly a knotted maze. He felt momentarily grateful that they were at the edge of the *sagra*, adjacent to the stairs. Fear was nipping at his ankles, and he was desperate to get the tourists out so he could join the townspeople fighting the fire. He held out his arms wide, as if herding spooked livestock, and ushered the group down the steps.

He shouted to be heard above the chaos, "Everyone, go to the *piazza*. Do *not* leave Santa Lucia! The fire department will need a clear road." Edo nodded at Giuseppe who was running into his butcher shop to grab his fire extinguisher. "You'll be safe in the *piazza*. Please, wait there." Seeing the mix of slow or no understanding on the faces of those looking at him, his ribcage clenched, "Trevor, translate? I need to go.

Those groves, they've been there for a thousand years. The soul of Santa Lucia is in those trees . . ."

Trevor nodded quickly. With his booming baritone, he relayed the information both in English and Italian to the assembled tourists, adding that they needed to clear the streets quickly so the townspeople could do their work. He aimed them to the *piazza*, and then snagged Edo's elbow as he fled Bar Birbo and raced up the castle steps, fire extinguisher in hand,.

"Let me help!"

"What? Oh, no, there is nothing, without an extinguisher there is nothing . . ."

"You don't have another one?"

Edo stopped, thinking. He nodded and ran back into the bar, snatching up the fire extinguisher at the door leading to the terrace. His gut tugged, as he thought of Chiara. Where was she? What if she'd gone into one of the open rooms of the castle and was trapped, a wall of flames preventing her escape? His breath grew shallow, and he launched the extinguisher to Trevor. "Let's go!"

The two men joined the gathering group of townspeople rushing up the stairs.

Edo felt a hand close over his wrist and startled. It was Chiara, standing with Magda. "Edo. You're okay." It was a statement.

"*Sì.* You?"

"Yes. I'll get the other one."

"No, I've given it to him."

Chiara's eyes followed Edo's to rest on Trevor, stymied in his attempt to crest the stairs by the wall of bodies moving down the stairs.

There was no time for questions. Chiara nodded, "Be safe."

"I will. You too. Stay out of here, okay, Zia?"

Chiara nodded, her attention caught by Magda's horrified expression as she backed away from the fire-lit steps.

Stella broke away from Vale, mid-kiss. He leaned toward her, his hand between her shoulder blades, bringing her back against his chest. She pulled away. "Vale? Do you hear that?"

"It's nothing, *amore*. Just everyone enjoying the *sagra*." His hands ran down Stella's back, lingering on the welcoming swell of her hips.

"Seriously, Vale."

"Mmm, yes, I'm very serious." Vale nibbled the base of her neck, and allowed his hands to run up her side, to her ample bosom. "I'm taking this very, very seriously." He cupped his hands around her and sighed.

A shout, closer now, stalled his caress. He jerked his head up.

They held their breath, listening.

Stella turned to Vale, "Do you smell smoke?"

"A little, but I always did . . . I think this room was once the kitchen of the castle."

"No, it's different."

Vale inhaled, "Yes, I smell it."

More shrieks cut the air.

Vale straightened, "I'll go check what's going on, you wait here."

"Vale!"

"*Sì?*"

Stella pulled him closer, "Please, be careful."

Vale looked into Stella's eyes, filled with warmth he easily drowned in. He leaned down and lightly touched his lips to hers. She pulled his head down, pressing their mouths together, and her passion enflamed him. No woman, ever, had set his loins trembling like this one. She may be middle-aged and a mother and married to that detestable mayor, but there was a vitality to her that quickened him more than he ever dreamed possible. Though he knew he needed to leave, he almost couldn't remember why. With his tongue he opened her mouth more deeply and drank her in, his hands pulling her up and against him. They were both moaning now, hands searching each other's bodies. Lighting like butterflies, then pressing with increasing fervor.

The voices in the doorway sounded like the memory of a dream. Until Dante's voice bellowed, "Stella! *Vale?*"

The townspeople bore down, fire extinguishers thrust out like armor. Giuseppe quickly located the violently burning thread of flame, shouting for assistance. The heat seared his face as he rushed forward, into the belly of the blaze. He loosed a blast of chemicals from the hose, howling as an ember branded his cheek. Patrizia joined her husband and soon many stood together, dousing the flames. Luigi, the owner of l'Ora Durata—who was so paranoid about fires that he had more than the strictly required number of extinguishers in his *trattoria*—called out to the waiters he'd outfitted. They fanned around Giuseppe, spreading out among the tables and twisted wisteria vines, shouting invectives at the fire. They held their collective breath as the blaze slackened in the face of the onslaught.

Meanwhile Edo and Trevor, along with Giovanni and Sauro, attacked the knots of fire raging within the arms of the olive trees nearest the castle. The flames, which had licked up at the promise of aged olive wood, submitted to the spray and began to falter.

Triumphal shouts rang through the castle garden. The common fist around their internal organs released its hold. It would be okay. Finally it could be okay.

The celebration cut off suddenly as the froth from the fire extinguishers slowed to a trickle. Despair filled the townspeople, they were out of ammunition. *Where were the fire trucks?*

Without the fall of liquid, the fire surged, redoubled. A tree exploded into flame. The one beside it quickly caught, the branches crackling for a moment before fire erupted through the boughs.

It would pain you to notice how the brilliance of the blazing trees made a mockery of the light that characterized Santa Lucia. The towns-people, of course, were spared that particular anguish. They were far too focused on the inferno before them. Every creak and moan of the trees as they shuddered with heat shot through their hearts. Their trees. Their trees were dying.

Just then, a dozen or more townspeople clamored up the stairs, shouting. They ran clumsily, buckets of water weighing down their arm. Shoving their neighbors aside, they rushed toward the trees and threw water at the fire.

"The falls!" they shouted. "More water!"

A brigade quickly formed, townspeople stretching between the trees and the falls, sending water up the stairs, past the castle, and into the groves. This nightmare looked to soon be over.

If only somebody had noticed where else the fire had caught.

A line of fire snaked through the dry grass raked to the side of the castle's clearing. Gaining strength, a burst of flames exploded out over the edge to rain upon the rooftops below. Most of the fire fell upon stone tile and, without fuel to burn, brightened momentarily before withering. But a few of those flames fell upon l'Ora Durata's wooden roof. An accumula-tion of dry leaves prodded the fire into greater strength, until it was robust enough to begin digging into the roof itself.

Unbeknownst to the townspeople desperately protecting the groves in the clearing above, the fire gained a new intensity as it began to devour the antique wood of l'Ora Durata's roof tiles. The flames lost their jittery sparkle and instead grew into long, languid tongues of heat, burning blue into orange like a depraved sunset.

In mere minutes, the flames extended their range, stretching out over the roof line. The roots of the fire began to crawl deeper, creeping down into the joists and beams of the building that had stood on that site since the early 1800's.

Bea—racing back to the castle with a fire extinguisher after shooing her chickens into the area under her house that was once a wine cellar and now functioned as a garden shed—stopped short at the sight of l'Ora Durata's roof alight with flames. She stood, uncharacteristically paralyzed. Bea scanned the nearby rooftops, noting that they were all stone.

From a distance she heard the sound of a siren. She offered up a prayer of thanks that someone had called the fire department. It sounded as if the truck was only now beginning the climb up the mountain, and once it arrived, it wouldn't be able to make its way through the street, would it? Bea lingered on the realization that she'd never thought to wonder how the *vigili del fuoco* would attack a fire on narrow streets.

A snap recalled Bea to the present. She bolted up the stairs to the castle, ignoring the stings of shock to her arthritic knees. Grabbing the first person she saw, she gasped, "L'Ora Durata! Fire!"

The face before her took a moment to register the news, and then turned to the crowd and bellowed, "Quick! To L'Ora Durata! She's on fire!"

Luigi, the owner, had feared this exact situation years ago when he bought the building and noted its uncharacteristic wooden roof. He fell to his knees. He knew he should have listened to his mother's warning about that roof. But no, he'd been so taken by the story of the builder constructing the edifice in the style his brother's Sienese monastery.

Edo yanked Luigi up, "Stop! We'll save it, but we have to move quickly! You there!" He shouted to a clutch of men surrounding the arbor that seemed to now be safe, "Run down to l'Ora Durata and see if you can contain the fire until the *vigili del fuoco* arrive. Take this!" He snatched Bea's extinguisher and flung it to the men. "And we need people here to contain it from above."

The crowd rearranged itself, snaking down the stairs to l'Ora Durata, and whipping toward the edge of the clearing. The men on the ground in front of the *trattoria* aimed their water buckets uselessly at the top windows of the restaurant. The outer walls were moistened, but they were stone anyway, and weren't in danger. Meanwhile, the fire continued down the sides of the inner walls, exploding out in bursts of flame and plaster, rushing over the spray from the one extinguisher the villagers had left.

Edo and his crew had slightly better luck from above, as they began to arrest the fire still spreading along the rooftop.

More townspeople arrived with buckets of water. Suddenly, they all stopped moving, their heads cocked at a distant wailing sound. They heard the siren enter the parking area at the edge of town, and then, remarkably, begin to make its way carefully through the street. But how?

In minutes that passed like hours, the spinning blue light of the fire truck flickered against the walls of Santa Lucia. Mingled shouts of joy and sighs of relief met the sight of the *vigili del fuoco*, who leapt out of their vehicle, which was as tall as the trucks that serviced Girona, but thin and short enough to navigate the streets of Santa Lucia.

The firefighters shoved the townspeople out of the way as they released ladders and attached fire hoses. A hush descended as the firefighters moved quickly to douse the fire in the building before racing up the stairs to assess the damage to the castle and threat to the groves.

"Magda! Where are you going?"

"I'm done with it, Chiara, done with it!"

"With what? Magda, you're scaring me."

Magda stopped abruptly and leaned against the stone wall of the alley. Breathing heavily she gazed up at the starlight, greasy now with smoke billowing from the castle. A sob threatened to choke her. She shook her hand to free herself as Chiara's footsteps staccatoed down the alley to rest beside her.

"Magda?"

"I can't do it anymore Chiara."

Softly, Chiara asked, "Do what?"

"I just can't. I can't fight it anymore."

"What are you talking about?"

Magda breathed deeply before looking up, her eyes shining in the darkness.

"Follow me."

She strode to her house, through the door, gesturing to Chiara to follow. Chiara waited uncertainly in the kitchen, as Magda continued to her room. She came back bearing a cardboard box, a bit larger than a shoe box.

Magda dropped it on the table and sighed, settling herself into a chair.

Chiara said nothing, waiting, hesitant to break the stillness that had descended around Magda.

Finally Magda began. In a whisper, and then gaining strength. "My parents. My parents were not good people. They . . . they were Nazi sympathizers. They hated Jews, but they didn't like much of anyone. Including me." Magda breathed deeply through the tears that welled into her eyes. "They wanted me to be more like them. Strong. But I, I couldn't. And they hated me for it."

Chiara dropped into a chair and put her hand on Magda's arm.

Chiara had a sudden image of Magda, as a little girl in Germany, hiding in the corner so her parents wouldn't beat her for coming second behind a Jewish girl.

Her vision was interrupted by Magda croaking, "It's all my fault."

At first Chiara thought Magda meant it was her fault for losing to a Jewish child, but then realized that image was her own construction. "What do you mean? What's your fault?"

Magda shook her head and waved away Chiara's question.

It hit Chiara like a clap of thunder. "The fire? The fire is your fault?"

Magda said nothing.

"Magda, that's ridiculous."

Chiara remembered that holding the *sagra* at the castle was Magda's idea. That she had browbeat everyone into agreeing with her. "Listen, Magda, the inspector approved the site, nobody could have guessed—"

"I bribed the inspector."

"Ah."

Magda nodded slowly. "Everyone was right about me."

"No, Magda! It was the inspector's job to be forthright. He didn't do his job. You just wanted the *sagra* to be a success."

As Magda stared at her hands clutched on the table, Chiara realized why it was so important for Magda to prove herself valuable.

A tear slid down Magda's cheek. "I ruined the *sagra*, and probably the castle. And all the homes. And the olive trees! And probably the whole town." She finished lamely.

"Let's not get carried away. It sounds like the fire is under control, and anyway, fires have hit the castle before, and it's still standing. Likely all that got damaged was the wisteria and the arbor. It's lucky that Santa Lucia is almost all built from stone."

"What if someone got hurt?"

"No one got hurt. It's okay, we saw everyone leaving, remember?"

Magda choked back a sob, and nodded obediently.

Chiara went on, "So what's in the box?"

Magda blinked back her tears and tucked her hair behind her ears a few times before answering. "My box. It's a box of reminders."

"Reminders?"

"Yes. My parents' things."

"You kept all of this."

"Yes."

"May I?" Chiara asked, indicating the box.

Magda shrugged and pushed it to her. Chiara sifted through photographs of stoic Germans, commendations handwritten on thin vellum, a patch with a symbol that matched the amulet. Chiara held it up, questioningly.

"It's a symbol, a sign among Nazi sympathizers of kindred spirits."

"Magda. Why would you wear that?"

Magda shook her head and wailed. "I don't know! I'm not a Nazi, I swear. What my parents did made me sick. I was an adult before I stopped having stomach aches, and even now it's not quite proper." Magda's hand flitted to her stomach before she shook her head again. "I hated what they did, Chiara. I don't know why I'd wear such a thing."

But Chiara did, or at least she suspected.

"How old were you when you started wearing the amulet?"

"Oh, I don't know. I was a child. The war was essentially over, but my parents' hatred, oh that lasted until their death."

"When did they die?"

"I don't know that either. They escaped Germany when the search for Nazis was heating up. They left me with my aunt in the country. She told me when I was in high school that they had died in a car accident. I think that's when I started wearing the amulet, actually."

Chiara was silent.

Magda mused in wonder, "Maybe that car crash never happened."

Chiara regarded her friend. "You let your parents define what you believe about yourself."

Magda hung her head. "Yes."

"How long are you going to let those people decide who you are?"

"I'm not. Not anymore. I want to get rid of this box. But, without this box, who am I?"

Chiara took Magda's hand. "Well, let's burn that damned box and find out."

Shouts of alarm were replaced with yelps of celebration, the air ringing with relief as the last of the fire was extinguished.

One by one, the townspeople thanked the firefighters, who piled into their cartoonishly proportioned, but heroic, truck, and backed out of Santa Lucia. The villagers dropped their weaponry and flung themselves to the ground around the castle yard. In groups of two and three chatter began, as voices catalogued their burns, the clothes that would never be the same again, the damage to the castle's groves, the impact on the coming year's yield. As runners in a relay, they passed the baton of thanks to the Madonna that the fire hadn't reached their trees.

The loss of the castle *uliveto* was heartbreaking, certainly, but don't people feel their own losses most of all?

As the villagers began brushing themselves off to return home to a well-earned sleep, speculation began churning at the cause of the conflagration.

Giovanni mused, "Such bad luck. The wind must have blown embers up to the vines."

On the far side of the castle yard, a voice answered. "Are you serious? The vines aren't dry enough to catch that way. Someone must have set this fire."

"*What?* That's insane!"

"C'mon, don't be stupid. Plenty of people could have done it."

A chorus of "No way!" echoed as more people realized the conversation in play and the speculation spread. The voices meshed and jammed in the darkness.

The accuser sat up, moonlight illuminating the side of his face. It was Fabio, the tuba player who worked at the hardware store. "Look what happened in Spain just a few weeks ago. You know the African population around here has been rising. You know what they are capable of."

"What? Impossible!" Giovanni retorted. "I know our immigrants. They come into the *alimentari* every day. They would *never* ever do this."

"Then who?" insisted Fabio.

"What do you mean, who? We had a fire out here around dry wood. Whose crazy idea was that?"

A voice next to Fabio muttered loudly, "The German."

Fabio snickered. "Ah, see. Maybe it was her. Maybe she started it. Mrs. Angry."

Giuseppe growled from his position lying down beside Patrizia, "Magda? You think she ruined the pipes in order to convince the mayor to have the *sagra* here just so she could burn it down? What's wrong with you, boy?"

Grumbles.

Fabio went on. "How about those tourists?"

Giuseppe sat up to glare at him. "Which ones? Why would tourists want to burn Santa Lucia?"

"*You* know," Fabio said. He stood and, backlit by the lantern light, he put one arm on his waist while jutting out his hip, and lifting his other hand to dangle his wrist provocatively.

"Fabio, don't be crude," Patrizia chided. She swiveled her head from side to side and startled, seeing Edo standing, rigid, in the moonlight reflecting off the castle wall.

Edo took a beat before pushing past his fellow impromptu fire fighters, headed for the steps. Trevor glared at the townspeople, pausing as if to consider saying something, then setting his jaw and following Edo. Marcello, changed now out of his *vigili* uniform, muttered to himself between gritted teeth before following Edo and Trevor down the stairs and into the bar.

One of the speakers whistled a deescalating swirl, "Nice going, Fabio."

"Well, how was I supposed to know that *finocchio* would be out here fighting the fire?"

The word sailed above the men and women. Innocent enough in the market, when one asks for fennel, here it was not innocent at all. The insult flew, sending shivers through the streaky moonlit air, clouded with smoke that heaved like a live beast.

Patrizia shook her head, "He was one of the first here. Maybe that's why you missed him."

A voice from the left, disengaged by the darkness, "Why would Edo do this, anyway, Fabio?"

"I never said Edo did it! I said *those* people! We all know what they're like. No morals."

"You have known Edo since the two of you were boys." Patrizia countered.

"What did I just say? I'm not accusing Edo, just the other homos."

Patrizia straightened her jacket and smoothed down her skirt. "If you ask me, that makes no sense."

Fabio grunted. "Anyway, okay so maybe it wasn't them. Maybe I was right the first time, and it was the Africans."

A groan rose up from the area closest to the orchard. Giuseppe measured his voice, "It was the wind. Why borrow trouble?"

Grumbling broke out around Fabio, as he raised his voice to be heard. "We have to watch our backs. All kinds of strangers and nutcases make their way through Santa Lucia."

Patrizia stood. "I don't think of our neighbors as nutcases. Or strangers." The cords of her neck tightened as gestured toward her follow villagers, "All of you? Are you listening to this? Is this okay with you?"

Murmuring voices.

Fabio laughed, "You are so naive."

Patrizia stepped to Fabio, slamming the side of her right hand against the palm of her left. "*Vaffanculo.*"

She stormed off to where the arbor once stood.

Giuseppe sat open-mouthed, having never heard Patrizia swear mildly, let alone the mother of all expletives. He leapt up and followed her, hoping she would ignore the guffaws. He caught up to his wife standing at the edge of the castle. She wiped her eyes furiously, and stammered to her husband, "I can't believe they'd say those vile things."

Giuseppe ran his hands up and down his wife's arms. "Hey, it's Fabio. He's alright, but he's quick to anger, and quicker to accuse."

Patrizia faced Giuseppe by the yawning castle doorway, her chin trembling, "I know. But still. When does it stop? And when do other people call him on it? Why is everyone just staying there as if he's right? Why aren't they *moving?*" She gestured angrily at the assembled people sitting, lying, or standing in the dark, continuing to mutter to each other with intermittent chortles and barks of protest.

Giuseppe considered. "I don't know. Maybe they're just tired. Maybe they are scared to disagree. But you know those people, Patrizia, you *know* them. You know there can't be more than one or two that agree with Fabio."

"But those one or two are rotting away the core of our town, like moldering grapes in a wine barrel."

Giuseppe ran a soot-covered hand through his hair.

Patrizia sighed, "Come on, let's go home. We'll stop by Birbo on the way and see if Edo is okay."

As she turned her body, her movement released the moonlight that had been building at her feet. It flowed into the recess of open room and her sight was caught by a blur on the floor. Patrizia stopped suddenly and pointed, her other hand stalling her husband. "Do you see that?"

Giuseppe peered in, and, unsure of what the rumpled shape on the stone floor could be, stepped closer. The hair on the back of his neck prickled. He swept forward, shouting over his shoulder.

"Call an ambulance!"

"Oh my God, Giuseppe. Is that a person?"

"Patrizia, go! Go now! Call an ambulance! No, wait! Get someone to meet me at the bottom of the stairs!"

"Okay, okay." With one last quick glance into the darkness, she ran from the door of the castle.

"Quick! Someone! Help!"

The people assembled on the lawn of the castle rose in unison and turned their heads toward Patrizia.

A voice called from the center of the group, "*Cos'è succede?* What's going on?"

"There's someone. Someone hurt or, or . . ." Patrizia couldn't say the word *dead*, "unconscious, not moving. We need someone to drive to the hospital!"

Sauro the baker stepped forward, "Who is it?"

"I . . . I don't know. Someone small."

"*A child?*" several voices gasped.

"I think so, I don't know. Please, who can drive us?"

Giovanni, his *alimentari* apron charred in places, plunged his hands into his pocket and pulled out his keys. "I can. I left my Ape in the *piazza* in case we needed to haul anything from the shop. I'll get it. Is Giuseppe here?"

"Yes! He's with . . . Please go now! I'll get Giuseppe to bring . . . to meet you at the bottom of the stairs."

Giovanni gave a tight nod and fled down the steps. Instantly, chatter broke out among the group. Conversation fragmented as the silhouette of Giuseppe carrying a bundle appeared at the edge of the clearing. Patrizia gasped and hurried to him. "Stay where you are!" Giuseppe called to the crowd who had begun to press in. He hooked his chin to the right to indicate that Patrizia should come closer. Before she could make out the features of the face nestled against her husband's broad chest, he whispered, "It's Fatima."

Patrizia's knees slid out from under her. She stumbled and regained her balance. "Fatima?" She breathed. "What was she doing here? Her family doesn't come to the *sagra*."

"I know. I was just talking to her mother about it yesterday. The smell of pork turns their stomach."

"But . . ."

"The smoke must have filled the room before she knew what was happening."

"Oh, Madonna, is she okay? Will she be okay?"

"I don't know. She's breathing, but she's not gaining consciousness, even after I poured water on her forehead and hands. Somebody is coming?"

"Yes. Giovanni. He's run to get his Ape, it's parked in the *piazza*."

"Good. I'll meet him, get our car, and drive her to the hospital."

"I want to come with you."

"There won't be room in the Ape, I'll call you when I get to the hospital."

"Giuseppe, what if she . . ."

"Don't say it. Just pray."

"I can't tell the others. You heard them. What if they say she started it, that it's her fault?"

"Nobody who knows Fatima would believe . . ." He couldn't finish the sentence.

"We know that, but those people." Patrizia gestured uselessly to the taut group of watchers straining to hear their whispers.

"I have to go. If they accuse her, we have to trust that it will blow over."

The rattle of the Ape cut through the sound of people milling through the town, aimless now without the *sagra* or the fire to pull them together.

Patrizia nodded, "Go! He's coming." Giuseppe pressed his cheek against his wife's.

"I'll call you."

Blinking hard, Patrizia nodded again. "*Sii con Dio.*"

Giuseppe effortlessly hoisted Fatima a little higher. He strode to the steps, carefully picking his way down while steadying his shoulder against the stone wall. Patrizia watched him walk away and focused on bringing air into her body. She slowly turned back to the castle lawn, filled now with low voices.

Fighting the tears that threatened to overcome her, Patrizia wondered if God could see fit to kill an innocent.

Isotta handed Luciano a cup of warm *camomilla*. He looked up at her candlelit face gratefully, his tense fingers stretching around the warm cup.

"*Grazie.*"

"Of course. Luciano, that sounds horrifying."

"It was. Thank the Madonna it was caught relatively early. When it started, it looked like it would take the groves down. L'Ora Durata was damaged, so of course Luigi is carrying on that this will ruin him. But he's forgetting that insurance will pay for it. Unless he's just looking for a reason to shut down the restaurant. I know it wasn't making him the profit he'd imagined when he moved here, and now with the prospect of repairs, perhaps he's just out of energy." Luciano sighed, "He may feel differently tomorrow. Maybe we all will."

Isotta sank into the chair beside Luciano and sipped her tea. "And nobody was hurt?"

"No. I stayed out of the way, but I was at the bottom of the steps when they called down that the fire was contained, and then over, and nobody was hurt beyond minor burns. Well, a child slipped on the steps in everyone's hurry to leave, but a skinned knee? That feels like a blessing compared to what could have happened."

Poor Luciano. When he finds out . . .

The two of them watched the stars glimmering tentatively from behind the veil of smoke.

Luciano murmured, "It's going to require a lot of cleanup. I'll head over there in the morning."

Isotta nodded, her eyes fixed on a winking star. "I'd like to help. Santa Lucia has come to feel like home. But I don't want to run into . . ."

"No. Of course not. And Isotta, I must tell you. I ran into Massimo."

Isotta's breath caught. "Does he know I'm here? I heard knocking but I didn't know . . ."

"He suspects, yes. We should have counted on the Santa Lucia gossip chain."

She leaned her head back and closed her eyes. "I guess it was only a matter of time. I'll need to leave in the morning."

"If you can stay for breakfast, I have some friends I'd like you to meet."

Isotta turned her head to Luciano. "Friends?"

"Yes, there are two little girls who come over once or twice a week. I tutor Elisa, mostly with math. She's taken to sharing her drawings with me, I think you'd really enjoy them, she has a unique vision. I wonder if that friend of yours you mentioned who teaches at the art school in Florence might be interested in seeing Elisa's work. And Fatima. Well, Fatima is like a dose of *asparina*, she has a knack for relieving tension. You'll like them. Maybe have your send off from Santa Lucia be the kind where you know you're always welcome back."

Tears pricked Isotta's eyes. "Oh, Luciano, it's going to take me some time to figure out how all this happened. How I was so blind for so long. And Margherita. I just don't know."

A banging on the door swallowed Isotta's next words.

"Isotta! I know you're in there! Isotta! Come out!"

Isotta breathed, "Massimo."

Luciano stood, "I'll take care of it."

"No. I don't want you becoming a target. This is my fight. I guess I was stupid to think I could leave without this happening. I'll go."

Isotta stood, and Luciano put a hand on her arm, "Isotta! I believe there's something wrong with him. I didn't tell you everything about what happened earlier tonight. He's not rational."

"He won't hurt me."

To Luciano's uncertain expression, Isotta added, "Okay, well, yes, he's emotionally wounded me, but—"

Luciano said in a rush, "He hit me."

"What?"

"He punched me down, kicked me. I'm telling you, I don't think he's in his right mind."

"Are you hurt?"

"My face is scraped, but I'll be okay."

"Scraped? Luciano, give me the candle, I want to see."

"No, it's fine. Please don't worry over me."

Massimo's voice called out again, "Isotta! Come out! *Isotta!*"

Isotta gave Luciano a searching look, trying to evaluate this wound through the dim light. She bit her lip before standing. "I'm going to go talk to him."

"Isotta, no!"

"I know he won't hurt me."

"How can you be sure?"

Isotta paused and squeezed Luciano's hand before letting go. "Because he couldn't hurt Giulia again."

To Luciano's puzzled expression, Isotta added, "It's okay. I'll be right outside. I'll shout if he lays a hand on me."

Luciano nodded, reluctantly.

She smiled and said weakly, "One way or another, at least it will be done."

She walked through Luciano's house and opened the door, just as Massimo was beginning to pound again. Before he could sidle into the house, Isotta stepped into the street and closed the door behind her with a sharp click.

Massimo, panting heavily, whispered, "You're okay."

"Of course I'm okay."

"The fire. Someone was taken to the hospital, someone . . . small. I was so scared it was you."

"Someone was hurt?" Isotta's mind darted. "Margherita?"

"No, not her. She's with Mamma. They never even made it to the *sagra*. Their train was delayed."

Isotta sagged with relief and leaned against the door. "*Grazie Dio.*" She took a breath and then straightened. "Well, now you know it wasn't me. Goodbye, Massimo."

"Wait! Why aren't you home? You're supposed to be home."

Isotta's laughed with shards of flint, "Supposed to? Come off it, Massimo. I know. I know about Giulia. I know about your perverted game. It's over between us."

"No! You can't mean that! We're married!"

"Marriages end, Massimo. That can't come as a shock to you."

"Not ours, Isotta! We're supposed to be together forever . . . till we . . . till we die."

Isotta's face contorted. "You're delusional."

"But I worked so hard, it felt so right—"

Isotta cried out, "*You* worked hard! I was the idiot who went along with anything you told me. Who believed you. Who let you control every bit of my life. I made it pretty easy for you Massimo. Now is where it gets challenging because you'll have to deal with the truth that Giulia is gone."

"I know she's gone!"

"Well, I'm not going to be her replacement."

"Is that what you think? That you're her replacement?"

"It's the truth. The truth that everyone is this town saw before I did."

"But I didn't . . . I never—"

"Goodbye, Massimo."

"Wait! What about Margherita?"

Isotta turned back from the door. She asked softly, "What about her?"

"She's asking for her mother. What am I supposed to tell her?"

Isotta reminded herself that this was Massimo's way of manipulating her. "You should have thought of that earlier. This is not on me."

"No! Isotta, you're right, I didn't start this for the right reasons, but I love you, I love *you!*" Massimo dropped to his knees in front of Isotta and wrapped his arms around her waist. He pressed his cheek against her and sobbed,"Please, *please* let me prove it to you. We'll start over. We'll start fresh. We'll move out! My mother. My mother pushed me into this. She was mad with grief when Giulia died. She convinced me—"

"You did this Massimo. You did. Only a weak man blames his mother."

"Okay! Yes! It's my fault, but I can make it right. Just tell me what you want, I'll do anything."

Isotta's hands hovered above Massimo's head as she fought the urge to thread her fingers through his hair.

Fabrizio wearily pushed open the door of Bar Birbo.

He stood in the entryway, waiting for Chiara to notice him.

"We're closed," she called over her shoulder, stacking the dishwasher.

"I know."

Chiara whipped around. "Oh. It's you."

"Yes, it's me. I'm sorry for intruding, I just wanted to make sure you were okay. I heard . . ."

"I'm fine. Well, not fine, strictly speaking, but," Chiara spread her arms and noted her clothes streaked with dirt and soot and charred bits of Magda's box. She'd been up all night. "I'll live."

"The girl who was taken to the hospital, someone you know?"

"A little. I've seen her, but she doesn't come in. Fifth graders don't have much need for coffee," Chiara smiled wryly. "But I've watched her. She came to Santa Lucia a couple of years ago, maybe? I can't remember. Luciano took her family under his wing, as he does with immigrants. I know he'd spoken of her with admiration. A sunny child. I hope she's okay." Chiara bit her lower lip and turned away. She ran the water over her hands and said, "But I'm fine. It was nice of you to check."

"Chiara, when the fire started and I couldn't find you—"

"I was with Magda."

"I didn't know. I just knew you had been there, and then you were gone, and I panicked."

Chiara's chin ducked down to her chest. She said nothing, but reached for a towel to dry her hands before slowly turning back to Fabrizio.

He stepped to the counter and reached across to her. Without meaning to, Chiara took his hand. "Fabrizio, I can't—"

"Yes, you can. Because I'm also done with secrets and holding back."

Chiara blinked, confused.

Fabrizio picked up Chiara's hand and kissed it. "I should have told you before Chiara. I'm not just here for vacation."

"I didn't think so." Chiara girded herself. A spy? A land developer? Mafia?

"I'm a writer."

Chiara released his hand, "A *writer?*"

"Yes. Books. I write books," he finished, lamely.

"What kind of books?"

"*Gialli*, mysteries."

"Why didn't you tell me? That doesn't sound like a terrible secret."

"Being a writer isn't, perhaps, but well, I'm here for inspiration. My next book is set in a small town, and I needed space to breathe and concentrate and imagine a life different than mine in Bologna. I just didn't want people acting differently because they knew I was watching them."

"But they did act differently."

"Yes, it took me awhile to realize that. I didn't count on the fact that inserting myself into a small town would change the way people behave. Like a pebble dropped in the ocean may not create any rings, but a pebble dropped in a still, small pond will."

The image struck Chiara, and she wondered—perhaps they were all pebbles, with interlocking waves creating a design beyond her imagining.

Fabrizio squeezed her hand, recalling her to their conversation. "Anyway, talking about my writing usually serves to fade it. It's hard to explain, but the more I talk about my writing, the less I'm able to actually write. I needed to protect that."

Chiara nodded and then startled. "Wait, how do I even know you're telling me the truth?"

"Given how reserved I've been, I figured you may not easily believe me. I know the rumors. People in Santa Lucia don't speak as quietly as they think they do. My favorite theory was that I'm really from Rivaldo, that town in Tuscany that also is big on *cinghiale*, and I was here to steal secrets about what makes Santa Lucia's *sagra* so popular."

Chiara arched her eyebrows, "I hadn't heard that one."

"It's less colorful that the mafia one. I admit, I've used these rumors about me as character development for my book. Which reminds me, I was saying—" Fabrizio released Chiara's hand to reach into the wide pocket of his coat. Sheepishly, he pulled out a book and laid it in front of Chiara.

She picked up the book. "You wrote this?"

He nodded.

Chiara ran her hand over the embossed cover, simple, no design, just the title, "The Blade's Edge" and a name "Fabrizio Mariani."

Gently, Fabrizio took the book from Chiara's hands, allowing his fingers to pause for a breath over her hands, before turning the book to the last page. Softly he said, "In case you don't believe me . . ."

Chiara looked down, and smiled at the photograph. It was taken a few years ago, surely, but it was unmistakably Fabrizio.

She looked up and grinned, "And you write mysteries."

He clasped her hands in his and leaned forward. "I'm tired of mysteries."

Edo took the steps down to the bar one at a time. At the bottom, he hesitated before pushing open the door.

"*Buongiorno*, Zia."

"*Buongiorno*, Edo. You're up early."

"Yes, I figured there'd be lots of business what with people heading up to the castle to clean." Edo looked around at the empty shop and gave a wan smile, "I guess not."

"Not yet, anyway. It was a late night, everyone may be sleeping it off. *Un espresso?*"

"Please."

Chiara nodded and began grinding the beans. She hummed tunelessly and smiled at some inner thought.

Edo pulled a stool up to the other side of the bar. "Zia?"

"*Sì?*"

"I have something to tell you."

Chiara switched off the La Pavoni and turned back to place the delicate white cup into her nephew's outstretched palm. "That sounds serious."

Edo nodded. "Maybe. I don't know."

Chiara rested her towel on the bar, and pushed the sugar container to Edo. "What is it?"

"I don't know how . . . how . . . to say this," he stammered. All in a rush he went on, "I don't like women. Well, I like them and all, I mean, I like you and my mother and Patrizia," Edo was stammering, now.

Chiara nodded, silently allowing him to continue without interruption.

Edo closed his eyes and took a breath, "I'm gay."

Chiara closed her hand around Edo's clenched fist. "I know."

"You *know?*"

"Yes."

"For how long?"

"Oh, I don't know. Looking back it seems like I always knew. But I guess I've only known that I've known for about a month. Or two maybe."

"Why didn't you say anything?"

"Why didn't you?"

"I was afraid."

"So was I."

"But . . . but . . . why should you be afraid?"

"Little person, if you weren't ready to tell me, what good would it do to force the conversation?"

Edo blinked back tears of relief and confusion. "But if you'd told me, I wouldn't have worried."

"You were worried?"

"Of course!"

"About what?"

"What do you mean '*about what*'? You've seen how this town treats . . . gay people."

Chiara tucked her hair behind her ear. "Yes. Santa Lucia is changing, but not quickly enough in some ways. But Edo, you couldn't have thought I would judge you?"

Edo stood straight and frowned, "Why not? People have been judging me my whole life, even when they didn't know, or I didn't know. Or at least I wasn't acknowledging it to myself."

"They have Edo, it's true. But not me. Not ever me."

Relaxing his posture Edo said, "Yes, I guess so. It was just easy to lump you in with the rest of them."

"Well, we never talked about the issue in general, so I can see why you wouldn't know where I stood."

"And, well . . . Zia? Where do you stand?"

Chiara sighed. "Edo, I'm in favor of more love in this world. And that's all there is to it."

Edo nodded, then wiped his eyes.

Chiara noted the gesture, "You okay, sweet boy?"

He nodded.

Chiara hesitated, "Edo? Have you told your parents?"

"No. I haven't told anyone." He paused as his thoughts skirted to Trevor and the bicyclists and the vague memory of the random mouths and hands in the clubs. "But last night, after we put the fire out and all of us were still up at the castle, some of the people were trying to figure out who started the fire—"

"What do you mean who started it? Wasn't it just the fire catching on something? The papers or the vines? Ava's been after us for years to clean up those vines."

"Yes, that's what I think too. But you know people, they always look for someone to blame. Anyway, someone thought maybe it was the group of tourists, some of whom were gay, and I just realized, by not saying anything, I'm basically allowing it to continue."

"Edo."

"No, it's okay, Chiara, I needed to figure it out, and I have. Or at least I'm working on it."

Chiara nodded. "They don't still blame the tourists do they? That's just absurd."

Edo shook his head. "No, by the time I was walking away, they'd circled back to blaming the Moroccan immigrants."

"*What?*"

"Yes. You know how it is. With that terrorist attack in Germany, it's easy for scared people to target them."

Chiara reached under the register and grabbed her car keys. "Edo, get my coat," she said, tension strangling her voice.

"Where are you going?"

"To the hospital."

Magda pushed on the door of Bar Birbo and startled when the door didn't swing open. She stood there, uselessly, her eyes roaming around the front of the shop, looking for clues. Her eye caught on the "*Chiuso*" sign. Leaning forward to shield her eyes from the glare of the morning sun, she peered through the glass.

"She's closed." The baker's voice called from across the street.

Magda straightened, frowned, and turned to Sauro, smiling genially as he leaned out from the beaded curtain.

"But . . . why? It's not Monday." Did Chiara go on vacation and not tell her? How could Chiara not share that with all the talking they did yesterday, warming themselves around the box burning on the rock of the waterfall before the current swirled around the fragments and swept them down into the swamp where they belonged.

The baker shrugged, "*Boh*." He smiled again and slipped back into the fragrant shop as he caught sight of Bea walking toward the bakery for her morning loaf of bread.

Magda's face creased into it's familiar scowl. What was going on?

Luciano turned the corner and saw Magda standing in front of Bar Birbo, unsure of where to go next. He called out, "She's closed."

"I have eyes." Magda spat back. She took a breath and tried again. "Yes, I see that." Better, softer. She smiled in appreciation of her effort. She saw that Luciano didn't look as pleased, so she added, "Did she go somewhere?" Magda couldn't help her eyebrow furrowing down again. She consciously tried to raise it.

Luciano tried not to laugh at the battle that was raging on Magda's face. What was happening to this woman? Her face seemed to be in the midst of some kind of gymnastic routine. He forced away the mental picture of Magda in a leotard balanced like an egret on a balance beam. "She's at the hospital."

"The hospital! Is she okay?" Luciano's face softened at Magda's panicked voice.

"Yes, she's fine. She went to see Fatima."

"Fatima? Who's Fatima?"

Luciano closed his eyes and wrestled with the emotion that fought to choke him.

"The little girl they found last night at the fire."

"The fire? Was she hurt? *Was she burned in the fire?*"

Luciano's voice seemed to shrink as he said, "No, not burned. They think smoke inhalation. She was in the room under the arbor, it must have filled with smoke before she even knew. Giuseppe found her."

Magda's eyes flew to the butcher shop.

Luciano said, "He's at the hospital, too."

The tension in Magda's body closed around her vocal cords, "How is she?"

Luciano shook his head. "They don't know yet. She hasn't regained consciousness."

"And the family, are they there? Somebody needs to tell them! Their Italian is terrible, they probably don't know what to do! We need to form a committee!"

"Magda. Yes, of course they are there. Patrizia went and told them right after Giuseppe took Fatima to the hospital."

Magda's eyes narrowed. "How do you know all this?"

"Because Patrizia came to see me first. She knows I worked with the family."

"And you're equipped to deal with this stress? Of course you're not. I'll take over."

"No."

"What?"

"No, Magda. I appreciate the offer, but the family trusts me, and frankly I think it best that they have someone around them that they know, and that knows their daughter's name."

Magda huffed. "Well, what are you doing *here* then? Why aren't you at the hospital? It doesn't look like you're taking your responsibility very seriously. Besides," she said as she peered at Luciano's cheek, "your face is bloody. You look ridiculous."

"It was a long night. But, Magda, why this sudden interest in a girl you don't even know?"

Magda blanched, and was silent. "I know. I'm sorry, Luciano." As she rubbed her hand across her eyes, she missed Luciano's eyes widening at her apology. "Look, I might as well say it. I'm sure everyone else will be saying it—the fire was my fault."

"What? No, it was the vines. The fire chief said so this morning."

"Whatever, it was my idea to have the *sagra* at the castle."

"And was it you that held a lit match to the vines?"

Magda head swiveled up, and she blinked up at Luciano, surprised as much by the softness of his tone as his refusal to blame her.

His voice gentled further. "Unless you blazed up those vines on purpose and forced Fatima in that room," his voice caught momentarily, struck by the image of Fatima collapsing, alone, in a space rapidly filling with smoke. "There were many people involved in that decision, Magda. It doesn't fall on the person who first spoke the notion."

Magda opened her mouth to argue, but Luciano held up his hand. "I can't talk more about this, I need to get back."

Magda nodded, rebuked. "But why are you going in this direction?"

"I need to get Elisa. Fatima's family is asking for her."

"Elisa Lucarelli? They're friends? Oh, wait, yes, I remember now."

Luciano nodded and then moved to proceed down the street.

"Luciano, please, no offense. Will they let her go with you? You know that family. Suspicious and angry, they remind me . . . well, never mind."

Luciano paused. He hadn't considered what would happen if the family didn't allow Elisa to join him. They didn't know him, or their relationship.

Seeing him hesitate, Magda rushed on, "Can I come with you? I'll talk to them for you."

Luciano's eyes narrowed.

Magda went on. "Please. I want to help. I promise . . . I'll be . . . well, I won't be like me."

Luciano surprised himself by laughing. "Okay, let's go get her."

"Maybe I should do the talking," Magda said, hurrying so much, she was several paces ahead of Luciano.

Luciano stopped walking. Magda, realizing that she didn't know where Elisa lived, paused. Luciano ventured forward while saying, "Magda, this is not your tragedy. This is mine. You can come and join in if I need you, but you'll have to not be in charge, and you'll have to restrain your combative tendencies, and God damnit, you'll have to trust me."

Chastened, Magda hung her head. "Okay."

Three more turns and they were there, in front of Elisa's door.

Magda moved to knock, but Luciano gently pulled her back with their linked arms. She bit her lip, nodded, and stepped backward with an slight squeak of passing gas. Luciano patted her shoulder and rapped authoritatively on the door.

The woman who opened the door wore a stained and shapeless dress. She brushed hair off her face that was last dyed perhaps three months ago, the brassy red at odds with the dark hair streaked with iron. "Yes?" She asked, querulously.

"*Buongiorno, signora.* I'm Luciano Sapienti, I used to teach at the *scuola elementare*, but now I am retired and have enjoyed the pleasure of tutoring your daughter in math from time to time."

Elisa appeared out of the darkness, her face taut. Luciano smiled warmly at her, and Magda, sensing that this was a moment that called for warmth, stretched her mouth across her teeth to approximate a smile.

Elisa's mother held the door open just a crack. "I can't pay you."

Magda's turned to Luciano to gauge his response. He stiffened but said, "I assure you, madame, there is no need for payment. Your daughter has an exceptional mind. It's a joy to work with her."

Elisa's mother's eyes narrowed. "Hrmph. Then what do you want?"

"Forgive me, *Signora*, but I wondered if I might have a word with your daughter?"

"Elisa? What for? She's busy."

Elisa wiped her hands on her apron. "It's okay, Mamma. He's my friend."

Her mother cocked her jaw and glared at Luciano. "Fine. Come on out."

Elisa sidled past her mother, who stayed propped in the doorway, her arm fixed fast across the entrance. Elisa stepped up to Luciano, her eyes searching his for a sign of what brought on this unexpected visit. She winced at the cuts on his cheek. He smiled sadly at her, and she registered fear behind his look of reassurance.

Luciano looked at Elisa's mother as if to beseech her for a moment of privacy, but her posture only stiffened. He cleared his throat, "Child. I have some bad news. There was a fire at the *sagra* last night."

Elisa nodded. "*Io lo so* . . . I know, everyone is talking about it. But everything is okay, right? Is your house okay?"

"Yes, yes, I'm fine." He took a breath. "It's Fatima."

"Fatima!"

Elisa's mother chimed in, "Who's Fatima?"

Luciano's gaze was locked on Elisa, so Magda cleared her throat. "A little girl in town. She and Elisa are good friends."

Grumbling, Elisa's mother muttered, "What kind of name is Fatima? They can't be that good friends if I've never heard of her."

Elisa whispered, "What happened to her?"

Luciano took a breath, "She was in a room that filled with smoke, and she is very, very sick."

Elisa moaned and pressed her hands against her temples, "Where is she?"

"The hospital. I thought you might want to see her. And her mother thought you being there might help Fatima in some way."

"You're not taking my daughter anywhere," Elisa's mother broke in. "You think I'd let her go off with a strange man? I've heard about you, you know. I'm not an idiot. You're probably drunk now, and just want to take my child to do God knows what to her."

The three on the front step regarded Elisa's mother with a mixture of shock and disdain. Magda swallowed the bile she felt rising in her throat. "Signora, I'm sorry I have yet to introduce myself. My name is Magda, and I own the Villa Tramonte in the *centro*. I'll be accompanying Luciano and Elisa to the hospital. I'll make sure she gets there and back safely, and can give you my phone number. We'll be back this afternoon."

Elisa's mother glared at Magda before sniffing. "Even so. I heard that fire was caused by the Muslims. I don't want Elisa mixed-up with that."

Elisa's pinched face flushed red. "Mamma, I'm not 'mixed-up' with anything. I need to see Fatima. She's my friend."

"Oh, Elisa, you're such a fool."

Elisa closed her eyes and then said, "I'm not a fool. And I will go to see Fatima."

"Ha! What kind of mother would I be if I let you go with strangers?"

"But you are not my mother."

"Elisa!"

The tension on the front steps mounted. Elisa sighed, "I'm sorry, Mamma, I didn't mean it that way. I just . . . I know you want to protect me, especially now, but Luciano is my friend, and Fatima is like a sister to me. I have to go. I think it might be my fault that she was there at all."

"Not your fault!" Magda said sharply.

All eyes turned toward her and she muttered, "Sorry. Carry on."

Elisa scratched her chin as she gazed at Magda curiously. She shrugged and turned back to her mother. "I'm going, and you can't stop me."

"Elisa! What are you saying?" Her mother looked around at the other adults and gestured as if to beg their understanding for her foolish daughter. Luciano and Magda gazed back, their faces like stone.

"Papà is gone, and he's not coming back. You made sure. We're safe now. But we can't go back to how we were." Elisa nodded to herself, satisfied, and went on, "I'm going to the hospital to see one of the few people in my life who doesn't make me feel like an idiot. Let's go." Elisa strode away from the door, not looking back to see if Luciano and Magda were following.

Her mother shouted, "Stop! You can't take her, I'll call the police if you try!"

Elisa turned around and inhaled deeply like Luciano had taught her to do when faced with what seemed an insurmountable problem. She tempered the steel in her voice. "I'm going. If they don't take me, I'm walking to Girona, or I'm hitching a ride. You can't stop me. The rules are broken."

She walked down the street. Luciano and Magda followed her with their eyes, and looked at each other, unsure of what to do.

Elisa's mother's sobbed and then said, "Well, what are you waiting for? You can't let her go alone. Go!"

Not needing to be told twice, Luciano and Magda followed Elisa up the road.

Luciano nudged open the heavy blue door. The faces assembled around the slight and shrouded figure on the bed looked up, nodding and shifting their weight before refocusing their attention on the girl, her face hidden behind tubes and an oxygen mask. As if by their sheer will, they could make her reanimate, return to them.

Luciano held the door open and Elisa walked in. She sobbed at the sight of her friend, and Salma made room for Elisa beside her. Elisa lurched forward, and curved into Salma, her tears flowing fast. Salma put an arm around the girl and pulled her closer. Looking up at Luciano she whispered her thanks for bringing Elisa.

Magda followed Elisa, but seeing the quizzical looks at her presence, she turned to Luciano, "I'll wait outside. The room is full. I can't imagine I'm needed here."

Nodding his assent, he softly told the group that Magda had helped him fetch Elisa, and would be in the waiting room should anyone need anything. Magda cleared her throat, "Unless there is something you need now?"

The unfamiliar faces shook their heads, the man in rumpled clothes standing next to Salma added, "Chiara has gone to get us lunch. Chiara and that boy—Edo?"

Magda nodded. "I'll be here if you think of anything." She stepped back out to the hallway, willing the smell of disinfectant to drift out of her nose, out of her pores. To have her vision not filled with the unmoving figure of that little girl. Seeing her had cued memories of those curious eyes in the bakery, that ready laugh in the *alimentari*. Her fault, her fault . . .

Magda stumbled to the waiting room and slid into the first empty chair, relishing the cool, hard, uncomfortable surface.

Back in the room, Luciano asked, "How is she?"

Elisa, hearing the question, gulped air in her attempt to stop crying and listen for the answer. Flooding images made it hard to concentrate. Fatima weaving necklaces from daisies while chatting about the smell of Persian roses, spinning tales of King Ferdinand and Queen Isabella from the books Luciano lent her, wearing the short-sleeve shirt under her family-approved wardrobe every day, placing her warm hand on Elisa's arm when she sensed Elisa's heart shivering in fear or sadness, lying on her bed with her hands under her head while the two of them swapped childhood memories of ghost stories and fairy tales, closing her eyes to savor whatever she was tasting, whether or not it included pork, before holding it out with a grin to share it with Elisa.

Salma said, "The same."

"The x-rays didn't come back yet?"

In halting Italian, Salma answered, "They did, but the photographs are difficult to read. They do not know how sick the lungs are. The doctor said the blood tests are finished. It is what they thought—she lost much oxygen."

Salma's father added, "They think she breathes chemicals from fire and it sleeps her. No, not sleep, but like sleep?"

Luciano smiled, "Faint?"

"Yes, thank you, faint. The smoke, it fills the room and . . ." Fatima's father gestured to his daughter, taking up far too little space in the big, white bed.

A man seated across the room, Fatima's uncle, Luciano remembered, said, "I thought I saw her moving a little while ago, but Salma thinks that was a shadow."

Fatima's father lowered his voice and asked Luciano. "And the fire?"

Luciano answered, "The fire chief confirmed it was started by an ember on the vines. There is no other story."

Salma's breath exhaled slowly, and she turned back to her daughter. "What was she even doing at the *sagra?*"

Elisa felt her stomach clench. Had Fatima been there to meet her? Had she been angry? Had she been ready to forgive her? Or had she just been there to watch the town eat and celebrate, to maybe sneak a bite?

Elisa looked up at Salma who wordlessly nodded her permission. Elisa caught up Fatima's hand—were those pomegranate stains on her fingers?— and pressed it to her cheek. "Fatima . . . please . . . I love you. Come back, my friend."

Thunder rumbled high across the greying sky. Shadows grazed the valley floor, meandering around stands of olive trees and leaping over stretching cypresses. The air thickened, gathered—an inhale before the storm.

One by one the figures filed past the Madonna glowing in her heavenly niche. Loaded as the villagers were with buckets, brooms, and bags, they paused to brush their fingers over the figure. She gazed upon each of them, her expression transcendent. They bowed their heads, breathed in, and climbed the steps. Like ants on a tentative trail, they followed each other up to the castle.

Chiara, newly back from delivering a pistachio yogurt cake and the news that the town was praying for Fatima, leaned on Edo for support. The two of them muted, intent on the task at hand. "What if it rains?" Edo asked.

"Then we'll go home. But it could blow over. These November storms are often more flash than substance."

Ava, who had heard about the English tourist, touched Edo's shoulder. He looked down at her and smiled. She couldn't help the way her stomach backflipped at his tender grin, but she was able to return his smile before the two of them strolled easily to the edge of the castle. They sighed in unison before gathering the charred remains of the vines.

Carosello, a piece of lettuce hanging from his right ear, trotted past Edo and Ava to nudge his nose against Fabrizio's knee. Fabrizio, who had just crested the stairs to scan the group for Chiara, greeted the dog. Carosello thumped his tail twice and then flopped on the ground, stretching across the top of the stairs.

Catching Chiara's eye, Fabrizio stepped over the dog to approach her. He reached out his hand, and Chiara took it for a moment before lifting their intertwined hands to kiss his fingers. Ignoring the whispers, the two of them began collecting the spent fire extinguishers to stack them by the steps. While Chiara was still troubled by questions about how to navigate this relationship when Fabrizio returned to Bologna at the end of the month, she tried to focus on this, now. This moment of fragile peace.

Dante stood in the center of the clearing, hands on his hips. Hearing a muted snickering behind him, he whirled and glared at Fabio. Fabio suppressed his laugh and looked chastened, plunging his brush into the bucket of soapy water.

Patrizia and Giuseppe made their way into the clearing. The butcher held his wife against him as her eyes welled with tears. When she saw Chiara standing closer to Fabrizio than strictly necessary, she smiled and moved to greet them. Giuseppe approached Dante and asked about the rumors that the owner of the castle had been in contact, angry about the news of the fire on his property. Dante nodded in affirmation, and said that the owner was planning to fly in from New York City to assess the damage.

Magda hugged the wall as she arrived, her face alert for any sign of suspicion or blame. Most faces slid past her, intent on their tasks, a few nodded perfunctorily, accepting her place among them. She breathed deeply to ease the tension in her chest and joined Giovanni and Rosetta, who were folding the unburnt tables and resting them against the wall.

Vale appeared briefly at the entrance to the castle, but spying Dante, he hung his head and retreated back down the steps. Stella was absent. She'd left Santa Lucia late in the night. Rumor was she'd moved in with her eldest daughter.

Sauro the baker arrived and helped Paola, the owner of the produce market, sweep ash and bits of coal. They paused to lean on their brooms as they gazed over the groves. Anyone who has loved an olive tree will empathize with the hammer to the chest at the sight of those burnt groves. No, the trees weren't theirs, but they were cousins to theirs. Paola blinked back tears. She turned her head to return to work, but her vision was caught by Luciano arriving with Isotta and Elisa. She watched them for a few moments, biting her lip, before she returned to her sweeping.

As they entered the clearing, Elisa's eyes glimmered. Luciano leaned down and reminded her of what the doctors said—it was very possible that Fatima would recover. She was stronger than almost anyone knew. They needed to keep thinking positively and sending her prayers. Elisa bit her lip and nodded. Isotta squeezed her hand. Elisa closed her eyes briefly, and then smiled up at Isotta. She accepted the rake Luciano held out to her and stepped to the edge of the groves to rake the burnt rosemary branches.

Along with the mingled images of Fatima strangled in smoke and lying in her pristine hospital bed, Elisa couldn't help scanning the assembled townspeople. Was her real mother here, now? Or her father? Did they know her? Had they stayed away from her all these years because they didn't care? Or were they waiting for an opportunity to talk to her? Was it someone she knew? What if it was someone she hated? What if it was someone she loved? Her mind was in knots, she wished she had Fatima to talk it out with. Fatima would find a way to make her laugh and wonder at the same time.

Now that Carlo was gone, Elisa wondered if she could persuade her mother to tell her the truth about her parentage. But not yet. Her mother was still broken and worried about how to support the household. Her brothers—the three of them agreed that no revelations about bloodlines would divide their sense of kinship, they would always be her brothers— maintained that their lives would only improve with Carlo gone. She was inclined to believe them.

Standing beside Elisa, Isotta searched for Massimo or Anna. Her argument with Massimo that had rung through the quiet streets of Santa Lucia seemed to have shamed him and his mother into staying home. Isotta breathed a sigh of relief, but she found herself regretting not seeing Margherita. After Massimo had left, she'd cried with Luciano, realizing that leaving Massimo meant leaving the little girl that had come to feel like her own. She struggled with feeling powerless in the face of a wash of regret. Could she still see Margherita, without seeing Massimo? Was Massimo willing to change, to see her for who she was? Could he really love her as herself and not the glimmer of his wife dead and buried as he'd insisted last night? Or was the whole relationship too rotten to ever recover? And, then her mind cycled back to the most painful question— could she keep Margherita in her life?

At the thought, her stomach lurched. She'd tried to quiet her nausea this morning with plain toasted bread, but she still felt the threat of bile rising in her throat. It must be nerves.

Unless . . . her hand fluttered to her belly and she began furiously calculating the days that had slipped by her, tangling, uncounted.

A wisp of wind, fresh as innocence itself, began moving between and through the townspeople. Arching into the sky, the breeze, more confident now, thinned the bulky heft of the clouds, stretching them into a hazy veneer. The sky seemed to twist on itself, opening a circlet in the shifting veil. For a brief moment, the edges of the aperture glowed brilliantly around a stretch of sky the exact blue of the Madonna's niche. A cascade of light flowed through the rippling air to warm the assembled faces, lifted in greeting. All around, gnarled branches swayed and bowed, tossing glints of silver into an endless sky.

THANK YOU FOR VISITING SANTA LUCIA!

Luckily, like any great small town, something wonderful waits just around the corner. *The Silent Madonna: Book Two in the Santa Lucia Series* *(mybook.to/TheSilentMadonna)* has hit bookshelves, so you don't have to wait to discover what happened to Fatima, Isotta, Chiara, and the rest of the villagers.

Santa Lucia is a four book series, so make sure you sign up to receive advance notice of new book releases, promotions, and giveaways *(michelledamiani.com/SantaLucia)*. As a thanks for stopping by, you'll also get Chiara's famous pistachio-yogurt cake recipe. Perfect alongside a *cappuccino* and an afternoon of reading.

One more thing, could you leave a review of *Santa Lucia* on Amazon.com *(mybook.to/SantaLucia)* and/or Goodreads? It only takes a few moments, and reviews are like gelato on a summer day for independently published authors.

If you enjoyed the world of *Santa Lucia*, might I recommend *Il Bel Centro: A Year in the Beautiful Center (mybook.to/IlBelCentro)*. It is the story of my year in Umbria, which served as the inspiration for *Santa Lucia*.

Now, don't be a stranger! Stay connected via Facebook, Instagram, Twitter, and *michelledamiani.com*.

Until then, keep dreaming,

— Michelle

ITALIAN WORDS IN THIS TEXT

∿

CONVERSATIONS

a doppo/ *a presto/alla* *prossima volta*	see you later	*buonasera*	good afternoon
		buongiorno	good morning
allora	well now	*cara*	dear
amore mio	my love	*castello*	castle
anch'io	me too	*che succede ?*	what happened?
andiamo	let's go	*ciao*	hello and goodbye
arrivo	I'm coming	*come no?*	why not?
aspetta	wait	*comunque*	anyway
(un) attimo	just a moment	*davvero?*	isn't that right?
auguri	congratulations	*eccoci qua*	here we are
basta	that's enough	*fa un* *freddo cane*	literally "it makes a dog cold", used to express that it's freezing outside
bella	beautiful		
bentornato	welcome back	*fidanzato/a*	fiance/e
boh?	no real translation, similar to "who can say?" and often given wth a shrug	*gita*	field trip
		grazie	thank you
		lo so	I know
bronzato	tanned		
		ma dai!	Come on!
buono/a	good		

maestro	teacher, often used as an honorific	*ragazzi*	guys
moda	fashion	*salve*	greetings
nascondino	hide and seek	*senza pelli sulla lingua*	without hair on the tongue (plain speaking)
nonno/a	grandfather/mother	*sono d'accordo*	I agree
paesano	country boy	*stronzo*	bastard, piece of crap
per favore	please	*tesoro mio*	my treasure
piacere	nice to meet you	*tutto bene/ tutto a posto*	everything's okay
poverino/a	poor		
prego	you're welcome	*va bene*	it's okay
pronto	literally "ready" but used as "hello" when answering the phone	*zio/zia*	uncle/aunt

~

ABOUT TOWN

alimentari	shop that sells cheese and cured meats, as well as some other basic foodstuff and household supplies	*palazzo*	palace
		palazzo comunale	seat of civic authority, like a town hall
Ape	a three-wheeled truck with a small motor	*Perugino*	Umbrian Rennaisance painter; his paintings (or those of his students) adorn many Umbrian buildings
comune	where administrative aspects of the town happen		
		piazza	town square
farmacia	pharmacy	*polizia municipale*	police department
festa	celebration/party		
forno	bakery	*rosticceria*	shop to buy pizza by the slice, and sometimes cooked items for takeaway like fried rice balls (arancini)
fruttivendolo	produce shop		
macelleria	butcher shop, often with other fresh items		
		trattoria	informal restaurant

FOOD & DRINK

albicocca	apricot	*lampredotto*	tripe sandwiches
aperitivo	cocktail	*latte caldo*	hot milk
Barolo	a red wine from the north of Italy	*mandarino*	mandarin orange
biscotto/i	cookie/s	*panino*	sandwich
buono/a	good	*pecorino*	sheep's milk cheese, sold at different levels of ripeness; Pecorino is also a kind of white wine from Le Marche
cacio e pepe	pasta with grated cheese and pepper		
caffè	espresso specifically, or coffee more generally	*lumaca*	snail
caffè lungo	espresso pulled slowly so that there is more water and a fuller cup	*normale*	my usual
		prosecco	bubbly wine, Italy's version of champagne
cappuccino	espresso with milk	*salumi*	cured meats, like salami and prosciutto
cenone	a big, festive dinner		
ciambella/e	donut/s	*tagliata*	sliced, grilled beef, often scattered with rosemary and olive oil
cornetto/i	Italian croissant/s		
cornetto con marmellata	Italian croissant filled with jam	*tagliatelle*	fresh pasta, cut similar to linguini
cornetto con crema	Italian croissant filled with cream	*tartufata*	black olive and truffle
farro	an ancient grain, similar to barley	*torta*	cake
		vigili	police officers
frizzante	bubbly water	*vino*	wine
frutti di bosco	literally fruits of the forest, mixed berry		

A WORD ON ITALIAN MEALS

Italian meals are divided into appetizers (*antipasti*), first course of pasta or soup (*primi*), second course of meat or fish (*secondi*), side dish of vegetables (*contorni*—also the name of the newsletter you should sign up for at *bit.ly/Contorni* so you receive news of the next book in the *Santa Lucia* series) and dessert (*dolci*).

ACKNOWLEDGMENTS

I first conceived of this book as a serial, publishing three chapters a week on my website. I envisioned *Santa Lucia* as a telenovela in *espresso* form—a sort of caffeine-loaded, dialogue-heavy, plot-driven story that draws the reader into a sweeping narrative.

The next step was editing the story into the novel you hold in your hands. I would not have been able to translate my vision onto the page without the patience, grace, and talent of Emily Morrison, who shepherded Santa Lucia through draft after draft (after draft after draft) to pull out the best in me. Other friends generously offered their editing skills and I am endlessly grateful to: Paul Ardoin (without him, the fire would have all the emotional intensity of a sluggish barbecue), Christina Ball who corrected and improved my Italian (and Italian-isms), and Kristine Bean and Nancy Hampton who offered their discerning eye to every misplaced comma and typo, as well as sharpening my writing. I don't know what I did to deserve such a stalwart team.

Bless my family for shoving me out the door to write and for believing in me when my own confidence flagged. My children—Nicolas, Siena, and Gabe—bore the brunt, but Keith is the one who would hear the quaver in my voice, shove everything aside, and walk me through each and every impasse.

It was with my family that I experienced life in Umbria for a year. My children's stories about their days in Italian public school, Keith's misadventures pushing paperwork, our lives intertwining with our beloved Italian neighbors all rested in my soul like seeds. Those seeds deepened and shifted and bloomed into this book. And so I offer thanks the town of Spello, for nourishing my soul and inspiring my story.